RAINBOW KNIFE

Sally Bennett Boyington

Tales of the Watermasters
Volume 2

Wordsmith Pages

To

everyone who encouraged me to complete
Rainbow Knife

Also by Author

Homegrown Muse
(as Sally P. Bennett)

Swallowing the Sun
(#1 of Tales of the Watermasters)

Coming Soon:

Bitter Wind
(#3 of Tales of the Watermasters)

Find out more at www.wordsmithpages.com

Contents

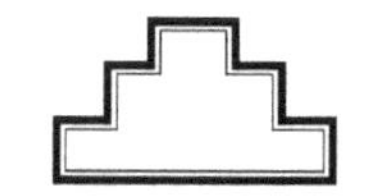

Prologue

When Serpent gnaws the bones of the earth
and Buzzard pierces the sky,
when all the green ribbons have dwindled to dust,
the rainbow knife will fly.

—PROPHECY OF THE PEOPLE OF TWO RIVERS

Waterstrider fought off panic as everything around him darkened.

He lay on the ground, breath knocked out by a fall from the red rocks on which he and his friends were playing take-the-hill. Laughter and shouts above him broke a strange hush. Birds had gone quiet, their songs and calls and whistles stilled. The dogs too seemed to know something was amiss, for they had run off and no longer barked and snapped at the boys' bare feet scuffling on the rocks.

The air pressed in on him. No clouds hung in the sky, and Brother Sun was too bright to gaze at directly, yet daylight faded. When Waterstrider blinked he saw red and black spots. He closed his eyelids and rubbed the heels of his hands into them. *One heartbeat. Two. Three . . . If I can count, does that mean I'm not going crazy?* After ten heartbeats, he took his hands away and found that the world had descended into twilight. His stomach clenched.

Tagalong leaped off the rocks and knelt by his side. "You see it too?" Tag asked, his normally deep-copper cheeks pale.

"Yes." Blood pounded through Waterstrider's head. He searched the sky for smoke, dust, anything that would explain why Brother Sun still shone but gave off hardly any light. As the air cooled and a breeze puffed past, gooseflesh lifted on his arms.

"What's happening?" Tag asked.

One by one the others came to surround Waterstrider. Their wide eyes begged for an answer to Tag's question. Rivulets of sweat ran down dust-coated bare chests onto cotton loincloths. Tangles of black hair torn loose from braids stuck on damp, red-brown skin nearly the same color as the rock outcrops.

Only Cloudface stood apart, arms crossed and a sneer on his thin lips.

Waterstrider climbed to his feet. He told himself it was the dusty odor of bursage that made his nose itch, his eyes water. He pinched his nostrils between thumb and forefinger, then swiped the back of his hand across his sweaty upper lip. Westward, past his friends' worried faces, a dark wall of wind-borne sand mounted into the sky from the desert flats. Though nearly as tall as the Greasy Mountains toward which the southerly wind swept, the top edge of the sandstorm hung several hands below Brother Sun, so it was not blocking the sunlight.

Waterstrider's belly twisted with a growing sense of wrongness. He turned his gaze northward, toward the rounded ridge known as Mother Sleeping. At the front of the broad, arched cavern in the middle of the ridge, several Skywatchers pointed upward, their pale blue robes distinct against the shadows of the Belly of the Mother behind them.

Waterstrider frowned. At this moment, the Skywatchers, celebrants of the upcoming ceremony to mark the turning of the sun, should be cloistered in the Belly of the Mother, hidden behind the tall stacks of wood that Waterstrider and his friends had delivered for the midwinter sun-festival. The Skywatchers should be singing to Brother Sun and smoking tobacco in reed pipes, letting the smoke waft upward through the sun-hole at the top of the cavern as they prepared for the New Fire ceremony. They should be getting ready to light the fires that would be seen all over the valley, a sign that days would soon grow longer again. Instead the Skywatchers stood outside, watching.

Do something! Waterstrider cried out silently to them. Their stillness made him wonder whether they felt as helpless as he did. He chanced another look at the sky, where Brother Sun was disappearing into the maw of a black monster.

Waterstrider swallowed hard. Whipping up his courage, he gestured toward the Skywatchers and said to his friends, in a strained voice he hardly recognized as his own, "If there was anything to fear, they wouldn't be so calm."

"They're fools." Cloudface, who had seen only one winter more than Waterstrider's thirteen but always claimed to know everything, crossed his arms and puffed out his meager chest. His beaky nose lifted. His yellowish eyes, flat and expressionless, fixed on Waterstrider. "Silly old men."

Tagalong shifted a worried gaze between Cloudface and Waterstrider. "The ceremony . . ." His voice choked to a halt. He stared at Waterstrider beseechingly as the younger boys started to cry.

Waterstrider could barely see the Belly of the Mother now, so quickly had the light fled. Though he had no more idea than his friends what was happening, he cleared his throat and told them, "The sun is waning like the moon does, nothing more. Like the moon, it will return." If not, his reassurance wouldn't matter, for none of them would survive to accuse him of a lie. That realization made his heart pound, shaking his whole body.

Cloudface unfolded his arms and stabbed a finger toward the darkening sky. "You've never seen anything like that—admit it. You're scared."

"What if I am?" Waterstrider retorted. "Anyone would be."

"I'm not," Cloudface declared.

"Liar."

"I'm *not*." The other boy's strangely light-colored eyes narrowed into slits. "Only babies admit to being scared. Are you a baby? Do you want to run home to your mother? Oh, I forgot—you don't have a mother." He laughed, though it sounded forced.

Some of the others smiled uncomfortably. A few laughed along. Waterstrider stared them into silence.

"Anyway," Cloudface went on, "I'm not afraid. My life-path leads to greatness."

Waterstrider might have pointed out that Cloudface had no way of knowing what was to come. But the other boys, distracted from their earlier fear, were now paying attention to the squabble, not the growing darkness. Waterstrider forced his hands to stay open, though he wanted to knock that sneer off his tormentor's mouth. "Bickering like this is stupid. Those of you with little brothers or sisters, they'll be needing some comfort. Let's go back. See if there's anything we can do to help."

He turned and headed down the slope, first at a light jog, then with increasing speed in a vain attempt to outrun the dread that weighed down his heart. A glance over his shoulder once he reached level ground showed that only Tag followed him. The others remained behind with Cloudface. What they do doesn't matter, he told himself. But why had they looked to him first for reassurance if they were going to be guided by Cloudface in the end?

A twisting breeze kicked up dust around him to sting his eyes, pelt his skin, clog his nose and throat. He took the most direct route from Mother Sleeping, a plunging, steep and dangerous trail in the dark rather than the longer one they'd come up bearing wood. Spiky greenthorn trees grabbed at his arms, slicing his skin. He wished he'd thought to pick up his shirt before leaving the rocks. Distracted, he nearly ran into a saguaro cactus that loomed at a crook in the trail.

After that, he forced himself to slow down. Tag didn't catch up with him; Waterstrider hoped that meant his friend was being careful.

By the time he reached the village of Serpentgate, the darkness had begun to lift. Still, the sprawling village was stirred up like an anthill. Parents called for children, who ran heedlessly. Cursing and wailing and shrieking filled the air. Someone cried that she had looked overlong at the rim of brilliance around the darkened sun and now couldn't see.

Waterstrider did what he could to soothe terrified children and get injured people seated out of the way until healers could tend them. Later that day, after spotting Tag and other friends, Waterstrider tried to convince himself nothing truly bad had happened: Brother Sun came back, everyone he cared about was safe, and life returned to normal. Yet shivers ran through him each time he noticed the sun's warmth on his face and remembered how quickly and inexplicably Brother Sun had changed.

Later still, the sun dropped into a notch in the distant western mountain range. It cast flames of orange and pink across the sky as it slipped below the horizon. It would set in the same position over the next days, its dying gleams sending up a thin wedge of light framed by dark mountains. Maybe that night, maybe the next—Waterstrider didn't know how the exact day was determined—the Skywatchers would light the fires in the Belly of the Mother to mark the midwinter sun-festival. Waterstrider wondered whether Brother Sun's dimming would prove a dire sign, maybe that the Skywatchers' prayers for longer days and stronger sunshine were going to fail.

As true twilight fell, Waterstrider was summoned to Cloud Mountain, the great mound at the south edge of the village, by his father, Longflute. Waterstrider waved at the man stationed at the gap in the adobe wall surrounding Cloud Mountain and was passed through without comment. *Did you see it?* he wanted to ask the watchman, as he'd wanted to ask everyone he'd encountered since the swallowing of the sun. Instead he held his tongue. He knew where to find his father, for Longflute was the assigned watcher tonight, keeping an eye on the Belly of the Mother for the lighting of the New Fire.

Waterstrider climbed the steps to the top of the mound, then wound his way through the maze of roomblocks, plazas, and towers. The darkness made him shiver, and he sped up. He hoped Sister Moon would soon rise to end this day with something normal.

Didn't anyone foresee the darkening of the sun? he had wondered many times as the day wore on. There were plenty of priests and priestesses and others, like the Skywatchers, who claimed to speak with the goddess and other divine beings. And most of the People of Two Rivers went questing when young to find their own spirit-guides, who would show them their new adult names and speak to them in dreams for the rest of their lives. None of the spirit-guides had warned that the sun might go dark? Mother Ge had never suggested to her priestesses that her son, Brother Sun, would become diminished and then creep back to life? The Ta'atchul, the Beloved Spirits, had never told their priests that Brother Sun might be dying?

Through the day Waterstrider had kept his thoughts to himself. Enough people were already spreading rumors when they had no more answers than he did, and the speculation seemed to make everybody more upset. Upon hearing that Longflute had sent for him, a spark of hope had flared—maybe his father had heard something. Maybe his father would tell him everything was working out according to the will of the mother-goddess.

Longflute looked up from his work, hands stilling over braided yucca cord and a plumb-bob. "I expected you back right away, after delivering the wood."

Even though Waterstrider chose his words carefully, mere mention of the disappearance of the sun prompted Longflute to arch a brow and tell him that the goddess's mysteries were none of his concern. "We're heronfolk," he reminded Waterstrider. "Practical-minded. We don't claim to understand the doings of Mother Ge." Waterstrider had heard that his whole life. He knew exactly what his father meant: the heronfolk were Watermasters, and that meant getting water into the canals and moving it to the fields where it was needed. "Leave knowledge of things unseen to the priests and priestesses," Longflute said.

Waterstrider came to believe, as the days slowly grew longer, that the Watermasters should have dealt head-on with the inexplicable rather than ignoring it. Long after the sun's return, life remained unsettled. Disturbingly, people began to blame the Watermasters—rather than, say, the Skywatchers or the rain priests or even Mother Ge's priestesses—for the sun's disappearance. The accusations became more unreasonable as time wore on. Anything bad was the fault of the heronfolk: accidents, illnesses, stored food getting moldy, failed hunts, even women dying in childbirth. Waterstrider wondered how much longer despair, anger, and suspicion could smolder before flaring up into a destructive blaze.

Nobody but him seemed interested in dousing the flames of rumor. And he had no notion of where to start.

⌃

A few moons later, Waterstrider sat on an outcrop below Mother Sleeping, near where he and his friends had been playing before the sun went dark. He looked southward over the familiar clanlands, the canals that drew from the broad river glinting in the sunlight, and in the distance, beyond the river, the Greasy Mountains. He sighed. *Will I ever see them again?* The rains had come, late but strong. The air smelled of resinous shegoi, brittlebush, and rocky soil. Green shoots had emerged, pretty layers of yellow and orange and pink and blue flowers covered the foothills, and the sky glowed with an intense clarity that hurt his heart.

The scrape of a sandal on the rock behind him warned of someone's approach. Waterstrider scrubbed a hand over his cheeks to wipe away any telltale moisture lingering there. He looked up and saw Tag, whose round face was creased in worry.

"I looked for you by the river," Tag said.

Waterstrider didn't trust his voice, so he shrugged in reply.

"There are Watermasters from downcanal passing through the village." Tag started to lift a hand as though to touch Waterstrider's shoulder, then dropped it back to his side. "Is it true—the heronfolk are leaving the valley? Ditchrunners, ditch bosses, women and children, everyone?"

"Not leaving. Just getting everybody in one place to keep them safe. Find out what's going on down at Earth River, that's all." Waterstrider hoped the words, forced through a dry throat, sounded sincere. He couldn't bear Tag's sympathy. "Give the farmers a chance to calm down. The River Council will think of a way to make the priests back off and stop causing trouble."

Tag nodded, but his frown deepened. "I heard some of the heronfolk of Earth River got hurt. I heard they killed the Rainsinger of the Temple of Mist."

That was what Waterstrider had heard too. But Longflute claimed it was a priest of the Rainsinger's own temple who had killed him. Whatever the truth, women and children in a Watermaster settlement had been attacked.

Waterstrider said, "It may seem a big problem now, but I guess that'll pass when the rains stop and the farmers need help getting the canals running."

"If there isn't any danger, why do you have to go somewhere safe?"

Waterstrider eyed Tag. "Better to be careful, don't you think?"

"Cloudface isn't going. He told me so."

"He doesn't have a choice. He'll do as the rest of the heronfolk do."

"He says he'll stay here, with his mother's clan. You could do that too."

Waterstrider snorted. He didn't even know which clan his mother belonged to, for her people had wanted nothing to do with him. Not that he could blame them. His father had never stopped running around with other women, and his mother had drowned herself soon after Waterstrider was born. Waterstrider's friends knew his story as well as he did: He'd been put to the breast of a woman whose newborn had died. After being weaned, he'd been fostered in a Watermaster family that shared no blood with him. Only when he became useful had his father taken him back. Waterstrider had a low opinion of the ties of kinship others took for granted.

Tag smiled nervously. "You could stay with us, me and my family—" His gaze darted to Waterstrider and away.

For a moment Waterstrider was tempted. As he wavered, he thought about how closely Tag had been following him lately, how difficult it had been to peel himself away and be alone. He guessed, too, that Tag hadn't asked his mother and father how they felt about bringing a Watermaster into their home. "Turn my back on the heronfolk?" He shook his head. "No. I won't do that."

"You aren't your father. You don't need to follow the heronfolk."

"I want to."

"I don't want you to go!" Tag rubbed his sandal against the closely packed gravel.

"You talk as if the Watermasters are going away, never to return. That won't happen. Everyone says so." Waterstrider hoped everyone was right. "The farmers can't keep the canals and ditches in repair by themselves. Even if they did, they don't know how to coax the water where it needs to go. And the clans can't agree on which fields need the irrigation most. The farmfolk would starve to death without the Watermasters."

"I'm not sure they agree. My gran says too many are listening to the priests and believing their promises."

"It's not goodbye, not really. I'll be back. I promise."

Tag nodded, but Waterstrider could tell he didn't believe it.

Too soon, the time came to leave Serpentgate, cross the river, and head south to the place where the Watermasters were assembling. Waterstrider stepped out of the cool shadow of the adobe room on

Cloud Mountain where the boys who were ditchrunners kept their belongings and slept all together. The thought that he might never return to it made him shiver despite the sun's warmth on his skin and the cotton tunic and leggings he wore.

Cloudface stood in a dark alcove between buildings. He caught Waterstrider's eye and raised the back of his hand to his mouth, signaling silence. Waterstrider took a quick look over his shoulder and saw the other ditchrunners clustered together, debating how many of their belongings to bring on the journey. He walked toward Cloudface, who hissed, "Go away."

"You can't stay here by yourself," Waterstrider said.

"Why do you say that? You'd as soon be rid of me."

"That might be so. But staying behind isn't right."

Cloudface sneered. "I'll decide what's right in this."

Waterstrider shrugged. He was about to turn away when Cloudface said, "Don't tell anyone."

"Who would I tell? No one cares whether you go or stay."

"Promise." Cloudface caught at Waterstrider's wrist, gripping it painfully.

Waterstrider tore himself free. "Fine, I'll promise not to tell. You do as you please."

He turned away and fell into step behind the other boys of the heronfolk, following them through plazas and passages, down the uneven steps, out the gate in the outer wall, and away from Cloud Mountain. They walked in silence along the wide path that led toward the river crossing. Others of the heronfolk caught up and merged in, separating Waterstrider from the rest of the boys.

In the group, large and loose as it was, no one would notice Cloudface's absence. *"You'd as soon be rid of me."* That was true enough. Waterstrider put Cloudface out of his mind.

As the house compounds dwindled at the edge of the village, he wondered how long it would take the farmfolk to figure out how badly they needed the Watermasters. The path crested a hill, and he craned his neck to take one last look at the village of Serpentgate. Not a last look, he told himself, for he would surely come back, as he'd assured Tag.

The brush of a hand against his arm startled Waterstrider out of his reflections. He found himself in a knot of giggling girls. The contact of skin on skin as he passed through their midst made peculiar sensations run through him. He smiled at an especially pretty girl. Her face softened in a way that made him think of his mother and the other unhappy women left behind by his father. Waterstrider looked away.

He spotted a younger girl who watched him intently from a small group of children playing a stick game in the dust. She seemed all arms and legs. Below a mat of black hair was an impossibly wide mouth showing a gap-toothed smile. Between hair and mouth, a pair of eyes peered out of the dirt-streaked face, piercing him and laying him bare.

Waterstrider flushed. Then Longflute caught up with him, clapped a hand on his shoulder, and pressed him onward with the other heronfolk.

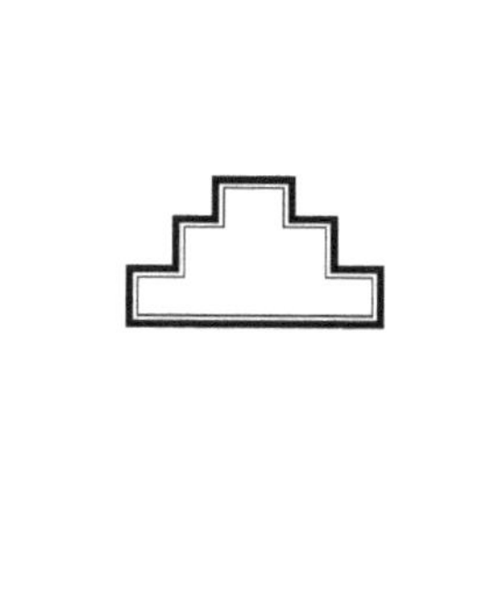

Brother Sun hears our song from the notch in the mountains;
tomorrow he comes wrapped in fire.
A new turning dawns, our hearts soon to gladden
as Brother Sun leaps ever higher.

—FROM THE SONG OF NEW FIRE

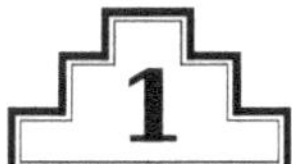

Cobble fixed his gaze on the heat-cracked stones of the fire ring, within which flames flickered pleasantly as the autumn day faded. He took a steadying breath as he considered the Namer's question: Was Cobble ready to give up the name he had borne throughout his boyhood? Was he ready to become a man?

He ached to answer *no*. His heart quailed at what the Namer, the elderly man seated on the other side of the fire, would learn from his tale. Yet the hope that the Namer might be able to tease out what was real in the naming-quest from which Cobble had just returned drew forth a whispered "Yes, uncle."

Raising his head, Cobble looked at Dustwind, who served as the Namer for the tiny village of Lastwater. The old man's face was broken and seamed, as dark as the rocks in the mountains on which long-ago people had pecked away the age-darkened varnish to leave behind images of Mother Ge's children. Travelers said the shapes of animals, humans, sacred beings, and strange spirals and lines could be found all over, wherever outcrops rose above the valley floor. Cobble supposed he might have made some of his own rock pictures during these past few days. He couldn't remember.

Dustwind said, "Cobble was a name well suited to a boy of your bloodline. But as you step forth on your life-path, you need a new name."

Cobble nodded, though he wished things didn't need to change. He folded his quivering lips together to keep from begging for everything to stay as it had been before his vigil in the mountains.

"Then start your tale in the traditional way, as these stories are supposed to be told. Tell me, what did the boy named Cobble see during his naming-quest?"

Obediently Cobble began, telling his story as though he'd observed it from outside himself. "After five days of having no visions, the boy named Cobble, hungry and thirsty, headed toward home." That left a lot unsaid: Shame over the failure of his quest. Fear that he would never have his own family, for what girl would trust him to keep her and their children safe, if no spirit-guide walked through life by his side? Worry over what he was lacking. He wasn't ready. Hadn't fasted enough. Hadn't prepared himself. Hadn't opened his mind to the visions Mother Ge must have sent him.

At the memory of what had happened, Cobble's stomach twisted, making him wonder if he would throw up the bit of food his mother had given him before sending him to Dustwind's compound. He clutched his belly with a hand that felt weak and unsteady. Sweat broke out on his palms and forehead. What if the Namer thought he was making it up?

Cobble ducked his head and continued the story: "The boy rounded a bend and saw"—*in the shadows of the rocks, malevolent yellow eyes stare out of a black beast's face, above a mouth filled with jagged white teeth*—"a jaguar." The simple words didn't half capture the dread he'd felt, but he kept talking. *Crouching in darkness, it waits still and quiet, all except its tail. Draped across the path, the snaky tail twitches. I flinch as I try to stop. My foot lands badly, half off the path. My ankle turns and my knee collapses, dragging me sideways and down.*

I wobble on the loose scree and then, losing my balance, topple over. My hands are caught in the folds of my cloak, so I can't catch myself. I sprawl on my side, half blinded by tangles of hair. Dust makes me cough. I start rolling downward. I struggle to free my arms, but I'm going too fast to stop. All I can do is shield my head.

Down and down I slide and tumble over and over. I cry out once but force myself to be silent: a man wouldn't yelp and whimper, and I must now find a man's courage within me. The jolting fall seems to last forever. I don't stop until I roll halfway across the dry wash at the base of the ridge and fetch up against a boulder.

Cobble realized he had stopped talking at some point. He shot a look at Dustwind, whose wrinkled chin rested on his leather-clad chest.

"Go on." The Namer's voice offered no clue about what he thought of the story. "Cobble saw a jaguar and fell. What then?"

"In the fall, Cobble"—it felt strange to refer to himself that way, but he supposed that was the point, to separate himself from the name —"must have hit his nose, for when he wiped it, his finger came away bloody." He remembered wrapping a trembling hand around the finger to hide the scent of blood. He'd felt exposed in the open wash, with nowhere to hide, no way to defend against tearing fangs and raking claws. Dizzy with fear, he'd scanned the slope for any sign of the jaguar but saw nothing.

Cobble wondered whether Dustwind believed his story. Most people knew of jaguars only from tales told by Far-Traders and other travelers from the southlands, for the powerful hunters seldom came this far north. Cobble didn't dare mention that the one that he'd seen wore a black coat, even more rare than the spotted kind. What could it mean that such a fearsome beast had appeared to him?

No spirit-guide had revealed itself in the four days Cobble spent fasting on the highest peak—consuming nothing but herbal infusions by mouth, burning tobacco and breathing the smoke, rubbing pungent medicine-bundles over his naked, chilled flesh—all to bare himself to Mother Ge and her sacred children. During those seemingly endless days of doing exactly what he was supposed to, all that happened was that he went from hungry and miserable to famished and desperate and ashamed.

Only after he'd exhausted the waterskins and started home had Cobble experienced anything that could be considered a vision. But how could the jaguar, fierce hunter and unafraid, be a spirit-guide for Cobble, who was nothing like that? Cobble remembered being in the wash and wishing he knew what lay in wait for him on the narrow mountain path above: was the jaguar really there hunting prey, or was it a manifestation from Mother Ge . . . or nothing at all, made up out of his own fear?

I rest against the big rock, taking shallow breaths through my mouth. There's a sharp pain in my chest with every heartbeat. I worry it might be a broken rib, or worse, but as my pulse slows, the twinges subside. I push away from the rock and lie on my back. I test hands and arms, knees and ankles, neck and shoulders. Though I hurt all over, everything moves when told to.

"What was around Cobble after he fell?" Dustwind asked, drawing Cobble out of the painful memory.

Patches of stiff arrowweed and brittlebush grew along the banks of the wash. The crisp odor of plants he'd crushed on the way down mixed with the scents of blood and dust on his skin. Sunlight pierced the slit of sky that showed overhead. A bird let out a harsh one-note call somewhere up the slope.

"There was a noise," Cobble said. The buzz had jolted his nerves. "Cobble turned his head to find a sidewinder close. Too close."

It holds its head up and flicks its tongue in and out. I'm unable to breathe or swallow. A man would smash the lurking snake. I fumble for a rock to toss at it. Before my hands find anything, it twists away, up the bank and into the arrowweed.

Relief leaves me lightheaded. I gasp for breath and try to blink away the returning dizziness. All over, I feel bruises, cuts, scrapes, cactus thorns stuck in tender places. And cold, though the fill of the wash feels warm under me. My cloak is gone.

Cobble's fingers traced the welt that extended from one shoulder to his breastbone. His pronghorn-hide shirt had ripped during the fall, and the leather ties of his woven rabbit-fur cloak had sliced his upper chest. A man would have gone back for it.

Dustwind's eyes followed Cobble's movement. The old man frowned. "You tell me nothing of what filled your heart during this journey home."

"Is that important?" Cobble asked.

Tilting his head, Dustwind eyed Cobble. "You saw a jaguar, you fell into a wash, you scared away a snake."

"That is what happened." To Cobble's ears, the plain facts were enough. What would Dustwind think if he exposed his childish worries?

"Hmmph." With a wave of his hand, the Namer urged Cobble to continue.

"Cobble became hungry again." Though embarrassed to admit to his boyish weaknesses, Cobble said, "He awoke that morning with an aching head, cracked lips, and cramping muscles from lack of water. And so he started for home, but he got scared by the jaguar and . . ." Cobble cleared his throat. He reminded himself that he'd returned safely from his quest. So why should telling familiar old Dustwind what had happened seem as dangerous as the naming-quest itself?

Cobble said, "He remembered thinking his stomach was grumbling. As the rumbling grew louder, he realized it came from overhead, not his stomach. Gray clouds were building in the bit of sky he could see." Over and over, as far back as Cobble could remember, his father had drummed into him the danger of getting caught in a deep wash in the mountains. You couldn't see whether rain was falling in higher country, droplets becoming little rivulets joining into streams and then, with incredible speed, filling every channel carved out between rocky walls. Flash floods were strong enough to sweep away everything in their path, including fools who didn't pay attention to the subtler signs of rain. Even massive rocks sometimes got uprooted and pushed downstream when that wall of water and mud and debris hit them.

I gaze at the slope I rolled down. I see no path, not even a game trail. If anything larger than a rabbit or skunk goes down to drink from a spring or a seep in the wash bottom, no sign of its passage is visible. A glance toward the other side of the wash shows a nearly sheer rock face rising out of a tangle of arrowweed. The lower part leans inward, over the wash.

Thunder rolls again. "All right!" I shout at the heavy sky. Lightning flashes in the cloud bank. The tang of damp stone and the nose-itching smell of rain-swelled clay come to me on a breeze.

I wonder whether my bruised hands will be strong enough to grab onto twisted bushes to steady me as I climb. Not that I have a choice. I must get higher; only then can I rest. I step toward the knee-high bank. A buzzard sails above the cliffs, wingtips buffeted by wind currents I can't feel. I stop, stuck in place by fear, face and hands twitching. If carelessness or weakness kills me, scavengers like the buzzard will peck the flesh from my bones.

The hot sizzle of lightning makes my skin crawl. The ground trembles beneath my feet. I run to the bank and climb up it on all fours, using my hands to steady myself as the edge crumbles under my knees. I grab for the largest bush I can reach.

"Tell me about the storm."

Caught up in reliving the experience, Cobble had forgotten what he'd last said. He blinked, unsettled by Dustwind's glittering eyes. What was there about a rainstorm in the mountains to interest the old man, who had to have witnessed thousands of storms?

Cobble began the last part of the story. "Cobble fell again, startled by a flash of lightning." He had jerked, and the rock under his moccasin had broken away. His forehead hit the slope as he started to slide down again, his shirt riding up painfully so his belly grated over the dusty scree. Then he'd felt nothing but cool air until he landed in the bed of the wash and had the breath knocked out of him. Again he had lain flat on his back, staring upward.

"There was a darkness as of night, broken by flaring stars. Then the blackness lifted to reveal"—Cobble doubted he could describe it well enough—"a band of sky covered by clouds, inside of them giant faces like masks, with sharp-fanged mouths and round unblinking eyes. They whispered to Cobble in voices that echoed and overlapped. He couldn't tell what they were saying, but he found himself on his feet and walking down the wash and around a bend, then another."

Away from the jaguar, Cobble had hoped. "Farther along, there was a huge stone. When he ran his fingers along its curve, he found a lip that broadened as it went up."

The sensation of coolness on his feet had caused him to look down. Water, rising as he watched, trickled into the indentions left by his moccasins. He'd looked up at the stone again. *All you have to do is get up there,* he'd told himself. "Cobble jumped up again and pulled himself onto that little ledge. From there," where he'd rested, leaning against the warm rock face, "Cobble could see a little trail winding back and forth across the mountainside."

The whispering masks, faces in the oncoming storm, had led him to safety. He'd thought at the time that his adventures were fortunate, for they gave him a story to tell the Namer. But after he'd returned home, while eating the rabbit stew his mother had set aside for him, when he'd looked back on the jaguar and sidewinder and the masks in the clouds, his heart had turned over with a great thump. None of those things seemed like any spirit-guide he'd ever heard of.

"And now Cobble's story is done." His father had told him to finish with those words. Cobble's lips felt so dry, they stuck to his teeth. He reached for the waterskin his mother had given him for this meeting. As he swigged the water, it cooled the back of his mouth and cleared some of the cottony sensation from his throat.

Cobble waited what seemed like a long time. Every now and then he cast a sidelong glance at Dustwind, whose eyes were closed in thought. The old man's wrinkled, bony hands rested on his thighs. The only indication that he was still alive was his thin chest rising and falling with the occasional breath. Cobble wished the Namer would say something, even if it was to chide him for making up such a story.

Dustwind stirred and briefly opened his eyes. Nodding, he said, "Yours will be the last name I ever give."

Cobble's mouth dropped open. He shut it with a snap. He hadn't thought about that, but it made sense. There were no boys younger than him in the village.

After the departure of the Watermasters, places like Lastwater slowly died. Farmers had been the first to leave, as one by one the canals failed. Then makers of baskets and pottery had left; no one in the village had extra food to trade for new things. Only people who relied on the western mountains had stayed—for the game animals, special herbs, and stone quarries found there and nowhere else. Ten winters or so after the departure of the Watermasters, Cobble had been born, one of the few children at Lastwater. The others, those who'd survived, had already left.

Why tell me I'm the last? Cobble wanted to ask, but his father had cautioned him against speaking too much. *"Wait until the Namer asks a question,"* his father had said. *"Interrupt his thoughts, and the name could come out badly."*

Not wanting a weird or embarrassing man's-name like Spots or Snakehead or Clumsy, Cobble bit back what he wished to say: *Must I too leave this place? It's where I belong.* He waited. He wiped beads of sweat from his forehead. He licked his lips, then pulled his lower lip between his teeth and scraped at the dry patches. He twisted his hands together and noticed several of his knuckles were swollen. His skin pulled against the dried blood of cuts and scrapes. He ran a finger along the welt on his upper chest and wished he'd been brave enough to go looking for his cloak.

Cobble wanted to cross over to Dustwind, whose eyes were half closed under spiky white eyebrows, and press on one shoulder to see if the old man was still awake. Instead the boy sat by the fire and fidgeted.

At last Dustwind brought his head up with a jerk. "Can that be it?" Eyes widening, he gazed at Cobble for several heartbeats. The elderly man turned his craggy face to the sky. "Mother-of-All-Creation, I hear you. May you give this young man the courage, discipline, and strong mind he will need if he is to safely walk the life-path you have laid out at his feet."

Cobble lost his breath as the Namer's prayer to Mother Ge rang in his ears: he didn't want a name that required courage. His heart beat as it had when he'd seen the sidewinder. Unable to remain silent, he blurted, "What is my name?"

"Skyblade."

Cobble stared at the Namer. "Skyblade?" He shuddered at the sound of it.

The old man's deep-set eyes held Cobble's. "Skyblade is a powerful name. It will serve you well."

Skyblade. Uncomfortable under that penetrating stare, Cobble looked away. He couldn't escape the name, echoing over and over in his head. *Skyblade. Skyblade.* "Uncle, how did you choose that as my man's-name?"

"It's not I that chose it," said Dustwind in a kindly voice. "Your spirit-guides did."

"My spirit-guide?" Cobble had been certain that no one walked by his side to help him through the quest. Day after day, hungry and confused, he'd been all alone in the mountains. Hadn't he?

"Mother Ge sent you not one spirit-guide but many. Jaguar, its spotted coat a sign of rain, gleaming fangs and claws that mean lightning. Sidewinder, horned serpent with raindrop scales, lightning fast in strikes and movement. Faces in the clouds, whispering to you of rain and flood, wind and storm, promise and danger wrapped up together."

Cobble pressed trembling fingers to his head. Such frightening beings were his spirit-guides? He shrank from the prospect of such a life-path unwinding before him. Through lips stiff with fear, he mumbled, "Skyblade doesn't sound like a name for Lastwater." His village was a place for quiet names, calm and ordinary.

"I have seen much in my many days. Born the same winter the rain priests came to the valley, I became a man in time to help build their temple and enjoy the peace and plenty that followed."

Cobble's gaze flickered toward Dustwind. He'd never heard that before, about the old man's time in Serpentgate, where the priests' temple stood.

"These old eyes tell me you grow impatient, as any young man would: 'What do they matter, these things long buried in the past?' you ask. It is because the past is not dead. The sky warns of changes to come: in the darkness of a clear day, in the streak of starfire brightening the night, such things as marked the rain priests' coming and the Watermasters' leaving. It's the sky that needs young men to understand it, not the bones of the earth."

Cobble clamped his mouth shut to keep from interrupting. The bit about impatience was the only part of Dustwind's rambling words he understood. He was afraid to find out what the old man meant by darkness in day and brightness at night and understanding the sky.

"You're not meant to stay here in Lastwater," said Dustwind, "waiting until all others have died or fled. Mother Ge has laid out a different life-path for you."

"What do you—" Embarrassed by the mouse-squeak of his voice, Cobble didn't finish the question. He forced out a single word: "Where?" Where was he supposed to go?

"From the story a youth tells of his quest, a Namer discovers only his true name, not where it will take him. Go now, Skyblade. Speak with your father. He sees what lies within rocks, where they will break, how to sharpen an edge. Trust him to see what is within you, too." Dustwind tapped his own chest, thin and shrunken with age. "In here, where your soul-spirit lives."

Cobble scrambled to his feet, frightened of what his father might tell him. This wasn't how he had expected his naming to turn out. He bowed his head in respect to Dustwind and took his leave with the sensation that a trap had closed on him, though he supposed he should be reveling in his freedom, his release from the dying village in which he'd grown up, a place from which his few childhood friends had already departed.

As Cobble walked through the village, he tried to look at it as if this was the last time he would see it. The oldest houses, rounded like brush-walled field huts and originally plastered with thick layers of adobe built up over generations to be deep as a man's arm, had collapsed into untidy lumps. With every rain, mud from the curved walls had been deposited on the ground in uneven mounds. Mesquite support posts stuck up like bare arms from a headless torso. Branches that had been woven together to make up the roof now surrounded the posts like disheveled skirts. Even the newer rectangular house compounds, separated from their neighbors by adobe walls taller than Cobble's head, bore signs of neglect. Patches of plaster still clung to the eroding walls, but large chunks had fallen away. Rooflines sagged. Walls had begun to lean.

As Cobble drifted through the village, he thought about what it would mean to stay in Lastwater. Almost everyone else was between Cobble's parents and Dustwind in age. People had their aged parents to support, not children. As a boy, Cobble had been able to help only in little ways, but as a man, he had expected to do more. He would grow stronger as his parents became weaker. He would carry heavy core stones from the quarry for his father, make long journeys gathering herbs and food for his mother. He would hunt deer in the distant mountains and haul the whole load of meat home.

Cobble shook his head at the thought of leaving his parents alone. Who would take care of them if not him? There was no one. If he had to leave Lastwater, would his parents agree to go too? Surely so.

Sunset hung over Cobble's head with brilliant hues of coral, shell, sulfur, and cinnabar painted on the blue of skystone. He told himself the sky would surely look as beautiful elsewhere, for it arched over the entire Valley of Two Rivers and would make everywhere seem familiar. He would have his parents there to ease his way into a new life. All would be well.

Yet as he trod the desert pavement, packed tight by generations of forebears who had passed down something of themselves to him, he didn't think he could call somewhere else home. He didn't want to leave. And why should he go? The name Skyblade might be an awkward fit for Lastwater, but surely it would feel right after a while.

At last Cobble—Skyblade, he reminded himself—came to the gap in the high wall that enclosed his family's house compound. His tentative confidence began to evaporate as he wondered how to tell his parents the name they would have to call him. He peered into the work-yard that lay between the main building and the storage room.

His father, Flintspark, sat under the vatto. Its roof of branches filtered the fading sunlight into blurry shadows that reminded Skyblade of the jaguar's spotted coat. A large stone core rested on the work mat in front of Flintspark, but he had hammered only a few thick pieces off it in the time his son had been with the Namer. His big hands were still, his head bowed.

Waiting for me. Waiting to hear my new name. "Father," Skyblade said in greeting.

Flintspark looked up with a smile. His eyes widened as he saw his son's face. He set down his tools beside his right leg, in a small pile of stone detritus that would be swept up later. The way he placed his stone chisel, two flakes stuck up around it like the horns above a sidewinder's eyes.

Skyblade glanced away.

"Is he back?" his mother called from inside the sleeping-quarters. She hurried out, wiping her hands on her dress. "I'll get him more stew . . ." Bluesage's voice trailed off as she, too, caught sight of her son. She took a few steps forward, then stopped and stared at him.

Both of his parents had seen him earlier, when he came stumbling out of the mountains. He'd braced for questions then, even a bit of a scold. A toolmaker was supposed to draw strength from the mountains, not get himself torn up. That was for farmers, flatlanders, who spent their naming-quests in the little hills and ridges that broke the sameness of the valley floor. His parents had said nothing then. What showed on his face now, he wondered, that would turn them speechless again?

Skyblade's mouth and chin quivered as he gazed at his parents. He clenched his back teeth and fought to control his expression. *The Namer didn't say I have to leave,* he reminded himself.

His father rose and walked up to him. Flintspark swallowed up Skyblade's cold hand in one of his massive paws and wrapped the other around Skyblade's elbow. "Do you have a name?"

Before answering, Skyblade had to clear his throat and blink quickly against moisture that prickled behind his eyes. "The Namer says I'm to be known as Skyblade."

His mother's face paled. Her deep-brown eyes went round with shock. She rushed forward and grabbed his shoulder with one hand, his father's with the other. "Not *that* name!"

Skyblade and Flintspark stared at her.

"Why not?" Flintspark asked his mate in a carefully neutral voice.

"It means priest-killer," she said.

Skyblade's blood chilled. He knew the story, though he'd never heard the name. Many turnings ago, when the rain priests first came to the Valley of Two Rivers, his mother's great-great-grandfather had been blamed for the death of one of the priests and was sent into exile. The rest of the family had moved westward, all the way to Lastwater, as far from the priests as they could get. No one outside the family was supposed to know the secret of their past.

Yet the Namer, the one tasked with looking into a boy's soul to discover who he truly was, had bestowed that infamous name on him. Dustwind might have known the story of the priest-killer, for he'd lived in Serpentgate and helped build the temple. Was that why old Dustwind had given Skyblade this man's-name? Or was the name given because of what had happened on his naming-quest? He couldn't describe the events of the past few days for his parents—the experiences could be shared with no one but the Namer. Nor could he think of any words of reassurance or comfort for his mother. However painful it might be, she had no choice but to call him Skyblade. No one refused a man's-name once it was bestowed.

"Surely you misheard," Bluesage said.

A muscle jumped beside Flintspark's mouth. He released his son and turned to his mate, taking both her hands in his. "Lay your worries aside for now," he told her gently. "We'll think about this over food. Your son is hungry. He hasn't eaten for days, remember, other than the little bit you gave him before he went to Dustwind."

She didn't respond immediately. Then she took a breath and asked, "What did the Namer say about your life-path?"

"He said to talk to Father about it."

Bluesage turned her face away and dropped her chin. Without looking at either of her men, she freed her hands, cleared her throat, gave a little sniff, and said, "We'll sit you down with stew first. Then I'll tend to your injuries. There wasn't time before you went to the Namer . . ." She continued to chatter as she bustled around.

Skyblade might have helped with the chores, but he wasn't sure a newly fledged man should do a boy's tasks. Bluesage motioned for Flintspark to add water to the special pot she used for simmering herbal infusions. Flintspark caught his son's gaze, held up a finger, and shook his head in warning. Did that mean *Say nothing* or *Sit still?* Skyblade wondered. And what was his mother thinking in this moment?

She knew how to fix broken bones and ease the pain of gashes and bruises and torn muscles. Before the farmers left, they'd called on her often. She'd explained that they got careless as they tried to grow more and more food in fields that wanted to yield less and less. Once the farmfolk were gone, she still had hunters and others who relied on her gifts. More recently, though, there were so few people living in Lastwater, hardly anyone needed her care.

We could leave, he wanted to tell her. *Go somewhere you could be more useful.*

Then what would his father do? These days, fields were unreliable except near the river, in the bottomland. Going where there were enough farmers to make his mother feel useful would take his father away from the quarries in the western mountains that had sustained generations of stoneworkers in his family. Skyblade sighed. If his mother was willing to leave Lastwater, would his father choose to stay here?

Skyblade thrust that idea away from him. His mother and father were lifemates, bound to each other by blood and vows, a bond marked for all to see by matching tattoos encircling their wrists. If he had to go, they would both go with him or both stay, of that he felt certain. But if they stayed, who would take care of them as they got older? Skyblade sucked in his lower lip and gnawed on it.

As his parents prepared dinner, they spoke in low voices and cast occasional glances his way. Skyblade wanted to believe they could figure out a life-path for him that would keep them all together. *Is it up to them to find a way forward?* a hesitant voice inside him asked. *Or do you need to do that yourself?*

Twilight gradually shrank his world to a small corner of the house compound—two walls and the darkness that lay outside the glow of the small cook-fire. Skyblade sat on a reed mat beside the fire ring and watched his parents come and go, passing each other in a dance they had perfected over time. For this name-day they had prepared a feast. Stew simmered in a corrugated cook-pot, creating a tantalizing song of scents. Waiting in almost unbearable hunger for his parents to join him, Skyblade gnawed on jerky his father had placed in a basket near his right hand. Mesquite-flour journeycakes and thin slices of baked agave heart appeared in another basket. His mother settled near him and began to drizzle corn paste onto a comal to make the piki bread he liked.

As tears threatened, he squeezed his eyes shut. Leave this place? Leave them? It seemed impossible.

"Have some stew," his father said.

Skyblade opened his eyes and looked at the heavy-walled bowl held out to him. After blinking a few times to keep telltale moisture from spilling down his cheeks, he took the warm bowl. His hands trembled, and he caught sight of his reflection, distorted by ripples across the surface of the broth. Who was he, now that he was no longer Cobble? What was he meant to do? He remembered the buzzard soaring over the wash, slicing the wind with its wings. Buzzards were solitary birds, not part of a flock. They came together only over a carcass, and then they fought and squabbled.

At the thought of a buzzard's solitude, his stomach lurched. His appetite faded. The scab on his forehead pulled against the skin around it, reminding him of the dangers on his homeward path: jaguar, sidewinder, steep walls that trapped him in the wash. Skyblade held the bowl awkwardly. The last part of the Namer's insight gnawed at him. He blurted, "Dustwind said I should leave Lastwater."

Silence fell. As Skyblade waited to hear his parents' response, his pulse beating in his ears was the only sound he heard: it drowned out the nightbirds' call, the shush of the wind, the crackle of the cook-fire.

Flintspark nodded. "We expected no less. After all, what is there to keep you here?"

"There's you! Both of you!"

In a resigned voice, Bluesage said, "You need to go where you're meant to be."

"I'm meant to be here," he told them. "You shouldn't be all alone as you get old." He had no brothers and sisters; none had survived infancy. A few had come out early, no bigger than a baby rabbit. Others had died of milk fever. He had vague memories of his mother cutting her black hair short in grief a few times after her big belly suddenly became small again. The three of them—he and Bluesage and Flintspark—were all that each other had in the whole world.

"It might be . . . there surely would be a better life for you somewhere else," his mother said sadly. "You're growing fast, with a big appetite."

Skyblade looked at the feast laid out in his honor. No longer hungry, he reached forward and set the bowl of stew on one of the flat warming-rocks inside the fire ring. "I can help you gather my share of food. And cook it, too. I may be little, but I'm strong." As Cobble, he had mostly followed his father around, asking questions and learning the stoneworker's craft. As Skyblade, he could make himself more useful to them both, especially his hardworking mother.

"It's not that you're a burden to us." Bluesage bit her lip and sighed.

Skyblade could see that he *was* a burden. For one thing, he ate more than his parents did. His mother picked at her food, birdlike. His father didn't eat much either, often working with one hand while grabbing jerky or journeycakes with the other. Skyblade studied them, for the first time aware of crow's-feet at the corners of their eyes and gray in their hair. Their faces seemed thin.

Skyblade knew that life had gotten harder in Lastwater after the Watermasters left. Irrigation water had once flowed all the way to the village, but as time passed, the main canal could no longer feed the ditches that took water to the fields, and they went dry, one after another. In dusty fields, the crops failed. The deer that had formerly come to steal corn retreated to the desert, making venison a rare treat. Even rabbits and plump-breasted quail became hard to find. Greens were picked early; if any survived to set seed, those seeds were eaten instead of being left to ripen and fall and grow new plants again. A few people started agave patches and planted nopal cactus, but those dryland crops had been eaten up faster than they could regrow. Everybody in the village had to walk farther and farther for wolfberries, cactus fruit, even mesquite beans, because the mesquites nearest the village had been cut for wood. Skyblade knew all that.

What he hadn't considered until this moment was what the daily struggle to feed him meant for his parents. Leaving Lastwater might be the best way to help them. But how could he bear it? Skyblade had sometimes yearned to have friends and adventures, neither of which could be found in the village. Now that he was being urged to leave his parents behind, he regretted ever letting such a yearning lodge in his mind. He pressed a palm against his rib cage and laid his other hand over it, as though the pressure would keep his heart from shattering like a dropped cook-pot.

His mother reached out and patted his uppermost hand. "We've talked about it, your father and I. Perhaps you could go somewhere for a time and then come back."

Leaving for just a little while sounded less scary. Skyblade felt a stirring of hope. "Where am I supposed to go?"

His parents didn't answer right away. Bluesage looked down at her lap, while Flintspark gazed at the fire ring. At last he directed a sidelong look at his son. "The name *Skyblade* would suggest that your life-path leads to the rain priests."

Fine hairs lifted on Skyblade's nape. The priests prayed to the Ta'atchul, mysterious spirits of the sky. Skyblade remembered the muttering voices, the sharp-toothed faces in the roiling clouds of his naming-quest, and shivered. If those were the Ta'atchul, he wanted nothing to do with them.

"Perhaps Mother Ge has given us a chance to set things right," his mother murmured, her face turned away so he couldn't see her expression. She took a deep breath and let it out slowly. "To repay a debt of blood."

Skyblade folded his arms as the ache in his chest deepened. Though he knew he was being unfair, he asked, "Am I to be sacrificed to the sky-spirits for something done long before I was born?"

His mother lifted her head. She gazed at him with tear-filled eyes. "Don't look at this as a punishment. The priests have a good life."

Skyblade pushed to his feet. He opened his mouth to protest, then shut it as his father said:

"They have young men join them as Seekers, stay for a turning, and then return home. Or remain nearby and become craftsmen or even farmers, mated to girls of some clan. Not all who go to the temple take the vows."

Skyblade lifted his chin toward the blanket of stars overhead, only half seeing them. He considered the possibility of returning home after an adventure he would remember forever, as Dustwind had done. Or finding a lifemate of his own and producing a new family in a place where living was easier. Or taking vows that would bind him forever to the sky-spirits.

Flintspark said, "There's a trade day soon, at Rabbitbrush. Come with me. We'll talk to the village priest and see what he has to say."

"In the end, it's my choice, isn't it?" Skyblade said. "Let me think on it a while." He sat again and reached for the bowl of stew.

The trade day arrived quickly. While stars faded in the false light that preceded dawn, Skyblade walked along the canal path. His mother's burden basket, its yucca-fiber net straining against the weight of the stone tools in it, dug into his back. He reached behind and wrapped his hands around the saguaro-rib stanchions. A slight upward lift eased the pressure on his head where the tumpline rested, a wide strap that went from one saguaro rib to another and helped steady the load.

The previous evening, he and his father had sorted through the baskets and hides that held finished tools and preforms, which would receive their final shape and edge later. Under Flintspark's watchful eye, Skyblade had carefully folded the more delicate examples in rags, checking them for flaws, before placing them in pouches. Skyblade had been impressed by the treasures his father brought out of the storeroom. There were chert belt knives he remembered having admired when he was no taller than his father's waist, a graceful greenstone ax head he'd been allowed to peck away at during one long winter, even a set of flensing and butchering knives of different sizes to strip flesh from carcasses.

He now bore those beauties upcanal as gifts for the rain priests to convince them to let him serve in the temple. He wasn't sure whether to hope the tools would be tempting enough—or wouldn't. His father was a canny trader, used to getting enough food for the next winter by making tools the previous one. For the upcoming winter Skyblade was allowing himself to be traded away, and his parents would not even gain food from it.

That first night after receiving his man's-name, Skyblade had reconciled himself to the idea that he had to leave. His parents were right:

there was no life for him in Lastwater. Whether that meant his life-path lay with the priests was another question. In the confusion that had clouded his mind immediately after becoming Skyblade, he'd been sure it didn't.

Now, as he walked beside the empty canal under a slowly brightening autumn sky, he wondered whether the fact that his name had belonged to an ancestor who wronged the rain priests meant something. If the tools he carried made the priests accept him, he could restore his family's honor by giving his hands and his service to the temple for a time.

He'd been afraid, in those first moments of being Skyblade, of leaving his parents and everything familiar. Yet that was part of becoming a man, and so he had given in to his father's suggestion of going to Rabbitbrush to speak with the village priest.

His fears had subsided with each step out of Lastwater, as he remembered the vision Mother Ge had sent him of the rain-spotted jaguar, the lightning-strike sidewinder, and the great black bird borne on thunder and wind. She had shown him terrifying faces in the clouds—and protected him from his fears both on the earth and in the sky.

But during the last part of the journey upcanal, after crossing Snakewallow Wash and entering lands where clan flags marked the extent of fields, Skyblade had begun to doubt again. Wouldn't the priest at Rabbitbrush take one look at him—an outsider, clanless and unknown—and turn him away? Or even recognize his tainted blood, descended from a priest-killer?

Flintspark was confident that the finely crafted tools would win Skyblade a place in the Temple of Lightning. It might not happen, Skyblade told himself. Then what? *Then you go home and make yourself so useful to your parents, they can't imagine life without you.*

Distracted, he caught his moccasin on a protruding root. Skyblade jolted forward. He kept himself upright by shifting his balance lower and quickly placing his hands on his knees. The tumpline slid partway off his forehead on one side. The sudden uneven pressure wrenched his neck. "Aiii! By the goddess!"

His father, leading the way, turned and asked, "Are you all right?"

"Fine." With his thigh muscles and back protesting the awkward position, Skyblade fumbled with the strap and managed to right it.

"We can rest if you want."

Skyblade straightened slowly. He looked ahead. Smoke from the cook-fires of Rabbitbrush drifted in the breeze, though the gentle curve of the canal and the low willows and reeds that lined its course hid the village walls from view. "It's not far. I'll be fine."

The sun rose behind a blanket of clouds as Skyblade followed his father into Rabbitbrush. The village was the same as he remembered, contrasting painfully with Lastwater. Here, walls of houses stood straight and proud, supporting sharp rooflines, the plaster coating mostly fresh. And Rabbitbrush, at least twice the size of Lastwater, held a lot of people. Hundreds. They all seemed to shout or whistle or sing or laugh. The noise made Skyblade's head ache.

He pulled the tumpline away from his forehead to ease the strain on his neck. With his head free, Skyblade could see more of the village.

Once every moon, Flintspark would set off before dawn on a trade day, laden with tools to exchange for food. As Skyblade had grown, he'd carried a waterskin and a belt pack with journeycakes for his father, then added quartz crystals, skystone beads, nodules of obsidian, arrowheads, knife blades, and spearpoints, all lighter items that could be rolled up and placed in a carry-sack. This was the first time he had borne a loaded burden basket—granted, it was his mother's smaller one and weighed a lot less than the one on his father's back. Carefully he settled the tumpline onto his forehead again, relieved that he would soon be free of the load.

Flintspark strode onto the trade ground, a large open space at the foot of the plastered wall surrounding the big platform mound, the tallest structure built by men that Skyblade had ever seen. Other traders laid out their wares on blankets and furs while sharing stories and jokes. One came and took the burden basket off of Flintspark. After a word of thanks, Flintspark did the same for Skyblade.

"I can—" Skyblade bent toward the basket, which balanced upright on the four saguaro-rib stanchions. As he did so, he saw a thin piece of chert poking through a hole in the netting. Skyblade bit his lip, afraid the knife tip had sliced through the twisted-yucca cord. If so, it would be his fault; he was the one who had wrapped the blades before putting them in his mother's basket. A second glance showed him that the netting was still knotted properly. Still, his carelessness could have required a repair. Not a good start to his new life as a man. "I can take care of my basket," he finished.

"Leave it." Flintspark waved him away. "The trading will wait."

The same trader who had freed Flintspark of the larger basket overheard. "You have somewhere else to be?"

"My son has been called to serve the rain priests. We're going to hunt up old Hawkleg."

If the pride in his father's voice hadn't prodded at his own heart, Skyblade might have contradicted him. Called to serve? Hardly. He realized that he hadn't considered what this life-path might mean to Flintspark. Did his father think *My son is special?*

The trader looked askance at Skyblade but said nothing. Skyblade turned away and lifted the waterskin to his mouth, drinking deep to soothe his dry throat and help ward off the headache that wanted to sneak back.

As Skyblade lowered the waterskin, Flintspark clapped his hand on his son's shoulder. "Let's go."

They walked to the end of the mound, where a set of crude stairs led up to the flat top. The mound top consisted of a maze of walls, many crumbling like the ones in Lastwater but still tall enough to keep Skyblade from seeing what lay behind them. He imagined dark rooms filled with clouds of smoke from tobacco and whispered songs that would draw down the clouds and call the rains. He shivered as his eyes darted from side to side. Through narrow passages Flintspark made one turn after another, following walls that allowed only one route.

The walls opened onto a plaza, in the center of which burned a good-sized fire. The scent of mesquite carried sharply to Skyblade's nose. Beside the fire on a bench made of gnarled wood sat an old man. Basking lizardlike in Brother Sun's warmth, the elderly priest didn't look up to see who had invaded this place in which he rested alone.

On the priest's cheek, Skyblade saw a zigzag tattoo of lightning, its heavy line swallowed by deep wrinkles. Skyblade pressed his lips together as he wondered whether he would someday have the same mark pricked into his skin with cactus thorns and colored with mesquite charcoal. Have the sides of his head shaved close, his remaining hair pulled to the back of his head and wrapped around with ribbons into a club, like this priest, whose fallen-in face seemed as ancient as the mound around him.

Skyblade's parents believed that their son was capable of pursuing a life of magic and prayer, learning rituals that would bind the Ta'atchul to his will. Skyblade hadn't been able to envision that future for himself. Whenever he thought of the Ta'atchul, he could see only the glaring eyes and tooth-filled mouths that lurked in the clouds during his naming-quest. Becoming a priest had seemed out of reach, pulling down the rain from the sky too big a role for one such as him. As he studied this wrinkly, broken-down old man napping by the fire, Skyblade for the first time considered the possibility that the priests were men like any others.

"Greetings, O Hawkleg, honorable uncle," Flintspark said.

The ancient priest by the fire looked up with rheumy eyes. He shifted on his bench as though to see them better. "Who comes?"

Skyblade kept his eyes averted from the rain priest's left leg. Below the knee, the leg was withered and twisted, the reminder of a rattlesnake bite from many turnings ago. In his youth, Flintspark had explained earlier that morning, the gray-haired priest had been a shadowdancer, one of the ritual performers who danced with live snakes during the spring sun-festival. He apparently disliked having his deformation noticed and could become bad-tempered if someone commented on it. Skyblade pitied the crippled priest but understood the pride that might make him sensitive.

"Honorable uncle, I am Flintspark of Lastwater, maker of stone tools. This is my son, Skyblade."

With a single glance up and down, Hawkleg took Skyblade's measure. His gaze returned to Flintspark. "A large name for such a small boy." His voice plainly said, *Why are you bothering me?*

"Skyblade is his man's-name, newly bestowed. It's a name worthy of a Seeker."

Hawkleg's bushy eyebrows drew together. "Many boys believe they've been chosen."

I don't believe I was chosen, Skyblade thought. *That's not why I'm here.* But as he remembered the jaguar, the sidewinder, wings on the wind, and faces in the clouds, his pride stirred. The name Skyblade had come from that vision, after all.

Hawkleg waved a gnarled hand. "The priesthood doesn't need any more Seekers. Go away." He couldn't be persuaded, even with Flintspark's promise of tools with which to keep the mound and the buildings on it in good repair. The old priest snorted. "Tools? Useless to me."

Flintspark hesitated but at an unrelenting glare from the priest nodded and made a respectful farewell. Hawkleg bent his head toward the fire and closed his eyes.

Skyblade followed his father back through the maze to the steps. Wordlessly they descended, Skyblade trying to figure out whether he was disappointed or pleased by the priest's rejection. They were crossing a small plaza when a challenge came from behind: "Boy! What brings you here?"

Skyblade spun around.

A large man approached, tall and broad, wearing a wide-sleeved cotton shirt belted in place over a kilt. Respectfully, Skyblade lowered his head. So muscled were the man's legs that Skyblade thought a single thigh had to be as thick as his own waist.

"I asked what you are doing here."

Skyblade stole a sideways glance. A frown twisted a scroll tattooed on one cheek and a streak of lightning on the other, marking the man as a rain priest, though far more imposing than crippled Hawkleg atop the mound.

Skyblade gulped. "I—"

His father answered on his behalf. "Greetings of the day, honorable uncle. I am Flintspark, of Lastwater. This is my son, Skyblade."

Skyblade suppressed a shiver when a pair of glittering dark eyes, as reflective and depthless as obsidian, turned his way.

Flintspark extended his hand politely, palm outward. The hard-faced priest didn't lift his hand to press against the one being offered to him.

"The stone trader," the priest said with a lift of his brows. His long hair, too, like Hawkleg's, was held in an upright club at the back of his head, wrapped with a yellow ribbon. The sides of his head were shaved, but a short fringe along each side hung down to cover the shaved part.

"Yes," Flintspark said. "And you are . . . ?"

"Thorn."

Flintspark inclined his head respectfully. "Thorn of the Stormbringers. I've heard the name. You come to Rabbitbrush to collect tribute for the temple, don't you?"

"That is correct."

The priest turned his attention to Skyblade, scrutinizing him from head to toe more carefully than Hawkleg had done. "Skyblade. And Flintspark, of Lastwater. What made you disturb Hawkleg's slumbers this day?"

Flintspark smiled. "My son would become a Seeker."

"Why?"

"Lastwater has nothing for young people. Soon enough it will dry up and blow away—"

Thorn interrupted. "Only a few Seekers become Stormbringers, but merely becoming a Seeker changes everyone. Going home to a small, quiet place once he gets used to Serpentgate may be difficult. Have you considered that you are likely to lose him forever if he comes to us?"

Skyblade felt the urge to promise that he would never turn his back on his parents, but he had given his word to stay silent during his father's introduction of him to the priests. He pulled his inner cheek between his teeth and ran his tongue over it to keep his mouth shut.

"Returning to us would be his choice," Flintspark said. "If he decides—"

"It is not for Seekers to decide whether they are worthy of taking their vows."

"You'll find him worthy," Flintspark declared.

The priest swung his head toward Skyblade again. "This scrawny boy hardly resembles you. Is he your mate's son rather than your own, and you want him out from under your roof?"

"Go to the trade ground," Flintspark told Skyblade. "Bring back your mother's basket."

"But—" Skyblade swallowed his protest and started off.

"Feed him up well," Flintspark said right before Skyblade turned the corner and lost sight of the two men, "and he'll grow fast. I did at that age."

Skyblade stopped, unable to resist hearing what was said about him.

"Your son, then. So you and his mother are lifemates." For a moment, Thorn the priest said nothing more. Then he added, "You know such a pairing is impossible for a Stormbringer? If your son became one of us, he would be vow-bound to the Ta'atchul, never a woman. Though he would lie down with many, none could ever be his."

Skyblade knew the priests ritually coupled with the women who served Mother Ge, but he'd never imagined himself doing that. He flushed as the thought stirred his blood. He reminded himself of the plan: spend a turning as a Seeker, then leave the temple and find something to do near Serpentgate that would allow him to bring his parents upcanal and take care of them as they became old. But girls! For a moment he lost himself in imagining the beautiful Cornmaidens.

Thorn's deep rumble broke that vision. "If you care for your son, you should take him and return to Lastwater. We seldom accept boys from the outer villages."

"But you do sometimes," said Flintspark. "I know this is true."

"When there is something special about them. I do not see this with your son."

It was no more than Skyblade had told himself earlier that morning. Still, hearing it stated so plainly stung.

Flintspark said, "From what I've heard, the advantage of Seekers from Serpentgate isn't that there's anything special about them. It's that along with them, you gain food and cotton and strong young backs to labor in the fields. But you also need to keep your temple and other buildings plastered and in good repair. Skyblade has a knack with stone and earth. Besides, he's a good worker: diligent, careful, obedient."

Skyblade drew back at the emphasis he thought he detected in his father's voice on that last word, as though Flintspark knew he was listening. An obedient son would have obeyed his father already and be halfway back with the tools. Skyblade headed for the trade ground and tried to set aside what both priests he'd met today thought of him: small, weak, a forgettable boy from a forgotten place. Instead he pictured the soft curves and soft skin and soft voices of Cornmaidens.

As he entered the plaza, he saw a few villagers poking around the goods laid out for trade. Scattered among tall water ollas and thick-walled cook-pots were rawhide packets of salt from the Great Water far to the west, huge granaries he could nearly stand up in, robes from the curly-haired humped beasts from the plains beyond the Mountains of Sunrise, and massive metates and mesquite grinders, each one so heavy it would have been its own load. Skyblade pressed his lips together. If a puny thing like him became a trader, he would have to specialize in lightweight goods, like dried herbs and brilliant macaw feathers from the City of Birds in the southlands.

On one side of the trade ground, Skyblade saw a group of girls, pretty, with dimpled cheeks and long hair flowing over their shoulders. They chattered to each other and giggled at him. He knew what they saw: an awkward boy, thin, shorter than most of them, sweaty, covered in travel grime. Skyblade set his back teeth and tried to march along, straight backed and proud.

He stopped in front of his mother's burden basket. Earlier he'd been proud of his effort, walking with that weight on his back. As he looked at the basket now, all he could see was that it was less than two-thirds the size of his father's and was filled only halfway. Mostly what he'd been carrying was air. Not that the girls would know that. But Thorn the Stormbringer would, as soon as it came time to unload the basket. The priest was the one Skyblade had to impress, not the girls.

Skyblade took the top bundle of tools from his father's basket. He placed the thick otter-hide packet, tied securely with yucca-fiber cords, in the smaller burden basket, then added two more. The three bundles of tools came to within a hand's-breadth of the top ring of the burden basket. Determined to prove that he was strong despite his small size, Skyblade sat in front of the fully laden basket and put his arms through the shoulder straps. He straightened the tumpline and let the strap fall over his shoulder where he would be able to reach it once he was up and balanced. He placed his feet under him and tried to stand. With the help of his braced arms, Skyblade managed to get his butt off the ground, but he feared that if he tried going any higher, he might overset and crush the basket under his body as he wallowed as help-less as a turtle tipped onto its back.

"What are you doing?" his father's voice snapped.

Footsteps pounded up to Skyblade from behind. The weight of the burden basket vanished so quickly, he found himself standing on tiptoe as Flintspark stripped first one strap and then the other down Skyblade's arms to pull the basket off his back. Skyblade settled onto his heels and turned. Blood rushed into his cheeks as he watched his father place the basket on the ground—with one hand, Flintspark had held up the full basket while freeing Skyblade from the straps. Skyblade's impulse to prove that he was stronger than he looked had made him look foolish.

Beyond Flintspark stood Thorn, a witness to Skyblade's humiliation. The big priest said, in a voice almost gentle, "Let us see what you brought."

Flintspark jerked his head at Skyblade, who leaped to obey the wordless order. Removing the tool packets from the burden baskets meant he could hide his burning face.

"Agave and corn knives," said Flintspark. "Trowels for plastering. Plus preforms for thin blades and nodules for points, some chunks of pretty stones for beads and mosaics, even flint for starting fires."

The priest grunted. "Anything heavier?"

Skyblade bit his lip on a snappish observation about how heavy these tools were, when you had to carry them on your back.

Flintspark's hands unknotted the cords on a large skunk-hide packet. He spread the black fur wide and separated the pieces of gleaming chert, roughly shaped into long blades but not yet sharpened for use. "What do you have in mind?" he asked.

"Scrapers and choppers. Axes."

"I can bring some," Flintspark said.

Skyblade stilled at the finality in his father's voice. Had they come to an agreement? With his arms deep in the basket, ready to take out the last fur-wrapped bundle, he couldn't see his father's expression. He released the tool packet and straightened. Flintspark stood feet apart and hands behind his back, staring at the rain priest.

The priest bent low and examined a few of the blade preforms. Then he rose to his full height and locked eyes with Flintspark. "Is he worth five loads to you?"

"Three."

"Four, and done."

"Four, then," Flintspark agreed.

The two words echoed in Skyblade's ears.

"Delivered when?" the priest asked.

Flintspark folded the skins around the blades again and prepared to tuck them away. "These two, you can have now. I'll deliver the last two to you at the time of the New Fire ceremony. At Serpentgate. Along with your new Seeker."

"At midwinter, then. We will expect everything to be of the highest quality." The warning was plain: there could be no turning back from this bargain. "I will send someone for these two loads."

Skyblade stared after the priest's broad back as the big man left. Less than three moons in which to say farewell to his parents, his home, his village, and the mountains that had brought him the man's-name that set him on this life-path. He told himself that day was a long way off—no point worrying about it yet.

Time passed quickly for Skyblade between the trade day and the midwinter sun-festival. There were tools to be made, food to be gathered and prepared for winter storage, goodbyes to be said. Then a long day's travel along the canal from Lastwater through Rabbitbrush and on toward Serpentgate, where the priests' temple stood. With each step Skyblade took toward Serpentgate, he found himself less anxious about what it would be like to live among the Stormbringers and more excited about being with boys his age, seeing what generations before him had built, and witnessing the ceremonies that kept the world in balance. Then finally he was there—not at the temple yet but near enough to see it.

He stood gazing up at the broad cavern called the Belly of the Mother, north and uphill from the village of Serpentgate. Earlier, while sunlight seeped through bands of clouds, Skyblade had learned from a trader named Blackstar, a friend of his father's, that the flames of the New Fire ceremony would long ago have been lit by a group called the Skywatchers. The Skywatchers had diminished until they were too few and too elderly to perform the sacred rites, so Stormbringers were now the ones who turned Brother Sun back in his journey along the horizon, making the nights shorter and the days longer.

As Skyblade waited for the ceremony to begin, blood pumped hot and edgy through him. He figured all those who stood watching felt the same, despite the chilly drizzle that rolled off their faces and oiled cloaks. But his excitement had a different cause: he might someday be one of the celebrants bearing torches in the Belly of the Mother.

In the silence, with his father on one side and Blackstar on the other, Skyblade heard his breath rasping in his ears. The long, throaty note of a ram's horn sounded. Its echoes came back from the red cliffs. On that signal, the torches dipped toward the cave's floor. Flames whooshed up from the tinder—fluff from cattails, another thing Blackstar had explained. In a burst of scarlet heat, the Belly of the Mother came alive with the blaze of the New Fire.

Skyblade, eyes stinging from the brilliance, tore his gaze from the wall of flames and looked southward, toward Sky River. More fires winked into existence in every direction as far as he could see. Watermasters had once been the ones to pass along the fiery assurance of spring to everyone in the Valley of Two Rivers, lighting signal blazes on all their high mounds overlooking the canals—but now it was the priests who made the promise.

He heard the rise and fall of the Stormbringers' deep voices as they began casting the song that would put an end to the rainy, gray days of winter. These were the men he was bound to serve, for at least one turning. Maybe the rest of his life, if he proved worthy. He imagined himself as one of the singers, one of the robed men who lit the fire, someone who helped return Brother Sun to his proper path and set the world in order. That possibility gradually became a yearning: *That's what I want.*

Feeling guilty in the next moment, he glanced at his father, who stood beside him. What would his parents do if they lost Skyblade to the priests, as Thorn the Stormbringer had warned might happen?

Flintspark smiled fleetingly and reached for Skyblade's elbow. Callused, scarred fingers pressed, warning Skyblade to silence. But Skyblade hadn't been going to say anything; Blackstar had made it clear that nothing but the priests' song should be heard during the ceremony. Tomorrow's feast day would be the time for noisemaking and gaiety. "Finally," Blackstar had grumbled. "Everyone's tired to the bone of this wet winter." As Skyblade listened to the rise and fall of the Stormbringers' voices, he wondered whether the priests could call on the Ta'atchul to stop the rains, as well as to bring them.

In every community Skyblade and his father had passed through between Lastwater and Serpentgate, they'd heard about the damage to the canals from flooding, and the expectation of more to come, given the depth of the snowpack in the mountains to the east where the river originated. Along the eroded canal path, they'd had to cross many unrepaired washouts. Skyblade's back still remembered the weight of the burden basket, which held one of the last two loads of tools that would complete the bargain with the priests. On the uneven footing of the path, top-heavy from the basket, Skyblade had imagined himself losing his balance and tumbling into the cold water that pooled in the canal depths.

"So why hasn't anyone filled the washouts and replastered the canal banks?" he'd asked during a rest break while they were munching journeycakes and staring into the canal.

Flintspark had replied, "Why bother with repairs when floods are likely to tear through them when the snow melts?"

To keep them from getting worse, Skyblade had thought. Trudging onward behind his father, Skyblade had recalled the ancient prophecy of the rainbow knife: terrible days when the canals would fail utterly and the People of Two Rivers would be cut loose from their fields and forced to wander the desert, homeless and reliant on whatever food Mother Ge provided for them. Was the prophecy coming to pass? But no, he'd thought, the priests wouldn't allow such a thing.

The closer Flintspark and Skyblade had come to the river, the worse the path had become. Finally his father had suggested that they leave the canal and cut across the desert toward Blackstar's compound north and east of the village of Serpentgate. The going had become easier in the wide spaces between shegoi bushes and stands of bristling cactus. They'd arrived early enough to shrug out of the baskets, have some warm stew, and get into a good position from which to witness the New Fire ceremony.

Skyblade had thought it would be harder to say goodbye to Lastwater and his parents. But as he'd walked along the canal and had seen other little villages like Lastwater, interspersed among clusters of isolated stick-and-mud houses set in fields, he'd thought about what Thorn had said: *"Becoming a Seeker changes everyone. Going home to a small, quiet place once he gets used to Serpentgate may be difficult."* Skyblade hadn't been able to imagine what Serpentgate might be like or why going back to Lastwater would be a disappointment.

Then he had arrived at the Belly of the Mother and, by the light of the setting sun, had seen the massive mound at the south end of the village of Serpentgate. He'd gotten his first look at the three-story Temple of Lightning, gleaming in the sunset at the north end of Serpentgate.

With the flames of the New Fire at his back and the song of the Stormbringers in his ears, he peered through the gathering darkness toward the place where the temple stood, but he could no longer pick it out. After the ceremony, that's where he would live. Not in the temple proper but in a set of rooms nearby where the Seekers slept and ate all together as brothers. Skyblade found himself eager to get there and see what this new life would be like.

Smoke, thick and roiling, stung his eyes. He squeezed them shut, but still they burned. Skyblade wondered at the intensity of the burning sensation, for he was far below the fires in the Belly of the

Mother and far above the mound of Serpentgate where the nearest signal fire burned. A strange odor made him cough. It smelled of tobacco and something more. As another spasm of coughing struck him, the hair on the nape of his neck stirred.

Around him, even inside him, Skyblade felt a presence. His skin tingled and became hot. Sweat beaded on his torso before rolling down his chest, under his deerskin leggings, and into his rain-dampened moccasins. He shook there, engulfed in smoke and soaking wet inside his oiled cloak, burning up despite the drizzle that should have chilled his exposed face and hands.

"What is it?" his father asked from beside him.

Skyblade opened his eyes. He couldn't say anything, couldn't move, couldn't breathe. As the sooty haze began to dissolve, he saw in the wisps of smoke the faces of a lovely girl with clouded eyes and a woman with a glowing smile. The earth trembled under his feet.

Flintspark grasped his arm with hard fingers, steadying him. Skyblade blinked down at the hand biting into his flesh. When he looked up again, the women were gone. Had he imagined them? he wondered. Or had he been given a vision, this time without the fasting and herbs he'd consumed during his naming-quest? The evening breeze played over Skyblade's skin, drying the sweat and cooling him.

Who were they, those two? No answer came to him on the breeze. There was only the song of the Stormbringers.

Skyblade swiped the granite trowel through the plaster in the waterproofed basket beside him. With swift strokes, he spread the plaster over the wall he knelt in front of. He wished his father had never told Thorn that Skyblade had a knack for working with stone and clay.

Since arriving in Serpentgate a few moons earlier, Skyblade had been tasked with replastering walls. *"It's important work,"* Thorn had told him. The priest's words had inspired Skyblade for a while. But as spring neared, the thrill of being somewhere different, having new responsibilities, and the expectation of making friends had been replaced by loneliness and the fierce ache of missing his father and mother. Though thinking about his parents made the heartsickness worse, Skyblade found himself doing it more and more, even talking out loud sometimes when alone, as though one of them could hear him.

"So it's boring. Does that make it unimportant?" he imagined his father asking. "It's not what I expected to find myself doing," he muttered, as he thinned out the plaster, carefully feathering the edges.

He wasn't learning anything about the ceremonies conducted by the Stormbringers, wasn't trusted to handle any of the ritual paraphernalia. He wasn't even working with stone, which he appreciated for its permanence, its unyielding nature. Instead he spent his days with clay, changing it from one form to another. Not the sticky red clay used to make pottery but heavy caliche, strong enough for adobe walls and plaster.

There was an endless supply of caliche in the ruins atop Cloud Mountain, the greatest mound his people had ever made, higher than the tallest mesquite tree and eighty strides long. The structures atop the mound had collapsed into rubble, the branches that once formed their ceilings long ago burned in cook-fires or reused in other buildings. Day after day, Skyblade walked to the mound, where he gathered up chunks of adobe and placed them in a burden basket, hauled the heavy load through the village to the temple, crushed the adobe into powder, mixed the powdery caliche with cactus pulp and water to make plaster, and applied that to walls within the temple precinct.

Taking wood and caliche from the ruins seemed disrespectful, like disturbing a grave. But the Stormbringers considered it necessary, and he supposed that meant it was important.

No one cared how he felt about what he was doing. Or anything else. For the hundredth time that day, Skyblade wished he could share his thoughts with his parents. He ran the trowel through the basket to pick up more plaster as he considered what he would tell them if they were there. He would probably talk about the canals. Lately they intrigued him more than the Temple of Lightning and the Stormbringers.

"From the top of Cloud Mountain, you can see the main canals really well," he said. "The river too." The river, filled with debris, had been scary even from a distance. Stronger-than-usual winter floods had torn out the weirs that normally tamed the river, holding back the water and pushing it into the broad main canals. The weirs couldn't be rebuilt until the canals were repaired, and fixing the many washouts along the canals took the biggest, strongest farmers.

That meant they wouldn't have time to prepare their fields for the spring planting. With the promise of an extra share of the harvest, the Stormbringers had sent most of the Seekers to the fields. Skyblade, who lacked experience with such work, was instead prettying up the temple precinct for the spring ceremonies. His initial pride at being given that responsibility had quickly worn off. Going to Cloud Mountain for adobe was the only part of the task he enjoyed.

From the mound he was able to watch the work crews shoring up the banks of the main canals as they laughed and teased and shoved each other while shouting instructions back and forth. He envied their comradery.

Skyblade scraped out more plaster and smoothed it with the trowel. "It could be worse," he said, still imagining his father was there to hear. "I could be slogging through muddy fields or clearing ditches, with somebody ordering me around all the time." Instead, each day he had a section of wall to work on and no one standing over him to criticize.

Heavy downpours hadn't only flooded the canals: one rainstorm after another had sloughed away swaths of plaster from the temple walls. "Turns out, I'm pretty good at mixing plaster. And I don't complain about doing the same thing over and over." That evidently set him apart from other Seekers. "Thorn even praised me once. He said, 'At least that boy from Lastwater doesn't whine. And he does as he's told.'"

Skyblade had nearly finished replastering the building nearest the temple. It hadn't been easy. His hands were raw and blistered. His back and shoulders ached constantly. His mind was numb from boredom. "It would be nice to hear that I've done a good job," he said to his absent father as he swept the thin chert trowel one last time over the fresh plaster.

Sitting back on his heels, he placed the trowel on the ground and wiped his brow with his sleeve. He looked at the section of wall he'd finished. Smooth and glossy, the plaster was starting to dry to its final creamy color at the edges of the patch he'd laid in. Skyblade stood and stretched, linking his hands behind his back, then tilting his head to one side and the other. He lifted his face to the cloudless sky, so pure a blue that he couldn't imagine anything more beautiful.

Looking back to the wall, its deep crevices and fine cracks and bare spots smoothed into an unbroken surface, Skyblade wished its perfection would last, though he knew it wouldn't. Still, it should look good for the upcoming ceremonies. It would have time to harden before raindrops beat down on it. The prickling of his skin, a weather-sense that had developed since his naming-quest, told him rain was coming—not today, but tomorrow. He sighed and unlinked his hands, shaking them out at his side.

Time to go back to the mound and get some more adobe.

"Hey! Lastwater boy!"

Footsteps crunched behind Skyblade. Recognizing the voice, Skyblade spun around to face Puckermouth, the Seeker who'd been on the other end of Thorn's compliment about Skyblade working without whining. The thin-faced older Seeker was flanked by a few others, who followed Puckermouth around like dogs, ready to snarl and snap at anyone who showed weakness.

"What are you doing here?" Puckermouth walked up to Skyblade and shoved him.

Skyblade staggered back. His shoulder blades came up against the remains of a wall, steadying him. Glad that Puckermouth and his gang wouldn't be able to circle around behind, Skyblade trained his gaze on the ground. What were they doing here on the mound? he wondered resentfully. This was his place.

"Look at me when I'm talking to you!"

He knew better than to obey. A direct stare would earn him a kick in the shins or a punch to the nearest shoulder, while refusing to look into the older youth's ratty face would bring only insults.

"You're supposed to be working at the temple. Not the mound!"

Seeing a movement out of the corner of his eye, Skyblade flinched. Puckermouth and the others laughed. Skyblade flushed, which set off a slow burn of anger inside.

Puckermouth had special privileges not offered to the other Seekers, and Skyblade figured that must have made Thorn's mild criticism rankle more. Puckermouth, who ran errands for the Storm-bringers, bragged about being the only Seeker allowed to enter the temple. He bragged about having touched the crystals that focused Brother Sun's light, the ram's horns that announced the beginning and end of ceremonies, and the flutes, drums, rattles, and roarers that sent music winging into the sky for the Ta'atchul. He bragged about being a particular favorite of the Rainsinger, the highest-ranked priest in the Temple of Lightning. But he couldn't brag about being a good worker.

"I'm here for adobe," Skyblade said.

"A scrawny thing like you?" Puckermouth sneered.

One of his butt-sniffers said, "He looks scared. Think we oughta give him something to be scared about?"

Puckermouth said, "Nah. He's quivering like a baby already. Bet his pecker's all shriveled up from fear."

Under lowered lids, Skyblade saw moccasin-clad feet pad nearer and circle toward his right side.

"He don't need to wear a loincloth," a high, girlish voice said. "Nothing to hold in place."

"Balls no bigger than hackberry fruit." Puckermouth's breath felt hot on Skyblade's left cheek.

Skyblade turned his head quickly to see what his tormentor was up to. The hem of his tunic was lifted. Puckermouth fumbled for the ties of his loincloth. Skyblade, uncertain how far Puckermouth might take today's humiliation, smacked the older Seeker's hand away. "Leave me alone. I've got work to do."

The older Seekers didn't move to let him pass, but at least Puckermouth stopped pawing at him.

Someone asked, "Think he's ever been with a girl?"

Puckermouth leaned closer and made kissing sounds toward Skyblade, who drew his head back and turned it away. "Shiningdawn says he doesn't watch her when she goes by," Puckermouth said. "That tells me everything I need to know."

"Now there's a woman could make a dead man stand up and sing," another of his followers said.

"Funny this one doesn't think so. What's the matter, baby boy? Don't know what to do with a woman?"

Skyblade muttered, "She's not a woman. She's a Cornmaiden." One of the young women whose ritual coupling with the Stormbringers ensured the fertility of the crops. Only full priests were permitted to even see a Cornmaiden's face, let alone the rest of her. To keep men and boys from lusting after them, Cornmaidens were veiled whenever they left the priestesses' compound. Anyway, Shiningdawn wasn't the one Skyblade dreamed about at night. If she wasn't swaying her hips suggestively in hopes of catching somebody's gaze, she was rubbing her breasts against any male within reach in a crowd.

Though Skyblade kept his face turned away from Puckermouth, his nails dug into his palms, so tightly had he fisted his hands. He imagined himself uncoiling and smashing one fist into the older Seeker's nose—and being sent straight back to Lastwater. Over a girl he didn't even care about.

"What are you doing?" demanded Thorn's deep voice. "Get to work. You are to help with the plastering, not squabble among your-selves."

"This isn't over," Puckermouth said quietly to Skyblade. He and his butt-sniffers drifted away.

Skyblade, embarrassed by the trembling of his mouth, set his back teeth and pressed his lips together. He started to follow the other Seekers.

"Not you, Skyblade," Thorn said.

Startled, Skyblade stopped. He glanced at the big Stormbringer.

"A friend of your father's has come to see you."

Skyblade eyed Thorn, who stood stiff-legged, his arms crossed. Thorn jerked his head toward his right shoulder. Behind the glowering rain priest, Skyblade spotted a familiar face: Blackstar. The trader passed Thorn and came up to Skyblade. Grasping him by both elbows, Blackstar gazed at him with red-rimmed eyes.

"A Far-Trader came through from the west," Blackstar said. He swallowed hard. "He brought word of your parents . . . nearly every-body at Lastwater . . . they're gone."

Thorn said, "They took sick. Gut troubles, the kind you can't throw off."

"What do you mean—gone?" Skyblade asked.

"They've joined the Ancestors," Blackstar told him.

The words made no sense.

"A few still live," Thorn said. Skyblade looked at him. "They were taken to Rabbitbrush, to the healers there. Your parents weren't among the survivors."

Skyblade shook his head. "No." He yanked free of Blackstar and wound up facing the head-high remains of a wall. "No!" Wanting to break something, smash something, Skyblade laid hold of a cracked section of adobe. He pulled on it, but it wouldn't give.

Sickness churned his insides. He looked at his hands, white-knuckled where they wrapped around the adobe. Slowly he made himself release his grip. He stumbled away, overwhelmed by the heat of his blood, the storm in his head, sweat pouring out all over. He braced his hands against the wall and started kicking it. One long swing with his leg made a welcome pain run up from toes to spine. He'd only struck twice when Blackstar dragged him away.

Hugging Skyblade so tightly that he couldn't move his arms, Blackstar said, "Stop. Hurting yourself won't bring them back."

Tears burned down Skyblade's cheeks. He heard Thorn say, "Let him go." Hard hands pressed in, shifted. Blackstar grunted and released Skyblade.

Skyblade fumbled for his belt knife with one hand. With the other, he reached for his hair to cut it to mark his grief.

Thorn twisted the knife from his grasp. "Be still, Seeker," the big priest told him. "Remember, you are ours now. You left your life in Lastwater behind and vowed to serve the Ta'atchul. This is where your parents wanted you to be. Because they sent you here, you still live."

But they don't! Skyblade's desire to destroy something, to punish this world by taking something out of it, built up like floodwaters behind a brush dam, piling higher and higher until he felt he would be torn apart by the force of his desire. *"Be still."* It seemed impossible. Yet he stood frozen in place, unable to get his feet to move, as something tightened around his chest, squeezing the air out of him. Skyblade closed his eyes. His father's face came to mind, his mother's. Never see them again? Never hear their names spoken? His eyes popped open. "I have to go—"

"No," Thorn said. "You are bound in service to the Stormbringers until we release you. There is nothing you can do for your parents. We are your family now."

Skyblade stared at Thorn. He wanted to spit in that tattooed face.

Family? My family is dead, he wanted to shout.

Blackstar walked up to Skyblade. "They've been taken care of, don't worry." He placed a gentle hand on Skyblade's shoulder and added, "People from Rabbitbrush went to Lastwater to sing the spirits of the departed to the Ancestors. The Stormbringer is right: there's nothing more for you to do. You'll be best off staying here and keeping busy. That'll help take your mind off their passing."

Skyblade dropped to his knees. Shivering, he retched and puked until he felt as if his stomach would come out through his teeth. He'd left his parents and come here to make their lives easier. Now they had no lives at all. When he finished his turning as a Seeker, there would be no one to go home to. No Flintspark. No Bluesage. No one to care for as they grew old. Their spirits had left meat and bones behind, to moulder away in their cotton wrappings and slowly become dirt. Skyblade's tears joined with his sweat and vomit, pooling in the old, broken plaster of the mound.

Several days later, Skyblade stood on the edge of a crowd watching the Stormbringers bring order to the world during the River-Binding, the spring sun-festival. He looked through eyes hot and swollen. Dull misery choked him at the thought that his own world would never be right again. *"We are your family now,"* Thorn had said. *"You are ours."* Skyblade had been permitted no way to express his grief, no time to see his parents' bodies and prove to himself that they were truly gone. His sorrow might eat away at his innards and flood him with memories, but every day he had to pretend that his service to the Ta'atchul gave him reason enough to go on living.

It is enough. It has to be. It's all you have left, Skyblade told himself. *You have a task to do. Go do it.* Yet he couldn't force himself to move. Three moons ago, at the winter sun-festival, he'd had his father at his side. Now he was surrounded by strangers. Skyblade shook his head and took as deep a breath as his tight chest would allow.

Behind him, on a platform built by some of the other Seekers for this ceremony, one of the younger priests danced behind a screen of fine yucca-fiber netting. The sun rose behind the dancing priest, casting his long, spidery shadow onto the wall of the Temple of Lightning in a series of dizzying swoops and arcs. The many small braids on the shadowdancer's head twisted and writhed as if alive. Deep-voiced drums boomed and echoed like distant thunder. Over the steady rasp of basket drums and patter of gourd rattles, the eerie hum of wind-roarers rose and fell.

Skyblade knew the wind-roarers were only slabs of painted wood spun around and around on a cord, but their sound lifted the fine hairs on his nape and made his back teeth ache. The drums rumbled through his bones. Trying to ease the disturbing sensations, he shifted his weight just as the rhythmic music of the instruments faded. At the oddly loud scuff of his moccasin on the hard-packed ground of the plaza, he froze.

The gestures of the shadowdancer slowed, until the young priest stood as though carved of stone, head bowed and arms lifted in supplication to the Ta'atchul. Skyblade hardly dared to breathe for fear of disturbing the crystal quiet of the spring morning. A ram's horn blasted, and the Rainsinger, the most powerful of the Stormbringers, appeared at the top of the Temple of Lightning. Three stories above the plaza, the Rainsinger seemed no larger than a child. The openings that normally gaped black and deep, one directly above another along the center line of the temple's massive walls, had been covered with hides nearly the same color as the walls. To Skyblade, the temple seemed impenetrable, a sheer cliff made by the hands of men.

At the pinnacle of this made-mountain stood the Rainsinger, whose yellow robes shone in the new light of day. Macaw feathers of the four colors of beauty—red, green, blue, and yellow—surrounded his head like rays of the sun, with yellow at the top, green and blue on each side, and red covering his neck. White clay had been painted in a large circle on his face, covering the tattoos of lightning and speech on his cheeks. Black streaks ran down to his chin. In the center of his forehead, the Rainsinger wore a mica mirror that caught the light of the rising sun in unpredictable flashes. He held in one hand the ancient lightning-staff of his office, a single piece of limberwood twisted into a zigzag form and studded with flashing mirrors.

Skyblade couldn't stop staring at the priest, who seemed a creature from a tale of the First Days rather than a mere man. The weight of the moment sent a shiver through Skyblade. Cast forth from the great height, the Rainsinger's song echoed against the walls of the plaza below:

> *In the morning's stillness now we gather to beseech thee*
> *To calm thy rushing waters and flow into the canals.*
> *With pure and hopeful hearts we come together to beseech thee*
> *To calm thy anxious waters and flow gently to the fields.*
> *With unity of spirit now we all as one beseech thee*
> *To calm thy flooding waters and search out the waiting seeds.*
> *For in the sun's warmth they lie under the earth, and thy touch*
> *   they thirstily seek.*

As if the song called them forth, Skyblade felt the Ta'atchul around him, tickling his skin, stroking his hair, whispering in his ear: *"The witch is ours. Bring her to us."* His heart stuttered. The ram's horn sounded again, and the Ta'atchul drifted away on the echoes.

A few days ago, a rumor had begun to circulate among the Seekers: the Rainsinger had traced witchlight in the canal from Lastwater all the way back to Serpentgate. Skyblade had heard several versions of the story. A witch had released poison into the canal. Or had cursed everyone in Lastwater. Or had released a malevolent spirit accidentally, and instead of the ghost hanging around Serpentgate, it had drifted downcanal. *What's wrong with Lastwater, that a witch would want to destroy it?* Though the other Seekers never asked Skyblade outright, he'd felt the question in their avid eyes.

Merely coming from a place connected with witchcraft was enough to mark someone. People seemed to think the victims of the witch must have done something to earn their fate.

Anger at that attitude had sliced through the fog of grief around Skyblade. He'd gone to Thorn to find out if the rumors were true. The big priest had replied that a woman from Serpentgate was indeed accused of being a witch. *"Why would she want to harm anyone at Lastwater?"* Skyblade had asked. Thorn had shrugged and told him that only the Rainsinger could find out whether she had anything to do with it. *"She may be* a *witch without being* the *witch,"* Thorn had said. Looking straight into Skyblade's eyes, he'd asked, *"Someone needs to seek her out and summon her to the Rainsinger for his judgment. Will you do it?"*

At those words, an image of himself plunging a knife into the witch's heart had flashed dreamlike into Skyblade's mind. He could avenge his parents' death!

But that would never happen: without knowing for certain that this woman had harmed his mother and father, he didn't have the confidence to walk the path of vengeance. What he could do was take her to the Rainsinger and let the truth come out. *"I will,"* Skyblade had vowed.

Standing in the plaza, with the Ta'atchul plucking at him and urging him into motion, he should be eager to bring the witch to justice. So why was he reluctant to do so?

The ram's horn blared out again, marking the last verse of the Rainsinger's song. Skyblade forced himself to move through the crowd, craning his neck, bumping into people, and leaving muttered apologies in his wake. At last, along the edge of the plaza, he spotted a woman matching the description Thorn had given him: small and slender, with a single white streak snaking through a long braid wrapped around itself and held at the back of her head with a pair of bone pins. A narrow deerskin cape slipping off her shoulders covered the upper half of her pottery-red skirt.

Skyblade eased toward her. According to Thorn, the woman—a potter named Firesister—stole pots from ruins and worked some kind of witchcraft with them. Skyblade wondered why anyone would do such a thing. Then he remembered his mother talking about people of the old blood, who felt that using tools and goods of those who had departed this world was a way of honoring them. Skyblade thought of his mother's grinding-stones and choppers, her jars and bowls and cook-pots, her roomful of lovingly gathered herbs. Would this woman, this witch, have wanted people dead so she could take their things? But then why was she still at Serpentgate instead of at Lastwater poking through the houses of the ones she had killed?

From a few steps away, Skyblade studied the witch covertly, keeping his face turned upward as though watching the Rainsinger's performance. In profile, her nose and chin were strong, framing a wide mouth with well-shaped lips. He'd seen that face before—she had stood beside a girl at the Belly of the Mother during the New Fire ceremony three moons before.

The Song of Binding ended with one more reverberation from the ram's horn. As the echoes faded, the shadowdancer began moving again. His arms looked different now, bearing strange lumps and swellings. Skyblade knew the ridges were illusions of a sort; they weren't actually part of the young priest's body. While people were distracted by the Rainsinger's song, the shadowdancer had been brought rattlesnakes, placid in the morning cold. The dancer held their heads as the snakes wrapped themselves around his arms. There were no drums now, no rattles or wind-roarers, not even the usual waking sounds of the village. Everyone seemed to be holding their breath. Everyone except Firesister.

She turned and began to leave the plaza. Skyblade hurried to catch up with her. Once free of the crowd, he charged ahead of her and blocked her path. He readied the words he was to deliver.

Then she looked at him. Her warm eyes caressed Skyblade, sweeping him up into her joy. Her mouth curved into a smile, so sweet and loving that he felt humbled before her.

Skyblade said, "The— the Rainsinger . . ." He faltered, suddenly doubting that such a joyous woman could be a witch.

He remembered something his mother had said once, when a neighbor had the bloody flux and thought he'd been cursed: *"Illness always follows the floods. No need to look for witches when it's just bad water."*

Skyblade shook off an inexplicable reluctance to carry out his task. The Rainsinger had sent him here for the sake of the entire community, he reminded himself. Whether his mother believed in witches or not made no difference. This woman's happiness might even come from the pleasure she took in harming others. Yet as he looked at her, he had trouble believing that such a terrible thing could be true.

She asked, "Are you a Seeker, then?"

The doubt in her voice pricked at his pride. With as much dignity as he could manage, he delivered the words he'd been taught: "You've gathered up pots from old places. You must bring them all to the Rainsinger so he can free the spirits trapped in them."

She cocked her head to one side, birdlike. "Must I? Why is that?"

"If you fail to do so, those you care about will suffer when your dark secrets are exposed."

Her smile faded. Her eyes narrowed, and she caught his gaze with hers, unblinking.

An exclamation from the crowd freed Skyblade from her searching eyes, which threatened to strip him bare, down to his soul. He turned his head and followed everyone else's gaze to the temple.

The shadow of a serpent's head reared back and froze for a moment, a monstrous crescent poised against the shadowdancer's arm. The snake's triangular head shot forward and buried itself in the blackness. Skyblade gasped as the shadows twisted and separated, long crooked lines shooting away from the dancer's body. The young priest shuddered and fell, leaving the watchers to gape at the faint pattern of empty netting cast upon the temple's wall by the sun.

Skyblade crouched in a scatter of potsherds, basket sections, pieces of rope, chunks of mud, cane segments. Overlaid on the debris, like a reflection on water, was the indistinct image of the shadowdancer falling, black against the temple wall. Skyblade closed his eyes against the memory as he struggled to piece together what had happened after. The more he thought, the smaller the storage room seemed to become. Every shift of his foot, every rustle of his clothing echoed off the adobe walls surrounding him. The memories came slowly, as though reluctant to emerge from the dark corners of his mind.

Time had passed; that much was obvious. The ceremony had started at dawn, and the sun now stood high overhead, piercing the wood-framed rectangular opening that was the room's only entry. Skyblade remembered climbing through the opening and down a ladder—gone now—to get into this storage room, a compartment in a long, narrow structure along the base of Cloud Mountain. Before that, he'd walked here on his own two feet, though not of his own choice. At each elbow, gripping him hard enough to bruise, was one of the warders who protected the Cornmaidens in their comings and goings from the House of Quickening. Before that, what?

A few flashes of memory: *The plaza, lit by an undimmed sun. Ashen faces around him. A mutter of* "Kissed by the serpent" *passing from one mouth to another. The Rainsinger beginning to speak words that couldn't undo the horror of the serpent's strike.*

Looking at the shaft of sunlight that led up to the real world, Skyblade could recall only one thing the Rainsinger had told the crowd: "If you believe, if you truly believe, then the Ta'atchul will save the one who has fallen." Skyblade had wondered how many people would have to believe, and then voices had begun to whisper on the wind and everything around him had become hazy.

He scrubbed at his forehead. A dull headache hung behind his eyes, an ache that worsened with his touch. Had he fallen? he wondered. But his fingers encountered no bruise. The rasp of skin against skin echoed off the shadowy walls. A few more memories returned. *Stumbling to the gate of the temple precinct. Seekers and priests standing in the plaza, asking each other what happened to the shadowdancer, where he's been taken. I pass them all, saying nothing, and go to the Seekers' quarters.* Skyblade couldn't remember what he'd done from then until sometime later, when Thorn came and got him and took him to the Rainsinger. He wondered whether he had slept or simply lost time, as had happened during his naming-quest.

Legs unable to support him any longer, Skyblade sprawled in the debris on the floor of the abandoned storage room. The Rainsinger, his painted face a dead-white circle from which his unusual yellow eyes gleamed, had wanted something from him: a lie. Skyblade's stomach churned. The headache became worse as the memory sharpened. He rolled onto his back, arms at his sides, and allowed himself to remember.

"It was the witch's doing," the Rainsinger had said. "She cursed the shadowdancer. You must tell everyone that."

But it hadn't been her doing, couldn't have been. As the first serpent struck, Firesister had been talking with Skyblade, her attention not even on the ceremony. Skyblade had told the Rainsinger that, had refused the command to blame her for the disaster that had cut short the ceremony, which since the First Days had bound the river to the will of the people, sending its water into the canals.

Staring unseeingly upward, Skyblade recalled his mother's face, earnest and beloved, as she'd said goodbye to him that last time: "Seek the truth," she'd said, "and you'll never go wrong. Hold fast to what you know to be real." Skyblade laid his forearm over his eyes. His thoughts spun into another memory. *If you truly believe,* the Rainsinger had told the crowd in the plaza. Was that true? Did the Rainsinger—the one who had demanded that Skyblade lie about Firesister—care about truth? How could anyone know what was true or real here in Serpentgate, with its ceremonies and priests and witches?

The mound is real, Skyblade told himself. But it's crumbling and needs repair, like the canals. Like the people, too. Long ago, before Skyblade was born, the People of Two Rivers were split asunder by words that might not have been true, exiling the Watermasters over nothing more than rumors. The same kind of rumors that had sent Skyblade's family to hide in Lastwater. True or not, words have power, Skyblade thought, and it seemed that the people who could best control their words had the most power.

Rubbing his temples, Skyblade thought about his attempts to describe to the Rainsinger what he'd seen in some people's expressions in the first moments after the shadowdancer's fall. It wasn't fear or shock. Maybe hatred or resentment? Something like it showed in Puckermouth's eyes when looking at Skyblade. If people resented or even hated the priests, could there even be enough believers in the plaza, in the entire village, to save the shadowdancer?

Instead of listening to Skyblade, the Rainsinger had interrupted him. "You let the witch escape," the high priest had said, fixing Skyblade with pale flinty eyes, which measured him and found him wanting. "You have proven worthless as a Seeker. Worse, disobedient."

Skyblade had stared at the ground, a spark of anger flickering in his heart. He hadn't disobeyed the Rainsinger. He'd lost track of Firesister after the shadowdancer was struck, but who wouldn't have gotten distracted?

Thorn had defended Skyblade: "He failed today, yes, but offers no excuses. A Seeker who honors the truth may be of some use in the future."

"Disobedience must be punished."

"Separate him from the others, then," Thorn had suggested. "Let him think about what he has done."

That was when the warders had come for Skyblade and brought him to this storage room next to Cloud Mountain. Skyblade curled up on the hard-packed floor in a solitude he hadn't sought but now found to be a relief, as overstrained nerves began to relax.

"Things take on a part of the souls of their makers," his father had once said. Pots, baskets, knives, jewelry, they all were alive in a way. The tools made by his father still held a piece of Flintspark in them. Was that why Firesister collected old pots—to have some connection with the people who had made them? Skyblade groped after that idea, which seemed familiar, but it drifted away.

When he blinked into awareness in the soft dimness of twilight, he realized he was lying face-up in the debris with his arms thrown wide. The edge of a potsherd pressed into his back below his ribs. His cheeks felt wet. The flex of the ceiling told him someone was walking overhead. Dried mud and feather-light dust rained down around him, but the ceiling held. He sneezed and scrambled to his feet.

"Who's there?" Skyblade called out.

A figure appeared. For a moment the silhouette against the dusk-purpled sky reminded Skyblade of the shadowdancer's fall. He blinked away the memory and focused on the form squatting at the hole. When the visitor held out a gourd canteen from which water dripped, Skyblade's gaze fixed on the canteen. He hadn't had any water since dawn. The dryness in his throat seemed suddenly unbearable.

"Rest easy," Skyblade heard Puckermouth say. "You'll be here for a while." Skyblade waited for the gourd to be carelessly dropped, but instead the older Seeker lowered it on a cord. Then Puckermouth tossed down a small cloth-wrapped packet. Skyblade supposed it held journeycakes or cactus-fruit leathers, enough to keep him alive until he was released from the storage room.

Puckermouth sneered. "I was supposed to bring you a hide to sleep on and a cover, too. Forgot. Maybe tomorrow." He disappeared.

The ceiling began to creak, and dust again drifted down.

"Hey!" Skyblade said. "What are you doing?"

In answer, a heavy door made of saguaro ribs was pushed across the opening. "Why are you closing me in?" Skyblade's chest tightened and shivers ran through him as the small patch of light shrank and finally vanished.

No answer came back. Skyblade leaped upward. His fingers struck the door hard enough to jam his knuckles, but the wooden door didn't give. "Ayeee!" he yelled, wordless in frustration. He jumped higher, struck the door with his right fist, then dropped awkwardly to the ground. Skyblade threw his head back and yelled again and again, uselessly.

After a while he stopped, so parched he thought his throat might crack open. Disgusted by his body's weakness, Skyblade felt around for the canteen and the packet of food. Once he found them, he went back to the wall and shoved aside the debris. He sat cross-legged with his back guarded by Cloud Mountain and ate the journeycakes, washing them down with water. The mound radiated cold. He shifted against it, scraping his backbone. The lack of blankets would guarantee him an uncomfortable night. Maybe a lot of them, he thought, if the Rain-singer decided to keep him isolated until the priests found some use for him.

Anger rising again, Skyblade got up and paced back and forth. A large, rounded piece of pottery broke under his moccasin. He stomped on it until he felt nothing more breaking, only pebble-sized bits. Skyblade found another and did the same thing. He yelled some more, broke a few more potsherds, and finally exhausted himself.

"If I'm useless anyway," Skyblade shouted, "let me go home and grieve like a proper son." Echoes off the walls were his only answer.

"Do not doubt yourself."

Skyblade awakened in a dark place with those words ringing in his head. He wondered where his sleep mat was before he remembered he was being held in the storage room, until the Rainsinger set him free. As he lay there, chilled on the bare ground, he heard a man say, "The River-Serpents have taken their revenge for the exile of the Watermasters. The canals are dying, and so are we."

A different voice, cracked with age, replied, "The canals are flowing now."

"Only while the river is high. When the rains stop and the snowpack melts, there won't be enough water in the river to sustain the canals. They'll dry up, no help for it. I tell you, it's the rainbow knife prophecy come true."

The voices sounded faint and far-off. Skyblade wondered where the two men were: if they stood on the mound above him or next to the storage room in which he lay, or if some trick of the wind carried their voices from farther away.

"The Stormbringers—" the older man began.

"Their poison washed downcanal and killed all those people! That's why Mother Ge felled their shadowdancer."

Skyblade imagined poison flowing invisibly downstream to Lastwater, like the "bad water" his mother had spoken of. At the thought of her, loss and guilt stabbed his heart. He sat up and pressed a fist against his breastbone. As he shifted, the gourd canteen scraped against the wall.

"What's that?" the younger man asked. There was a pause.

The older man said, "I hear nothing." He went on, "Remember, we owe everything to the Stormbringers. They promised us rain if we proved faithful to their Ta'atchul—and the Long Thirst ended. They promised to make the fields yield generously if we built the House of Quickening and brought the Cornmaidens to them—and we've eaten well ever since. When the Watermasters left, the priests promised to make the rains so plentiful, the canals would no longer be needed. In your worry about an old prophecy, have you forgotten all this?"

The younger man's voice came back again, filled with frustration. "In Serpentgate, that might be true. The people downcanal won't be so lucky. This winter's floods have ruined the canals beyond repairing. The River-Serpents haven't only torn out the weirs, they've gnawed their way down to bedrock near the canal heads, so there's nothing to secure the posts in. Even the rocks we placed last spring didn't hold."

"Then you do it over. Eventually the rains will have to stop. The floods can't last forever."

"I'm telling you, even after the floods recede, the canals won't run! Since the day of the dark-sun, everything has gone wrong."

"You were too young back then to understand—"

"I remember everything about that day," the younger man said. "And the days that followed. The priests call the rains . . . but can they stop them?"

"The Ta'atchul will answer our prayers. The rains will end, the floodwaters will recede, and there will be a way to fix the canals. It may take more men, more time, but it will be done."

"We don't have the knowledge. For that, we need a Watermaster."

Silence fell again. Then the older voice, sounding weary, said, "Even if you summoned them, why would they come? We drove the heronfolk away."

"Not *we*. Anyway, they're still our people. To save us, they would come home."

"You cannot go back to what was."

"Waterstrider would come."

The silence was longer this time.

The older man said, "He may have been your friend once, but he owes you nothing now. What makes you think he would return?"

"I'll tell him what Cloudface has become."

"Don't be a fool!"

"You're too late to stop me. I've already sent a message to Waterstrider with one of the Far-Traders from the City of Birds."

The older man asked, "How could you do that without giving the council a chance to discuss it?"

The younger man said something Skyblade couldn't make out.

"This was not your decision to make."

"It's the only decision possible. I knew you would want to bring it up to the council, and they would talk it to death, and then the Rainsinger would tell everyone what to believe. There's nothing now that can be done to stop it. Waterstrider will return. Please. I need you to stand with me on this. Don't tell the council."

"You ask me to choose between my own blood and my responsibility as an elder."

"Face the truth, Father. The Rainsinger will destroy us all. I saw the end coming with the shadowdance. Mother Ge will have her vengeance on the priests and those who believe in the Ta'atchul."

Someone called out, and for a while Skyblade heard the tramping of feet going past the storage room. No more confidences passed between the two men, father and son.

Skyblade rubbed his chest, as though that could ease the clenching of his heart. It hurt too much to think about his parents dying and passing from the world, let alone try to figure out whether they had died from malice—through poison or a curse—or had simply taken ill, as his mother would argue. How was he to know what was true?

"Seek the truth," his mother had said. Skyblade thought about that advice. The Rainsinger had asked him to lie, and he'd refused. Now, in possession of information that others wanted kept secret, Skyblade understood that remaining silent would be the same as a lie. He could probably end his confinement if he told the Rainsinger what he'd heard. Make himself useful to the priests. That was obviously what he should do.

Yet he saw, over and over, the shadowdancer struck by the serpents and falling to the ground. *"Mother Ge will have her vengeance."* What if the younger man who'd said that was right about the priests? What if they were the ones, not Firesister, who was to blame for his parents' deaths? *How can you believe that?* asked a small voice from a kernel of loyalty deep inside his mind that he hadn't known was there. *I've been here for three moons, working hard, and this is how they treat me?* he argued back, overcome by a sense of injustice: the daily stings of Puckermouth's abuse, the assertion that he belonged to the priests and couldn't properly grieve for his parents, the unfairness of this punishment.

Skyblade drew the knife from his belt. He pulled the top section of his hair up and wrapped it around and around with the cord from the gourd canteen. He pulled out one section of hair and cut it with his knife close to his scalp. Then he unwound the cord and let the rest of his hair flop down. Thorn had stopped him earlier from cutting his hair as a visual sign of his loss, but Skyblade could do this much to mark his grief. Hidden by his remaining hair, it would be a secret.

Skyblade pulled his knees up close to his aching chest, folded his arms over them, and dropped his forehead. Braced against the wall of Cloud Mountain, he shut out thoughts of what he should do in the future. Instead he buried himself in pleasant memories from the past in which his mother and father still lived.

The night passed slowly. Finally a dim light filtered through the slats covering the opening of the storage room. Skyblade's hips and knees felt stiff. His hands and feet ached with cold. Rising to his feet, he yawned and stretched. He found a corner to piss in but winced at the touch of his icy fingers.

He was hungry. Thirsty. Cold. Sad. But he had survived the night.

He wondered whether the shadowdancer had been as fortunate. He hoped so. The whole community would suffer if the shadowdancer died; there already seemed to be growing dissatisfaction with the priests. What if some group of malcontents decided to get rid of the Stormbringers, as had transpired with the Watermasters? Skyblade frowned as he considered whether that could really happen.

It occurred to him that losing the Stormbringers might not be a bad thing, if they really were corrupted by evil and had earned the wrath of Mother Ge, as the younger man from the previous evening had said.

A moment's reflection convinced Skyblade that such a rift in the community would indeed be terrible. It would pit father against son, clan against clan, at a time when the canals were ruined, perhaps beyond repair. What would the people of Serpentgate do with no canals and no rain, as might happen if Mother Ge fought outright with the Ta'atchul? Not that there was anything he could do about it, even if he was free.

With nothing to do but wait, Skyblade went back to sitting against the wall of Cloud Mountain and thinking, miserably, about what the future might hold.

Puckermouth eventually came. The older Seeker dragged the heavy cover off the opening of the storage room and lowered a waterskin. When Skyblade went to untie it from the cord, Puckermouth tossed down a woven-reed bedroll. The bedroll struck Skyblade over the shoulders. He grunted.

"What's the matter, Skyblade from Lastwater?"

Skyblade kicked the bedroll out of the way and finished untying the waterskin. A heavy deerhide cover came next. After flinging it off his head, he glared up at Puckermouth and said, "I need to speak to the Rainsinger."

"Not likely." The older boy's smug tone made Skyblade itch to slap that pointy jaw.

"He'll want to hear this."

"The Rainsinger doesn't talk to Seekers at the best of times. You think he'd lower himself to exchange a few words with you?"

Skyblade tried to keep his voice even. "You'll get in trouble if you're the one who keeps this from him."

He could almost hear the other Seeker thinking. He knew Puckermouth believed him when the older boy asked, "So, what is it?"

"I'm not going to tell you." He knew better than to trust Puckermouth with a message. If it wasn't "accidentally" forgotten, it would be garbled beyond recognition. Anyway, Puckermouth had brought a hide and bedroll. There would be no need to make Skyblade comfortable unless someone important would be coming to check on him soon. Probably Thorn. "What about food?"

"Food?"

"Don't I get any this morning?"

"I spilled it on the way."

"Of course you did." Skyblade gritted his teeth to keep from saying anything more.

Puckermouth glanced over his shoulder, then back into the storage room. "Hand me up the canteen." His sudden cheerfulness put Skyblade on guard. "I'll go get you some food."

Skyblade stooped and picked up the empty gourd. He lifted it not quite to arm's length, forcing the older Seeker to lean over the hole and extend his arm to grasp it. Puckermouth muttered something under his breath, then vanished. Thorn stood beside the hole.

"How is the shadowdancer?" Skyblade asked the priest.

"Hanging on."

The answer chilled Skyblade. He thought about Hawkleg's twisted body, marred for the rest of his life by snakebite. The elderly village priest, crippled and immobile, had seemed pitiful to Skyblade. But Hawkleg had survived. The young shadowdancer had to as well.

"Your mother was a healer," the big priest said. "Do you know how to cure snakebite?"

Skyblade's eyes widened at the question, even as the thought of her made his throat go tight. "Why? Surely the healers—"

"Did you ever help your mother?"

"Gathering herbs, yes. But not in the sickroom."

"That is unfortunate." Thorn turned to go.

"Wait!" Seeing an opportunity to free himself from Puckermouth's mistreatment, Skyblade set aside the distracting thoughts of the shadowdancer and focused on proving his loyalty to the priesthood.

Thorn slanted his head to look down into the hole. He looked mildly irritated to be stopped.

Skyblade said, "I overheard something last night that the Rainsinger needs to know. It's not for anybody else's ears."

Thorn hesitated, then came back to the opening and knelt beside it. "Are you saying I cannot be trusted with it?"

The Rainsinger relied on Thorn's counsel, Skyblade reminded himself. Telling Thorn this secret would be the same as telling the Rainsinger. "There were two men talking last night. A father and a son, I think. The son said he'd summoned a Watermaster to come back to the valley and deal with the canals. They wanted to keep it secret from the Rainsinger."

"A Watermaster? Did you hear his name?"

Skyblade groped in his memory. "I'm almost certain they called the man Waterstrider. Because the name was so close to Water*master,* I didn't think I heard it right the first time. But then they repeated it."

"So," the priest said. "So." He looked off into the distance. Toward the temple, Skyblade guessed. "We shall see what the Rainsinger has to say about that," Thorn murmured.

"Was that useful enough?" Skyblade asked.

"What do you mean?"

Skyblade felt awkward. "My being here is some kind of punishment, until I prove myself useful. Wasn't that what you said yesterday?"

"Be patient. It is not over yet." The big priest shifted his weight, and the ceiling groaned.

As bits of mud streamed down onto the bedroll, Skyblade said, "Wait!" There had to be something that would persuade Thorn to let him out. He thought quickly. "Knowing the Watermasters are coming back, doesn't that prove I can be useful? Nobody ever pays me any attention. People talk over my head all the time because I'm so small, I look like a child. You could send me out into the crowds during the rest of the sun-festival, and I could listen to what's going on, bring you more information about the Watermasters—"

Thorn shook his head. "The Watermasters know better than to come back. Even if these men you heard talking got word to them, none would be fool enough to return." His voice became almost kindly. "Let me give you some advice. Do not mention Watermasters to the Rainsinger. If he believes you, he is likely to blame you for giving him such a message. You could find yourself in this storage room until your hair turns gray. If he does not believe you, no telling what he might do." Thorn stood.

Drop me into some hole and let me rot? Skyblade tried to bury his resentment. The Rainsinger, servant of the Ta'atchul, did what was necessary to make the priesthood strong. If that meant reminding a Seeker who it was he served, so be it.

Not long after Thorn left, Skyblade heard a ram's horn signal the beginning of the public ceremonies for the second day of the sun-festival. He listened to the Rainsinger's voice, today cast forth from Cloud Mountain rather than the temple. The words were startlingly clear, as though spoken just for him. Some trick of the wind, Skyblade supposed. Or the Ta'atchul making sure he heard?

"In ancient days," the Rainsinger intoned, "when our forefathers guarded the secret of growing cotton, our lands stretched out along the wide rivers from one mountain range to another."

"Yes, it was so," came the rote response from the crowd assembled in the large plaza beside Cloud Mountain.

Skyblade wondered how many people had come. Enough to keep the shadowdancer alive?

The Rainsinger continued, "In ancient days, our forefathers prayed to the Ancestors, who watch from the sky. They walked in the clouds and sent down the rain, but then they faded away."

"Yes, it was so."

"For a time, Mother Ge heard your prayers on the wind; her Smokemothers stood tall and proud. Fertile were fields, and the canals all ran full, but those days too are no more."

"Yes, it was so."

"We must let them pass and feel no regret, no thoughts of what might have been," said the Rainsinger. "With the Ta'atchul astride the sky, we need never fear drought again. With the Ta'atchul binding the rivers, we need never fear flood again."

"Yes, it is so."

"Green ribbons in the desert shall bring the water to our fields. Breath of sun's fire shall pass its spark to our seeds. The waiting earth shall drink deep and then burn with life. To see this all come about, you only need believe."

"I believe," the crowd answered. "The Ta'atchul walk among the clouds. Their voices echo in my bones. My hands shall do their will."

Skyblade found himself moved by the ritual words. He swallowed against a lump in his throat. As another blast from the ram's horn sounded, he realized that he wanted to be a Stormbringer. He wanted to have faith that the world was orderly, that things happened because they were meant to. He wanted to believe in the Ta'atchul and have them answer his prayers.

Believe in the Ta'atchul, Skyblade told himself. No matter whether the Rainsinger tells the truth or you hate the other Seekers or you're afraid you're going to be stuck here in this storage room forever, believe in the Ta'atchul. Skyblade lifted his hands in supplication to the cloudless sky and began to pray for the shadowdancer to revive. It was a simple enough thing for his first prayer, not like taming the river or filling the canals or turning the sun. "You come to me in whispers on the wind," he said. "So I am whispering to you. Save the shadowdancer who is vow-bound to you, who fell while serving you honorably. Keep him alive, I beg you. If you're near, if you hear me, stoop to his side and breathe life into him."

Skyblade supposed the Ta'atchul were accustomed to better prayers, but he didn't know any. He kept praying until his throat felt raw and his words were too faint to be heard by his own ears.

Mistlight

This bowl has drunk from the bones of the Mother
the power to call back the soul.

—FROM THE CURING SONG OF THE MAMAKAI

Torches flickered, flames bending and scattering, as the door to the prayer room swung outward. The unexpected movement startled Mistlight, who sat cross-legged within, skirt hiked up higher than was proper With one hand she fumbled for her veil to shield her damp, flushed face from whoever dared enter the room where she was tending the shadowdancer. The chanting of the priests under the vatto outside became louder, drowning out her healing song, one that her mother had sung over childhood bumps and scrapes: "When Mother Ge made up this land, she made us plants to fill our hands . . ." Forgetting the next words, Mistlight hummed instead. "Hmm hmm, willow bark and bindweed, something else and cactus seed . . ."

She lost her place in the song as sweat trickled down one temple. "The decoction is still plenty warm," she said. She peeled an herb-infused cloth off the shadowdancer's arm. "You can wait a while longer before changing out the heating-stones."

"Ya! Girl!" Instead of the Stormbringer's masculine voice she expected, an old woman demanded, "Is that how you speak to me?"

Mistlight's hand jerked. She lost her grip on the cloth, which slipped into the pot holding the hot herbal decoction. A few wayward drops stung her bare thigh. She hissed and rubbed at the spots where they landed. When she looked up, she saw the stooped figure of the Childcatcher, midwife to the Cornmaidens and Smokemothers, in the doorway.

On a normal day, Mistlight reflected as the tingling of her skin faded, she would have been with the Childcatcher, helping gather herbs, grinding roots, preparing decoctions and infusions, tending to women in the moontime hut, and whatever else the old priestess needed. But these weren't normal days. The shadowdancer had been struck down in the middle of the Binding of the Serpent, and the whole village was waiting for the world to be put back to rights.

Mistlight flushed as she thought about how important she had suddenly become. As the Rainsinger had told her, by saving the shadowdancer, she would undo the terrible omen that had disrupted the sun-festival. She was thankful that the veil hid her pinkened cheeks from the Childcatcher's sharp eyes. Pride and vanity were unbecoming for a Cornmaiden, the old priestess often said. During the first few moons of being a Cornmaiden, Mistlight might have agreed. Now she would argue that having something to be proud of was the only way to get noticed.

"Revered grandmother," she said. Folding her hands on top of the folds of her skirt, she ducked her head in the gesture of respect owed to the four high priestesses.

As the Childcatcher came closer, Mistlight made out a lumpy carry-net across her sunken chest. Stringy white hair slipped from the scarf looped around the priestess's head and shoulders. Her tattered deerskin dress and leggings hung on her like a half-shed snakeskin. Mistlight shuddered at the thought of snakes.

The Childcatcher peered at her. "Lift your veil, girl, and let me look at you."

"The door—"

"None of the Stormbringers will see your face. They are busy at their prayers."

Mistlight lifted the loose netting and folded it back across her hair.

"You need to rest," the old midwife said. "Your eyes look like two coals burned into your face." She took off the carry-net and placed it on the ground next to the reed mat on which Mistlight sat.

Mistlight wrinkled her nose as an unfamiliar odor drifted past, borne on a cool breeze from the door. "I'm all right." In truth, she was so tired, she felt shaky. She'd worked through the whole night without sleep.

"I brought you some food."

The Childcatcher dug in her belt pack and handed Mistlight two journeycakes in yucca-fiber wrappers. The old priestess then went to the shadowdancer, crouched next to him, and pulled aside the cloths on one arm. She gasped at the sight of the purple, swollen skin, scored by deep cuts someone had made across the bite holes to suck out the venom before Mistlight had been called to tend him. Laying a hand on the young priest's forehead, the Childcatcher frowned at Mistlight. "Who told you to apply hot compresses?"

Mistlight remembered how pale and clammy the shadowdancer had been, staring blindly up at her, when she'd first seen him the previous day. He'd seemed to welcome the heat, judging by his sighs of relief every time she laid on a new cloth. "Hot for healing, as you taught me, to draw blood up to the skin." Mistlight gathered from the Childcatcher's tight lips that her reasoning had been wrong. She stared down at the wrapped journeycakes.

If you had been here, she thought, *you could have told me what to do.* A moment later she felt embarrassed at her pettiness. The Childcatcher had been called to attend a difficult birth in the village. And anyway, Mistlight had agreed to take care of the shadowdancer by herself.

"Fool girl!" The Childcatcher stood and placed her hands on her hips. "When the skin is swollen like this, you need to cool it."

Mistlight glanced at the shadowdancer briefly before her gaze skittered away from the accusing flesh. She concentrated on unwrapping the journeycakes, though she had little appetite.

The Childcatcher sighed and shook her head. "Of course, you are not the one to blame." She returned to the carry-net, lowered herself to the floor beside it, and fumbled with the ties. "This burden should never have been placed on your shoulders," she grumbled. "He should have been taken straight to the healers." The Childcatcher took two stoppered jars and a pitch-sealed basket from the net. The odd smell became stronger as the priestess placed the basket, its lid secured with ties, next to Mistlight's knee.

Mistlight said, "Healers have only the knowledge of men. I'm the one chosen to be the hands of Mother Ge while the Stormbringers pray to the Ta'atchul for their vow-brother's deliverance."

"I hear the Rainsinger's words. They sound strange and awkward in the mouth of one who serves Mother Ge."

Mistlight lifted her chin and met the Childcatcher's chiding gaze. Above the bristly white eyebrows were tattooed flames marking the number of children the old priestess had borne. The flickering torchlight twisted the six tattoos into grotesque triangles that reminded Mistlight of rattlesnake heads, mouths open to strike. She looked down and away from the sight and shivered, chilled despite the warmth of the room.

"I could not believe it," the old priestess went on, "when I left the birthing hut—the mother will live, thanks to Mother Ge—and found out what happened during the ceremony."

"Was the baby . . . ?"

"Stillborn. Breech, and strangled by the cord."

Mistlight felt a pang of sympathy for the mother: how terrible, to hope for a child and lose it before it ever took a breath.

The Childcatcher asked, "Why did you let the Rainsinger talk you into this?"

Mistlight didn't know how to answer. She felt sure this dried-up husk of a woman could never understand how alive she felt when she was with him. How fast and hot her blood ran. How she yearned for him when he wasn't near, would make up excuses to go to the temple for a glimpse of him. How every smile and pleasant word gave her hope that his heart would someday be hers.

"I'm the only one he could trust," she said, "out of all those purified for the sun-festival." The Rainsinger could have chosen any of the Corn-maidens, because they had undergone the same rites of cleansing. In the end, she was the one he had sent for. That had to mean something.

The Childcatcher scowled. "We will talk about your foolishness later. The important thing now is to make sure this young priest survives until the end of the sun-festival."

"The shadowdancer is vow-bound to the Ta'atchul. They'll save him." Mistlight placed the journeycake wrappers on the ground beside her and set the crumbly mesquite cakes on top. Her stomach cramped at the thought of food. As she brought her hand back, it brushed against the bulge of the earthflower love charm that hung on a leather cord around her neck, covered by the scarf. The sweet smell of earthflower, secured within a small cloth pouch, overcame the odors of the sickroom and eased the twinges in her stomach.

The old priestess said, "The Ta'atchul may be able to call down rain, but life is for Mother Ge to grant. The Rainsinger has no command over her. Or you."

"I do this because he asks, not that he commands."

"Better if you did it for the sake of the village," the Childcatcher snapped, "or even the shadowdancer, than as a favor for the Rainsinger." She twitched aside Mistlight's scarf. Quickly Mistlight drew it back into place to hide the leather thong and the bruises visible on her neck from the last time she had lain with him in the House of Quickening.

The priestess said, "You know you are the only one who goes to the Rainsinger of her own will."

"Yes, I do go to him, and proudly!" Mistlight shot back. "So should the others. It's our duty to bear children, not enjoy the getting of them." Yet she did enjoy being with Eaglefeather, as the Rainsinger had told her to call him. His roughness excited her in a way none of the other Stormbringers ever did.

Self-conscious under the steady look the old priestess was giving her, Mistlight popped a journeycake into her mouth and chewed. Saliva burst into her mouth so painfully that she couldn't force herself to swallow. She realized she hadn't eaten anything for a couple days. Before the start of the sun-festival, the Cornmaidens had fasted for their purification rituals in the mountains. And once word of the shadowdancer's fall spread throughout the Smokemothers' compound, Mistlight had been too anxious to eat. She'd danced with the other Cornmaidens at midday and had been summoned by Eaglefeather right after that. Since then, she'd been here tending the shadowdancer. No one had thought to offer her anything to eat. Swallowing, she wiped crumbs off her mouth.

"A duty as yet unfulfilled," the Childcatcher reminded her, "after nine moons."

Mistlight pressed her lips together. She knew very well that she had only until the midsummer sun-festival to quicken. If she failed to get with child in the next three moons, she would be sent away, no longer a Cornmaiden—which meant no chance to become a Smokemother. And becoming a Smokemother was the only way she could continue to be with Eaglefeather. A lump came into her throat. Her eyes felt tight and hot with tears she couldn't allow to fall. She reached for the smaller of the two jars—multicolored, with a design she couldn't make out—and removed the wooden stopper.

The Childcatcher warned, "Don't drink that. It's snake venom, not water."

With trembling hands, Mistlight put the jar down and resealed it. Before the shadowdance, the snakes' fangs were supposed to be milked, so a stray bite wouldn't harm the shadowdancer. She had supposed, given his condition, that the snakes had been at their full spring potency. But now here was the venom. "What's this for?"

"The Rainsinger asked for it," the Childcatcher said. "I offered to deliver it to him. It gave me a reason to come to the temple precinct and see the shadowdancer's condition for myself." She frowned. "I will tell the Rainsinger to have a Stormbringer take your place here."

"The Rainsinger said only I have the purity of heart to tend the shadowdancer."

"You are not the Rainsinger's creature. Today you must rejoin the Cornmaidens for the basket dance. That is what you purified for and practiced."

"They don't need me. He does!" Mistlight pointed at the shadowdancer just as he coughed and began to twist about, wracked by spasms.

The Childcatcher bent over him and held out her hands, palms down, above his chest. She shivered all over. Her wasted body seemed ready to collapse, as if she had let some of her life-force flow into the body of the shadowdancer, who gradually stilled. She drew back her quivering hands. "Girl, you must keep him in this world until I can get you out of here. This task is not for you."

"I won't go! I promised the Rainsinger!"

"If the shadowdancer dies, people will see his death as an evil omen. Do you imagine the Stormbringers will allow themselves to be blamed for it?"

"The Ta'atchul will save him."

The priestess glared at her. "You place too much faith in the prayers of the Stormbringers. If they were effective, this boy would be growing stronger, not weaker. Until I return, you need to cool his fever and draw down the swelling."

"Cool him? With what?"

"I mixed up a clay poultice." The Childcatcher pointed to the basket.

Mistlight unfastened the coiled lid and tipped it back. The acrid odor of the mixture, released into the close room, made her head swim. "What's in it?"

"Things the healers say should help pull out the venom. Stroke it on gently, then cover it with cool, damp cloths. Change out the cloths when his body warms them, and rinse them in plain clean water. Put on more of the poultice whenever you can see his skin through the mixture. But first, open up this room and get rid of the torches and the hot rocks."

Breathing through parted lips to avoid the nasty smell of the poultice, Mistlight listened to the old priestess's instructions with mounting resentment. The Childcatcher made it sound as though she had done everything wrong. But how was she to have known? A faint voice in her head said, *That's why he should have been taken to the healers.* She snapped her mouth shut with a click of her teeth.

"I must go," the Childcatcher said. She grasped Mistlight's wrist with her clawlike hand. "Keep him alive!" She shook Mistlight's arm for emphasis. "I will try to convince the Rainsinger to release you from your promise."

"But—"

"Do what you can. Courage!" The old woman grabbed up the smaller of the two patterned jars and left.

After the Childcatcher's skinny back disappeared through the doorway, Mistlight took up the remaining jar, red and white and black in a dizzying pattern of swirls and fine lines. She unstoppered and sniffed it, then took a cautious sip. Finding only water, she drank greedily, letting it wash the crumbs of the mesquite journeycakes down her throat. She replaced the stopper and set the jar down.

Mistlight dipped her forefinger into the basket, swirled her finger around, pulled it out, and looked at the clinging mixture. It glistened with dark flecks and contained fragments of feathers and leaves. She brought it close to her nose. It smelled mostly like damp clay and river mud along with something that reminded her of burnt hair. She reminded herself that Eaglefeather hadn't told her what to do for the shadowdancer, just that he trusted her to tend the boy. Following the Childcatcher's advice couldn't hurt.

After pulling the veil over her face again, Mistlight used an otter skin to carry the hot decoction pot out of the prayer room. She set the vessel down outside the door, then did the same with the rocks that had been keeping it warm. The Stormbringers seated in a ring under the vatto seemed so involved in their prayers that they didn't speak to her, and she saw no reason to tell them what she was doing.

When Mistlight reentered the prayer room, she looked over her shoulder at the door and considered leaving it open. She decided to close the door so she could take off the veil to see better. Unfortunately, that meant she had to leave the torches in place, which kept the small room too warm for comfort. She blotted sweat off her forehead with the end of the scarf she wore around her neck.

Mistlight began applying the stinky poultice to the shadowdancer's angry, weeping skin. It worried her that he didn't seem to feel the touch, not the way he had yesterday when she'd first been called to tend him. After coating his wounds with the thick mixture, she laid on some of the cloths that earlier had been soaked in the decoction and left to chill on the plastered floor. She closed up the basket and watched him closely, hoping to see his breathing become less labored.

The room soon became stifling even without the hot rocks. Mistlight stood and stretched, blotted her forehead again, then pulled the veil over her face and opened the door. A cool breeze floated in, making her shiver. As she heard a scraping sound behind her, she whirled around and saw the shadowdancer's limbs moving weakly. Two quick steps took her to his twitching body. She knelt and carefully reached out, almost touching his shoulder. When he seemed to flinch away, she jerked her hand back. "Heya," she said to him. "Are you awake?" His eyes remained closed, and he made no answer.

Outside, she heard a woman's voice. The prayers of the Stormbringers faded, and a man said something that sounded angry.

Mistlight looked up, prepared to ask the Childcatcher whether the shadowdancer's restlessness was a good sign or bad. This time, though, when the light streaming through the doorway dimmed, it wasn't the Childcatcher who stood there. Mistlight scrambled to her feet as she recognized the scariest of the four high priestesses, the Truthspeaker, whose stern face jutted out of a tightly wrapped headscarf. Mistlight ducked her head respectfully and murmured, "Revered grandmother."

The priestess paused in the doorway. She didn't respond to Mistlight. Her gaze rested on the shadowdancer. She took one step forward, then another. In her smoke-colored robe, she blended into the sunlight that angled through the door. Behind her, dust particles borne on the shaft of light swirled and twisted.

Reminded uncomfortably of snakes again, Mistlight asked, "Aren't you needed for the Blessing of the Seeds, revered grandmother?"

The Truthspeaker glanced at her. "I am on my way there now." Instead of leaving, though, she drifted closer to the shadowdancer.

"Did you, too, come to check on me?"

The silence stretched on until Mistlight thought maybe the Truthspeaker hadn't heard her. At last the priestess said, "I granted permission for you to be here. Do not tempt me to change my mind." She bent over the shadowdancer and brushed the back of one hand across his cheek.

The gesture seemed so motherly that Mistlight blurted out, "Is he your son?"

"All babies born to Smokemothers belong to the village." The Truthspeaker pushed a damp hank of hair off the shadowdancer's forehead. "You know that."

She did, yes, just as she knew that should she someday bear Eaglefeather's baby, she would have to give up that little squalling bundle—and she would undoubtedly be glad for the future she would gain by doing so. Most of the other Cornmaidens pretended it would be a difficult choice. "Did you come out of motherly love?" Mistlight pressed. "Is that why you gave me permission to take care of him?"

The Truthspeaker straightened and cast a fierce look at her. "What would you have done had I refused?"

She moistened her dry lips. Though she could not admit as much, she would have come anyway. The love she felt for Eaglefeather was too powerful to be bound by rules.

"That is what I thought," the priestess said. "Whether he lives or no will be up to Mother Ge, not your efforts."

The light from the doorway was blocked by a big, masculine body, startling Mistlight into emitting a birdlike *eep* before she slapped a hand across her mouth.

The new arrival said in a deep voice, "Truthspeaker, you ought to be praying that he lives."

Mistlight peered at him and picked out Thorn's squared-off chin and blade of a nose, easily recognizable. Behind him, only half visible, was the slight figure of a Seeker.

The Truthspeaker snapped, "Praying to the Ta'atchul, as the Rainsinger says? I think not."

"Did I say 'to the Ta'atchul'?" Turning his head toward Mistlight, Thorn said, "I have brought a Seeker to take your place here."

"No! The Rainsinger told me to do this!" Mistlight hurried toward him and laid a hand on his arm.

He covered her little hand with his own rough one. Gently he told her, "Show Skyblade what you have been doing, then go take a well-deserved rest."

Mistlight shook her head. "I'm not so tired. I don't need to rest."

"Good," the Truthspeaker said. "Now that the Stormbringers have decided to do more than pray to save one of their own, you can join the rest of the Cornmaidens to help give out the seeds. Show the Seeker what to do here."

Thorn told her, "The girl has been up all night."

The priestess straightened, back rigid. "Whose fault is that? Listen to the drums: even as we speak, her sisters are out there performing the basket dance."

Once the Truthspeaker said that, Mistlight realized the rumbling beat of the cottonwood drums had begun. The Cornmaidens would be dancing light-footed in a long line in the plaza, each holding a broad basket against her chest, winding into a spiral and out again, spinning with the basket overhead. She should be there. They'd been practicing the dance over and over to get their movements uniform and the spacing precise. For a moment, Mistlight actually wished she could be out there, just another Cornmaiden, without this responsibility, without the arguing, without the desire to have something more in the end than custom would allow.

Thorn said, "You can see exhaustion in her face. She deserves better from you."

"Who are you to tell me what I owe to one of my own?"

Mistlight felt awkward, caught between the two powers: male and female, priest and priestess, Ta'atchul and Mother Ge. Her hand crept up to the earthflower pouch that hung under her clothing.

Thorn sighed. "That is not my intent." Gesturing toward the shadowdancer, he told Mistlight. "Show Skyblade what you are doing."

Mistlight looked at the Seeker, a slight boy no taller than herself who bore the unlikely name Skyblade. She caught him staring at her as though he could see through her veil. His flushed cheeks suggested he was as embarrassed by the argument between Thorn and the Truthspeaker as she was. Out of sympathy for him, not because she had any intention of letting herself be replaced, she returned to her mat at the shadowdancer's side and gestured for the Seeker to join her. He knelt on the other side of the basket that held the clay poultice mixture. She took the lid off the basket and was gratified to see his nose wrinkle.

"That looks—" he began.

"Hush!" she told him as she strained to hear what the Truthspeaker was saying to Thorn.

"—think to tell me how to treat my people."

Mistlight was glad she wasn't the target of the Truthspeaker's anger this time. She and the Seeker traded troubled glances.

Thorn said, "You should be grateful I brought someone to take over from her."

"Grateful!" the Truthspeaker responded. "It was your ceremony spoiled, not ours. An ill omen for the Stormbringers: perhaps Eagle-feather should never have been selected as Rainsinger. The way he treats her servants, Mother Ge has much to be angry with."

"Do you want people to blame the shadowdancer's death on Mother Ge? The Rainsinger did what he could yesterday to overcome people's fear: Pray to the Ta'atchul, he said. Have faith. All will be well. Instead people should worry that Mother Ge has forsaken them?"

"No one will believe that." The priestess's nostrils flared.

Thorn bent closer to the Truthspeaker. "The Binding of the Serpent is needed to make the canals flow. The canals are needed to make the crops grow. Do you think even seeds blessed by Mother Ge will yield food without being watered? What will you say to your starving people this fall?"

"Are you telling me that the Stormbringers will fail in getting the canals running again? Then you had best make sure the summer rains are even and plentiful. Come, Mistlight. We will leave these—"

The shadowdancer exhaled with a long, heavy, shuddering breath. He lay still, with none of the spasms that had afflicted him earlier. His chest no longer rose and fell.

Mistlight could almost see his spirit rising from his heart like a wisp of smoke. She scrambled away from the body, but her feet tangled in her skirt and she fell awkwardly on her hip. She found herself nose to nose with the young Seeker, only her veil separating them. His eyes looked as round as the moon. He pulled back, rose, and helped her up with steadying hands on her shoulders.

Before she could thank him, Thorn grabbed him by the arm and spun him away. "Go! Hurry! Tell the Rainsinger he is needed here."

The Truthspeaker reached the door before the Seeker, and both hurried out. Frightened at being left behind, Mistlight started after them as Stormbringers began flooding into the small room. Their broad shoulders bore her backward, toward the shadowdancer's corpse and his untethered spirit. She flung out her hands and tried to push her way past the wave of priests, to no avail. "Let me through!" she called.

Someone jostled her, knocking her against the wall. She lost her balance and dropped to hands and knees. Through the forest of legs, she saw a thick-bladed knife begin to carve an X in the plaster floor in the doorway—the track of the runnerbird, meant to lead the spirit out of the room. One deep voice started singing: "Death it comes now for our brother, death comes soon for me." Others joined in with "The harder I struggle against my fate, the sooner it comes for me."

Stray gleams of light reflected off knives being slipped out of belt scabbards in front of Mistlight's eyes. Imagining a carelessly wielded blade taking off her ear, she backed away and forced her trembling legs to bear her up. To her horror, the knives seemed to follow her. She flattened against the wall, cringing away from the sharp edges. Breaking the rhythm of the death song, they sliced back and forth through the cotton ribbons that held each Stormbringer's hair in a club at the back of his head. The pale ribbons fell, twisting through the air. Hanks of hair soon followed, a section cut down to the scalp of each dark head to mark the loss of one of their own. "Ashes of despair they fill my mouth as the soul sheds its mortal skin," the priests sang. "Sorrow must follow the memories we share as the spirit flies upward in triumph."

Mistlight felt their anguish like it was her own, though she'd never really known the shadowdancer. Countless times she had touched him throughout the night, brushing her fingers against his hot skin as she laid on cloths and removed them. Her hands, red and chapped, were the last he had felt in his life. Tears came into her eyes, welling up so quickly that the moisture surprised her.

She wanted out of that prayer room, away from death and failure and guilt. But between her and the freedom she craved stood an unbreachable wall of yellow tunics with loose black hairs cascading down them. Mistlight sighed out a despairing breath and reached under her veil to dash away the useless tears.

The Stormbringers began to move, leaving a clear space between Mistlight and the open door. To escape, all she would have to do was step over the shadowdancer's body. She gazed despairingly toward the sunlit plaza, so near yet unattainable. A few of the Stormbringers nearest the door slipped out, but only to make room for others to enter. The newcomers bore between them a litter like hunters used for deer carcasses. They placed it on the plastered floor next to the shadowdancer and moved his limp form onto it.

Mistlight's stomach lurched at the sight. She tore her gaze away and stared straight ahead, wishing she could have gotten out along with the Truthspeaker and the young Seeker. In the plaza, a man in yellow ceremonial robes walked toward the prayer room. The way he moved told her it was Eaglefeather. A trembling hand lifted to touch the earthflower pouch that hung between her breasts. One part of her knew the Rainsinger couldn't show any preference for her in public, but another part, the one that had made her agree to take care of the shadowdancer, hoped for some acknowledgment of all that she had done . . . because the man she loved had asked it of her.

She met Eaglefeather's unusual yellowish eyes as he paused outside the door, but only for the space of one heartbeat. Then his gaze dropped to the shadowdancer's body, and he began to sing the death song in unison with his priests. Six of them lifted the litter. In time with the rhythm of the song they marched out of the room. The rest of the Stormbringers followed.

Frozen by her lover's coldness, Mistlight watched them go. She wanted to run after him, tear off her veil, and make him *see* her. Instead she cautioned herself to patience and patted the earthflower charm. With that she would win his heart, she was positive. All she had to do was spend a few nights alone with him in the House of Quickening.

Mistlight plodded across the temple plaza, every step an effort. She wanted to hurry back to the Smokemothers' compound, but her body wouldn't obey. Her limbs felt heavy and clumsy.

Voices from overhead drifted down. She paused and looked up at the top of the massive temple. A few Stormbringers passed to and fro behind the half wall there, only their heads visible from below. Another priest knelt on the roof of the small room that capped the temple. He was dragging a bundle of sticks up with a rope. Mistlight realized the branches, jerking and bumping against the plastered wall as they rose, were for the shadowdancer's funeral pyre. She shuddered and tore her gaze away as she imagined the flames that would soon consume his earthly body. Once again she felt trapped in the hot, stifling room she had just left.

Mistlight forced herself into movement again, but the reminder of death pursued her, and her hands began to shake. Despite all that she had done, the shadowdancer's soul had slipped away. His passing hadn't been her fault, she would swear to it. No one could accuse her of having done any less than her best. She was only supposed to keep him comfortable until the Ta'atchul saved him. If anyone had failed in their duties, it was the Stormbringers, whose prayers had proven useless.

The dark opening in the wall that surrounded the temple precinct seemed to recede with every step she took. As though her scarf were tightening on her neck, she struggled to breathe. She pushed onward, driven by desperation. At last she reached the shadowy chill of the precinct wall. It seeped into her skin and drew out some of the heat that was suffocating her. Beyond the wall, she breathed more easily.

As Mistlight walked the well-worn path toward the Smokemothers' compound, she heard the drums of the basket dance, felt the beat pulsing through her. Her heart ached in her chest, and her head felt so hollow, she couldn't imagine executing the whirls and swoops of the dance.

No one else was around when Mistlight entered the Smokemothers' compound. Stripping off her veil and unwinding the scarf from her neck, she headed for the sleep-room she shared with the other Cornmaidens who had not yet quickened with new life. She paused in the doorway, remembering what the room had looked like the previous summer when she and her vow-sisters had first entered it: so many sleep pallets, there was barely space to walk between them without stepping on another Cornmaiden. Now there was more bare floor visible than bedding.

She crossed the room and collapsed onto her pallet face-first, barely catching herself with her arms. The warmth and softness of the deerhide cover came as such a relief, she pressed herself into it. Then she rolled to her back and pulled a rabbit-fur blanket up from the foot of the pallet to cover herself. She lay there, closed her eyes, and waited for sleep—glorious, long-awaited, restorative sleep—to take her.

It didn't come.

She couldn't make her eyelids stay shut, couldn't keep her mind from tossing and turning. Though her body remained still, her thoughts kept shifting back to the shadowdancer. In an attempt to fool herself into believing it was time to sleep, she flung one forearm over her eyes to block out the daylight. That didn't help—and produced an unpleasant mixture of odors besides. Poultice. Herbal decoction. Torch smoke. Infection. Sweat. She moved her arm to her side and lay there, determined to fall asleep.

The thick adobe walls of the maidens' sleep-room muted outside noises. Mistlight realized she could no longer hear the drums of the distant dance. Bird calls and voices vanished. So did the sighing of the wind. As quiet descended on her, she watched dust floating in the dim light that filtered through the open doorway.

Pulled from sleep, Mistlight heard a woman outside the room say, "Not me. He gives me the shivers."

Mistlight gathered that she had slept through the Cornmaidens' dance and that her vow-sisters had returned. She sat up, blinked sleep from her eyes, and tried to figure out whether she felt rested enough to deal with the questions she expected about the shadowdancer.

"I'll go," another Cornmaiden offered. "I haven't been with him yet."

The words told Mistlight who was speaking—Shiningdawn, a Cornmaiden who seemed determined to couple with the entire priesthood before her service to Mother Ge ended. Mistlight rose and straightened her clothes.

"Really?" said someone else. "That's surprising. He must be the only one."

Mistlight began to smooth her hair, tucking stray locks into her braids, as Shiningdawn said, "No, there's a few more."

Mistlight's throat tightened, and she dropped her hand. The other Cornmaiden had said, *"He gives me the shivers."* Of all the Stormbringers, only the Rainsinger prompted that response. Mistlight hurried to the doorway. Outside she found some of her vow-sisters clustered together, still veiled and indistinguishable in their ceremonial finery. One said, "You don't have many more moons to finish bedding them all." Several giggled. A few laughed outright.

"If it's the Rainsinger you're talking about," Mistlight declared, "I'll go to him." The laughter died down as veiled heads turned toward her. She tried to stand tall and confident. She couldn't risk letting Shiningdawn take her place as his favorite. "I'll go."

Coming up beside her, the Seedkeeper murmured, "Not you. You didn't sleep last night." She placed a thin, clawlike hand on Mistlight's shoulder.

Mistlight twisted away. The high priestesses, with all their rules and admonitions, were so far removed from love—if they had ever felt such a fiery emotion—that they could never understand how important it was for Mistlight to be at Eaglefeather's side now. "Revered grandmother I rested today while everybody else was busy." Mistlight met the elderly priestess's probing gaze without flinching.

The Childcatcher entered the Smokemothers' compound through the narrow opening in the enclosing wall. She circled around the group of Cornmaidens and halted next to the Seedkeeper. "Why are there warders waiting on the path?" the Childcatcher asked the other priestess.

The Seedkeeper said, "The Rainsinger has called for a companion to join him in the House of Quickening."

"During the sun-festival?" The Childcatcher gave an exasperated huff. "He has become unreasonable since rising to his office."

"Some of the Cornmaidens are willing," the Seedkeeper said.

The Childcatcher eyed Mistlight. "Are they, indeed?"

Mistlight said, "Revered grandmother, I said I would go."

"So did I!" Shiningdawn folded back her veil, revealing a determined expression, as she hurried toward the high priestesses and Mistlight.

The Seedkeeper shook her head and clicked her tongue in disapproval. "Fighting over him!"

Startling Mistlight, who hadn't seen her enter, the Truthspeaker said from near the entrance to the compound, "Whoever goes will be unable to participate in the rest of the ceremonies. She would need to be purified again."

"Then I should be the one, revered grandmother," Mistlight said. "You already told me I've been corrupted." Eaglefeather had to have known that touching the shadowdancer would leave her impure. Why else would he have sent for someone today, unless he wanted her, specifically?

Her brief flare of pleasure faded as the Truthspeaker slashed a hand through the air and said, "No. We must not encourage the Rainsinger in this outrageous demand."

The Childcatcher grabbed the Truthspeaker's sleeve and tugged the other high priestess toward herself and Mistlight. Softly, so no one else could hear, the Childcatcher said, "We might consider allowing it, since Mistlight is willing."

Mistlight pressed her lips together to keep from saying anything. Though startled that the older of the two high priestesses was taking her side, she had enough presence of mind not to insert herself in their quiet argument.

The Truthspeaker looked exasperated. "Why should we break with tradition and set aside customs that have so long pleased Mother Ge?"

"Perhaps Mother Ge brought down the shadowdancer," the Childcatcher said, "because she is no longer pleased with the old ways."

The Truthspeaker's head jerked as though she had been slapped. But she recovered quickly. "Are we to do whatever the Rainsinger commands?"

The Childcatcher murmured, "Not for his sake but for hers, we might send Mistlight to him. Mother Ge has not yet favored her with a child. Her bleeding ended several days before the sun-festival. This might be her time."

Mistlight locked her hands together in front of her. She was half afraid to breathe for fear of calling attention to herself.

"Giving in to his demands may set a dangerous precedent," the Truthspeaker said. "Will we appear to be serving Mother Ge or the Rainsinger?"

The Childcatcher shot back, "Is that any reason to punish Mistlight, who did her best through a long, lonely night?"

The Truthspeaker said, "Many would consider being sent to the Rainsinger a punishment—"

"Not this one. She is willing." To Mistlight, the Childcatcher said, "You are willing, are you not?"

She nodded vigorously. "Oh, yes, revered grandmother."

"Come now, sister," the Childcatcher said to the Truthspeaker. "You see? There is no need to let him divide us. If Mother Ge blesses Mistlight with a child, it will be a sign that she still holds the Mother's favor."

Mistlight wanted to rush out of the Smokemothers' compound immediately and run straightway to Eaglefeather, but going to the House of Quickening required preparations to be made with the help of her vow-sisters. Putting on the sleeveless wrap-around dress. Dusting her face with corn pollen. Braiding her hair with strings of turquoise, obsidian, and shell beads, symbolizing the union of sky, earth, and water. Smudging with sticks of smoldering tobacco and bursage to drive off bad thoughts. Singing a prayer to gain Mother Ge's blessing. The familiar ritual dragged on until she wanted to scream with frustration. At last she was deemed ready.

Veiled and robed, she left the compound and joined the warder who would take her to the temple precinct. His hand cupped her elbow as they strolled along the path. The pace seemed horribly slow to Mistlight, but scurrying to the House of Quickening was beneath a Cornmaiden's dignity.

As the temple grew larger in her view, the sunset breeze filled with smoke from the shadowdancer's funeral pyre. Mistlight coughed and stumbled, breaking the warder's gentle hold. He stopped to let her recover. A few more coughs cleared her throat, but her first deep breath brought her the smell of singed flesh on the wind, an unbearable reminder of the shadowdancer's death. She began to breathe through her mouth, panting like a dog.

When she would have gone on, the warder grabbed her wrist. She blinked at him in surprise, having almost forgotten he was there.

He asked, "Why are you doing this?"

"Doing what?"

"You stayed up all night with the shadowdancer."

It sounded like an accusation. Puzzled, Mistlight said, "The Rainsinger sent for me." She tugged against the warder's grasp. He released her but didn't move, so she didn't either. "I'm the only one who could come—the others have to remain untouched for two more days."

"Two days." The warder looked down at his feet. "The Rainsinger can't wait even that long."

"Why is this any of your concern?"

He shot her a sidelong look of misery, and Mistlight realized that of course he was upset—one of his vow-brothers was dead. Her gaze drifted to the section of hair that flopped over his temple. The Stormbringers in the prayer room had cut their hair too, in mourning for the shadowdancer. She bit her lip. If she could hardly bear to be reminded of his death, how much worse must it be for his vow-brothers?

The warder shook his head and said under his breath, "It's not right, Stormbringer and Cornmaiden during the sun-festival. Things were already strained enough before, and then the shadowdancer . . ."

Mistlight didn't know what to say to that. *I'm sorry* didn't seem right. Neither did *You must miss him.* Feeling helpless, she tentatively reached out a hand and patted his arm.

He said, "If Thorn was the Rainsinger, my brother would still be with us. Milk a rattlesnake's venom properly, and it becomes powerless."

Mistlight sucked in her bottom lip and ran the tip of her tongue over it. Was this young priest blaming Eaglefeather for the shadowdancer's death? She remembered the jar of venom that Eaglefeather had asked the Childcatcher to bring him. Surely that meant he knew the snakes had been milked. Thorn as Rainsinger could have done no more, she thought loyally.

The warder lifted his gaze to her veiled face. "Even if my brother's passing hadn't happened, the Rainsinger shouldn't break with tradition. I should get to watch the ceremonies, at least. Catch a glimpse of clan-sisters and brothers. Old friends. We all came to the temple from clans we can never return to."

Mistlight's chest tightened so that she could hardly breathe. She closed her eyes. His words stabbed her heart, painful reminders of the fundamental difference between her and everyone around her: she had no clan-sisters and brothers, no clan ties at all. She'd been raised at the Children's House, with orphans and other unwanted children coming and going as their situations changed. Mistlight had seen herself as apart from all of them, for her mother had been in charge there. But then she became one of the orphaned children of the house. Tears burned behind her eyelids, and she shuddered, squeezing her eyes more tightly closed.

The warder kept talking. "For vow-brothers, our family is now here, with the Ta'atchul. Instead of seeing people I once knew, I will do as I am bid and take Mistlight to the Rainsinger."

Mistlight pushed away the familiar despair, shoving it deep into her mind where she could ignore it. "How did you know it was me?" she asked in a voice that sounded rough to her ears.

"You all move differently. Different heights, different builds."

"You're not supposed to know. That's the reason for this—" She gestured at her veil and robes. "To make us all the same."

The warder grinned. "No one else chatters like you. Besides, you smell good."

Mistlight thought about the sweet-smelling earthflower hidden in a pouch under her dress. But he couldn't mean that, for she had gathered it only recently, when the Cornmaidens went to the mountains to purify themselves. She shook her head, worried suddenly that he might notice a change in the scent she bore. To distract him, she asked, "How do you know our names?"

"There's somebody in the vow-brothers from nearly all the clans. The younger ones usually recognize the new Cornmaidens."

"We should go," Mistlight said. She felt strangely conspicuous as he took her elbow again and they started walking. She remembered the expression on the Seeker's face when he'd come into the prayer room with Thorn. Did he, too, recognize her? The thought was unsettling. Did everyone know she was the one who had let the shadowdancer die? She found herself wishing for the dark of night to conceal her.

Snatches of flute and drum drifted in the air, telling her that in the dance plaza, unmated young men and women had begun to dance in a large circle, clasping hands with one partner, then spinning away to encounter the next. Kin and strangers and friends alike came together and parted. Some pairs would feel a mutual stirring of hearts from clasped hands. They might look for an opportunity to slip off together and explore where that attraction would lead. She was fortunate that she no longer had to imagine herself someday finding the one who made her heart pound. Mistlight had found him already and was going to him. With the help of the earthflower love charm, she would catch his own heart.

Her lips curved into a smile that lasted past the gate and the guardtower, across the temple plaza, and to the quickening room, lit by rushlights, where Eaglefeather waited for her. Strings of turquoise and shell necklaces draped around his neck, and earbobs dangled to his shoulders. Though he wasn't in his ceremonial finery, his magnificence dazzled her. He stared at her, and her at him, for ten heartbeats, or perhaps a hundred.

She pressed a hand against her chest, as though she could in that way keep her heart from beating through her ribs. Her palm rested on the softness of the pouch that held the earthflower, tucked out of sight beneath the dress and robe. As her fingers squeezed the charm, the sweetness of the love-herb rose into the air, along with the scent of her body's readiness for him. Mistlight felt certain that the earthflower would work its magic this night.

Without a word, Eaglefeather grabbed hold of her wrist and tugged her all the way into the room. He closed the woven reed door, then looped the fasteners over their pins so no one could enter unbidden. He turned back to Mistlight. In his eyes was a glitter she'd come to recognize during many nights past. He pulled off her head cover and veil, folded her in his arms so tightly she could hardly breathe, and bent close. Eaglefeather placed his lips against her neck. He inhaled deeply. She briefly felt his damp tongue on her skin before he nipped her, making her jerk in surprise.

"You smell like a woman ready for pleasure," he murmured.

Mistlight felt a stirring against her belly.

"Or perhaps you prefer pain," he went on. "You're a strange one. I can do anything I please, and you not only take it but beg for more."

He captured her mouth with his, then sucked on her lower lip and bit it. With his teeth still trapping her lip, he backed her into the adobe bench, wide enough for two but not quite long enough to sleep on. Abruptly Eaglefeather released her. She clutched at him to keep from falling, but he pushed her hands away. She sat with a jolt as she discovered that the bench was lower than she expected, with none of the usual padding.

"You refuse me nothing yet fail to give me what I most need." His voice was cool and smooth. "Time and again I fill you with my seed, and it dies in you. If I lie with you tonight, will my seed again go to waste?"

Mistlight searched his face for any sign of affection. Seeing nothing, she took off the robe and spread it behind her on the bench. Then she eased back on one elbow and swung her legs up, first one and then the other, as she stretched out invitingly. She was relieved to see his eyes following her movement. Positioning herself so that her breasts thrust forward and her knees were slightly raised and parted, she smiled and said, "The Smokemothers sent me here because it is my time."

Eaglefeather stood still. "I doubt that, after all these moons. It is more likely that you have offended Mother Ge. Else why would she fail to save the shadowdancer when I left him in your care?"

Mistlight brightened her smile and reached for his hand to draw him onto the bench beside her. He resisted at first but then turned and climbed on top of her, straddling her hips. With the hand that held hers, he pressed her arm onto the bench, while his other hand caressed her breast.

"Tell me," he said, "why should I not send you back to the Smokemothers and ask for another Cornmaiden for tonight?" He dug in his fingers and twisted.

Gasping from the shock, Mistlight braced for his hands to close on her throat, for the slow tightening that would take the breath away from her, leaving her lightheaded, black spots wavering behind her eyes. She still bore bruises from the last time he'd done that. His hands began to move—one along her arm, the other across her chest. As they drifted across her skin, she shivered, so sensitive was she to his touch.

One hand brushed against the earthflower charm between her breasts. He stilled and stared at her. His fingers traced the cord upward from the cloth pouch toward her neck. Slowly he slipped a forefinger under the cord, drew the pouch from under her dress, and examined it.

"No " Mistlight grabbed for the charm.

He snapped his hand shut around it. "What is this?"

"It's not what you think!" But she was suddenly afraid of what he might think. "You weren't supposed to find it! You weren't supposed to know!'

Eaglefeather shoved her hand away. He yanked the cord from which the earthflower charm was suspended. After a second attempt, the cord broke. He disentangled himself from her and stood, staring at the pouch. He tore open the packet and poured the grayish green bits of earthflower into his palm. "A charm to keep from bearing a child," he muttered.

"No!"

"Do you think me stupid? So many times I spilled my seed in you, yet you have not quickened." His eyes narrowed to slits. He burrowed fingers into her hair near her scalp and pulled hard. Pain shot through her head. Crying out in protest, she tried to pry his hand loose.

He demanded, "Or is this something worse? Some poison with which to sicken me?" He shook her.

"It's nothing but a sweet-smelling herb! That's all!"

His nostrils flared. He brought his fist close to his nose and inhaled twice. "What did you hope to achieve with this?"

"I want your child! I would never do anything to prevent that!"

"What else are you hiding?"

"Nothing!"

"You lie!" Eaglefeather slapped her.

Crying, she reached up to her smarting face. He dragged her wrap dress off one shoulder and thrust his hand under the dress, between her legs and up her belly, groping for anything else she had hidden there. She pulled away and caught up her robe, which lay crumpled on the bench. Holding it between them, she said, "I'm not lying! I love you, more than life itself."

Eaglefeather grabbed her by the wrist and hauled her toward the door. When he released her to undo the fastenings of the door, she pulled the armhole of her dress back up to her shoulder and grabbed the veil, throwing it carelessly over her head to cover her face.

"Listen to me. Please," she begged. "I meant no harm." Hot tears streamed down her cheeks.

He ordered the warder, who stood in the plaza looking stunned, "Summon the Truthspeaker. No, the Seedkeeper." The young priest nodded hastily, turned, and ran toward the gate of the temple precinct.

"Let's go back in," Mistlight suggested tremulously.

The Rainsinger glared at her. "Not another word. Not until I find out what you have done to me."

"It's not—"

He raised his fist. Sticking out of the bottom was the corner of the pouch.

Afraid he would strike her again, Mistlight closed her mouth. She tucked her stinging cheek against her shoulder and pressed her hands together. She watched him warily from the corner of her eye as they waited for the Seedkeeper to arrive. She couldn't think of anything to do that wouldn't make him more angry.

Soon the Seedkeeper hurried into the temple plaza, the Truthspeaker beside her. They looked disheveled and bad-tempered. Mistlight hunched her shoulders and tried not to catch the eye of either one.

Eaglefeather stepped toward the Seedkeeper. He opened his palm to reveal the earthflower. As the priestess cupped her hands, he poured the crushed pieces into them. "What is this?" he demanded.

The Seedkeeper sniffed, then bent her head and drew in another breath. "Earthflower."

"To stop a woman from conceiving a child?" he asked.

"It is said to stir love and desire," the Truthspeaker said quietly.

"A love charm." He looked from one to the other of the high priestesses. "Did you hope to control me through this? Exert your goddess's power over the Rainsinger?"

Mistlight couldn't hold back any longer. "Mother Ge makes babies more readily where there is love!"

"Quiet, girl!" came the Childcatcher's scratchy voice from behind Mistlight.

Mistlight whipped her head around and found the eldest priestess, who had followed the others and was now scowling at her.

Eaglefeather announced, "From now on, any Smokemother or Cornmaiden entering the temple precinct will be stripped naked and searched."

Appalled, Mistlight turned back to face him.

The Truthspeaker said, "You cannot hold all of us responsible for what this one silly girl tried—and failed—to do."

Mistlight began, "I only wanted—"

The Childcatcher told her, "One word more, you foolish child, and I will strike you!"

"You all are bound together in the service of your goddess," Eaglefeather told the Truthspeaker. "What one does, all do. When one deserves punishment, all do."

She replied, "You are being unreasonable. This is the sun-festival. Let us wait until it is over and revisit the issue then, with cooler heads."

"Do not think time will soften my resolve," he said.

The Seedkeeper stepped toward him. "The fall of the shadowdancer was a bad omen yesterday, and his death today has cast a long shadow over the sun-festival. People need reassurance that things will improve, that the seeds blessed by Mother Ge will grow and that the Stormbringers will call down the rains to ensure ample crops. The Smokemothers and Stormbringers must work together."

"Then prove that you can be trusted," Eaglefeather snapped. He cast a furious glance at the Truthspeaker. The priestess nodded once.

Without looking at Mistlight, he said, "Take her. Never let me see her again."

"Don't turn away from me," Mistlight pleaded. "I love you!"

The Childcatcher stepped between her and the man she would do anything for.

"No!" Mistlight tried to get around the old priestess. The other two high priestesses rushed toward her. Each of them grabbed an arm and held her in place. "Stop it! Stop!" she yelled. "Let me go!" She squirmed against their clutching hands.

The Childcatcher slapped her, and she froze in shock. "You are not his!" the Childcatcher declared.

The other priestesses pulled on Mistlight, tugging her toward the temple gate. Desperate for Eaglefeather to come after her, even if only to insult her again, she cast a glance over her shoulder and saw him walking away, toward his workroom. "No!" she wailed.

3

Tucked between the two eldest priestesses, who grasped her arms with surprising strength, Mistlight passed through the gateway of the Smokemothers' compound. Cornmaidens looking calm and happy sat on reed mats scattered around the little plaza. Some stared up at the sky, as though admiring the faint glow of twilight clouds or listening to the echoes of drums and flutes from the village dance. Others had their heads bent together in low-voiced conversations.

She dropped her gaze to the hard-packed ground as the Seedkeeper and Childcatcher released her and went ahead. Any hope of getting to the sleep-room unnoticed failed miserably, as someone called out, "Here she is." The others rose from their mats and crowded around her. "You're back so early!" "Are you all right?" "What happened?" "Did he hurt you?" They flung questions at her so quickly, her ears rang. She bit her lower lip and wondered what to say.

"Quiet down," Mistlight heard. An arm came around her shoulders. Out of the corner of her eye, she saw that her rescuer was Shiningdawn, who would never make the mistake of falling in love. Wishing she could be as sensible, Mistlight looked away. Eaglefeather's rejection burned in her heart.

"Do you want some?" one of the girls asked, holding out a seedcake.

Mistlight shook her head.

"Give her a moment to settle herself," Shiningdawn said.

Everyone went quiet, but Mistlight knew their curiosity wasn't gone, just waiting to burst out in more questions. "I'm all right," she told them. "I'm just going to change."

They cast doubtful glances at her but returned to their mats with no more argument, as though high priestesses escorted a Cornmaiden back from the House of Quickening all the time. Mistlight retreated into the sleep-room. She took a rushlight from the basket by the door and lit it with a spark from the firestone. All the while, she listened for whispers outside. If the girls were talking about her, the adobe walls blocked their voices. She placed the rushlight in a holder and went to her sleep mat to pick up her clothing. Although alone, she felt so self-conscious that she went into the screened privacy area to exchange the wrap dress for her usual tunic and skirt.

Mistlight folded her ceremonial clothing and laid the child-beads on the neat pile. She wrapped her hands around each other, closed her eyes, and bowed her head, offering the customary prayer to Mother Ge that would end her responsibility for the ceremonial regalia. Her throat tightened with rising tears, making each word an effort. Mistlight picked up the pile of clothing, then rounded the privacy screen to put everything away. She stopped short as Shiningdawn came in.

"You've been summoned to the Dreamwalker," her vow-sister said.

Incapable of forcing a response past the lump in her throat, Mistlight nodded. She busied herself with the dress and robe, opening the storage baskets where they were kept and tucking them inside. Her skin prickled from Shiningdawn's unrelenting gaze.

"It must be a good sign, right?" Shiningdawn asked. "That they've finished their discussion so quickly?"

Mistlight pushed past her and fled toward the door, emerging into the cool evening under the curious stares of the other Cornmaidens. She hurried across the plaza to the Dreamwalker's cell. She didn't believe it was a good sign at all.

In the precise center of the small room, a brazier gave off a heavy scent of herbs, tinged with tobacco from smoldering cane pipes. The four priestesses stood in the flickering light of oil lamps resting on three-legged stands in the corners of the room. Their shadows overlapped and multiplied in a tangled web.

Mistlight ducked her head respectfully and said, "Revered grandmothers, I have come." A long, nerve-wracking silence met her greeting.

The Dreamwalker spoke first. "Your heart is clouded now, and you must face the storm. Have courage. One day the clouds will clear."

Mistlight didn't try to make sense of the seer's words. The Dreamwalker's proclamations came from whirlwinds of the mind produced by dizzyweed potions. Only full priestesses, who spoke with

Mother Ge, had any chance of understanding. Mistlight clasped her hands together before her and waited as patiently as she could for the decision.

The Truthspeaker, straight-backed and unyielding, her thin face skull-like from shadows cast by the oil lamp near her elbow, asked, "Do you understand what you have done?"

Mistlight swallowed hard and managed to whisper, "Revered grandmother, I intended only to make the Rainsinger love me back."

"Love is not something for you to make happen," the Truthspeaker informed her. "Such a thing lies only within Mother Ge's power, not ours."

Recalling the teachings from the early days of being a Cornmaiden, several moons earlier, Mistlight said, "She makes babies best where there is love."

"For other women, yes, that is her wish." The Truthspeaker tapped a forefinger on her knee.

Mistlight couldn't look away from that tiny repetitive movement. She felt the words more than heard them, pulsing in her head. Conversing with the Truthspeaker was not for the unwary at the best of times, and for Mistlight this was becoming the worst time she'd ever experienced in her life.

"Our order exists for a different reason," the Truthspeaker went on. "To maintain balance. Male and female, light and dark, sky and earth. Mother Ge sends new life to Cornmaidens as a sign of her favor. The absence of a child in your belly shows that these moons you have spent in her service have not been enough to overcome your bad blood."

The last few words penetrated the fog in her mind. "What do you mean by that? What bad blood? My mother—"

The Seedkeeper interrupted. "Your mother is not at issue."

Mistlight tried to figure out what that meant. "My father?" she asked. But she didn't know who her father was; her mother never would say. Then she thought about how the Seedkeeper kept track of the couplings of priests with Cornmaidens and Smokemothers, careful to keep kin from coming together in the House of Quickening. Mistlight searched the Seedkeeper's wrinkled face. If anyone knew her father's identity, it would be that priestess, who had spent many turnings tracing bloodlines.

Who is my father? she wanted to ask. She held back, for this was not the time to indulge in curiosity. She had to find a way to convince the priestesses that Mother Ge did approve of her. That Mistlight should, at midsummer, take the vows of a Smokemother.

The Childcatcher leaned forward and told her, "I am truly saddened that it has come to this."

A weight settled on Mistlight's chest at the seriousness in the oldest priestess's voice.

"The Dreamwalker read the signs to learn Mother Ge's will," the Truthspeaker said.

Mistlight glanced at the Dreamwalker, whose pupils had expanded so far under the influence of dizzyweed that they were ringed by only a narrow band of brown. The seer held a bowl with complicated patterns in black, white, and red on the inside. Whatever designs the potter had made weren't the important part, Mistlight knew. Instead, the residue left in the bowl by a decoction of divining herbs told the Dreamwalker what future Mother Ge laid out for Mistlight.

The Truthspeaker went on, "That you remain barren, that you could not save the shadowdancer, those are not your fault, merely a sign of Mother Ge's disfavor. But that you attempted to work a charm upon the Rainsinger, that was your choice and no one else's." She fell silent.

For a moment that seemed to stretch out into eternity, no one said anything.

The Childcatcher was the first to break the silence: "Mother Ge cannot keep one such as you in her service."

The words echoed in Mistlight's head, becoming fainter with each repetition. Her knees buckled, and she fell to one knee.

The Dreamwalker said, "A single moldy ear of corn will spoil an entire granary and must be thrown out."

Then the Truthspeaker: "You are now released from your vows, Mistlight, and must leave us. The end of your service as Cornmaiden comes only a few moons early. We will allow everyone to believe that you made this choice yourself, so upset are you over losing the shadowdancer."

"Leave? No!" Mistlight crawled to the Truthspeaker and flung her arms around the Smokemother's shins. "Revered grandmother, the Rainsinger will send for me, I know he will! When he does, I have to be here. He may be angry now, but he'll let me explain—"

"It is not his decision to make," the Truthspeaker said. "This is Mother Ge's will."

Mistlight lifted her gaze to the high priestess's stark face and saw no softening in the implacable eyes. "I can't leave! I have to become a Smokemother!"

"Hush, child. The decision has been made." The priestess grasped Mistlight by her shoulders and drew her to her feet.

She staggered, losing her balance when the Truthspeaker gave her a slight shove toward the door. She looked from one to another of the high priestesses. Only the Childcatcher met her gaze.

"But where am I to go?" she asked in a small voice, unable to imagine life outside the Smokemothers' compound.

The Childcatcher suggested, "You could follow your mother's life-path and work at the Children's House to give others a better life. You had happy times there, did you not?"

Mistlight thought of how it had been when her mother was still alive . . . and the loneliness after.

"That would be the safest place for you," the Seedkeeper said.

Safest, she repeated to herself rebelliously. *From what?* What did the high priestesses know of life outside their compound? "If I am no longer a Cornmaiden," she argued, "you have no authority over me. No right to tell me where and when to go."

"We have every right to say that you must go now." The Truthspeaker pointed to the door. "Where you find yourself after you leave is up to you."

Mistlight glared at the Smokemother before her, then swept her hot gaze left and right over the other three. None of them defended her or showed any sign of relenting. Was there any point in arguing with these horrible old women? She turned on her heel and crossed the Dreamwalker's cell in three paces.

Outside, she halted to keep from running into a cluster of Cornmaidens near the doorway. Their shocked expressions told Mistlight that they had heard every word of her humiliation. She walked forward. They stepped back, clearing the way, as though the merest touch from her might taint them—all except Shiningdawn, who stood with her chin jutted forward, and said, "Let her stay for tonight."

"Mistlight is no longer your vow-sister," the Truthspeaker said within the room. "She cannot remain here."

Shiningdawn protested, "At least let her stay till moonrise. It's dark out there."

Mistlight saw the high priestesses' refusal in the Cornmaidens' faces.

Taking a step forward, Shiningdawn said, "Women who need our protection can stay here without being Cornmaidens."

"Not Mistlight. She will find peace only by leaving," came the Childcatcher's gravelly voice. "That is an end to it. See her to the gate."

Mistlight, with no choice but to obey, bent her head and walked past Shiningdawn. The other Cornmaidens trailed after her, but none of them said anything. Her eyes began to fill with tears she refused to let fall. The Cornmaidens weren't really her sisters, she told herself—or friends either. She wasn't sad to say goodbye to them. In fact, she resented them for having the life she wanted. With the passing of three more moons, she would surely have quickened with Eaglefeather's child. Now all that she had dreamed of had been stolen from her.

Shiningdawn ran up from behind. She squeezed Mistlight's hand, bent close, and whispered, "Go to Firesister. She'll know what to do."

"Why would I go to that woman?" Mistlight pulled her hand away. She walked through the open gateway and left behind the place she had hoped would be her home for many turnings, until she withered in old age and her spirit rose to join the Ancestors among the clouds.

She placed one unwilling foot in front of the other until she reached the main path through the village of Serpentgate. Left would take her to the Children's House, near the center of the village. To the right was the temple. Mistlight wavered at the junction, unable to choose. She felt a desperate craving, as though she were fasting and smelled delicious rabbit stew but knew she couldn't have even a taste. She was sure she'd seen the same starving look in Eaglefeather's eyes when he looked at her. He needed something only she could give him.

Yet how could she think of going to him now, in the midst of his fury over the earthflower charm, his grief over the shadowdancer's death, his frustration over the ruined ceremony? Rushing him like this would be stupid. She knew all that, knew she should be sensible and wait, and yet—he was the only one who might be able to convince the high priestesses to change their minds. That couldn't wait.

Mistlight turned her head and swept her gaze up the massive wall of the temple to the room at the top, where leaping yellow and orange flames shone in the night as they consumed the shadowdancer's body. There was nothing to be done about the ceremony or the shadowdancer, for those disasters were public and widely known. What had happened between her and Eaglefeather in the House of Quickening, that was another matter. No one else knew the details. If she could get him to demand that the high priestesses reinstate her as a Cornmaiden, she could still be with him. All she had to do was find out what he wanted from her.

She went where her heart led her, but the gate to the temple was closed. "Let me in!" she called up to the guardtower.

A face appeared at the tower's edge. "None are permitted to enter after dark," the guardian of the gate replied.

"Cornmaidens are," she said boldly. "Mistlight the Cornmaiden needs to speak with the Rainsinger!"

"A bare-faced girl? I see no Cornmaiden here."

Mistlight remembered that her veil was gone. "Just tell him!"

The guard didn't answer. He retreated into the tower.

Mistlight gathered her courage. Aware that she might never have another chance to speak with Eaglefeather, the only person with enough power to change her life-path, she ran to the gate and beat on it with the heels of her hands, rattling it against the frame. "Open up! Let me in!" Nothing happened. She struck the gate a few more times, even kicked it, but still it stood fast against her. "Open for me right now!" she demanded. "I must speak with the Rainsinger!"

The gate cracked open. Someone behind it said, "What are you—"

Mistlight rushed forward. She threw her weight against the gate, which swung wider as whoever held it grunted. She stumbled in, scraping her shoulder and cheek on the adobe wall. Before she could get all the way in, her wrists were grabbed and she was pushed against the wall. She squirmed to escape the priest who held her. "Let me go! I have to—"

He tightened his fingers upon her wrists until she cried out in pain. Twisting her arms, he pulled her from the wall, then backed her out of the gate and shoved her away.

Mistlight's ankle turned as she tried to avoid stepping on it with the other foot. She fell in a heap and watched the priest's legs disappear behind the edge of the woven-reed gate, which swept shut. Mistlight got up, hobbled to the gate, and pressed, but it wouldn't yield. "Open the gate! Open it!" She slapped the reeds again and again with open palms as hot tears streamed down her face.

She stood there and yelled until her voice gave out. No one came to her. No one spoke to her from the guardtower. No sounds came to her from the other side of the gate. As the evening breeze died down and a sluggish rain began, she became aware that her ankle throbbed. Mistlight slipped to the ground, her back against the adobe wall that separated her from Eaglefeather, and let the wetness from the sky mingle with her despairing tears.

If she left, she might lose all chance of reconciling with the man she loved, but she couldn't stay—the priests wouldn't let her in, not tonight at least. Though she knew she had to get away, her ankle made that seem impossible. Exploring fingers sent pain shooting up her leg. A bleak possibility struck her: if she slept in the open, perhaps she would become chilled and take sick and die, and all this awfulness would end.

"He-ya!" a man said, sounding surprised. "What are you doing here?"

When she blinked up at him, her damp eyes couldn't make out his face. Mistlight drew up her knees and locked her arms around them.

"Are you hurt?" the man asked.

She shook her head.

"Do you need help?"

She shook her head again and hugged her knees more tightly.

"Which clan do you belong to? I'll take you to them."

His question helped put her thoughts in order, for there was only one answer. "I have to go to the Children's House." She glanced at him, then away, remembering the Seedkeeper's comment that that would be the safest place for her. Safe from what? she'd wondered. Perhaps, she thought now, safe from strangers wandering the village making unwanted offers of help. "You don't need to come with," she told him. "You should get out of the rain."

"Come on." He held out his hand.

She dropped her chin onto her knees and closed her eyes. The next moment, his hand closed on one of her bruised wrists. She yelped and opened her eyes. His grip loosened enough that she pulled free.

"You said you weren't hurt." He sounded annoyed.

"Go away!"

"I can't leave you here. Get up."

It was an order. Though she might not want his help, he was determined to give it anyway. She shook her head.

He turned and crouched suddenly, offering his broad back. Drops of water clung to the loose ends of his two braids, plastering them to his leather tunic. "Climb on. I promise I won't grab you again. It's just . . . I'm not going to let you sit here crying in the rain."

Mistlight knew he meant it. She didn't have the resolve to refuse his offer or the strength to go on by herself. She moved the braids out of the way. Slowly she placed her arms over his shoulders and doubled them, one on top of the other, on his chest. She separated her knees and spread her legs, squirming to tuck her skirt around them, so that her thighs embraced the hard muscles on each side below his ribs. He hooked his elbows around her knees and rose. Carried like a child on his back, she felt every movement as he shifted under her. The sudden flush of heat that started in her belly and rose through her breasts, her neck, her cheeks and prickled her scalp embarrassed her. Turning her face away, into the cool rain, helped only a little.

He began to walk. The evenness of his strides reminded her of summer days in simpler times, when she and other girls from the Children's House would climb onto the backs of the strongest boys and have shoving matches in half-empty canals. The girls, bubbling with laughter, would try to unseat each other, while the boys would ram each other in an attempt to be the last team standing. She didn't remember ever winning, but splashing in canal water on a hot day was the point anyway. Exhausted, Mistlight rested her chin on his shoulder, closed her eyes, and lost herself in memories.

"You're that girl from the Children's House, yes?" the man under her asked, startling her into opening her eyes. "The one who joined the Cornmaidens?"

Light from the rising moon, glowing under the blanket of soggy clouds, showed Mistlight that they weren't headed toward the river. "This isn't the right way," she protested.

"Why were you at the temple gate, and without your veil and fancy clothes? It's not time for the choosing yet. You still have three moons until the new Cornmaidens are selected."

Mistlight tried to wriggle off his back.

"Keep still," he warned. "If I slip on the wet path, we'll both go down."

Biting her lower lip, she obeyed his sensible advice. "Where are you taking me?"

"The Children's House is too far." He was quiet for a few steps, then said, "You have the look of your mother about you."

Mistlight couldn't recall anyone saying that before. "How did you know my mother?"

His shoulders stiffened. After a momentary hesitation, he said, "I came from the Children's House too. Before your time, of course. After the hunters took me on, I delivered meat to the house for a while when your mother was in charge." He paused again, then said, "I was sorry to hear about her passing."

Mistlight accepted his sympathy with a nod, then tightened her arms to bring her head close to his, trying to see his face as she asked, "Then do you know anything about my father?" Although his steps didn't falter, she thought the question took him aback.

"No more than anyone else does," he said.

She supposed even if he did, he wouldn't tell her. Mistlight had never been able to breach the silence that shrouded her father's identity. She'd never worried about it before, but now—*bad blood,*" the Truthspeaker had said. "Turn around and take me to the Children's House. We're nearly at the edge of the village already. There's nothing more out this way but ruins."

"It's not as deserted as all that."

"I mean it!" She lifted a hand, wrapped it around one of his braids, and yanked as hard as she could.

"Owww!" He stopped, bending his neck so his head followed her insistent tugging. "Let go!"

She slid off his back, taking her weight on her good foot, and grabbed the other braid with her other hand. "Where are you taking me?" she demanded.

"To Firesister!"

He tried to pull his hair loose, but Mistlight took another wrap with both hands and held him in front of her. "Why?" she asked.

"It's someplace safe for tonight," he croaked out, twisting his shoulders in an attempt to face her. "Ow!"

She pulled harder, and he dropped to one knee. The braids snapped tight. Releasing her grasp on them, she felt her face flush. "Sorry." The brief apology sounded childish, so she sought something else to say. "I know you were only trying to be helpful."

He rubbed his abused scalp and glared at her. "That hurt, you vicious girl. What got you so upset? Why don't you want to go to Firesister?"

"She doesn't like me."

"Why would you say that?" The lines around his mouth deepened into a scowl. "She gets along with everyone."

"Ha!"

The man turned away from her. "We're close to her place. If you insist on going to the Children's House, you can go on your own. Otherwise, follow me." He pressed fingers to his head and grumbled, "For such a little thing, you have quite a grip."

Mistlight watched him stride off. She saw no good reason to go after him, this man whose name she didn't even know. It would be more sensible to go to the Children's House rather than hope for a welcome from Firesister. And yet . . .

Miserably aware that he didn't offer to take her on his back again, Mistlight limped after him. Though the rain seemed to have stopped, she figured the moon would soon retreat behind the clouds. She wasn't sure she could find her way to the Children's House in the dark. She ached all over, especially her wrists and ankle. She hadn't eaten for a while and found herself thirsty besides. This man, whoever he was, seemed confident of his ability to convince Firesister to take her in for the night. Mistlight told herself she was in no position to complain.

He walked along but not overly fast, as though easing his pace for her sake. Clouds scudded overhead, thinning and breaking up in a wind so high above her head that Mistlight couldn't feel it. The moonlight strengthened and stars began to sparkle. Reflections off wet bushes and puddles in the path caught her eye as she tried to keep up with her guide.

He walked along a line of ocotillos. The thorny stalks of the living fence were covered with leaves that looked black in the moonlight. The man stepped into a gap in the fence line.

Mistlight stopped, unable to enter the enclosure.

He turned and faced her. "What now?"

"The fence," she said. It was scary enough to think that Firesister lived outside the village. The fact that the potter surrounded herself with ocotillos made her seem a creature of the wild, not one of the farmfolk Mistlight had grown up among.

"Are you afraid once you're in, you won't be able to get out? Don't worry. The fence is there to keep animals away from her things, that's all. It's no different from the adobe walls around house compounds." He gestured for Mistlight to approach.

No different from a wall, she told herself, and forced her feet to move.

A few steps in, Mistlight spotted Firesister, who sat at the edge of a vatto with her face upturned. Mistlight had the fanciful notion that the potter was singing the clouds away.

"Wait here," the man told Mistlight. He continued to move forward and called out, "Firesister. It's me, Bearclaw."

Firesister turned her head and got to her feet. She approached the man and stretched her hands toward him. "Out enjoying this beautiful night?" she said, touching his forearms lightly. "Isn't it lovely, with the raindrops sparkling on the ground and the stars in the sky?"

Mistlight tucked herself out of Firesister's line of sight behind the man—Bearclaw, as she now knew. The welcoming smile wasn't for her. Bearclaw seemed a close friend of Firesister's. He could probably convince her to take in Mistlight for a time. Perhaps long enough to find some way to get back to Eaglefeather.

"There's someone with me," Bearclaw said.

"Bring him in too," Firesister said without hesitating.

Before replying, he flung a glance over his shoulder as though to make sure Mistlight was still there. "It's a her."

"Bring her, then."

Bearclaw walked back to where Mistlight stood wishing herself elsewhere. He placed one big hand on the nape of her neck and used it to press her into motion.

"Mistlight?" Firesister sounded shocked.

Not wishing to see Firesister's shock turn into hostility, Mistlight didn't look at the other woman. She glanced around the compound. She didn't find many straight, squared-off walls, the kind of houses and storage buildings she was used to. Instead there were curves and rounded shapes only partly visible in the dimness.

Firesister hissed in a breath. "Is this your doing?" she asked Bearclaw, waving her hand at Mistlight.

"Not me!" he rushed to say. "I found her like this, all weepy, near the temple. If anything, I'm the one who was abused."

Firesister approached Mistlight and gently touched her neck, her cheek. "Oh, you poor girl," she said.

Mistlight remembered that her neck was bruised from a few days earlier, overlaid by fresher bruises and maybe a little cut from the earthflower charm's cord. There were probably scrapes on her cheek from the temple wall. Self-conscious, she shifted away from Firesister's hands. "I'm all right. I wouldn't have come here, but he made me. I don't need to stay, if you don't want me to."

"Of course you're welcome here," Firesister said. She glanced at Bearclaw and teased, "This is an interesting excuse to come find me on a dancing night."

"I was on my way home, came across her, and brought her to you. That's all."

Firesister's mouth twitched. "Why were you going home when the moon is barely up?"

"The dance ended early," he explained. "Nobody's in the mood to celebrate, what with the rain and the shadowdancer."

Mistlight felt awkward between the two, as their conversation passed back and forth without her.

"You should have stayed," Firesister told him.

Bearclaw looked at her solemnly. "The only woman I want to dance with is never there."

"You know why."

"How long will you suffer?" he asked.

"With dear friends like you, how can you imagine I would be suffering?" Firesister placed her hands on Bearclaw's arm. "Thank you for bringing her to me."

Mistlight watched as she said goodbye to Bearclaw and sent him back out into the night.

Once he was gone, Firesister turned to her. "Let's get you cleaned up."

She couldn't bear the pretense a moment longer. "Why are you doing this?" Mistlight asked. "Why did you take me in when you hate me?"

Firesister stumbled back a step. One hand lifted to cover her heart. "I don't hate you," she exclaimed. "How could I? Why would you say such a thing?"

"Whenever you look at me," Mistlight said, "your eyes go hard and distant, like you aren't seeing me at all."

Firesister blinked rapidly. "Have I ever been mean to you?" Her voice sounded ragged.

"You're nice enough to me," Mistlight admitted, "but I never feel you really want to be. It's like you don't want anyone to know that you aren't as pleasant and friendly as you pretend."

"Wherever did you get such an idea? You're imagining things."

"Don't tell me that. I saw it in your face every time you came to the Smokemothers' compound to deliver food or tattoo a flame for a childbirth or a—" Mistlight stopped herself from mentioning the teardrop tattoo that marked the death of a Smokemother's child. She shivered and forced herself to go on. "Before that, too, when I was at the Children's House, you may have tried to treat me the same as the others, but your whole body showed it was a lie. Yet you took me in tonight without protest. Why would you do that?"

"Come to the vatto and sit down. I'll tend to your bruises and scrapes."

Frustrated, Mistlight asked, "How can I trust you to help me?"

Firesister gazed at her with a faint smile and held out a hand. "How can you not?"

Mistlight thought about the darkness outside the ocotillo fence and the long walk—alone, along paths she wasn't sure of—to get to the Children's House, where she didn't even want to be. Slowly she reached for the hand being offered to her. The skin felt dry and callused against hers, but the thin, warm fingers gave her a sense of comfort she hadn't experienced since her mother's death. Feeling disloyal, Mistlight drew her hand away. "You go first," she told the potter.

Mistlight tried not to limp as she followed the other woman to the vatto. Firesister motioned for her to be seated on one of the work mats placed around the fire ring.

The potter took a fire-starter drill from a gray corrugated jar and some bark fluff from a basket. She knelt near the fire ring and placed the fluff in the tinder plate, then began to work the drill efficiently. A spark flashed at the drill tip, and a tiny flame flared up. "Are you hungry?" she asked as she fed dried cornhusks into the growing fire.

"No." A grumble in Mistlight's belly contradicted her.

Firesister laughed. "Once I get a good cook-fire going, you can put some food in that unhappy belly." She lit a torch and placed it in a holder near Mistlight.

The bracing odor of pine pitch made Mistlight's nose itch. She rubbed her nose and glanced around. Outside the small ring of light under the vatto, the night seemed darker, as if closing in on her. But she wasn't alone. She had the potter promising food, comfort, and a place to sleep. She closed her eyes and let Firesister take care of her.

In a little while, she felt warm water being dabbed on her cheek. It stung as it seeped into her scrapes, dissolving the crusted blood. Opening her eyes, she found Firesister leaning close, intently focused.

"You're awake. Feeling all right?" Firesister squeezed out the cloth in a bowl of water by her knee. Froth from soaproot floated sluggishly on the water surface.

Mistlight's eyelids drifted shut as the other woman cleaned blood off her cheek. When the warm cloth went away, her skin cooled quickly, and she shivered. She heard rustling but didn't open her eyes to find out what Firesister was doing. Soon she felt the curved lip of a bowl beneath her chin. Water cascaded down her cheek, rinsing off the soap. Knots in her shoulder and back that Mistlight hadn't even noticed began to relax.

Firesister asked, "Why did Bearclaw find you at the temple? Don't the priests usually leave the Cornmaidens alone during the sun-festivals?"

Mistlight's slowly receding tension returned tenfold. "It isn't what you think," she said. "I wasn't there for the House of Quickening." *Because Eaglefeather didn't want me.* She thrust that thought away.

"Did they hurt you because you didn't save the shadowdancer?"

Mistlight locked her hands together in her lap and shook her head.

Firesister's voice softened. "I don't know what happened to you today. I won't ask you to tell me, though you can when you're ready. I know how hard it is when something goes terribly wrong in your life."

The words pricked at Mistlight's pride. She didn't want this woman's pity.

"All it takes is one mistake for your whole world to shatter," Firesister went on. "You feel like you've been ripped loose from all you know." She placed a hand on Mistlight's arm. "You have to be brave and face people no matter how you feel inside. Do you understand what I'm saying?"

She didn't, not really. Her cheeks felt cold and tight. She tasted salt on her lips and realized tears were flowing again. Inhaling raggedly, Mistlight drew away from Firesister and folded her arms across her chest.

"Are you cold?" the potter asked. "Let's get you inside. I'll bring you some nice warm stew in a bit."

With Firesister's help, Mistlight rose. That first step, even though she tried to be careful, caused pain to shoot up her leg from the twisted ankle. She cried out as her knees buckled. Firesister grabbed her and eased her down onto the mat. Mistlight pressed a hand to her ankle. It felt swollen, the skin hot.

Firesister bent close. "Your ankle looks bad." She sighed. "I don't have anything here to help with that. Should I go to the healers for some herbs?"

"No, don't leave me!" Unwilling to be left behind in this unfamiliar place, Mistlight grabbed Firesister's dress and clung to her, keeping the woman kneeling beside her. "Herbs aren't the only thing that can take down swelling," she said, remembering the strange-smelling poultice the Childcatcher had brought for the shadowdancer. "You have clay handy?"

Firesister tilted her head, and Mistlight realized what a stupid question that was.

"Clay, yes, I have that," Firesister said.

"Close by? Right here in the compound?"

At Firesister's murmur of agreement, Mistlight released her. "Bring me some. Please."

Soon the potter returned, carrying a cloth-wrapped lump that smelled of damp clay.

Mistlight asked for fresh water and more cloths. When Firesister brought those too, Mistlight added water to the clay until it became soft and sticky. Patting the wet clay onto a long strip of cloth, she felt the residue drawing on her knuckles as the edges began to dry. She folded the cloth a few times lengthwise and wrapped it around her ankle.

Despite having no idea whether the makeshift poultice would work on her sprain, she felt pleased. She had thought of something all by herself.

"When your whole world crumbles, sometimes work is the only thing that stops the crying," Firesister said. She wound a ribbon around the poultice and tied it in place. "I'll help you up now. Lean on me. Keep the weight off your ankle as much as you can."

The potter's even, practical voice reassured Mistlight, who found herself on her feet and limping toward an old-fashioned hut, oval in shape, with no abrupt corners. Even its low entryway curved at the top.

Firesister supported Mistlight's shoulders as they crouched to get through the short passage. One of the potter's hands lifted away from Mistlight. A moment later, the brush of soft hide against her face told her that her host had moved the deerskin curtain that kept out the chill in these mud-plastered huts. The interior was darker than outside, so Mistlight couldn't see anything. She had no idea where the roof poles or hanging shelves were. Nervously she raised her arms and swept the space in front of her.

"Just a few more steps," Firesister said, steering her to one side.

"All right." Mistlight pulled her arms back, but only a little. She didn't entirely trust the potter's guidance.

"Here. There's a bench."

Firesister shifted her grasp to Mistlight's waist and helped her sit. The bench flexed a little under her, as if there was empty space beneath her bottom. A storage bin, she guessed, covered by a woven lid.

"I'll go get a light. I'll bring you something to eat, too." Firesister's hands fell away.

Mistlight sat rigidly and listened to the woman's footsteps moving toward the entry. Once she was gone, Mistlight felt utterly isolated, blind in the dark.

Not even a whisper of breeze touched her skin to give her a sense of time passing. If not for the sound of her own breathing, she thought, she might be the only living thing nearby. Frightened though she knew she was being foolish, she began to count her breaths: *one, two, three, four* . . . After fifty, she lost count and decided not to start again. It wasn't so bad, she told herself, sitting in peace with no one demanding anything of her.

Footsteps approached, a thin vertical strip of light appeared, and the deerskin curtain was twitched back. Firesister came in, bent over, shielding a rushlight. Net bags dangled from her elbows. The tantalizing odor of stew accompanied her. She carried the gleaming rushlight toward a candle held upright in a painted jar wedged into the fork of one of the poles that supported the roof. After lighting that candle, she moved to the other roof pole and lit a second one.

She set one of the bags beside Mistlight on the bench, then drew the netting away from the bowl inside. "There isn't much stew left." She handed Mistlight a spoon made from bone. "I don't keep a lot of food around."

Mistlight's stomach growled again. She took up the warm bowl and dipped the spoon into it. The stew smelled so good as it came toward her nose that she almost cried when it filled her mouth. A painful burst of saliva kept her from tasting the first mouthful. She swallowed quickly and took another spoonful. This one she rolled around in her mouth: diced rabbit meat and gopher-root stewed together until soft, pot herbs for texture, chia for thickening, a hint of peppergrass seeds thrown in for flavor. No corn, beans, squash—none of the foods that Firesister always brought to the Children's House and the Smokemothers.

"Are you out of corn?" Mistlight asked before having another bite of stew.

"Frowning while you eat brings bad luck. Does your face hurt?"

Feeling self-conscious under Firesister's scrutiny, Mistlight chewed and swallowed. "No, I'm all right." She placed the spoon in the stew and twisted the handle in restless fingers. "I always wondered where you got the corn and beans from. You don't have any fields yourself, and you aren't part of a clan that would give you use-rights to clanlands."

Silence stretched out so long, Mistlight didn't think her question would get answered, but Firesister eventually took a breath, pursed her lips, and said, "I've been able to trade. Sometimes finished pots, sometimes teaching girls how to make their own. Or food I gathered. I spend a lot of time in the desert and foothills, collecting clay. It's simple enough to bring back gopher-root or shaadh, nut-sedge or pilkanyi grass, shuuvadh for pinole, hannam buds, cactus fruit."

"People like all that?" Mistlight asked in surprise. "They're willing to trade real food for it?" Hearing how insulting that sounded, she quickly filled her mouth again.

Firesister smiled. "What do you think of the stew?"

Mistlight swallowed and exclaimed, "It's good! I didn't mean . . ." She trailed off, not sure how to say what she meant. "It's just a lot of effort to go through for the Smokemothers. Unless you were ever a Cornmaiden?"

"No. Never a Cornmaiden."

"Then why do so much for the Smokemothers?"

"Shouldn't I? Aren't they deserving?"

After that, Mistlight didn't feel like talking. She finished eating as Firesister moved things around in the hut. "Not there," she said when the potter slung a hair-on deerhide over the bench. "I'm used to the floor." The bench had too much give in it to be really trustworthy, in her opinion. And what if she rolled off?

Firesister shrugged. She laid out a sleep mat on one side of the roof supports, indicating with a gesture that Mistlight should lie upon it. Mistlight complied, then accepted a rabbit-fur blanket. She should have been comfortable, with ample padding below and above to keep her warm, yet she found herself staring up at the curved roof wishing she still had the moon and stars overhead. When Firesister snuffed the candles, Mistlight felt darkness close around her. She lay there, unseeing, listening to Firesister's even breaths—and rehearing, over and over, the last gasp of the shadowdancer, the harsh parting words from Eaglefeather.

"I don't think . . . I don't think I can fall asleep," she said.

After a long silence that made Mistlight wish she had kept her mouth shut, Firesister began to sing:

A sleepy night with stars to light your way in gentle dreams,
The Great Star Path leads from the past, ahead the future gleams.
So rest now, child, close your eyes, let nightbirds soothe your mind,
'Til golden dawn creeps round again and Brother Sun does shine.

Mistlight closed her eyes. She concentrated on the old lullaby, in the hope that it would help her forget the terrible events of this long day.

When Mistlight woke, she was surprised by how rested she felt. She yawned and stretched. A glanced around the dim room showed that she was alone. She stooped and passed through the low entryway to get outside.

Leaning against the curved wall, she lifted her face to the mid-morning sun and closed her eyes to bask in the warmth. She tried to remember any night she had slept so soundly.

In the Children's House, there were always newcomers sobbing for lost parents, or childish grievances that got carried into the sleep-room after a day of quarreling. Nights had become even worse during her time as a Cornmaiden, for she often had terrifying dreams, though she never remembered the details upon sitting up in sudden wakefulness— only that they involved the temple.

In Firesister's sleep-room, the night had been filled with peaceful silence, followed by a slow waking.

Yawning again, this time feeling a pull on her cheek, Mistlight glanced around the compound. There she saw every kind of house. A small hut, round like an overturned basket, with woven sticks forming its walls. The old-fashioned oval plastered room she had slept in, with the vatto beside it. Next to the vatto, a rectangular adobe-walled structure opened onto a workspace littered with potsherds. A small square storage building was visible beyond that.

Mistlight shaded her eyes from the slanting morning sunshine. Next to the buildings were several clumps of nopal cactus. And around everything, a fence made of ocotillos.

"How's the ankle?"

Firesister's voice startled Mistlight. She jerked her head around to look at her host, who offered a brilliant smile. "It's better," Mistlight said without thinking. It *was* better—so much so, she'd forgotten about having twisted her ankle the night before. When she flexed it, she felt only a few twinges.

"Let's have a look," said Firesister, her eyes more gentle than Mistlight was used to seeing.

Mistlight let herself be guided to the vatto. Firesister helped her settle on one of the work mats, then untied the ribbon that held the poultice in place and peeled off the cloth wrapper with gentle hands. As the poultice fell away, dried clay flaked off. Mistlight brushed the dust from her leg. Reddish fold lines spiraled around her ankle and down to her foot, but the swelling was reduced to almost nothing.

With one finger, Firesister traced a line along Mistlight's neck. "You have a welt here. And bruises. Do you want me to—"

"They're fine." Mistlight grabbed the finger and moved Firesister's hand away.

Firesister sat on her haunches. "I always wondered why you went to the Smokemothers instead of the healers. You have a gift for healing."

Mistlight heard only sincerity in the compliment. Heat came into her cheeks, and she looked away, unable to meet Firesister's gaze. She thought, *If I really had a talent for healing, I would have saved the shadowdancer.* "This?" She gestured at her ankle. "I guess it wasn't hurt badly."

"You could go to the healers and ask them to teach you—"

"I'm going to regain my place as a Cornmaiden," Mistlight snapped.

"Why? Why would you want that?"

Mistlight stared at Firesister. How could she explain the craving that had come over her after her mother's passing . . . the clawing need to have a child, someone who would love her beyond all measure, as she had been devoted to her own mother? That was what had taken her to the Smokemothers initially. But the yearning for a child's devotion had turned into desire for a man. A man who had never made any promises to her, or any woman, but was bound for life to the service of the Ta'atchul. A man she had tried to make her own using a charm.

At the memory of his fury the night before, Mistlight's stomach clenched. Uncomfortable under Firesister's inquiring gaze, she cleared her throat, which felt hot and dry. "I've never seen a compound with so many different kinds of buildings. What is all this?"

Firesister looked from one end of her home to the other. "Most of it was here already. There were a lot of potsherds scattered around, and the adobe buildings just needed roofing. There was an old pit-house here, ready to be cleared out and new posts put in for the dome. Then it was a matter of tying the limbs together and weaving the brush into it."

"Were the ocotillos and nopales here too? Is that why you chose this place?"

"I planted the ocotillos," she said. "The nopales were here. Behind the compound there's a little stand of agaves, too."

"Why do you live out here all by yourself, so far from everyone?"

"I like it." Using one hand to brace herself, Firesister rose. She walked to the edge of the vatto and turned her face toward the sun. "Did you sleep well?" she asked.

"Yes, very much so," Mistlight said.

"Do you still plan to go to the Children's House?"

Mistlight was ready to agree. Then she recalled the flavorful stew of the previous night, her restful slumber behind the protective ocotillos, the quiet of the morning. She lifted her chin and squared her shoulders. "Why should I go back there? I'm no longer a child. If I'm welcome to stay here . . . ?"

Firesister's gaze passed over Mistlight from head to foot and back again. "As long as you're willing to work." Motioning toward the ground, Firesister said, "You can start by picking up the cloth and as much of the clay for the poultice as you can get. I'll reuse it for something."

Mistlight did as she was told. It was the first of many small tasks that day. Firewood had to be gathered, foodstocks replenished, water ollas filled at the river, meals prepared and eaten. The two women performed these chores in a companionable silence. As the day wore on, Firesister began crushing potsherds from strangely patterned old pots. She showed Mistlight how to knead clay to make it malleable.

Mistlight's hands tired quickly. She had to take frequent breaks to massage cramps out of the heel of her hand and the pad at the base of her thumb.

When the breeze brought the music of flute and drums again, she knew her vow-sisters were performing the basket dance without her, and she wondered how she could persuade Eaglefeather to help her regain her place in the Cornmaidens. She saw no way of reaching him during the sun-festival. She would have to wait until it was over.

And so she spent that night with Firesister, and the next day and the next, staying too busy to think or feel. Those days unfolded like the first one, focused on food and water in the mornings and turning to Firesister's projects once Brother Sun warmed the work area.

Mistlight's desire to be with Eaglefeather grew stronger with each day that passed. She wondered whether he had cast a love-spell on her without her knowing.

On the third evening she sat with Firesister, admiring the full moon as it rose.

"Tomorrow we'll pick hannam," Firesister said.

"All right." As Mistlight thought about it, she realized she'd never done that, had never gone out into the desert and plucked the hannam buds from the stick-like cactus on which they grew. That was the sort of thing clan-sisters did, a whole group of them together, laughing and chattering. Tomorrow, Mistlight reflected, it would be just her and Firesister working shoulder to shoulder, a few words passing between them. Mistlight had always imagined that Firesister had many friends, because everyone in the village seemed to know her—and like her. But in the days Mistlight had spent in Firesister's compound, no one had come to visit. The potter seemed to be a different person than Mistlight had always thought her.

Mistlight glanced at Firesister, who was smiling up at the moon, and wondered how she could have imagined that Firesister hated her. Firesister seemed perfectly happy with her around, spoke no more about her going to the Children's House. But Mistlight was impatient to get back to Eaglefeather, and she was resolved to spend only one more day with Firesister. They would pick hannam and laugh together, and then Mistlight would go.

She didn't tell Firesister what she had decided. They spent one more companionable evening together, and Mistlight fell asleep and didn't stir the whole night through.

Next morning, after they had fetched water and eaten lightly, Firesister assembled what they would need: a stack of broad, flat baskets; woven reed mats to scrape off the spines; saguaro-rib tongs to save their fingers as they plucked the buds from the cholla stems. She handed the scrapers and tongs to Mistlight. They were starting toward the entrance when several young men burst into the compound.

Firesister charged toward them. As she ran, the baskets flew out of her arms.

One smacked Mistlight above her eye. She flinched and cried out, though it didn't really hurt.

When she looked up again, she realized the men were Stormbringers, for their hair was tied up in a club at the back of their head—but she didn't recognize any of them. Her first thought was that Eaglefeather had sent them for her, and she started forward. Then she saw that their ribbons were white, not yellow. They were from the Temple of Mist, way down on Earth River. Confused, with fright growing in the pit of her stomach, she stopped and wondered whether she could find somewhere to hide.

Some of the priests grabbed Firesister by the shoulders and wrist. She screamed and began to fight, biting and kicking and twisting to get loose.

One of the Stormbringers strode to Mistlight and grasped her arm above the elbow, fingers digging in as though he expected her to resist him. He yanked her toward him and then onward. As she passed the storage room, she saw a man inside, tossing out pots to smash on the ground. Bowls flew from the doorway of the hut where she'd slept so comfortably.

Between Firesister's raging and the shouts of the Stormbringers trying to subdue her and the crashing of pottery, Mistlight couldn't bear the noise. It battered at her ears and echoed in her head.

The Stormbringer headed for the entrance to the compound, dragging Mistlight with him.

"What are you planning to do to me?" she asked her captor.

"Shut your mouth." He lifted his free hand as though to slap her if she disobeyed. As she cringed back, he pulled her onward so roughly that her teeth clicked together.

He didn't let go after they passed the ocotillo fence, not even as they entered the village. People gawked and chattered to each other, and children stopped wide-eyed in the middle of the path. "Where are we going?" she asked, hoping he would say their destination was the temple. Eaglefeather might be angry with her, but he wouldn't allow her to be hurt.

Instead she found herself being taken southward through the village, toward the river, drawing nearer and nearer Cloud Mountain until it rose like a cliff before her.

Mistlight anxiously swayed from foot to foot at the edge of the west plaza atop Cloud Mountain. Behind her were the crumbling remains of the Watermasters' mound-top buildings. Before her were three Stormbringers, standing feet apart and with arms crossed, blocking her view of what was happening. Every now and then one of them would shift, allowing Mistlight to catch a glimpse of people entering the plaza.

She recognized most. Clan heads, both men and women. Leaders of the hunters and healers. The remembrancer, who bore the memories of generations on his calendar stick. The four high priestesses. Each group kept to themselves. They sat in silence, their faces serious.

Mistlight clasped her hands in front of her and willed the Childcatcher to cast her a reassuring look. But none of the priestesses so much as glanced at her. Maybe they thought Eaglefeather was going to demand that they accept her back into the Cornmaidens.

Then she remembered his dark expression as he emptied the earthflower from the cloth pouch. He hadn't seemed like a man irresistibly struck by love. But he *had* breathed in the sweetness of the earthflower. Maybe, she thought, the days apart had allowed the love charm to work on him. Maybe he had discovered that life without her was miserable.

Her interlaced fingers tightened on each other, white-knuckled, and she waited to find out what he had in mind for her. It had to be his will that had authorized the unfamiliar priests to escort her here.

Before long, Eaglefeather strode into the plaza. He halted at the center. A mica mirror on his forehead flashed in the sun. Yellow robes streamed from his shoulders, marking him as the leader of the Temple of Lightning. He looked dangerous and splendid and every bit the Rainsinger. Mistlight thrilled at the sight of him.

"My cousins," he began, "aunts and uncles, those of you charged with the safety of your clans, of the village of Serpentgate, and even beyond, I stand before you humbled and saddened." He knelt on one knee and bowed his head. "I have failed in my sacred duties. Trusting in the goodwill of our people, I have allowed witchcraft to fester."

Mistlight's brow furrowed as she tried to figure out what that had to do with her.

"What do you mean?" a man asked.

"Is this why you called us here?" came another voice.

"Bring her," Eaglefeather said.

One of the Stormbringers in front of Mistlight turned and grasped her wrist, then placed a hand behind her back and moved her forward, almost like a dance. She stumbled a little and wished she could have been more graceful in front of all these elders. Bowing her head respectfully, she found she was looking down on the head of the man she loved. Her hands trembled. *Trust in him,* she told herself to steady her nerves.

"What reason do you have for summoning Mistlight before us, Rainsinger?" asked a man off to her right side. "Are you saying she's a witch?"

"Not a witch, not yet. But she has come under a malign influence," Eaglefeather said, still kneeling.

"What influence?" That voice sounded like the Childcatcher.

Mistlight kept her head bent as thoughts flitted through her mind. Suddenly it made sense, why Firesister had taken her in without question: what Mistlight had seen as kindness must have been something much darker. An inner voice tentatively reminded her of the comfort she'd received, the peaceful sleep. She smothered that voice. Eaglefeather had no reason to lie about such an important matter.

He rose and faced the seated elders. "Among us in this village," he began, "are people who blame others for their misfortune. Most are harmless, but a few have learned to summon the kind of magic granted by Mother Ge and the Ta'atchul to make seeds grow and rain fall. Of late, such divine gifts have been warped by evil intent into illness and death. Do not imagine the loss of the people of Lastwater to be an accident. No more was the shadowdancer's death by snakebite accidental. No," he said, in a voice that filled the plaza, "these were purposeful attacks meant to waken fear in our hearts."

"Why should the lofty Rainsinger concern himself with witches?" a crackly voiced man asked.

A few people laughed. Mistlight clenched her hands into impotent fists at the disparagement of Eaglefeather, but she kept her head bowed.

His eyes ranged over the crowd, from one end to the other. "Need I remind you of the last time Serpentgate had to deal with witches, when a priest of the Temple of Lightning was killed by witch-breath?"

The laughter stopped. Though that death from a mysterious sickness had occurred several generations ago, during the building of the temple, it still lingered in everyone's memory.

Mistlight's heart clenched at the thought of such a terrible thing happening again. Had the shadowdancer's death really been caused by a witch? If that was true, she reflected—and why else would Eaglefeather have said it?—then Mistlight couldn't be blamed for the young priest's death. It would also mean the prayers of the Stormbringers hadn't failed.

"Speak straight. Is Mistlight the one you accuse of being a witch?" the Childcatcher asked.

Mistlight's head snapped up. She stared at the old priestess, then back at Eaglefeather. *Say no,* she willed him. *You can't believe such a thing of me.*

He and the Childcatcher locked gazes. He said, "It seems I might have cause to do so."

"I'm no witch!" Mistlight exclaimed. Her denial drew everyone's attention.

Eaglefeather turned his attention to her. "Where have you been staying, since the Smokemothers threw you out?"

"You know who I've been staying with," she answered. He'd known she was at Firesister's compound, else the Stormbringers wouldn't have gone there to get her. But that meant— "Is Firesister the one you say is tainted?"

A hint of a smile played at the corners of Eaglefeather's mouth.

The remembrancer raised an age-gnarled hand and addressed him: "Rainsinger, do you accuse Firesister of being a witch? If so, why isn't she here to face her accuser?"

"She will be," Eaglefeather answered, without looking away from Mistlight. "Soon."

Recalling Firesister's violent struggles against the Stormbringers who'd laid hands on her, Mistlight shivered.

Eaglefeather went on. "For now, it is Mistlight's future that concerns me. She has been bent but not yet completely twisted. To save her, she must be removed from Firesister's influence and purified—"

The Childcatcher interrupted. "Who will undertake this purification? You? Purifying a Cornmaiden is not something that can be done by a Stormbringer. It is for Mother Ge to take care of."

"But she is no longer a Cornmaiden, is she?" Eaglefeather's smile broadened. "You cast her out."

Mistlight stomped on the impulse to insist she was no witch and didn't need purifying. Eaglefeather had taken her away from Firesister, after all. She had to trust him to deal with the Smokemothers too.

The remembrancer said, "Purifying a witch has never been done."

Eaglefeather nodded at the elder. "That is true. But if she is not purified, she must be exiled. Is that what you would condemn her to?"

"Only if she is proven a witch!" the Childcatcher exclaimed.

"She attempted to sway me with a charm," Eaglefeather said. "You know that as a fact."

Mistlight was shocked that he would reveal that to everyone. She stared at him, wondering if he really believed she was a witch.

Eaglefeather continued, "If Firesister is not to blame for Mistlight's transgression, then it must be the Smokemothers, the ones in whose keeping she has been for the past nine moons. Isn't that right?"

A voice resonated in her bones: *There is a way forward.* Mistlight, with sudden clarity, understood what she had to do. She stood straight-backed, head held high. "I wronged him," she told the elders, "and for that perhaps I should be punished. But after, may I not be redeemed as the Rainsinger says? Punished, purified, and shielded from any further transgression?"

The remembrancer was the first to reply. "In what way will you be redeemed? As a Cornmaiden, you were vow-bound to Mother Ge. That did not prevent you from working against the Rainsinger, if he is to be believed."

Mistlight said, "By herself Mother Ge wasn't strong enough to shield me from bad influences. Wouldn't she and the Ta'atchul together be more powerful than any witch? Let me serve them. Let them protect me from myself. Bring me into the temple. As a woman, serving Mother Ge. As an acolyte, serving the Ta'atchul."

"Impossible," the remembrancer scoffed. "Such a thing has never been done, never even dreamed of."

A man behind him protested, "Never is a long time. The Storm-bringers brought knowledge of the Ta'atchul only a few generations ago. There are those among us who still remember the building of the temple."

Someone else said, "Women cannot be Stormbringers. No woman has ever set foot in the Temple of Lightning, since the first course of adobe was laid down."

Slowly, speaking directly to Eaglefeather, Mistlight said, "Not as a woman, not as a priest, but as a healer. Let me atone for my failure to save the shadowdancer. I'll learn from the healers, dedicate my life to the Ta'atchul."

"There is only one way a woman can provide service to the Ta'atchul," Eaglefeather answered. "A service already performed by the Cornmaidens and Smokemothers." His eyes narrowed on her. "Yet there is the matter of purification." He addressed the remembrancer.

"A witch has never been purified, you say? Never allowed to walk free in the village after being exposed as a witch?"

"That is so," the remembrancer said.

"Yet I am the Rainsinger. I am the one who speaks with the Ta'atchul. If the Ta'atchul accept her in the temple, no elder of the village shall tell them nay. If the Ta'atchul will it that she be purified and take up her life again like any other clan-daughter, no one shall gainsay them."

Mistlight read doubt and suspicion on the elders' faces. "I will—"

Eaglefeather slanted her a warning look and slashed a hand through the air to cut her off.

She subsided.

He said, "If you see this woman walking free and unaccompanied in the village after today, it will mean the Ta'atchul have indeed purified her." He placed a hand over his heart and inclined his head toward the remembrancer. "An admitted witch, restored to her life-path through the will of the Ta'atchul. Be sure to record that on your calendar stick."

The Childcatcher addressed the other elders and protested, "You cannot turn her over to the Rainsinger. He will destroy her."

Beside the old priestess, the Dreamwalker said, "Mother Ge's hand is moving in this. She has long spoken to the girl. Let us send Mistlight to the temple as she asks."

"But—" the Childcatcher began.

Eaglefeather said, "It is not for anyone else to determine who enters the temple or how long they remain in the sacred space. As Rainsinger, this decision is mine alone." He motioned toward the other Stormbringers, who came to stand by Mistlight. "Take her to the temple where the Ta'atchul can hear her." To Mistlight he said, "Pray to them. See if they listen."

Mistlight plopped down on her bottom and squirmed until her back rested against the plastered half wall on top of the temple. Eaglefeather's order to expose her to the Ta'atchul hadn't meant she would be stripped naked, as she'd feared. Only that there would be nothing between her and them. Tipping up her chin, she gazed at the ragged white clouds drifting across the sky.

The priests hadn't rebuilt the room on which the shadowdancer's funeral pyre had blazed. At some point, everything—roof beams, funeral platform, firewood, and the corpse's ashes and bones—had collapsed into the room. The ashes and debris had been carefully removed, and streaks on the plaster showed that the priests had made an effort to wash off the soot, but the remaining walls still smelled of smoke and death.

Gazing at the open space above her head rather than the remains of the room before her, Mistlight reminded herself that Eaglefeather had saved her from whatever web of evil Firesister had been weaving around her. As soon as he finished at the hearing and came to her, she would make him understand her good intentions with the love charm—that it was not meant to trap him, simply to enable them to be together. There was no need for her to be purified.

Though perhaps, she thought, purification would rid her of the recurring dreams she'd been having since joining the Cornmaidens . . . especially the dream of Eaglefeather tumbling from the roof of this very room. She realized with surprise that she hadn't dreamed at all while at Firesister's compound.

Mistlight heard the scrape of a ladder in the room below. The uprights appeared through the square opening in front of her. Eager to see Eaglefeather, she scrambled to her feet, straightened her dress, and stroked her hair to smooth it.

His head came through the opening, rising slowly as he climbed. She wanted to run to him, wanted to beg his forgiveness—but had no idea how he would respond. Did he care for her . . . or at least still desire her? Was he angry about the love charm? She took a deep breath and tried to calm herself.

"Here," Eaglefeather said. He held out a packet of cloth.

She unwrapped it while he came the rest of the way up. She found a wrap skirt and breast band of undyed cotton.

"Change into these," he said.

Feeling awkward—for she had never appeared before him unclothed in daylight—she peeled out of her dress, wrapped the skirt around her and tied it, then draped the band around her ribs and back and over her breasts, securing it between them in a knot.

He gave her a waterskin. "Drink."

Mistlight removed the stopper and sniffed it. The smell was unmistakably dizzyweed. She pulled it away from her face.

He looked impatient. "You agreed to be purified, did you not?"

"Yes."

"Then drink, and let the Ta'atchul wash away the influence of evil."

Mistlight sipped and tried not to gag on the bitter brew. "I owe you much for rescuing me from Firesister," she said.

He barked out a harsh laugh. "Oh, she is no witch, though it served my purpose to have everyone believe it. For fifteen turnings I wondered how it would be to take a woman who was unwilling, as she had been when she was your age. Then you came to me, her daughter, accepting everything I did to you, without question or protest. I had very nearly given up hope that I would ever find the way to break you, for the priestesses protected you too well. But then you went running straight to Firesister once you were no longer a Cornmaiden. I am a fortunate man indeed."

The dizzyweed potion began to hum through Mistlight's veins. Sweat beaded on her chest, dampening the breast band. Her head seemed to be floating high above her shoulders, spinning. The waterskin slipped from her fingers. She tilted her head and gazed at Eaglefeather. "What are you saying about Firesister?"

He approached close enough that she felt his breath on her cheek. "She had two chances to save you—but refused both. This mother of yours, a woman who wanted you never to be born."

His words made no sense. Mistlight put a hand to her spinning head. "No. My mother was the head of the Children's—"

"The very sight of you served as a reminder of the violence in which you were conceived."

Eaglefeather's hands wrapped around her shoulders, and he shoved her to the wall, pressing her there with his body. He kissed her roughly once, then pulled his lips away far enough to murmur, "Like a lizard shedding its tail, she cast you off."

"Firesister is not my mother!"

"Oh, but she is. Everyone in the village knows where you came from."

As he lowered his head to her again, Mistlight tried to get her fists between her body and his, tried to squirm away.

"Yes, fight me!" A gleam of satisfaction lit his eyes. He grabbed one of her braids and held her still. "Had I known that the truth would be enough to turn you unwilling, I would have told you of your mother long ago."

Firesister

*Brother Sun and Sister Moon forever bound together,
doomed to pursue each other across a lonely sky.*

—FRAGMENT FROM SONG OF THE NIGHT

Firesister sat cross-legged in the storage room with her head tipped back. The square of sky above reminded her of the life she had made for herself: free to go where she pleased, do as she chose, be what she wanted.

Not long before, she had descended through that hole, climbing down a ladder that was then removed. She told herself she was not afraid. She had made herself too useful to the people of Serpentgate to be kept here long.

Daughter of the village, some called her. The warmth that usually enfolded her at that thought failed to drive off the chill in the dim storage room. Evidently other clanfolk resented or even feared her, since they allowed themselves to be so easily persuaded that she was a witch. Her future might depend on which group was more numerous. Or more desperate to please Eaglefeather.

She hoped it meant something that in order to drag her from her home and confine her against her will, Eaglefeather had to summon priests from the Temple of Mist, a few days' journey to the south. Perhaps some in Serpentgate's temple, such as Thorn, were coming to see their Rainsinger for what he really was.

She'd despised Eaglefeather from the first moment she laid eyes on him. He was young then—a Watermaster boy named Cloudface, cheating to win a race.

Firesister shook her head. "So long ago," she said, thinking of all that she'd endured since then.

"Firesister?" she heard, muffled. Then again, "Firesister?"

She scrambled to her feet. "Here!"

The roof supports began to creak. A trail of dust from the plaster ceiling marked someone's approach overhead. Something was dragged across the roof. Ladder legs appeared and slid down jerkily as the sinew wraps that held the rungs to the uprights caught on the branches outlining the opening in the roof. One small sandal and another sought the first rung, followed by a Smokemother's gray skirt, tucked up for ladder-climbing.

"Willowbundle?" Firesister asked.

"Of course. Who else?"

Willowbundle stepped off the ladder, turned, and flung her arms around Firesister, who accepted the hug gladly. Firesister clung to her friend longer than usual even though one shoulder protested the awkward position. Willowbundle swayed back and forth as one would comfort a child. Some of Firesister's tension seeped away with the soft warmth of the embrace.

Willowbundle pressed Firesister back a step and folded gentle hands around her cheeks. Tilting her face one way, then the other, Willowbundle asked with mock anger, "What kind of trouble did you get into this time? Didn't we promise to have only happy lives?"

Firesister forced a laugh. They had indeed made that vow, back when they were three girls with babies inside them: Firesister with Mistlight, Willowbundle with a son, and the third, the Cornmaiden who became Mistlight's foster mother after her own babe was stillborn. During those terrible days when Firesister had felt herself being swallowed by despair, Willowbundle's cheerfulness had been a beacon leading out of the dark maw.

Once, early in their friendship, Willowbundle had told her, *"It hurts me to see you so unhappy."* For her friend's sake, Firesister had learned to mask her feelings. The mask had become a part of her, as easy to wear as sandals. She made sure it was firmly in place now.

Willowbundle let her hands slip down to Firesister's shoulders. "Are you all right? The Truthspeaker said the Stormbringers had orders not to hurt you."

"A few bruises is all." And loose teeth that twinged when her tongue rubbed against them. "I got what I deserved for putting up a fight, I suppose. But I didn't recognize them, and they came in fast, with no warning."

The two women exchanged glances. Firesister knew they were both thinking of that long-ago day when she'd lost her innocence and nearly her life. So shocked had she been by the madman's attack, she hadn't fought back. Her lack of resistance hadn't lessened his frenzy. By the time her broken bones had healed, her belly had started to swell.

The elders of the village had held a hearing to decide how to punish her attacker. A stranger passing through the Valley of Two Rivers, he'd come across her, a young woman, alone in the ruins of the Near-Kin enclave. He'd done nothing wrong, he claimed, other than telling her she was pretty. She'd hit him first, he claimed—never mind that he bore bruises only on his fists. Exile, the preferred punishment of their people, would simply release him into the world, perhaps to assault more women. So the elders had ordered his hands smashed, to make him depend on strangers for his survival. If the attack was unprecedented, so was the punishment, done for Firesister's sake, while she was lying in a stupor with her mind wandering. She'd known nothing about it at the time, had learned about it many moons later.

Now, the elders who had gone to such lengths for her were discussing whether she should be punished as a witch. What would they do if Eaglefeather convinced them of her guilt? Would they mark her somehow and send her away? Or give her to Eaglefeather, as he demanded?

"The Rainsinger should have known better," Willowbundle said.

Firesister put on an easy smile, broad enough to crinkle the skin around her eyes. "I'm sure he's just doing what he thinks is best." *"Always smile and speak well of people,"* the Childcatcher had advised her once. *"It helps your friends and confuses your enemies."*

Willowbundle said, "I heard they brought word from their Rainsinger of some approaching danger."

"I don't know anything about that. I was . . ." *Terrified.* So scared that she couldn't remember how she'd gotten from her house compound to Cloud Mountain for the hearing. Couldn't recall the very beginning of the hearing. "I don't remember much."

Willowbundle's gaze drifted over her form, resting for a moment on her scraped knees. "Let me clean you up so you feel better. It may take time, but we will get you out of here. Be patient."

Firesister murmured vague agreement.

"Come over here." Willowbundle went partway up the ladder and began to take bundles of various shapes and sizes off the roof, naming them as she handed them down to Firesister. A sleep mat and bedding. Clean clothing. Packs of food. Water ollas. Everything Firesister would need for comfort. Except a declaration of her innocence. Firesister hoped that the Truthspeaker, with her ability to persuade, could accomplish that.

The Smokemothers didn't understand, though, how deeply Eaglefeather's obsession with Firesister ran. How could they? She'd never told anyone of his insistence fifteen turnings ago that because she'd survived the ordeal, she should devote herself to serving Mother Ge in gratitude. That she should become a Cornmaiden and give her body to the priests—of whom he was one by that time—in the House of Quickening.

Firesister had reason to suspect that Eaglefeather's plan to have her declared a witch was simply a way to gain power over her. Such a man would not easily give up his prey.

"Sit down here." Willowbundle patted the work mat in front of her. "Let me wash you off."

Firesister smiled and complied. With the first touch of a moistened cloth on one knee, she flinched, though she'd thought herself prepared. It wasn't pain that broke through her guard, for Willowbundle was being careful. It was a flash of memory—a priest had slammed his leg across the back of her knees, dropping her to the ground. Once she was no longer on her feet, she'd been subdued quickly. Firesister closed her eyes against the feeling of helplessness that rose in her again, as raw as it had been those many turnings ago. When would time heal that wound?

"I've seen you in much worse shape." Willowbundle rinsed the cloth and dabbed at the crusted blood on the other knee. Rinse and dab, rinse and dab. "Look there. Hardly broke the skin," she said. After pouring the tainted water into an empty jar, she took an olla of fresh water and motioned for Firesister to hold out an arm. Willowbundle wiped it from elbow to hand, removing the grime and leaving goosebumps behind on the wet skin.

Firesister looked at her other arm, her legs. Dirt covered her all over. Embarrassed, she drew her half-clean arm away from Willowbundle. "I'll do the rest," she muttered. "I shouldn't keep you from your other duties."

"The Truthspeaker said to stay with you until the healers come." With an expression that said *You're not getting your own way in this,* Willowbundle held out her hand.

Firesister submitted, extending her arm and resting her fingers on her friend's palm. Willowbundle worked the cloth up to Firesister's shoulder, touching a couple tender spots. Firesister bit the inside of her lip and refused to betray any sign of pain. As Willowbundle shifted to the other arm and tsked over the bruises on her wrist, Firesister was reminded of Mistlight's injuries a few days before.

"What became of Mistlight?" Firesister asked. "Did she go back to the Children's House?"

Willowbundle's hands stilled. She gazed in surprise at Firesister. "You didn't hear? She went to the temple."

Firesister went cold all over. "How . . . how did that happen?"

"Like you, she was brought before the elders and accused as a witch. The Rainsinger said she made a love charm."

Unable to move, stunned by what she'd just heard, Firesister groped through what little she remembered of the priests' invasion of her compound. She and Mistlight had been going out to pick hannam, and then these men had rushed in and laid hands on her. She'd seen no sign of Mistlight after being subdued and marched through the village, so she'd assumed that they had come for her and that Mistlight was safe.

After the long-ago attack, Firesister had been left with three reminders of that terrible day that she was sure would stay with her to the end of her life: the limp that she despised; the streak of white in her hair, which she didn't really mind; and Mistlight, whom she loved in a way that made her feel foolish and resentful and protective all at the same time.

Mistlight had been taken too? But why? A girl's attempt to capture her lover's heart hardly seemed like witchcraft. "How could the elders punish her for that?"

"I'm not sure it was a punishment. The Childcatcher said it was Mistlight's idea to go." Willowbundle shook her head. "A woman in the temple. Imagine." Paying close attention to Firesister's arm, she murmured, "Don't worry. She'll come to no harm."

Bile rose in Firesister's throat as she remembered the fresh bruises she'd seen on Mistlight's neck and wrists, marks left behind by men's strong hands. She swallowed hard.

Willowbundle added, "Mistlight is a good choice to be the first woman acolyte for the Ta'atchul. She's a seer. Many a night has the Dreamwalker accompanied her on the White Starry Path."

"Then why was she assisting the Childcatcher instead of the Dreamwalker?"

"They say she didn't gain her ability until after her first coupling with the Rainsinger in the House of Quickening."

"He never should've been allowed to touch her."

Willowbundle's eyebrows arched in surprise at Firesister's vehemence.

"Ah, well," the Smokemother said, "it's done now. Mistlight fancies herself in love with the Rainsinger. Like it or not, going to him was her decision." Willowbundle snapped her fingers. "Legs."

Firesister extended her legs for Willowbundle to wipe down. Chewing on the inside of her cheek, Firesister remembered the wild swings of emotions she'd experienced when she was Mistlight's age. From heights of adoration to depths of despair in moments. Crying, raging, loving . . . Everything had felt either glorious or unbearable.

If Mistlight's devotion to Eaglefeather was so strong that she had willingly placed herself in his power, what could Firesister do to extricate her? Firesister glanced around the storage room. From here, she could do nothing.

The Seeker's words during the spring ceremony came back to her: *"Those you care about will suffer."* Eaglefeather had sent the Seeker to her with a bargain, and Firesister had turned him away. At the hearing, too, Eaglefeather had said, *"Confess that you are a witch, and release those you have bound to your wicked heart."* Did he mean she could get Mistlight out of the temple by confessing?

"Stand up," Willowbundle said.

"What?"

"Up. I need to do the back of your legs."

Not wanting her friend to see the bruises the Stormbringer's blow must have left there, Firesister said, "I'll do that myself." She got to her feet and held out a hand for the cloth her friend had just re-wetted. "Give me those clean clothes, would you?"

While Willowbundle was digging in the pack, Firesister passed the dripping cloth over her thighs and calves and stripped out of her dusty dress. Willowbundle handed her a ragged-hemmed undyed cotton skirt, which she wrapped around her waist, tying it loosely. Then a long-sleeved shirt to draw over her head and let hang loose over the top of the skirt. She hissed in a breath as her shoulder protested.

"Are you all right?"

"Fine," she said through gritted teeth.

"Sit down again. I'll braid your hair in a circle around your face, as we used to do. It looks like a hawk's nest right now."

As Willowbundle combed out the tangles, Firesister's thoughts slipped back to Mistlight. She'd wanted to be a mother to Mistlight, but for many turnings she could only see the brutal father when she looked at her daughter's face. By then it was too late. Although most people in the village knew Firesister had given birth to Mistlight, the woman who fostered the girl-baby had become her true mother. Was Mistlight now suffering simply for being of Firesister's blood? Disturbed by that possibility, Firesister shook her head.

"Stay still." Willowbundle reinforced the command with a light tug at Firesister's hair. She smoothed out two strands and started braiding, picking up a third with a twist of her hand. "What happened during the hearing? How did you end up here?"

Firesister moistened her lips, took a deep breath, and released it, letting the hurt seep out with the air through her tight throat.

"Eaglefeather reminded everyone that I'm not a daughter of any clan, that most of my kin returned to the Mountains of Sunrise when the Watermasters left." Simply repeating the words made her dizzy. "That my parents died of the bloody flux, just like the people of Lastwater. He says I turned to witchcraft to avenge their deaths." The ridiculousness of it tasted bitter on her tongue.

Willowbundle shook her head. "He has always been unreasonable where you're concerned. What did you ever do to upset him so?"

I called him a cheat and a liar in front of everyone when he first came to the Children's House. Firesister shrugged. "Probably because I never wanted Mistlight to have anything to do with him. We need to get her away from the temple."

Willowbundle's hands jerked, yanking Firesister's head back.

"Ow!" Firesister grabbed at her friend's fingers, tangled in her hair.

"Sorry." Willowbundle's voice sounded tight. "I know you worry about Mistlight, but you can't interfere in this. She has to stay where she is."

Firesister, struck by a terrible suspicion, tightened her grip until Willowbundle squeaked. She had only Willowbundle's word that going to the temple was Mistlight's idea.

Drawing her friend's hand away from her head, Firesister asked, "Is this all the Smokemothers' doing? The shadowdancer, the love charm, even the accusation of witchcraft? Was it all to get Mistlight into the temple? And you, too. Are you here because you're my friend and concerned about me? Or are you worried I might do something to spoil the Smokemothers' plan?"

Sorting through the food after a distressed Willowbundle left, Firesister found little that she could eat. Almost everything needed cooking, and she had nothing to make a fire with.

The incomplete braid around her forehead began to come undone. When she went to brush the loose hair out of her eyes, a twinge in her shoulder stopped her, and she flinched. The rest of the braid slithered free. Bending her head and supporting her elbow on her knee, she managed to shove most of the dangling hair behind her ears. She wondered where she'd lost the long bone pins that normally tamed her braid and held it out of the way. She vaguely remembered yanking the pins from her hair and trying to stab the priests with them. The pins hadn't struck anyone—and the attempt to ward off her attackers had only made them more violent.

Firesister shivered. To distract herself, though she wasn't hungry, she went through what Willowbundle had brought.

At the bottom of one bag of food, she found a cornhusk wrapper. It contained fruit leathers, sticky from being squished together. She sat in the brightest part of the storage room and took one slow bite after another as she tried to settle her nerves by thinking.

Willowbundle hadn't answered her final pointed questions. That was . . . disturbing.

Firesister thought back to the parts of the hearing she could remember. Settled on a mat next to the Childcatcher, she'd been cautioned to silence—others would speak in her defense. She'd looked at the half circle of seated elders and told herself, *Don't let them see you're afraid*. She'd swallowed the lump in her throat and waited to find out who would take her side.

The Truthspeaker was the first to stand on her behalf. "If Firesister was that sort of woman," the priestess said, "she would not have helped make sure the Smokemothers had enough food. She would not have used her steady hand to tattoo our faces. Instead she would have blinded us."

To which Eaglefeather replied, "So she would spare the Smokemothers but harm everyone else." He turned to the assembly of elders. "Do you see the danger these priestesses of Mother Ge would inflict on the rest of you? For your protection, Firesister must be handed over to me. I will confine her where she can do no harm."

Fear, icy and brittle, lodged behind Firesister's ribs, stabbing her chest with each heartbeat.

Lightstone, the chief healer, stood next: "We mamakai disagree that Firesister deserves punishment. The Smokemothers and Cornmaidens are not the only ones who benefit from the generosity of this daughter of the village. She collects hard-to-find herbs and brings them to us. She makes us pottery vessels marked with powerful symbols that cure, not cause, illness."

"Power can be misused," said Eaglefeather. "Do you have certain knowledge that Firesister is innocent of the deaths in Lastwater? Proof that she did nothing to the shadowdancer? She has done very well at convincing the Smokemothers and healers of her sincerity and good will. But then, she is a sly woman, capable of covering her true intentions."

Some of the elders murmured to their neighbors. Others nodded.

Proof? How can there be proof that I didn't do something? Firesister squeezed her fingers together and used the pain to push away the mounting dread. She willed herself to keep her ears open. To have any hope of beating Eaglefeather, she would have to outsmart him.

The remembrancer, fingering his calendar stick, reminded the assembly that all the clans had long ago adopted Firesister as their clan-daughter and should not judge her harshly. "The village owes her," he said, "for allowing a monster to roam unknown and unsuspected, until the day he beat her and got her with child."

Firesister felt a gentle touch on her wrist. She looked down and found herself twisting her fingers so hard that her knuckles turned white. The Childcatcher's gnarled hand eased over hers and patted. Firesister forced herself to relax.

"Breathe, child," the old Smokemother whispered.

Eaglefeather spoke again: "Does the village owe her more than the Stormbringers and the Ta'atchul? What punishment should there be for killing the shadowdancer?"

Firesister wanted to scream *Don't believe the Rainsinger! You know me* but stifled the desperate plea. She had to trust that the elders would support her again, as they had before.

The remembrancer said sharply, "You have presented no proof that Firesister is responsible for the shadowdancer's death. Or that of the people of Lastwater."

"Can you promise that Serpentgate—nay, that everyone who lives north of the river—will be safe from her?" Eaglefeather's question drew mutters of concern from the elders.

The chief healer said, "Mother Ge gave Firesister several gifts after she recovered, not least the ability to cheer the stricken, raise up those who have fallen, and brighten the darkest heart." He looked straight at Firesister and inclined his head in respect.

She tried to smile.

The leader of the hunters stood next. "Firesister obviously has the favor of Mother Ge, since she was spared from death. Will you let the words of this priest sway you against one so favored?"

After putting their heads together, one of the elders declared, "We will consider all that has been said here. And will return in a few days, giving both sides time to uncover evidence of her innocence or guilt."

Eaglefeather asked, "What of the witch? Will you let her wander through the village unchecked?"

The elders then decided they could not take that risk, which was why Firesister had been escorted to the storage room and now found herself with time to think.

During the hearing, the Childcatcher had calmed her and the Truthspeaker had spoken up for her. Once she was secured in the storage room, Willowbundle had brought food and other things for her comfort. So why did she wonder whether the Smokemothers were really on her side?

Firesister peeled fruit leather off her back tooth with her tongue.

Something seemed to lie behind this accusation of witchcraft. Something she couldn't see. A dangerous current running under a placid surface. But what?

Did the Smokemothers hope to use Mistlight's devotion to Eaglefeather for some purpose of their own? But according to Willowbundle, going to the temple had been Mistlight's idea.

Then could everything be connected to the shadowdancer's death? Had that been a warning sent by Mother Ge, telling her people that they had strayed too far from the old ways?

Firesister stopped mid-chew and recalled seeing the serpents strike once, twice, again, and the shadowdancer fall. That day she had stood frozen in the plaza, unable to breathe, until the crowd's noise released her from her shock. Quickly she'd slipped away so no one could see her cry over him. Firesister was always happy, joyous, buoyant. It was the unspoken bargain she'd made with the village in return for bringing her back from the dead. No one should ever see her any other way, especially shedding tears for a young priest she didn't even know.

Firesister put the rest of the fruit leather back in the wrapper and spat the partly chewed piece into her hand. It tasted foul now. She knew she wouldn't be able to swallow it.

She tossed the bite of food toward one of the dark corners of the storage room. For a moment she stood looking into the darkness where it had fallen. The shadowdancer's collapse during the ceremony could possibly have been a warning for the priests, who kept trying to raise the Ta'atchul above Mother Ge. But the destruction of Lastwater? What reason could Mother Ge have for killing so many people? Firesister shook her head, ashamed of her suspicion of both the Smokemothers and Mother Ge. The mother-goddess brought life—she didn't take it.

As for the Smokemothers, even if she didn't understand why they were distancing themselves from her now, they had saved her before. She would have to trust that once again they were doing the right thing.

The shaft of sunlight had moved so that one of the water ollas rested in its warmth. Firesister squatted next to it. She poured a small amount of water into her palm and wiped away the stickiness left by the fruit leather.

A few drops spilled and made a dark circle on the floor. Absently she pulled a finger through the spot, drawing a line of lighter-toned dust over the dampness. Her moist fingertip left a brown streak on the floor beyond the curved edge. The shape looked briefly like an arrow piercing a heart. As the dust dried, the heart separated into two half-moons, which slowly vanished.

Firesister stared at the unmarked floor, then lifted her gaze to the sky. She thought of Willowbundle's sandals leaving the top rung of the ladder and disappearing. Who could she rely on if the Smokemothers weren't going to rescue her this time: The hunters? The healers? Or would she be left alone here, forgotten, until she starved to death and rotted away, as a witch deserved? No, she told herself, she was no witch. Mother Ge would reveal the truth.

Clinging to that certainty, Firesister rose and opened her ears to the world outside the walls of the storage room. The painful sweetness of a dove's call. Dogs barking in the distance. Men's voices, faint and echoing.

A runnerbird paused at the edge of the opening and leaned down, cocking its head as it fixed her with a black-and-white-ringed eye. It whined at her and clacked its bill.

"Shoo!" Firesister flapped her hands at the lean bird. "*You* can leave. Don't laugh at me just because I can't get out of here."

It chattered at her again. Then its head twisted to look at something. Spreading its wings and tail, it leaped into flight and was gone by the time she blinked.

Footsteps, heavier than Willowbundle's, approached on the roof of the storage room. Firesister backed away from the dust they released.

Huge shoulders and a head like a bear came into view, blocking out much of the light. The dark crouching form seemed featureless at first, but as she peered at it, she made out a white headband and a brownish shirt. A man, then, and not a beast. Still, her heart began to race, as it always did at the approach of any man when she was by herself.

The bear-man turned his head in almost the same manner as the runnerbird had done. He spoke over his shoulder, but Firesister couldn't make out the words.

More footsteps came across the roof. The bear-man pulled back. He was replaced by another figure, slightly less imposing but still broad shouldered enough to darken the room in which Firesister stood.

"Looks like you lost your ladder," the less imposing man said. "Want some help getting out?"

His deep voice made Firesister's bones hum. For the space of a few breaths, she felt like a rabbit caught between the paws of a coyote, fixed in place by its gaze. "No need," she finally managed to say.

"Oh? You're planning to stay in there a long time?"

Instead of answering, she retreated a step, but that didn't put enough distance between them. As she slid her other foot back, her heel struck the olla. A quick glance showed Firesister that although her movement had set the ceramic jar to rocking, none of the precious water had spilled. She sidestepped it and got to where she could no longer see this disturbing man.

"Mind telling me why you're stuck in one of my storage rooms?"

"Yours?" Firesister considered the words. Watermasters were the only ones who would speak of Cloud Mountain like that. Traders might stay a night or two in the ruins atop the great mound and village elders sometimes met in the mound's plaza as they had done today, but no one dared claim ownership in the many turnings since the Watermasters had left.

"If I'd known the People of Two Rivers used these rooms to keep women in, I'd have come home long ago." He laughed.

The tips of Firesister's ears became hot, and she was glad for the darkness that shielded her from his gaze. Neither of them said anything for a moment. Then she heard him shift. Dust began to rain down around her as several sets of heavy feet tromped across the roof, which groaned alarmingly.

Firesister hurried forward and looked up. She couldn't see the newcomers or the Watermaster—they all were too far back from the roof entry.

Another male voice, not the Watermaster's deep one, said, "This woman is our responsibility."

"Is it me you don't trust," the Watermaster asked, "or her? Most women don't need to be locked away—"

"She is accused of witchcraft."

There was a pause. Then, "Witchcraft, is it?" The Watermaster sounded contemptuous. "She doesn't look so dangerous."

"If you value your safety, you will not interfere."

"Threats, too?"

"Not threats. Advice. For your protection. The village elders are deliberating over what is to become of her. Until their decision is made, she must be confined."

"This homecoming becomes more interesting," the Watermaster said.

The ladder came down again, and the lighter-voiced man ordered, "Come up."

Firesister didn't recognize the voice, but the chance of freedom beckoned. She drew the back edge of her skirt between her legs and tucked it under the waist ties to keep the folds of cloth out of the way. Favoring her sore shoulder, she climbed the ladder and looked around for the deep-voiced Watermaster. Three of the priests from the Temple of Mist blocked her view. "Go on," one told her. He motioned for her to walk ahead of him to the edge of the storage room, where two more priests waited at the head of another ladder. They descended first.

"Down," a priest behind her said.

Firesister glanced back at three implacable faces. She swung onto the ladder and found the rungs with her feet. Once on the ground, she moved aside to give the last priests room to climb down. She looked up beyond the walls of the storage room to the top of the mound and saw two tall men standing shoulder to shoulder. They seemed to be staring straight at her. Bear-man and coyote.

She shivered and turned away, toward the cottonwoods that marked the riverbank. Two of the southern priests hurried in front of her, as if to block any attempt to run, while the other three positioned themselves behind. Feeling a crawling sensation on the nape of her neck, Firesister whirled around. Her long, unbound hair tangled in her fingers. Loose like this, it dangled nearly to her knees and caught on everything. Wishing she'd had the foresight to let Willowbundle finish braiding it, she slipped her fingers free and shifted the unwieldy hair to her back, then spared another glance at the men watching her from the mound.

"This way," said the priest on her left. He indicated the path that led straight through the village. North. Toward the temple. Where Mistlight was being held.

Firesister moistened her lips. "Where . . . where are you taking me?" She got no answer.

The priest who'd traded words with the Watermaster extended his arm toward Firesister, but she shrank from his touch. He didn't grab her. Instead, he gestured toward the north and said, "Quickly, quickly."

She found herself in the midst of five priests spaced evenly around her. As they urged her onward, the thought of escape rose in her mind. These were strangers to the village, unfamiliar with the surroundings. Maybe she could convince them to head east, into the desert, leaving the main path. She could slip away from them into the shegoi bushes and cholla cacti, following twisty rabbit trails until the priests lost sight of her.

And go where? a sensible voice inside her head asked. *Who in the village would take in an accused witch?* The only blood relatives she had were in the Mountains of Sunrise, and she hadn't seen any of them since she was seven or eight. *Not true. There's Mistlight. I have to find a way to save her, not to escape.*

The priests moved in rhythm with one another. Firesister's shorter legs didn't cover as much distance, so she had to hurry and even sometimes break into a trot to keep from getting stepped on by the men following behind. The jolting pace made her left leg ache where the bones had been snapped during the attack all those turnings ago. She'd been trying to run from her attacker and had caught her leg between two boulders. Caught between the memory—*he struck me, I fell, he dragged me loose, bones parting*—and the present, she caught at the shirt of the one who'd spoken to her. "I can't . . . go so fast . . ." she panted when he glanced over his shoulder. Firesister half expected him to snarl at her. Instead he ordered the others to slow down.

Limping along in their midst, Firesister caught glimpses of the old ballcourt and the plaza where traders offered their wares every trade day. People stared as the little group passed, but no one stopped the priests or asked what they were doing.

A white ribbon shone against the dark hair of the priest who seemed to be the leader, the one who'd spoken with the Watermaster. White, for the Temple of Mist. What had brought the southern priests north to Serpentgate? Why had Eaglefeather chosen now to accuse her of being a witch? Why hadn't she been left in the storage room at Cloud Mountain until the hearing reconvened?

As her heart knocked against her ribs, she caught the leader's sleeve. "Can we rest?" she asked.

"Not yet," he cast over his shoulder as he pulled free of her grasp.

Firesister couldn't accept that. She needed time to prepare for the encounter with Eaglefeather. "My leg got hurt when you came after me at my home." She stopped. Panting, she put her hands on her knees. "I can't go on. Just a little time to catch my breath."

He swung around to face her, bringing the group to a halt. "You—"

"Enough!" Striving to appear dignified, Firesister drew herself up straight. "The elders have not yet declared me a witch. You will treat me with respect."

They looked at each other, the expressions on their faces suggesting that they thought she was being unreasonable. One grabbed her shoulder, sending a jolt of pain down her arm. She whirled around with upraised fists and shouted, "Don't touch me!"

The leader said, "Then you will come on your own. Yes?"

Firesister's heart pounded. *Pretend to be a witch and curse them,* a voice whispered in her head. *Make them afraid.* A terrifying desire to be what she was accused of hung in her mind. She stood there, tempted by the illusion that she could walk a different life-path. Like a spark in tinder, she could flame up and consume her enemies. But she was not a witch.

Slowly she lowered her fists. "I will go."

The rest of the walk through the village didn't take long. Through it all Firesister felt eyes on her, as numerous and silent as the flowers on a mesquite tree: wary, thumb-in-mouth children, doubt-ridden mothers and grandmothers, suspicious men, they all seemed strangers to her. By now, the village elders would have shared what they knew with friends and relatives, and they with theirs, until everyone had a notion of what happened at the hearing.

Word would catch like fire in dry summer brush, racing from household to household, clan to clan. As quick as a lightning strike, Firesister had gone from being a respected daughter of the village to being a suspected witch. She forced a smile for the many watchers. If she was to save herself, let alone Mistlight, she had to pretend she was unconcerned by the accusation. Walk easily, as an innocent woman would do. And think of a plan.

Too soon, she approached the wall around the temple precinct. Behind it rose the massive temple. Firesister remembered the spindly black shadow of the young priest cast upon those high adobe walls. She shuddered. She'd promised herself she wouldn't return. Yet here she was, a few days later, passing through the gate under the guardtower. The southern priests escorted her across the plaza to the doorway of Eaglefeather's workroom, then left her alone to enter the dim space.

Eaglefeather stood behind an adobe altar cluttered by feathers and cords. Though his workroom was larger than the storage room she'd just left, dark patterns of lightning and clouds painted on the walls made it seem smaller, as though closing in on her.

"I know you dislike me," Eaglefeather said. He walked toward her with an unreadable face.

She forced herself not to retreat as he drew near.

"And despite everything," he continued, "you love Mistlight, though she may not understand that."

Firesister flinched, remembering her daughter's accusation, *"You hate me."*

"So you have a choice to make. Do you want her to continue living with me here until I am finished with her? When that day comes, when her wits are wandering like the Dreamwalker's, when she is barely able to fit two thoughts together, will you feel guilty?"

"Where's Mistlight?"

Eaglefeather held her gaze. "I told her of the lie. She knows, now, that you are her real mother. The woman who carried her and brought her into the world but could not be bothered to raise her."

Firesister absorbed that.

"Will you try to deny it?"

"Why should I? The harm has already been done. You've already revealed what everyone agreed to keep secret for her sake."

Eaglefeather shrugged. "If you believe nothing worse can happen to her while she is in my hands, there is no more to be said between us."

In a hunter's silence, he waited for endless moments, during which Firesister's heart thudded unevenly, beating hard and fast.

At last he said, "Did I misjudge you? Perhaps after all you lack a mother's instinct to protect your child." He began to turn away.

"Wait."

He halted his movement and bent a penetrating stare on her.

"Are you saying you'll let Mistlight go if I do what you ask of me? Even if she wants to stay?"

"Indeed." With a flash of anger, he added, "A woman has no place within the walls of the Temple of Lightning."

"What is it you want from me?" Firesister knew better than to trust any promise he made. This situation was a trap, like the ones boys caught birds in. Try as they might to escape, the captives were helpless. They could beat their wings and beaks against the sides of the trap until broken and bloodied, and still they would have no hope of getting free. And yet, for Mistlight's sake, she had to find a way.

"Kill the Watermaster."

Firesister crouched in a shadow and tried not to let her mind dissolve in fear. She flinched when a bat swooped close. As mournful cries of nightbirds echoed through the darkness, she shut her eyes and offered a quick prayer to Mother Ge: *Please grant me courage.* For sixteen turnings she'd asked for the same boon, and each time Mother Ge had given her the strength to go on. Tonight she added, *Thank you, Mother, for having him sleep.*

Taking a steadying breath, she opened her eyes and studied the Watermaster, his face lit by moonlight. Patches of plaster gleamed on the remaining walls around the plaza in which he lay. Men snored in the adjacent courtyard, but he was alone.

He was beautiful.

Mother Ge had made his face with strong lines and sweeps. His eyebrows were thick and black like the hair falling over his broad cheekbones. Firesister thought herself fortunate that his eyes were closed. Else she might not have the nerve to do what needed to be done.

As she rose from concealment and prepared to move toward him, a scuff of gravel, whisper-soft, sounded behind her. A hand clamped over her mouth. Another grasped her wrists and pulled them against her rib cage. Firesister struggled, but her captor tugged her close. The back of her head came up against hard bones. A man's breathing and heartbeat resonated through her, freezing her in place.

The Watermaster's eyes opened. Large and deep, they dragged her in like quicksand. He pushed himself up on an elbow and said something she couldn't make out. His voice, so deep it seemed like thunder, rumbled through her midsection.

In desperation she tried to tear her arms loose, but pain stabbed at her sore shoulder. The callused hand over her mouth slipped up to cover her nostrils. Panic flared, lending her strength as she bit and squirmed. She kicked back with her right foot, balancing awkwardly on her bad leg. Her lungs began to burn from lack of breath, and she felt herself weakening. Firesister sagged against the man who held her.

These aren't my people. She recalled the stories told by the Far-Traders of outlanders from far to the south, places with warrior-priests and skull racks, where beating hearts were cut out of living men to appease bloodthirsty gods. These men came from such a place. *Don't give up,* she told herself. But her body wouldn't obey.

The Watermaster said something more. Her captor's grip tightened for a moment, then released. The two men spoke back and forth as Firesister's gaze skittered from one to the other. Heart racing, she turned and backed away until she came up against one of the ruined walls of the courtyard.

The bear-man reached into the broad sash around his waist and pulled out the obsidian blade Eaglefeather had handed Firesister earlier.

She stilled, staring at the moonlit arcs along the knapped edge. She had tucked the knife into a crevice between two walls as soon as she got out of sight of the priests who'd brought her to the mound. *I should have smashed it to bits instead of hiding it.*

But no, she'd decided to warn the Watermaster that he was in danger —something he already knew. Why else would he have pretended to be asleep out in the open, alone? Rubbing her bruised wrists, she resented him for setting such a neat trap for her. Only . . . how had he known? "Did the Rainsinger tell you to kill me?" she demanded.

The Watermaster sat up straight, looking intrigued.

"Are you supposed to claim I attacked you," she went on, seeing how Eaglefeather might have planned everything, "and you were just defending yourself . . . ?"

Gesturing toward the obsidian blade in the bear-man's grip, the Watermaster pointed out, "You're the one who came after me with a knife."

"I threw it away."

"Or maybe you planned to retrieve it later." The Watermaster patted the sleep mat. "Sit here beside me," he invited.

Firesister stayed where she was. He smiled, innocent as a child. She remembered what she'd learned about putting on a smile: most people never looked past it to what lay beneath. *Careful. Be very careful of this man.*

"I can see why the Rainsinger might want me dead," he said. "If I get the canals working properly again, the farmfolk might decide they don't need rain priests anymore. But why would he want rid of you?"

The bear-man growled out a few words in a language that didn't quite make sense to Firesister. The words weren't important. She understood the menace in his tone well enough.

Nodding at the bear-man, the Watermaster said, "Don't mind Littlecliff. He doesn't appreciate people who wish me harm. Especially a witch."

"I'm no witch."

"Let's say I believe that. Then is this knife not yours?" The Watermaster's eyes seemed to darken as the eyebrows above them drew together, the outer edges lifting like the wings of a hunting hawk. He shifted and raised one knee, tucking the other leg under. His arms folded around the bent knee. He watched her closely. "I assume you were sent by someone. Was it the Rainsinger?"

She smiled, pretending a calm she didn't feel. "First I need a promise from you."

"Promises. I don't make promises to pretty women."

So good at lying. She knew what she looked like—dusty, weary, desperate, hair falling around her face in thick tangles. Even at her best, she wasn't a woman that people called pretty.

"Still . . ." she began. She lost what she planned to say when faces appeared over the tumbledown wall that separated the two sleeping-spaces. His men, awakened by the conversation, muttered to each other.

The Watermaster unfolded and rose in one smooth movement. He walked toward the narrow passageway she'd recently passed through. It led to the ruins that filled the north half of Cloud Mountain, where previous generations of Watermasters had slept and eaten and done whatever mysterious things kept the canals running. "Aren't you coming?" he asked without glancing back at her.

His way of walking stirred an old memory: a bounce on his heels, a swagger that started in his hips and carried through to broad shoulders. A thinner, younger version of him running with confident strides. Was this Watermaster the boy who'd been Eaglefeather's rival in that footrace she still remembered?

The bear-man—no, Littlecliff, he was called—rumbled out something.

The Watermaster held up a hand in acknowledgment. He turned and looked at her. "Do you really want my men to hear what you have to say?"

She stared into the dark passageway beyond him. Hemmed in by walls on either side, cluttered with fallen chunks of adobe, the narrow space waited. *This is for Mistlight. There's no time for cowardice.* Despite that, she couldn't bring herself to move.

"Well, come on." He beckoned her with a wave of his fingers.

Littlecliff came up behind her and touched her shoulder—just that, a feather-light gesture. Perversely, his presence made her braver. It meant she wouldn't be alone with a man whose name she didn't know. Slowly she followed the Watermaster from the plaza, with Littlecliff at her heels.

Not far down the passageway, they entered a building open to the moon, its adobe walls high and straight. The limbs that once braced its roof had been taken as firewood, leaving the floor rough underfoot with chunks of adobe and plaster.

The Watermaster reached the midpoint of the room, turned, and asked, "Who sent you to do me harm?"

"As I said, I'll tell you, if you promise to do one thing for me." The words reminded her of the bargain Eaglefeather had pressed upon her. Firesister gave herself a mental shake. *I'm asking only a small favor of this man.* Before he could speak, she hurried into an explanation: "The elders won't let me go home before my innocence is established. They allowed me to be confined in that storage room where you first saw me. But I need to be out talking to people, convincing them—"

"The priests took you to the temple. Did the knife come from them, along with orders to slit my throat?"

She shook her head. "It wasn't one of those priests. Please. I'll tell you everything if you just agree to . . ." Firesister trailed off as he folded his arms across his chest. "All I'm asking is that you keep watch on me."

"Keep watch?" He laughed without amusement. "You mean, let you wander around as you please, and if there's any trouble, it's me who will be responsible?"

She swallowed hard, accepting his suspicion as justified, and said, "Then set one of your men to guard me."

"I can't spare anyone, especially not over a village dispute. I'll need all the men I have, and more, to get the canals running again."

A village dispute. Was that how he saw her situation? An accusation of witchcraft meant so little to him? "It's not just for me." She heard her voice sharpen and tried not to allow anger to overcome good sense. She laced her fingers together. "My daughter, too, has been caught up in this. She's at the temple right now—"

"Why is this any concern of mine?"

"The reason the Watermasters were exiled, all those turnings ago. Didn't it begin with a simple dispute over a woman?" Firesister had been young then, but she recalled that much. "Without my help, your return could prove more difficult than you think. Dangerous, too."

His eyes narrowed. "Tell me why I shouldn't drop you back in the storage room."

Firesister wished she could return the Watermaster's threat with one of her own. *If only I really were a witch.* She knew nothing about him, which meant he knew nothing about her either. She ran her tongue over her lips and suppressed the urge to claim she could wield dangerous magic.

She had come here to form an alliance with the Watermaster against a common enemy. "The Rainsinger of the Temple of Lightning," she said. "He's the one who accused me of witchcraft. He's the one who sent me to kill you."

"Why?"

She hesitated before answering. She had nothing but a vague memory to go on . . . about a footrace long ago. A rivalry between two Watermaster boys. Not even rising to the level of a village dispute. Would this Watermaster remember that race? "As a boy, he was called Cloudface."

A muscle twitched in the Watermaster's cheek at the name.

"He stayed behind when the rest of you left. Took Eaglefeather as his man's-name and became a priest, and recently the Rainsinger of the Temple of Lightning. As for why, you probably have a better idea than I do."

"Why did you agree to it?" The Watermaster unfolded his arms and prowled toward her.

Firesister's heart began to pound. Littlecliff approached from behind so near that she felt his warmth.

The Watermaster stopped. His brows twitched as though startled. Frowning, he said something in the outlanders' language. Littlecliff growled back.

"I didn't agree," she said after a moment. "If I had, why would I have gotten rid of the knife and come unarmed to talk to you?"

The Watermaster's head tilted to one side. He studied her. "You might have planned to go back for it. After convincing me to trust you."

"That's not what I intended," she muttered.

"What did you intend? No, never mind that. What made you agree to come here, alone and, as you claim, defenseless?" Although he didn't move, he seemed suddenly larger, more intimidating, as though he'd absorbed some of the night shadows into himself.

She wet her lips. "The Rainsinger gave me no choice about coming. As I saw it, my only chance was to put my life in your hands and hope you would listen to what I have to say."

"I heard the claims made against you, starting with lurking in ruins and stealing things from the dead."

Firesister cast her mind back to the hearing and struggled to remember. While the accusations were being flung at her, she'd heard them only distantly, as though through someone else's ears. Her head began to ache from the effort of searching her hazy memory.

"Talking when no one is about." The Watermaster ticked off one offense after another. "Destroying plants from root to leaf. Vanishing as if on unseen paths. Ruining the spring sun-festival by killing the shadowdancer. Cursing an entire village."

"I did none of that," Firesister said.

"How are you going to disprove such things?" he asked.

"People will help me. I just have to speak with them."

His scowl deepened. Again he stepped forward, this time circling around her. With Littlecliff at her back, she couldn't turn to keep the Watermaster in sight. His footsteps passed behind, then along her left side.

She turned her head as he drew level with her shoulder. "I'm no witch. Nor am I a killer."

He paused, watching her. He stood there for so long, it felt like the entire night passed. At last he said, "Then why did the elders have you put into the storage room?"

"The Rainsinger didn't give them time to think about whether the accusations against me make sense." Though his face remained impassive, Firesister continued, "I didn't harm you. Why would I? I want you to get the canals running again. I want to help you put together work crews. I want the people I love to have an easier life, the way it was when I was a child."

"So you say."

She moved closer. Approaching this unapproachable man took all the courage she had. "If you help me clear my name, it will be good for you too," she assured him. "I can get every clan to send you workers, as many as you need. Give me an escort for five days." She managed to smile. "That's all the time I'll need to go around to every clan and convince them of my innocence."

"One day. I'll give you one day. But if you betray me—"

She swallowed hard at the threat.

He waved a hand around the space they stood in. "Sleep here tonight, and Littlecliff can go with you tomorrow."

"Sleep here?" She looked at the lumps of adobe and plaster on the floor.

"You'll have bedding. We brought up the stuff left behind in that storage room."

When Firesister forced her gritty eyelids open under the pale morning sky, she thought at first she'd woken in her own courtyard at home after an exhausting day of firing pots. A turn of her head revealed the jagged tops of ruined walls, and she remembered that she was on Cloud Mountain. She twisted farther and saw Littlecliff blocking the doorway. Though she'd expected his presence would keep her awake, she'd fallen asleep quickly. She guessed, after taking another glance at the sky, that the sun was about two handspans above the horizon.

One day. That was all she had. Firesister shoved the rabbit-fur blanket off, sat up, and went to stand, but her left leg buckled. She collapsed back onto the deerhide sleep pad, sending another spasm through the troublesome knee. With shaking hands, she straightened out her leg and began to rub the muscles around the joint.

A large sun-darkened hand came into view next to hers and took over the massage. Startled, she tried to pull her leg away. Littlecliff didn't pause in his movements. He rumbled something at her that sounded reassuring.

"Yes," she said. "All right." And after a moment, "Thank you."

He nodded.

Littlecliff seemed to know when the pain subsided, because he stopped exactly when she would have. She smiled her gratitude and stood, shaking her skirt around her shins. He rose too. Her stomach grumbled, and she pressed a hand to it. *Ignore it,* she told herself.

"Can I go?" She took a step toward the doorway.

With surprising grace for such a big man, Littlecliff maneuvered himself between her and the way out. He moved his hands in mimicry of eating.

"There isn't time for that," she said. "I have to see so many people . . ."

He shook his head and repeated his gestures, ordering her to eat.

"Did the Watermaster tell you to make me stay here?"

"No, I didn't" came that deep voice that had disquieted her the previous day. And again in the moonlit night.

Firesister looked past Littlecliff toward the doorway.

The Watermaster leaned against the wall beside it. He pushed himself upright when her gaze caught his. "Littlecliff decided that all on his own. He must like you."

As the Watermaster approached with that peculiar light-footed stride, her vision narrowed until he was all she could see. Don't let his voice unnerve you, she told herself.

"Waterstrider," he said. He stopped just before she flung up a hand to ward him off. "My name. It's Waterstrider. And you're Firesister."

She stepped back to gain a little breathing space. "How did you know . . . ?"

"The same way I knew what you'd done to get yourself accused of witchcraft. I have friends here."

Firesister absorbed that. It made sense as soon as he said it. Had the friends also informed him that the Rainsinger was Cloudface, his boyhood rival? Was that why he'd been prepared for someone to come after him? She told herself not to be curious. He had his problems, she had hers.

"You should eat." He turned away and threw a few careless words over his shoulder: "We cooked up some of the food left behind in the storage room."

"I don't—"

He was gone before she finished her protest. When she would have followed, Littlecliff stepped into her way with a worried look.

"Yes, yes, I'll eat," she promised, resolved to choke down a few bites and then go to the Smokemothers' compound to find out what could be done for Mistlight. The big man nodded and shifted aside. As Firesister walked through the doorway, he padded behind her.

Waterstrider's men lounged in the plaza, laughing and shouting back and forth, with steaming bowls in front of them. They were a rough lot, hard-faced and scarred despite their youth. Their hair was cut to shoulder length, as if they were all in mourning—the same as Waterstrider's and Littlecliff's hair, she realized with a glance at Littlecliff.

Firesister hesitated at the mouth of the passage. A few of the outlanders spotted her and stared, drawing the attention of the rest. Her skin tightened. When Littlecliff came to her side, they returned to their breakfast. Quieter now. Subdued.

Littlecliff touched her arm and pointed toward the other plaza, where Waterstrider had pretended to sleep the previous night.

"All right," Firesister said. She entered the empty plaza, while Littlecliff headed for the breakfasting men. Seeing no sign of Waterstrider, she wondered where he was. She thought he'd turned this way after leaving the room where she'd slept. There was no way off the mound on this end, and it was steep as a cliff and too high to jump from. The ladder that led down to the storage rooms was the other direction. It could only be accessed using the passageway she'd just come through. Puzzled, she continued through the plaza to the thigh-high wall that ran along the edge of the mound.

Voices caught her attention. When Firesister looked down toward the storage rooms that ran along the base of Cloud Mountain, she saw Thorn and a few other men. Yellow ribbons binding their hair and sewn on their shirts marked them as priests from the Temple of Lightning. Standing separate from them, his arms crossed, was a tall man with the shoulder-length hair of the outlanders. Waterstrider.

Thorn said, "I came looking for the woman who was here." He pointed toward the hole in the roof of the storage room where Firesister had been the previous day.

Waterstrider answered, "Did your Rainsinger tell you she'd be found there?"

Firesister somehow caught his attention, because he lifted his head and fixed her in place with his gaze.

"Firesister!" Thorn called.

She broke free of the Watermaster's stare and looked at Thorn, who frowned up at her.

Firesister scowled back. Eaglefeather couldn't have expected her to be in the storage room, she told herself, because he had sent her to kill the Watermaster. Had Eaglefeather known she wouldn't do it? Or had he assumed she would be caught by Waterstrider or his men?

She braced herself on the half wall, chilled by the thought of what could have happened to her if she'd really tried to kill the Watermaster. "The Rainsinger told you wrong." Firesister kept her voice steady and clear. "I've been up here since last night."

Littlecliff came to stand beside her. In his massive hands he held two bowls. An experimental sniff told her the contents were corn gruel mixed with some kind of meat. Her stomach grumbled again.

"I will come to you," Thorn said. He took two steps away from the storage room's opening.

Waterstrider uncoiled his arms and moved to block Thorn with his body. "No priests on top of Cloud Mountain."

"Firesister was entrusted to the Stormbringers."

"All the worse," said Waterstrider without budging, "if you lot were trusted with making sure she stayed put—and promptly misplaced her."

Thorn's expression darkened. "That is not what happened."

"No?"

Firesister was almost sure Thorn didn't know why Eaglefeather had released her. Among all the priests, he was the most honorable, remaining true to his vows and imagining everyone else was the same. He would have made a much better Rainsinger than Eaglefeather.

Thorn said, "I will be taking her now."

Firesister exclaimed, "No!" The two men stared up at her. She told Thorn, "Leave me here."

"The Rainsinger said—"

Waterstrider bared his teeth. "Your Rainsinger . . ."

Don't tell him, Firesister willed. Waterstrider glanced at her as if he'd heard her thought. *No one would believe such a terrible thing.*

Returning his attention to the priest in front of him, Waterstrider continued, "He was the one who accused her of being a witch. I can't blame her for distrusting him."

"What will you do for her, then?" Thorn challenged. "Will you demand that she be declared innocent, and if not, you will refuse to work on the canals?"

"Witchcraft is a village matter. I have no interest in it, one way or another." Waterstrider's deep voice sounded cold and hard. "She asked only for a chance to prove her innocence. I'll give her that. So leave her here with me. Go back to your Rainsinger and tell him he misjudged my resolve."

Without looking away from the Watermaster, Thorn said, "Firesister, come with me."

"No."

Thorn's gaze skimmed over her, from her mussed hair down and back up. "Are you staying of your own will?" he asked, studying her face. "Or did he threaten you? That big man next to you, is he there to make you say what the Watermaster wants?"

Startled, Firesister turned her head. Littlecliff stood there holding the bowls of corn gruel. She'd forgotten about him. "This is my choice," she said to Thorn with simple honesty. "Go back to the temple."

He continued to watch her.

"Truly," she said.

"It was handled badly," he admitted, "sending strangers to take you to the hearing. You must have been frightened. Were you hurt?"

She shook her head. "I'm fine. Let me stay here and do what I need to do."

"I didn't know until after." His voice was apologetic.

"I believe you." Firesister felt awkward saying such personal things so publicly. "What about Mistlight? Is she all right?"

"She is safe in the temple," Thorn said.

Waterstrider commented, "The temple doesn't seem like someplace a girl would be safe."

Firesister agreed with him, but she could hardly say so. "Thank you for worrying about me," she told Thorn. "You should go now."

He inclined his head toward her, then walked away, followed by the other priests. She watched him out of sight.

Littlecliff nudged her arm and held out a bowl.

"Yes," she told him, accepting it. "But let's eat quickly. I need to go."

He blinked, looking confused. She pointed toward the passageway. He shook his head and again made a show of eating.

Firesister sighed. "Yes, I'll eat first."

Firesister paused at the head of the ladder that would take her off the mound. She recalled the cold fear that had clung to her the previous night as she climbed the ladder, one rung after another, her legs and shoulder protesting, obsidian knife in a pouch suspended from the sash around her waist. The priests from the Temple of Mist had stood below and watched her go. She wasn't supposed to come down until the Watermaster was dead—though she doubted that her guards knew what Eaglefeather had told her to do. She had a notion, maybe just a wish, that the Rainsinger hadn't dared to discuss his plot against the Watermaster with anyone else.

Littlecliff rumbled a question.

"I'm going," she said. She swung onto the ladder and descended carefully, letting her good knee take most of her weight. Once down, she set off for the Smokemothers' compound. Through the village she passed, Littlecliff behind her. This time the watching eyes were not all hard and suspicious. Though the big outlander attracted wary stares, most people cast sympathetic glances her way. Pretending to focus on her hair rather than the watchers, she smoothed the tangles as best she could at the top of her head, then pulled the fall of hair to the front and braided as she walked. The skin of her arms and hands felt tight from grime, and she could see streaks of plaster dust on her skirt each time a knee swung forward under the cloth.

She hadn't worried overmuch about her appearance since that awful day many turnings ago, but she had washed regularly and kept her hair and clothes neat. Now she felt ashamed of the way she looked. Her legs ached. Her shoulder did too.

As Firesister drew near the entrance to the Smokemothers' compound, she turned to Littlecliff. "Stay here." She showed him what she meant by extending her arms, palms out, as though to shove him away. He seemed to understand, for he walked to the compound wall and leaned against it. Firesister went to the entrance. One stride took her inside the thick adobe wall, into a world of women where even the air smelled different—filled with eddies of herbal tonics and tobacco smoke along with lingering reminders of a meaty breakfast stew.

The aromas shifted as she crossed the plaza toward the workrooms of the high priestesses: herbs and tobacco became stronger, drowning out food. It had been the same when she'd lived here so long ago. She could have found her way through the buildings using her nose alone.

As usual, no one stopped her to ask what business she had there. Firesister was a regular visitor, though usually she carried a burden basket filled with food. Some of the Cornmaidens sent her furtive looks. The Smokemothers going about their duties took in her presence without comment, barely giving her a second glance. Firesister took comfort from their acceptance. If only the rest of the village would be that way . . .

Willowbundle appeared at her side. "Firesister," she whispered. "What are you doing here?"

"I came to meet with the Truthspeaker."

"Do you expect to get any more help from her than she already—"

"I'm here to ask about Mistlight. You said she's at the temple."

"Ah. Yes." Willowbundle hesitated, then added, "The Truthspeaker may not want to see you. The Rainsinger's accusations make it hard to let you come and go here, as a trusted friend."

Firesister recalled the harsh words she'd thrown at Willowbundle the previous day. Were they still friends? "Do you find it hard to trust me?"

"No, of course not."

The reassurance sounded weak. Firesister regretted voicing her suspicion as she watched her old friend walk toward the partly open woven-reed door of the Truthspeaker's workroom. A moment later the Truthspeaker called her in.

The Childcatcher was in the workroom too. After Willowbundle left, Firesister looked from one of the high priestesses to the other. The tension in their faces made her suspect that she'd interrupted a discussion neither of them was enjoying.

"Why are you concerned about Mistlight?" the Truthspeaker asked.

The Childcatcher opened her mouth as if to say something, then closed her eyes and shook her head. Her wispy hair glinted in the sunshine like motes of dust.

"I question what the Rainsinger is up to," Firesister said. "Why would he break with tradition and let a woman stay in the temple?"

The Truthspeaker shook her head. "It was not his choice. This was Mother Ge's doing."

Firesister rubbed her cheek, trying to remember exactly what Willowbundle had told her. "Why would you say Mistlight's offer to go was Mother Ge's doing? It seems she got tangled in a web that was woven to catch me."

The Childcatcher cleared her throat. "This is nothing to feel guilty about."

"No," the Truthspeaker agreed. "Having Mistlight in the temple may be vital."

"Why?" It made no sense, Firesister thought. The Smokemothers' order was much older than the Stormbringers', and the two religions rubbed uneasily together. Priestesses were stingy with their ceremonial knowledge, sharing no more than prescribed by Mother Ge for sun-festivals and ritual joinings at the House of Quickening—the latter only because Cornmaidens and Smokemothers needed male essence to bear children. Why would the priestesses suddenly be eager to have women in the temple?

"Joining with the Rainsinger has given Mistlight some of his power," the Truthspeaker said, her eyes glittering. "Mother Ge has gifted Mistlight with something more important than a child. True-dreaming. Visions."

Again the Childcatcher shook her head.

Firesister guessed the old priestess disagreed. "Visions of what?"

The Childcatcher said, "We had no plan to get her into the temple. She did it on her own."

Firesister asked, "If I change Mistlight's mind and get her out, would you take her back as a Cornmaiden?"

"You know nothing of what took Mistlight to the temple," the Truthspeaker said coldly. "You have never felt desire for a man, much less the one-sided love that fills Mistlight with courage."

"No need to worry about Mistlight," the Childcatcher added. "She is under Mother Ge's protection."

"As I was?" Firesister asked. That was something she'd heard often after the attack: *"Sleep. You're under Mother Ge's protection. No one will hurt you here."* She'd wondered, back then, why Mother Ge hadn't protected her before the attack, when she really needed it.

The Truthspeaker said, "Mistlight is different from you. She is like raw clay, which can be worked into many shapes, over and over. Mistlight is like that, while you are a fired pot, a vessel unchanging and brittle. Easily broken."

Firesister understood the priestess's argument. But she'd been raw clay like Mistlight, too, before she was shattered.

"We will watch over her," the Childcatcher said. "The Dreamwalker will go to her daily and train her to call forth visions. Help her read them. The Rainsinger will have no chance to harm her, even if he desires to do so."

Firesister had to be content with that, for in the next moment she was dismissed. Right before she left the Truthspeaker's workroom, the priestess surprised her by adding, "One last thing. If you wish to persuade the clan elders of your innocence, you will need to look respectable."

Willowbundle was in charge of that. She took Firesister to the room where the ceremonial robes for sun-festivals and other rituals were kept. Firesister goggled at the fancy doeskin dress her friend pulled from a storage bench. Dyed quills and beads in the colors of a spring sunrise formed intricate patterns in bands down the front.

Desiring a closer look, Firesister started to reach for it. Who had created such a wonder, so much more elaborate than the pottery designs she painstakingly painted on the bowls and jars she made?

"Not this one." Willowbundle laid it aside and pulled out another carefully folded garment. It was a simple doeskin tunic, open at the sides and with a laced slit at the neck. It wasn't completely plain: fringes of yellow feathers hung from the shoulders. They were attached to leather strips that Willowbundle removed before handing the tunic to Firesister. Cotton leggings followed, then moccasins that looked to have been worn only a few times.

"These should do." Willowbundle directed a chilly smile at Firesister. "You can wash up and change here. Once you finish, find Shiningdawn. She can help you with your hair." Willowbundle turned on her heel and left the room.

Firesister guessed her old friend was still upset by the words that had passed between them in the storage room. Later, when time wasn't so short, she would have to think of a way to make amends. Quickly Firesister cleaned herself and put on the clothes.

Shiningdawn came in as Firesister was tying a sash around her waist. "I was glad when Willowbundle said you wanted me to braid your hair," the pretty Cornmaiden said. "We haven't seen you much. Besides, I was bored." She sorted through the pile of reed mats near the door. "There isn't much I can do here. It seems my only useful skill is pleasing men."

Shiningdawn found two mats she liked and, still chattering, motioned for Firesister to follow her out. "You know the other Cornmaidens don't care much for me. I've missed your company." She placed the mats in a sunny spot and sat on one. "That rising-sun tattoo you made on my backside isn't sensitive anymore," she said, motioning for Firesister to sit in front of her. "It's all healed up. Thanks for keeping it a secret."

When Shiningdawn's string of words paused, Firesister put in, "I don't understand why you asked me for such a silly thing, much less why you don't want anyone to know about it."

"The less the other Cornmaidens know about me, the better." Shiningdawn began to ease a comb through Firesister's hair. "You've seen how jealous they are."

"You shouldn't tease them by flirting."

"Why not? Flirting is the most amusing thing I can do outside the House of Quickening." The comb encountered a knot that Shiningdawn's fingers quickly picked apart. "Why should I care what the Cornmaidens think of me? In a few more moons I can leave this boring place and won't have to try to get along with them."

Firesister heard the younger woman's hurt under the stream of words. She said, "Things change as you get older. It becomes more difficult to make friends. The friendships you find here, when you're all living together, are tighter, more enduring."

"Like you and Willowbundle?"

Firesister closed her eyes and sighed. *Believe it or not, Willowbundle is my closest friend*. She vowed to make things right with the other woman as soon as she got her life back.

"Seems like everybody is getting all round with child and rosy-cheeked from happiness—except me. Not that I mind." Shiningdawn's fingers worked efficiently as she talked. "If I had a baby, that would be fine, too, but I'd rather not, just yet. Come midsummer, I'll be done here. My mother says the earlier the better to start having children. Though they're healthier when conceived in love."

Keeping her eyes closed, Firesister let the conversation flow over her as the nimble fingers moved at the nape of her neck and down her spine.

"She also says men are more nuisance to have around than they're worth. Put them to work on the canals so you don't see them for days at a time and when they finally come home they're too tired to complain, that's what she says. She thought a life-path as a Smokemother would be good for me, having the fun of men without actually living with them. Only, I like men better than women. Not you, Firesister. I like you. You're different. Most women are so gossipy, without meaning half of what they say. Now, men don't say half of what they think. Not that they need to talk much. Just one look back and forth and you know exactly what they're thinking, most times. Of course, generally it's about making babies . . ."

legs forced apart, agony

At the unwelcome flash of memory, Firesister's eyes flew open, and her lolling head jerked upright. "Are you done?" she asked.

"Almost. Just let me tie this off." Shiningdawn soon patted her on the shoulder and said, "There."

Firesister rose and turned toward the young Cornmaiden. "I'm grateful for this, truly." Though tempted to caution the younger woman, maybe *Don't think you know what is coming in your life,* she decided not to offer advice. She simply added, "Be well."

A few moments later, when Firesister left the Smokemothers' compound, she was surprised not to find Littlecliff. She glanced around, but instead of his hulking form, she saw only a boy in the garb of a Seeker. As the boy approached, she recognized him as the one who'd come to her during the sun-festival . . . the Seeker who'd passed along Eaglefeather's warning about accusing her as a witch.

Littlecliff appeared from behind a wolfberry bush. He was on the Seeker in two steps and flung an arm around the twiggy neck. Bending his arm at the same time he straightened, Littlecliff lifted the Seeker off the ground. The boy choked and flailed.

Horrified, Firesister rushed forward. "Put him down!" she commanded. Slowly Littlecliff complied, though he left his arm draped across the boy's shoulder.

The Seeker twisted away and flung off the heavy arm. Panting and wide-eyed, he stood his ground. "It's about Mistlight," he said.

3

Firesister got between Littlecliff and the Seeker. She placed her hands on Littlecliff's broad chest and pushed him back. "You can't go around attacking people," she scolded. "He's just a boy."

Littlecliff's gaze traveled from her hair to her face and down her dress. Slowly his eyes returned to hers, and he smiled. When she would have drawn away, he placed his hands over hers. *Stay,* his expression said. A cold and lonely place behind her ribs loosened. For the first time in her life, a man's admiration didn't frighten her.

Someone seized her wrist and yanked her away from Littlecliff. As pain blazed in Firesister's shoulder, she cried out and curled her free hand around the joint.

The pressure on her wrist vanished as quickly as it had come, the agony in her shoulder lessening until she no longer felt as if her arm were tearing loose. Panting, legs trembling, she looked around wildly.

Littlecliff's massive paws swallowed up Bearclaw's hands, which were twisted so far toward the forearms that Firesister feared his wrist bones would break. The muscles in his arms bulged with effort as he was forced to the ground.

"What are you doing?" She stepped toward the men and slapped Littlecliff on the shoulder, and again. "Yah!" she cried, striking him with her open palm until he blinked at her. "Let him go!"

Littlecliff tilted his head with a puzzled look.

"You're not stupid. Let go!" She worked to pry his hand open, but it felt solid as a rock. "Bearclaw is my friend. Friend!" She grasped Littlecliff's arm to shake it. Pain flared in her shoulder. As she whimpered and clutched at it, tears welled up, blinding her. She heard harsh breathing, the scrape of moccasins on the ground.

When her eyes cleared, she found that Bearclaw had escaped Littlecliff's hold. He held a chert knife, one of the heavy, sharp ones he used for butchering deer and bighorn. He waved the knife back and forth, occasionally making little feints toward the outlander, who watched the movements of the blade with no sign of fear.

Firesister wondered how to end the fight before blood was shed.

"Come with me," Bearclaw said without shifting his attention from Littlecliff. "I'll make sure he doesn't hurt you."

"Stop it!" she ordered. "This kind of messing about will only make things more difficult. Put down the knife."

"You're taking his side?" Bearclaw asked.

"No. He's on my side, where you should be too."

"I came to rescue you. You should be thanking me. Being alone with a man, a stranger . . . When have you ever allowed that?"

Since this morning, Firesister realized, as she thought about it. Three times now she'd been attacked by strangers. Each attack had less impact than the previous one. This latest time, when Littlecliff grabbed her in the dark, she hadn't been hurt, and only a little scared. Walking out through the village with him had felt . . . comfortable. She rubbed a thumb over her breastbone, an unaccustomed warmth blossoming deep inside. "Sheath your knife, Bearclaw," she said quietly.

She squeaked as Littlecliff charged Bearclaw low and fast, ramming his belly and driving the air out of his lungs. Bearclaw fell to the ground, Littlecliff on top. The two men grappled and rolled, grunting with effort, occasionally striking with a hand or knee or foot.

Darting forward, Firesister looked for the knife on the ground where they'd been standing. It wasn't there. She spun around and scanned Littlecliff, hoping she wouldn't see the rawhide-wrapped hilt sticking out of him. He seemed fine, not bleeding to death. Anger building, Firesister started toward them.

A touch on her arm halted her. She looked up to see Shiningdawn beside her, veiled as always when outside the compound but recognizable by her curves and her way of standing.

"Leave them," the Cornmaiden said. "They won't thank you for interfering."

When Firesister would have gone anyway, Shiningdawn's hand closed around her wrist. "Don't get in the way. Haven't you ever seen two men fighting over a woman?"

Firesister stared at her in astonishment.

Shiningdawn said, "Men want to be admired by the woman they like. Let them settle it themselves, if you don't want one of them hurt."

"But—"

Stepping between Firesister and the brawling men, Shiningdawn told her, "The Childcatcher sent me to remind you of something. Being driven from the village, going into exile, that's not the only alternative. You can choose the old way. Let Mother Ge decide what becomes of you."

"What do—"

"Stop!" a man's voice boomed behind Firesister.

She twisted around and saw Thorn striding up the path.

The priest inserted a foot between Bearclaw and Littlecliff, then grabbed Bearclaw by the neck and hauled him off the big outlander. "I said stop!" Thorn shoved Bearclaw away and turned to Littlecliff, who sat and lifted his open hands peaceably to shoulder level, as though he hadn't been fighting a moment before. Bearclaw snarled a curse but subsided when the priest shot him a quelling look. Littlecliff rose nimbly to his feet.

Relieved to see that he didn't seem to be favoring any part of his body, Firesister released a breath she hadn't realized she was holding.

"What is going on here?" Thorn demanded.

"None of your concern," Firesister said. She walked toward the priest and stopped midway between the two fighters. "What are you doing here?" she asked Thorn. "Did the Rainsinger send you?" She noticed that the Seeker seemed to have disappeared. Had Thorn and the Seeker been sent to delay her, she wondered, to keep her from talking to any of the clan elders?

"I was worried about you," Thorn said.

Bearclaw shoved past him. "Worried? Ha! Your Rainsinger is the one who put her in this position. Come on, Firesister." He reached for her wrist, the one he'd yanked before.

Snatching it out of reach, Firesister backed away. She bumped into Shiningdawn, who said, "I need to get back to my duties."

"Go on," Firesister told her. "I'm fine."

The Cornmaiden retreated into the Smokemothers' compound. Firesister noticed that all three men watched with interest. Once Shiningdawn's swaying hips were no longer visible, Thorn said, "The Rainsinger didn't send me this time. I came on my own."

Firesister asked, "Why?"

"I felt sorry toward you. Am I not allowed?" Thorn asked.

"I don't need you." As Firesister said this, hearing the bite in her own voice, Littlecliff's hand settled feather-soft and soothing on her shoulder.

Thorn said, "The elders entrusted you to the Stormbringers. They will be more likely to listen to you with a servant of the Ta'atchul along."

"The clan elders will speak with me because of who I am, not who's with me." She hoped that proved true.

"Do you distrust me?"

"Why shouldn't I? Go back to your temple and your Rainsinger, Thorn the Stormbringer, vow-bound to the Ta'atchul. I will solve this on my own or not at all."

He tried arguing more, but Firesister resisted, with Bearclaw throwing in the occasional unhelpful insult, and at last Thorn gave up.

"You should send away this outlander, too," Bearclaw told her as Thorn strode off.

"If you can't bring yourself to accept him, you can leave," Firesister said. "At least he doesn't keep yammering nonsense at me."

Bearclaw glared at her, then turned away. He walked over to a yellow-flowered brittlebush and dug both hands into its foliage, releasing its spicy aroma. After a few moments of rooting around, he straightened up, chert knife in one hand. He cast a baleful look at Littlecliff and carefully ran the flats of his fingers along the blade. "Won't leave you to him," Bearclaw muttered as he stuck the knife into the leather sheath attached to his sash.

"Then come on." Firesister caught Littlecliff's gaze and jerked her chin toward the main path. He nodded. She started for the path, Littlecliff following her.

After a few steps, Bearclaw appeared at her side. They walked shoulder to shoulder on the narrow path. "Where to first?" Bearclaw asked.

It was a good question. She ran her tongue over her upper lip as she considered her choices. "Squashblossom Clan," she said at last. A man of that clan was said to have been friends with some of the younger Watermasters. His father was one of the clan elders, his grandmother perhaps the oldest woman in all the villages north of Sky River, born before the arrival of the rain priests. That Squashblossom gran might remember the old days fondly, when canals flowed as far west as Lastwater, thanks to the Watermasters. Someone who grew up when the priests weren't needed might be willing to stand up to them now.

"You look so serious," Bearclaw said with a grin. "Where's your smile? I almost can't recognize you these past days."

"Why should I smile? What is there to be happy about?"

"Is your arm still paining you?" Bearclaw asked. "Was it the priests who did that or the outlanders?" He twisted his head to look back at Littlecliff.

"You grabbed me," she reminded him.

"I didn't know you were hurt. I'm sorry about that. Let's go to the healers first. They'll take care of you."

"No time for that."

"It just won't feel right until you're happy again. Your smile is like a bright morning after a drizzly day."

She stopped. Behind her, she heard Littlecliff's footsteps halt too. Staring at Bearclaw, she said, "Stop talking." Ignoring his hurt expression, she went on, "I need to think. I need to figure out how to persuade the Squashblossom elders that I'm not a witch. I don't need to ease your guilt about yanking my arm half out of joint. I don't need that."

"Firesister."

"If you want to come with me, to protect me from Littlecliff, fine. Then be quiet."

"Firesister."

"Can't you be quiet and let me think!" Out of the corner of an eye, she saw Littlecliff move forward. She turned her head and told him, "And you, leave Bearclaw alone!" She held up a warning hand. "Fighting with him isn't going to help me at all." She looked from one to the other and found them staring at her. "Both of you, stop—" *making this harder for me!* she wanted to say, but what good would it do?

Closing her eyes, Firesister ran a hand up her forehead and down the back of her head. She grabbed the braid at the nape of her neck and tugged fiercely, welcoming the distraction of the sting of her scalp. This was no time to make a fuss. *Hold fast to what must be done.* She had to escape from the Rainsinger's accusation of witchcraft and then free Mistlight. At the thought of her daughter in the temple, she shuddered, unable to throw off the memory of that day so ago when her life-path had been forever altered. Mistlight was that same age now. No matter what it took, Firesister had to protect her daughter from Eaglefeather.

But how to do that, when Firesister didn't understand what was happening? It was like being trapped in a treacherous undercurrent, swept this way and that, bobbing to the surface to take a single desperate breath while, all around, people stood on the bank calling to her: the Seeker, Shiningdawn, Thorn, Bearclaw, Waterstrider, Willowbundle, the Truthspeaker, the Childcatcher, all chattering at her, rattling off words, saying things she didn't understand. Only Littlecliff, the silent giant, offered respite from the confusion. He rose above the rest, a bridge across the torrent. If she could get to him.

"Come with me," Firesister said, her gaze steady on Littlecliff. "Help me. I can't do this alone."

As Firesister walked along the canal path toward the Squashblossom Clan enclave, the sun beat down on her head, making her wish for a scarf to ward off its rays. Heat tangled in her obsidian-black hair, and the air sucked moisture from her skin.

"It's hot," Bearclaw grumbled. "Feels like spring is over."

Firesister glanced at him. Beads of sweat clustered on his temples and at the back of his neck. Hunters, like their prey, seldom ventured out midday. "You don't have to do this."

"I said I would, didn't I?" Bearclaw tossed a squint-eyed look over his shoulder toward Littlecliff.

Firesister sucked in her lower lip, moistening it with her tongue, and quickened her pace. Bearclaw was doing her a favor. The least she could do for him in return was get him off the sun-baked path and into the shade, and relative cool, of a compound as quickly as she could. "It's not far now," she said, more for her sake than his. She was ready to sit down and rest—her crippled leg was protesting.

The side path leading down from the canal bank to the cluster of Squashblossom compounds soon came into view. Firesister motioned for Bearclaw to go ahead and turned to make the same gesture to Littlecliff. With one leg shorter than the other, she had learned to go down the bank sideways, keeping most of her weight on her sound leg. It was ungraceful and she preferred to be last, so no one was behind her to watch.

Littlecliff didn't budge. She tried again, waving him on. Still he offered her that blank stare. Firesister sighed in exasperation and walked to where the slope became steep. She twisted around, lifting one moccasin off the canal bank in preparation for that first sideways step. Littlecliff moved quickly in front of her and squatted in a position to carry her, like a child, on his back. Firesister froze.

Bearclaw looked up at them. "Yah!" he exclaimed.

Distracted by Bearclaw's protest, Firesister found herself perched on Littlecliff's broad back with her thighs supported by his elbows. He lurched into motion downslope, and she wrapped her arms around his upper chest so he wouldn't fall with her. As soon as the ground leveled out, Firesister pried his hands loose and slid down. Her legs felt more unsteady than she expected, so she clutched at his shirt. He looked down at her with a shy smile that warmed her cheeks more than Brother Sun.

She released her hold on Littlecliff to stand alone in front of the two men, who stared at each other. Shiningdawn's words came back to her: *"Haven't you ever seen two men fighting over a woman?"* She shouldn't like it, shouldn't feel flattered. After all, what use did she have for one man, let alone two? Firesister turned away and fanned her face for a moment as she gathered her wits. Then, "I'm fine," she told Bearclaw. "Let's just go."

The well-used path wound between shegoi bushes and knee-high fishhook cactuses plump from the ample winter rains, leading into the cluster of house compounds of Squashblossom Clan. Firesister wasn't sure which one belonged to the headwoman, Gran Squashblossom, but she assumed it would be an older one, maybe near a central plaza. There were no children at play, no sounds of grinding or pounding to lead her to some clan-daughter or matron to ask for directions. Farther along the path she heard men's voices, raised in what sounded like anger.

"The Squashblossom elders live that way." Bearclaw gestured toward where the voices were coming from. "I've taken meat to them." He started along the path as though oblivious to the dangers of intruding on a family argument.

"I don't think—" Firesister said, hurrying after him.

A voice made creaky by age said, "... too late to worry about the canals." The elder's next words were unclear, and then Firesister heard, "... blessing of Mother Ge on seeds and fields. We must start planting."

A younger man replied, "You said the Watermasters wouldn't come if sent for. You were wrong about that."

Bearclaw slowed. Firesister wondered if he just now realized this would not be the best time to interrupt the conversation.

"One lone Watermaster," the older man scoffed.

"One Watermaster who brought his own work crew," the younger pointed out. "Let the farmers take care of what they need to in their own fields. Waterstrider has men enough to rebuild the weirs and upcanal headgates before the heat of summer. Even if we have to haul water one olla at a time from the main canals, isn't that better than having to go all the way to the river?"

"We must trust in the Stormbringers."

"Stormbringers. The ones who say 'Only those who truly believe in the Ta'atchul will have rain fall on their fields—and anyone whose crops fail for lack of rain deserves it.' Who say 'Have faith in the Ta'atchul, not Mother Ge.' Trust in them still, after what happened to the shadowdancer?"

"We cannot blame them for a witch's doing."

Firesister grabbed Bearclaw when he would have charged around the corner toward the voices. "No," she said, as quietly and definitely as she could manage. "Blustering at someone won't change his mind. And I have to do this myself."

"Don't be a fool, child."

Startled by the sound of an elderly voice from behind, Firesister spun around to see Gran Squashblossom approaching on the arm of a girl—a great-granddaughter, perhaps, or even great-great-grand-daughter—on the edge of womanhood.

"Let him be your brave defender if he wants," the Squashblossom headwoman told Firesister. The old woman tried to pull away from the hand supporting her elbow, but the young clan-daughter gripped more tightly.

"It's the witch," the girl whispered.

"I can see who it is! My eyes work fine in the light of day."

The girl loosened her grip.

Gran Squashblossom tottered toward Firesister. "Why are you stand-ing out here rather than going in? Polite won't get you what you want." The headwoman latched onto Firesister's arm and urged her into motion.

Carried forward by the old woman's will, Firesister proceeded around the corner of the many-times-plastered adobe wall and slowly walked toward an entryway that looked larger and darker the nearer it came. Inside, as she drew close, Firesister saw two men seated under the vatto. The gray-haired one was Deeproot, the clan headman, Gran Squashblossom's eldest son. The other was Deeproot's son, born of a Squashblossom woman and thus bound to the clan on both hands, as the saying went when father and mother were of the same clan.

Gran Squashblossom eased ahead of Firesister to pass through the narrow gap in the high adobe walls. "You're quiet now, Deeproot?" she said to her son. "Your granddaughter came to get me because you were arguing with Tallcorn again. Over what?"

Deeproot eyed Firesister with distaste.

"The same old thing, if I have to guess," Gran Squashblossom continued. "Whether to take the side of the Watermasters or the Storm-bringers."

"The witch is not welcome in my compound." Deeproot rose to his feet, his head nearly brushing the branches that roofed the low vatto. He was a compact man with the callused hands and ropy muscles of a farmer used to digging and hauling and clearing brush. Age might have diminished him in size but had given him more authority, and Firesister felt small before him.

The elderly woman said, "You would force your feeble mother to stumble all the way back to her own house? I have something important to discuss with this clan-daughter—witch or no."

Deeproot's gaze dropped under his mother's withering glare. "She may stay, then," he muttered.

Gran Squashblossom pressed Firesister toward the vatto.

"But not them." Deeproot gestured toward the entryway.

Firesister glanced over and saw Bearclaw hovering in the gap, Littlecliff behind him.

"The outlander may not enter," Deeproot said. "Nor the hunter. Neither of them has business with the clan."

"I—" Firesister began. Gran Squashblossom squeezed her arm to silence her.

The old woman lowered herself to one of the mats under the vatto and waved a thin hand at Firesister. "Tell your overlarge men to remain outside."

Firesister shooed Bearclaw and Littlecliff away. She glanced at the two men nearby: the one, face dark and sullen, sitting across the firepit from his grandmother; the other, angry, as he seated himself on a mat next to his son. Was the anger for his son or because of the intrusion? Firesister wondered.

Addressing his mother, Deeproot said, "Why should you speak with this witch? For so she must be; the Rainsinger wouldn't accuse her without certainty."

"If I'd been born to Squashblossom Clan," Firesister said quietly, "would you believe me rather than him?"

"Am I obligated to listen, as I would a real clan-daughter?" Deeproot asked his mother.

Gran Squashblossom said, "Firesister is a real clan-daughter, so, yes. The Rainsinger's suggestion that we keep her isolated was granted for her own safety, not to punish her." She turned to Firesister and motioned her to sit. As Firesister complied, the old woman said kindly, "There are those who would harm you, after all. Many lost kin at Lastwater."

The unfairness of it burned in Firesister's gut. "Lastwater has nothing to do with me. Why would I have wanted to harm people I didn't know, in a far-distant place I've never been?"

Deeproot spoke to her for the first time. "As the Rainsinger says, to avenge your own family. You blame others for every misfortune in your life."

"I've never been resentful, only grateful," Firesister said. "I can't deny I've done things that may seem like witchcraft. But let me explain them."

"What explanation could you have for taking cracked, weathered old pots, like as not haunted by spirits?"

Tallcorn, across the firepit from Firesister, asked, "Why go out in the ruins at all?"

Because that's where the most interesting pottery can be found, she might have said. *Beautiful designs long forgotten. Birds in flight. Turtles and lizards. Pictures of a world that still exists around us, if only we would open our eyes to it.* Instead she stuck to the practical. "Potsherds from old pots are the strongest temper material," she said. "For water ollas, for storage jars, for cook-pots, there is nothing better." Unable to help herself, she added, "Besides, the Ancestors left their dreams behind in the ruins to help those of us who live on in this place."

"The Ancestors," Deeproot scoffed. "Whose ancestors? Not yours. You're Near-Kin, an outlander as surely as the one waiting for you outside. No blood ties to any clan."

His mother chided him, "The Ancestors speak to me, not you. To me, they have revealed that the time has come to choose a side. Today I will hear what Firesister has to say."

"The Rainsinger—" Deeproot began.

Holding up a hand to silence him, Gran Squashblossom said, "Only a fool would mouth the words of the Rainsinger. The priests' promises are like mirages that vanish as you walk closer. It's always rain tomorrow, when the growing corn needs it today."

"Those are dangerous words."

As the conversation rolled on, mother pitted against son, Firesister wished she could curl into a ball and sink into the hard-packed dirt of the work area. She glanced at Tallcorn, who looked as uncomfortable as she felt.

"Say, rather, true words you don't want to hear," Gran Squash-blossom said. "I prayed all night to the Ancestors. They bade me set the world back as it belongs, with everything in balance."

"No. There's no way back. The Stormbringers—"

His mother glared at him. "Have you forgotten the story of the River-Serpents, how they left the rivers and taught the first Watermasters to build canals? The Binding of the Serpent, that ceremony—do you imagine it can be done properly by priests instead of Watermasters?" Her nostrils flared. "No, never. The Ta'atchul, those beings of the air, cannot bind the River-Serpents."

"Watermasters." Deeproot snorted in disdain. "Why do you talk of Stormbringers and Watermasters instead of witches, with this one sitting right here?"

Gran Squashblossom pointed at him, her finger crooked and shaky. "Witches? A distraction. The priests are nervous now that there's a Watermaster on Cloud Mountain again. The Watermaster trusts this woman. He sent his man to make sure no harm comes to her."

Not trust, Firesister thought. *Guarding from me, not guarding me from harm.* But she didn't dare interrupt this argument. Even if she had been bold enough to do so, she knew Deeproot wouldn't believe her claim to innocence, much less that the Rainsinger wanted the Watermaster dead.

"She's the one who killed the shadowdancer," Deeproot said.

His mother said, "The shadowdancer is the first of the priests to die because of their arrogance."

"It was the Stormbringers who ended the Long Thirst."

"The rains came for untold generations, long before the priests entered the valley, and will continue to fall once the priests are only a memory. It's Watermasters we need, not Stormbringers."

Tallcorn leveled a stare at his father. "There's one here now—a Watermaster, I mean. The Watermasters took care of all of us. They never said, 'Only those who believe deserve to have their crops survive.' They never told us to ignore Mother Ge's teachings, to follow their orders at the cost of giving up everything that has sustained us since the First Days."

"Silence!" his father commanded.

Tallcorn looked away from his father, hauled in a breath, and said to Firesister, "The Rainsinger says he saw witchlight in the canals and traced it back to you, yes?"

She nodded.

Tallcorn directed his next words to his father: "That gives him a reason to argue that the canals be left empty."

"The Rainsinger has never suggested such a thing." Deeproot's mouth twisted with anger.

"Not yet. We still have time to restore the canals. With Waterstrider here, there's hope of a return to the old ways, from the days before the Stormbringers came. But only so long as the Rainsinger can't point to the canals as a source of illness and death. His accusation of witchcraft must not be allowed to stand."

"I will insist," Deeproot said, "that the Rainsinger's advice be followed with regard to this witch."

In a tight voice, Gran Squashblossom told him, "Don't imagine I'll allow you to take the clan down such a path. You're only headman of Squashblossom Clan because I gave birth to you."

"Mother!" Deeproot looked stunned.

"You think I couldn't cast you off?" the old woman asked. "This matter is more important than the love of a mother for her son." To Firesister she said, "Go back to Cloud Mountain and rest. I'll speak to the other clans myself, on your behalf."

"But I—"

Gran Squashblossom didn't allow her to finish. "There's more at stake than just you. This is a matter for the clans to resolve."

"But—"

"Since the day the sun went dark, nigh on twenty-five turnings ago," the old woman said, "we have become lost. Fearful, we pushed the Watermasters away. Now the reckoning has come, and our very existence teeters at the edge of a cliff, awaiting a nudge to send us to oblivion."

Gran Squashblossom's faded eyes glistened with upwelling tears. She shook her head and blinked a few times. "Trust me, child. I will undo this. I will see your reputation restored, so you can once again walk through the village without being pursued by whispers. Go back to Cloud Mountain." She touched Firesister's hand. "Trust me."

Deeproot looked furious, but he didn't contradict his mother again. Tallcorn was watching his grandmother with an expression Firesister couldn't read.

"Will you trust me?" Gran Squashblossom asked.

"Yes." What choice did she have? She had come to Squashblossom Clan to find allies, and here was the strongest one she could have hoped for, saying, *Trust me, I will save you.*

Firesister struggled to keep her left moccasin from dragging as they returned, all three of them—herself, Bearclaw, and Littlecliff—on the canal path. Tiny shells and fragments of larger ones glinted white and pink and silvery against the dusty gravel of the bank. Her gaze followed a drift of shell detritus across the path and down into the depths of the canal. These days, the canal's broad, flat channel was only knee-deep with water. Firesister sighed. She didn't see how the Watermaster could fix it; when she was young, she recalled, three man-heights the canal used to run when full, and so wide that a felled cottonwood trunk would barely span it.

Ahead she noted movement, concealed by the resinous foliage of shegoi bushes on the flats below the canal bank. She halted, peering through the bushes. Bearclaw walked on, but Littlecliff stopped beside her.

What was it she'd seen, Firesister wondered—a flickering of shadows on pale clothing? Unlikely, she thought, for although encountering people along the canals was common enough, they normally kept to the level paths atop the canal banks, as she was doing. The warning about people who might want to harm her rose into Firesister's mind, and a chill ran up her spine.

From the vantage of the canal banks, she should be able to see what was going on down on the flats. Unless whoever was there didn't want to be seen. Someone, perhaps, concealed behind the canal bank where it curved southward. Waiting for her?

Littlecliff placed his hand on her shoulder and wordlessly asked a question. The warmth and kindness in that touch began to thaw something deep inside, frozen so long in the dark that she'd nearly forgotten it.

She shook her head. "It's nothing," she said. "My knee is aching . . ." Rather than admit to having let Gran Squashblossom's words shake her, Firesister started to offer an excuse, then remembered he wouldn't understand it. She shook her head again.

Shouts rang out ahead, and solid, thumping noises, like digging-sticks breaking through caliche. Bearclaw started to run toward the disturbance, descending the steep bank in three great strides, then stopped, head held high as though sniffing the air. He turned and loped back toward her.

"Can you see anything?" he called.

"No!" Firesister answered.

Bearclaw motioned for Littlecliff to come to him. They met at the base of the canal bank. The two big men put their heads together for a moment, and Firesister wondered what her silent giant would have to say. Not much, evidently, for he immediately raced toward the noise.

Bearclaw scrambled up to Firesister.

"What is it?" she asked, frightened by the grim set of his jaw. Without waiting for his answer, she started down the bank.

"No, don't." He pulled her back to him, wrenching her arm again in the process. Firesister cried out, and Bearclaw wrapped himself around her in a tight hug. "I'm sorry," he said. "But you can't go. This isn't your fight."

Unable to see over his shoulders, she stopped resisting and listened closely. Bearclaw released her after a moment. She stepped around him and tried to find what was happening below.

The clamor grew louder, shouts of rage and pain. A few times she heard the clatter of stones striking each other. Knives? Axes? Firesister watched Littlecliff run across an open space, his shoulder-length hair streaming out behind him.

He raised his fist and slammed it down on something—someone—hidden from her sight. Then he crouched, as her heart thudded heavily in her chest. He rose, blood dripping from his hands, and reached into his belt. He pulled something out, took a step, jolted, and fell backward, a patch of red staining the front of his shirt.

Firesister's vision narrowed to that dark, spreading stain as a chasm opened before her. Then a man's muscular arms wrapped around her, obscuring Littlecliff's body from sight, and she found herself held tightly as her knees gave out. Firesister struggled to breathe. She twisted her head to the side, and he pulled her closer. One part of her knew it was only Bearclaw, but in her rising panic all she could think was that he was too strong for her, she was alone once again, helpless. In vain she tried to get free, pounding on his back with ineffective fists.

At last Bearclaw loosened his grip.

Firesister stepped away and caught her heel. She teetered off balance, then fell, hitting the ground with her tailbone and hands. The shock of the impact snapped her head back. She collapsed, staring up at the sky, where Brother Sun still shone, unaffected by the tragedy below. Her cheeks were wet, palms and elbows stung, and her spine ached, as did her neck.

"Are you all right?" Bearclaw knelt beside her.

Firesister climbed to her feet and stumbled toward the edge of the canal bank.

"Don't," he said, coming to join her.

"I have to see."

"Then let me go first. You stay here and—"

"No." Littlecliff was her friend, not his, she thought fiercely. She did accept Bearclaw's help to get down the canal bank, and then it came to her that Littlecliff might still be alive. Firesister swallowed hard, staggered by that hope. "Go," she said. "Run, fast as you can, and find out— Run!"

She limped after Bearclaw as quickly as she could manage, cursing under her breath that she'd overused her bad leg. Rabbit trails led her through the shegoi bushes toward where she thought she'd seen Littlecliff fall, but she didn't find him. "Bearclaw?"

"Here. Follow my voice"—so she did.

She discovered Bearclaw standing over Littlecliff, who lay still in a bloody pool. Nearby was Waterstrider, on whose temple a long gash wept blood. Unable to bear the sight of all that blood, Firesister dropped her gaze to the desert floor.

Tiny shells lay in the gravel, washed down from the canal bank. A scattering of potsherds, disturbed so the original shape could no longer be guessed at. Rabbit pellets. Firesister drew a deep breath, steadying herself.

"We should go to the bonemenders," Bearclaw said. "The Watermaster is still breathing."

She numbly accepted that. Waterstrider, alive. Littlecliff, dead.

Firesister looked around. There were only the two men, Waterstrider and Littlecliff, out of all the outlanders. "Where are the rest?"

"They were gone already when I got here. Whoever downed . . . your friend . . . must have been the last one. Staying behind to finish off the Watermaster, maybe."

"You think the outlanders did this?" Firesister limped toward Waterstrider. Her feet felt big and clumsy like river cobbles, and the sunlight made her shiver.

"Who else?"

Those southern priests. Under Eaglefeather's orders. When I didn't kill Waterstrider, he found another way. "Go to the bonemenders," Firesister said. "Leave me here. I'll do what I can." She bent over Waterstrider and began to untie the sash at his waist.

"Alone? What if those outlanders . . ." At her glare, Bearclaw trailed off. "What if whoever attacked him comes back?"

"Do you want him to die? He's the only Watermaster in the entire valley—that makes him more important than I am."

"Not to me," Bearclaw muttered.

Firesister tugged the sash from under Waterstrider. "You can get to the village much faster than I ever could." But a bonemender wouldn't do. It had to be someone high enough to not fear the Rainsinger. The chief healer, then. "Go straight to Lightstone. Tell him what happened."

"I can't leave you here by yourself." Bearclaw's eyes strayed to Littlecliff's body. He swallowed hard. "I won't."

Firesister guessed he was worried about Littlecliff's soul, untethered from its flesh, but she didn't share Bearclaw's worry. The dead had never caused her to be afraid; only the living had ever done that.

Besides, restless spirits cut loose by violence would hunt for the hand that had killed them, not simply the nearest person.

"Do as I say," she told him, "or I will gut you with the same knife they used on Littlecliff." Breathing heavily, Firesister stood. She lifted her chin in challenge. "If you come back without a healer or get here too late to save the Watermaster, I will kill you myself. I swear to Mother Ge, I will send you to the Ancestors by my own hand."

Bearclaw backed away. She watched him disappear into the shegoi bushes.

Firesister's knees collapsed under her. Other than making sure she didn't fall on Waterstrider, she didn't fight her sudden weakness. She sat on her left hip and tucked her legs to the right. Gently she lifted Waterstrider's head into her lap. Determined not to look at Littlecliff's limp form, trying not to think about the man who had suddenly come into her world, shifted it, and departed it just as abruptly, Firesister eased back Waterstrider's hair, sticky with blood, and began to wind the sash around his head to bind the wound.

A place in his scalp felt soft. She probed at it, wondering if the bones were broken, and what that would mean. If his skull were a pot, she could glue it back together. She hoped Lightstone could somehow do the same with Waterstrider's head so all his thoughts and memories would remain.

Firesister remembered the canals from when she was a little girl, before the Watermasters' departure from the valley—channels flowing deep with water, reliable even in the heat of summer. The canals didn't sustain only crops, of course. Fish could be netted above the headgates; waterbirds and turtles were caught in box-traps set among the cattails and reeds. Those days had been joyous ones. Then everything changed.

The Watermasters left. That first winter without them, floods tore through the canals. The farmfolk did their best to repair the damage, but it was never enough. Neighbors fought over the merest trickles of water in the irrigation ditches. As the main canals diminished, the villages farthest from the river shrank too, and the clans increasingly relied on the priests' promises of rain. Through it all, most fields got enough water to produce at least some crops—until Eaglefeather became the Rainsinger and began to turn the farmers against Mother Ge.

"*A return to the old ways,*" Gran Squashblossom had said about Waterstrider's return. But to do that, he had to live.

And not just survive. Within his broken skull, he carried the secrets of the Watermasters. He was the only chance the people of Serpentgate had of restoring the canals to their former bounty.

Firesister closed her eyes and prayed to Mother Ge that Lightstone would come quickly.

Soon, too soon for Bearclaw to have reached the healers' compound, she heard stealthy footsteps approaching from the direction of the canal. Firesister looked for a rock, a branch, anything within reach to defend herself and Waterstrider, but she found nothing. No knife had fallen from his sash when she'd removed it, and no digging-sticks or staffs lay nearby. The only thing she could use as a weapon was the blade sticking out of Littlecliff's chest. Too far away, even if she dared touch it.

A slight-framed boy emerged from the bushes.

She stared at him, at first seeing only the topknot bound with pale ribbon and thinking he was a priest, come back to finish off Waterstrider. Then she recognized him as the Seeker who had confronted her in the plaza during the sun-festival and this morning had spoken to her at the Smokemothers' compound. His gaze left hers and drifted down to Waterstrider, then along the tall Watermaster's length. Protectively Firesister placed a hand on Waterstrider's blood-crusted cheek and laid her arm across his chest.

The youth looked at her, then away. His eyes widened, and Firesister followed his stare to Littlecliff's body. "Is he dead?" the Seeker asked in a hushed voice, face twisted into the same expression he'd worn when the shadowdancer fell.

"If you fear wandering spirits," she told him, "you should leave now."

The Seeker swallowed hard. Without taking his eyes off Littlecliff, he asked, "Is that the Watermaster . . . ?"

Firesister patted Waterstrider's chest. Through his shirt, he felt hot. "This is him."

"He's still alive?"

She nodded. She thought the boy was relieved. *"Kill the Watermaster,"* Eaglefeather had told her. If this Seeker seemed happy that the Watermaster was still breathing, did that mean Eaglefeather had changed his mind and didn't want Waterstrider dead after all? But then who could have struck him down? Could Bearclaw be right, that the outlanders had turned on him? But that made no sense.

The Seeker asked, "Do you need help treating his wounds?"

Though she would have liked to do something for Waterstrider before Lightstone arrived, Firesister couldn't bring herself to trust the boy. Vow-bound to the Ta'atchul, he was expected to obey every order from the priests. *There's no way he could betray Eaglefeather, his own Rainsinger.* "No, the healers are coming. They'll be here soon," she said.

"Then . . ." Head bent, the Seeker scuffed the toe of one tattered moccasin on the finely graveled desert floor.

What had he said at the Smokemothers' compound, before Littlecliff and Bearclaw's scuffle? "You have something to tell me about Mistlight?"

"I'm afraid for her," the Seeker said.

"Why?"

"No one has seen her since she arrived. She was taken to the room on top of the tower, where the shadowdancer's body was burned." His eyes, darkened by dread, turned toward Littlecliff. Hastily he looked down at his feet again.

Firesister resisted the temptation to believe this youth, who feared witches yet had approached her during the sun-festival, and evidently feared ghosts yet stood his ground so near a body. But he had no reason to do anything to help Mistlight. His professed concern for Mistlight was likely another of Eaglefeather's attempts to manipulate Firesister through worry about her daughter. Mistlight had been at the temple less than two days—surely Eaglefeather couldn't have done anything to harm her yet, with the Smokemothers promising to look out for her.

"The Smokemothers say Mistlight needs to stay at the temple," Firesister said. "And the Rainsinger has agreed to it. So why have you come to me again with this matter?"

"If I get her away from the temple, will you take her in?" His boyish voice sounded tight, almost tearful.

Firesister's suspicions flared higher. Choosing her words carefully, she answered, "That would do her no good, not yet. Not as long as your Rainsinger is poisoning people against me."

The Seeker's hands came together in front of him, just below the belt wrapped around his middle. "I— If it would help," he said, "I can stand as witness for you in front of the elders."

"Why would the village council allow you as a witness?"

"My parents are among those who died at Lastwater, so I can claim the right to speak at the hearing. I could tell them to believe what you say rather than the Rainsinger."

Her eyes narrowed. A Seeker turning against his own could indeed make a difference, if she could trust him.

But she shouldn't need such a thing, for Gran Squashblossom had promised to persuade the other elders of Firesister's innocence. Granted, that was before Waterstrider was struck down. What if the Watermaster didn't recover—would the farmfolk go back to believing that the priests offered the only choice for this summer's crops?

Firesister wished Waterstrider had come with a whole group of Watermasters, as many as had left the valley twenty-some turnings ago, rather than at the head of a party of outlanders. But he was alone, and at the moment his life was in her hands. Trust in Mother Ge, she told herself. Trust Gran Squashblossom.

"You can't do anything for Mistlight if you're no longer a Seeker," Firesister said. "Go back to the temple. Wait there and watch. See if your suspicion that she's in danger is correct. If so, then once my innocence is established, bring her to me." If this boy was telling the truth, she wouldn't have to figure out a way to rescue Mistlight herself. If not . . .

The boy's head came up proudly, nostrils flaring. He nodded once, turned, and ran into the brush. The noise of his footsteps faded.

Silence wrapped around Firesister. Then a songbird warbled a call to its mate, a lizard scuttled from one bush to another, and life in the little desert space returned to normal, as though no humans rested quietly nearby.

A shadow seemed to pass across the face of the sun. Firesister looked up and saw a buzzard soaring high above. Had the scent of Littlecliff's death already been carried on the wind? she wondered. Or was it his soul, calling to the animal-spirits to consume his body? She had no idea what Littlecliff's people thought of death, how the earthbound form was to be treated, what became of the inner essence of a man. Tears rose, burning, behind her eyes, and she wished she knew what to do for her fallen giant.

Firesister eased herself out from under Waterstrider. Straightening her legs and back took some time, so stiff and sore were they. Dried blood caked her hands. She would have liked to wash them, but her waterskin held barely enough for two people to drink, assuming she could get some water in Waterstrider to help keep him cool—cleaning her scrapes and his wounds would have to wait for the healers.

Firesister removed the stopper from the waterskin and approached Littlecliff. "If what I am about to do is wrong," she told him, "I'm sorry. I'm not much of a singer." Firesister hoped he would see the sincerity in her effort and not judge her harshly if she fell short, for their brief friendship had proven his heart to be as large as himself, generous and open.

She knelt near his shoulder, singing the Song of Farewell to him. As she sang, she tipped the waterskin and poured some of its contents into her palm. Firesister dipped a finger into the pink-tinged liquid and traced it over Littlecliff's lips, then picked up more and closed first his left eye and then the right with the moisture.

When she finished the funeral song, she rested a hand on his shoulder, recalling the times he had done the same to her. "You left too soon," she said. "But you saved your friend. You did well." Firesister grabbed the hilt of the knife that had struck him down. She pulled it free of his body as she rose to her feet. Holding the blood-encrusted blade to the sky, she said, "I will keep this in your honor, and hold you in memory forever."

A slight breeze moved the shegoi branches and plastered a few wisps of hair against her damp neck. Firesister turned her face like a sunflower toward Brother Sun's light, drinking it in, drawing strength from it. The thin shade of the shegoi bush over Waterstrider would soon pass, exposing him to the midday sun. She would need to move him before that happened.

But how? Roll him over? Oh, yes, that would be good for his head. She sucked in her lower lip. A big man like that, he was too heavy for her to lift. Firesister remembered her first sight of Waterstrider through the roof opening of the storage room, a broad-shouldered shadow against the sky. She would have to drag him across the gravel. *And rip up his back just like your hands?*

"I couldn't do it at all if it were you," she said, as though Littlecliff could still hear her.

A beam of light through the bushes caught her eye as something glinted on the ground. She walked over and found the obsidian knife Eaglefeather had given her, the thin blade shattered into several pieces. It lay next to the skeleton of a saguaro that had fallen so long ago, the pulpy flesh had melted away, leaving the ribs behind.

An idea twitched in the back of her mind: instead of moving the man, move the shade. Firesister pulled ribs from the fibrous tangle holding them in place. Some were too weak and broke upon being touched, but several came free with enough length to be useful. She took the saguaro ribs back to Waterstrider and started building a framework.

Bearclaw took so long getting back that she was glad she'd put up the shade structure, weaving shegoi branches over the top to keep the sun off Waterstrider. Again and again she soaked her sash and squeezed water from it into Waterstrider's mouth, but his skin became flushed and hot, his breathing labored. The shadows lengthened around them as Brother Sun began to fall toward the horizon.

Finally she heard Bearclaw calling her name. "Here!" she answered, standing and waving to him over the bushes. "But—" when no one followed him, "where is the healer? Even if Lightstone couldn't come himself, he must have sent someone to the Watermaster."

"Lightstone refused, and no one else was willing. There's no kin-right where the Watermaster is concerned. No one knows what clan his mother came from."

"Gran Squashblossom—"

"She said no, too. The Watermaster has no people now that the heronfolk are gone. He's an outlander."

Firesister placed her hands on her hips. "He's no outlander," she snapped, daring Bearclaw to disagree. "Even Far-Traders, when they fall sick or get hurt in the valley, are taken care of. Surely a Water-master deserves better than traders."

"Traders have allies here. The Watermaster has only an enemy—the Rainsinger."

"Then what can we do? Look at him!" Firesister pointed at Water-strider, his chest rising and falling the only sign of life. She heard his breath rasping and realized the desert was too quiet.

She scanned the area, twisted to look all around her. In the direction of the village she saw a few dark heads moving quickly. Unstrung bows and spear points bristled amid the approaching party. Firesister grabbed for the knife she'd drawn from Littlecliff's chest, but Bearclaw stayed her hand.

"They're friends," he said, "come to help."

"With what?" Firesister asked, thinking of the weaponry.

"They're bringing a litter to carry the Watermaster back to Cloud Mountain."

Obviously there were more men than needed to carry Waterstrider. But perhaps there were bonemenders among them, with more experience than Firesister had in tending wounds. For now, she saw no better choice. "Are you sure it's safe to move him?"

Still holding onto her hand, Bearclaw said, "Once we get him to the village, you won't have to concern yourself with him anymore. You must think of yourself now and get free of this accusation of witchcraft. If you don't, you're likely to face exile. What will happen to Mistlight then?"

The men—hunters, she realized—emerged from the brush a few at a time. Uncomfortable with the way they seemed to fill the space, Firesister stepped back, away from Waterstrider, away from Bearclaw, into a gap between shegoi bushes. "Two litters," she said upon seeing the poles with netting connecting them. "The others are here for . . ." She stopped herself before saying Littlecliff's name and gestured toward him.

Bearclaw nodded. "For the other one. We can't leave him lying out here. Don't worry about them." He waved at the men lifting Littlecliff's corpse onto the litter. "We hunters have ways of dealing with death spirits."

Death spirits, yes, she thought. *You take care of Littlecliff. But Waterstrider needs people who can keep the soul in the body.*

With a flaming sunset filling the sky over her head, a desperate Firesister knelt with bowed head in the Squashblossom Clan's plaza. A little earlier she'd gone to Lightstone herself and begged him to come to Cloud Mountain to tend Waterstrider. When he'd refused, she had asked him to send someone else, anyone who could take care of a broken skull. He'd turned her down on that as well. As Bearclaw had said out on the desert flats, Lightstone saw no reason to step in. So Firesister had dragged herself back to the Squashblossom enclave on aching legs to ask another favor of the clan's elders.

Gran Squashblossom leaned on her staff and repeated her question: "Did you see who struck down the Watermaster?"

Firesister shook her head.

Deeproot said, "Then you can't be certain it wasn't his own men. How dare you accuse the Rainsinger of doing such a thing?"

Firesister drew a breath and addressed Gran Squashblossom. "You took care of me when I needed you. And I wasn't important to anyone. Reviving our canals will be impossible without the Watermaster, isn't that what you said earlier, this very morning? You said, too, that the priests aren't to be trusted. Yet you're standing with them?"

The old woman closed her eyes as though exhausted. "We have no right to take care of the Watermaster. He has no kin ties here."

"No more did I," Firesister said, "sixteen turnings ago."

Gran Squashblossom said, "The village let you down. It's different for the Watermaster. He brought his own danger with him. We need admit no fault in that."

Tallcorn stirred, a restless motion that caught Firesister's eye. *You're a friend of Waterstrider's from childhood. Say something in his defense.* But Tallcorn remained quiet, though color rose in his face.

Inwardly cursing him for respecting his elders more than he supported his friend, Firesister responded, "Even if he brought danger with him, does it matter, if we need the Watermaster so that we all may live?" Her words had no visible effect. She hesitated, having prepared only one more argument—one that she was reluctant to even utter, so likely was it to lead to disaster for herself if not for Waterstrider.

Firesister took in Deeproot's hostile expression, Tallcorn's silent shame, and Gran Squashblossom's worn, tired face. Slowly, committing herself to a risky venture, she said, "You're wrong about his ties to the village."

Deeproot's scowl deepened, and his eyebrows snapped together.

"Waterstrider is my man." Firesister couldn't bring herself to look the listeners in the eye as she lied. Instead she stared at the nearest compound wall. "I'm your clan-daughter and what's more, daughter of all the clans. That makes the entire village responsible for my mate as well."

Deeproot sneered. "Words cannot force the clans to accept an absurd claim of kinship—"

Firesister extended her left hand and turned it over to show the inside of her wrist, which she'd sliced with the obsidian knife to convince everyone of her sincerity. "This goes beyond words," she said. "We are blood-bound, Waterstrider and Firesister. Lifemates." As soon as the situation became less urgent, she resolved to tattoo a bracelet on herself, with a matching one on Waterstrider, as additional proof.

Tallcorn said, "Waterstrider would never bind himself to a woman for life. He vowed a long time ago to remain free."

Deeproot talked over his son's last words, asking, "Are we to believe he fell in love . . . with you?" Disbelief sharpened his crackly voice. "When? When would that have happened?"

"Not love," Firesister said, lowering her arm, "but gratitude for saving his life. The Rainsinger wants the Watermaster dead—and sent me to do it. Instead I warned Waterstrider. I kept him alive a few days ago. I'll keep him alive now, too."

Deeproot declared, "The Rainsinger would never go so far."

Firesister hadn't really expected anyone to believe her without proof. She thought of Waterstrider in the moonlight, making himself bait in a trap for whoever Eaglefeather might send for him. He had listened to her and accepted her warning. That meant he trusted her somewhat, though such an uncertain trust would likely be shattered by this claim of a blood-binding once he learned of it. But what else could she do? Firesister shrugged. "The Watermaster sent his man with me. Why would he—a stranger—do that, unless there was some bond between us?"

"Preposterous," Deeproot grumbled, but Gran Squashblossom said, "If you're truly lifemates, then the clans do indeed owe the Watermaster the same kin-right as you."

Firesister gazed at her. "Waterstrider rescued me from the Rainsinger, as my man. As his woman, I've given you justification to act. Please send for Lightstone to tend Waterstrider. If he survives, it will be a sign of Mother Ge's favor . . . proof that I am not a witch." Firesister hoped that as soon as she was deemed innocent, the suspicion that had fallen, by extension, on Mistlight would be lifted too.

"And if the Watermaster dies?" Deeproot asked.

"If he dies, after Lightstone has done everything possible to keep him alive, then it will show that I, as his lifemate, am not worthy. In the end, I will be judged by Mother Ge, not the village council. There will be no need for you, Grandmother, to persuade the other elders of my innocence. Instead, convince them to accept Mother Ge's judgment."

Gran Squashblossom's mouth twisted. "Are you so sure that Mother Ge will favor you?"

"Yes."

"Because if she doesn't, the Watermaster will suffer the same judgment as you," Gran Squashblossom said. "It could mean exile. Then what will become of everyone north of Sky River?"

Through a dry throat, Firesister said, "Mother Ge will pull him through." She prayed she was right.

Waterstrider

Herons fly, slow beat of wings, pleading with a sunset sky:
Show a place where fish still swim, all shining scales and glinting tails.
Dried to dust, the river deep lies dreaming of the hunter's feet.

—FROM A SONG OF THE HERONFOLK

Waterstrider lay on his back, surrounded by darkness. A ghostly flicker teased at the edge of his vision, vanishing when he focused on it. No sounds came to his ears, no shuffle of feet or whisper of cloth, only that hint of movement in the shadows. He struggled to move his arms, his legs, roll over, sit up, but his body wouldn't obey.

Is this death?

With fear clawing at him, Waterstrider searched for his last memory. Clear sky, shegoi bushes, fine gravel underfoot. He and his men were out inspecting the main canals, and there was laughter. Then . . . nothing. His heart gave one massive thump before settling into a steady rhythm that sent blood pounding through his head.

That meant he hadn't passed from the earth, for a dead man's heart would no longer beat. Waterstrider concentrated on breathing. The dusty tang of plaster stuck in his throat. His face and body felt hot.

A few more memories trickled in: a cool, gentle hand on his forehead, the comforting murmur of a woman's voice. Or maybe those were just a dream. He'd dreamt of his mother doing such things many times before, the mother who had drowned herself in a canal before he was old enough to remember her. As he'd grown into manhood, the dreams had lessened, but now he wondered whether his return to the valley had stirred up some forgotten yearning.

The pale flicker drew his eye again. Cloth, maybe, or a flash of teeth. But no real person seemed to be there, in the stillness of the dark. Could it be a visiting spirit, sent to guide his feet to the realm of the Ancestors? Was his life-force ebbing, heart and breath slowing, soul detaching from body?

In desperation he sent a questing awareness out from his center. If he found his fingers, felt something with them, got them to twitch or curl, maybe it would hold him here . . .

Rustling in the shadows made his breath hitch. Waterstrider turned his head that way but saw nothing. "Someone there?" he croaked out through a dry throat. He moistened cracked lips with a swollen tongue.

"I'm here," came an answer from the dark.

It was a woman's voice, gentle and reassuring. Relief flowed through him, rising like a spring in the desert. He might not know where he was or why he lay so still, but he sensed no immediate danger.

Footsteps approached, moccasins sliding over a smooth floor.

Waterstrider's lingering fear faded with each step, for the noises marked her as a living person, not a disembodied spirit. But he couldn't make out her face. "Why so dark?"

"You said the light hurt your eyes."

"When? When did I say?" Waterstrider's voice trembled. He cursed himself for revealing his weakness. "Who are you?"

"You don't remember? I hoped . . ." She trailed off, then said, "I understand what it is to be broken, to lie helpless in the shadows, at the mercy of hands you can't avoid. Don't be afraid. No harm will come to you."

Broken. Helpless. The words revived his unease. His pulse began to race again, bringing rhythmic twinges to his temples. "Where am I? What happened?"

She sighed. "You were attacked—a blow to the head. It kept you on the edge of death for several days. Since then, you wake up every now and then, ask me what happened, and forget everything I tell you."

"No," he said. "If I . . ." The rest of the thought wouldn't come to his tongue. His throat tightened with frustration, and he stared ahead at nothing.

"Don't worry. You're getting better."

He didn't believe her. Couldn't. If he'd been struck hard enough to be knocked out, why didn't it hurt? Waterstrider tried to put his hand up to feel for bandages or tender spots, but again his body wouldn't respond. This time he thought he felt resistance, as if he was tied up. "Can't move."

"There's a net over you," she said. "You were thrashing around."

"Want it off."

"I don't think—"

"Take it off!" Waterstrider rolled to his left, raising his right shoulder a little, testing the net. He sank back, then braced on his heels and lifted his hips, flexing the net across his thighs. Again he did that, and again, pressing against the netted cords. Shoulders. Hips. Shoulders. Hips. Over and over he pushed against the net.

"Stop, before you hurt yourself on the stakes!"

A weight came down on his chest, too much to push against. Waterstrider resisted, but then, strength gone, he gave in.

"Have you really come to your senses?" she asked.

Waterstrider tasted warm, sweet breath on his lips, felt a heart beating quickly near his, a familiar softness separating his ribs from hers. The woman had thrown herself on top of him. He froze. "Who are you?"

She pushed herself off his chest. "What's the last thing you remember?" Her voice came from a distance above him.

Again Waterstrider tried to call up that memory. Walking in the desert flats on his way from one canal to another. His men trailing behind, single file, trusting him to find a path that avoided cactus spines and ocotillo thorns. Something moving off to one side, barely visible through the shegoi branches. After that, nothing.

Waterstrider forced himself to remain calm. "Let me loose."

After a long pause, she knelt beside him. She traced a cord over his shoulder. A moment later it popped free. She skimmed down his arm to his hand, then his outer thigh, knee, lower leg, foot. His blood heated from those glancing touches. Even injured, Waterstrider's body stirred in response to a woman whose face and form he couldn't see. It was his father's legacy, the source of his mother's despair, an affliction Waterstrider had never managed to escape.

"Are you still awake?" the woman asked.

"Yes. Can I move now?"

"Not yet."

A slight weight shifted off his legs, but something immediately flopped across his hips and chest. Though impatient, he waited for her to clear the net from his upper body too. His fingers touched his bare thighs. Waterstrider realized there must have been a cloth lining the net.

"My clothes?" he asked.

The net and liner slid off his chest, leaving him naked. Sounding uncomfortable, she said, "You threw up. Several times."

Waterstrider was glad for the darkness that hid a flush of humiliation. Assuming he could believe her—and what reason did he have for doubt?—he'd been unable to control himself for days. He couldn't have fed himself or slaked his thirst. Someone must have done all that for him, then wiped him clean after the food and water left his body.

"Who are you?" He knew he'd asked before, but if she'd answered, he couldn't remember what she'd said. He despised himself for the weakness of mind and body that had made him utterly reliant on this woman whose name he didn't know.

"Firesister."

A woman he'd seen only three times in his life—and most recently had sent off with his closest friend.

"Where's Littlecliff?" he asked.

An indrawn breath told him he wouldn't like the answer. "You shouldn't utter his name," Firesister said quietly.

Waterstrider's heart lurched. The People of Two Rivers refused to speak the names of the dead. That meant Littlecliff had passed from the world.

An old memory surfaced from twenty-four turnings earlier, when Waterstrider had met Littlecliff on the first day of the Watermasters' arrival in the City of Birds. The two youths had quarreled over something—the details were long forgotten—and both had come away bloody. Soon after, they'd become fast friends, seldom far apart. If Littlecliff's name was never spoken, who would remember him?

"It's not his true name." Waterstrider couldn't bring himself to ask what happened. "They called him by another word in the City of Birds. 'Littlecliff' is the closest translation in your tongue."

Firesister took Waterstrider's hand. "He fell defending you. Sometimes after I tell you this, you say you wanted to know. Other times it makes you cry. Please hold it in your memory, so I never have to tell you of his death again. And be careful who you say his name to."

Waterstrider tried to remove his hand from her grasp, but she held fast. His fingers twitched. He didn't want any of this to be true. Days had gone by since Littlecliff's death, according to her. Days when he'd been wandering in his mind, waking for short times, then losing memories in sleep. Would he remember this time? Darkness wrapped around him as his eyelids grew too heavy to hold open.

"You must have worn yourself out fighting the net," Firesister said. "Rest now." She patted his hand, then let it go and bent over him, settling the cloth around him again.

With his last bit of strength, he said, "Don't tie me down."

She hesitated, then promised, "I won't."

Waterstrider woke again to find the place still hot, still shadowy. Odd, he thought. It shouldn't be hot and also dark. The days of early spring might be overwarm, but the ground chilled quickly once the sun set.

He felt groggy, and that seemed odd too. He'd been sleeping for days, Firesister had said. She'd claimed he forgot everything she told him. Not this time. This time her words had stuck with him. Littlecliff was dead. Died defending him, she'd said, and from that Waterstrider guessed he himself had been left for dead. What of the rest of the men from the City of Birds? Waterstrider struggled to bring that to mind. Maybe she'd told him, but he couldn't remember it now.

He lay on his back. Something under him gave when he breathed, while something else tightened around his chest—a tunic, he guessed. Waterstrider strained to hear the desert night-sounds of owls or coyotes. Nothing. Probably he was in a room. With thick adobe walls and a mud-chinked roof that blocked out noises and the light of the moon and the White Starry Path. Small enough to hold in the heat of his body. It could be anywhere in the village.

Waterstrider tried to roll onto his side. Nothing happened. He remembered that experience from the previous waking. He'd been tied down then. This time, he didn't feel a net around him. Just . . . his body wouldn't obey. His stomach knotted as dread began to seep into his blood.

People could survive blows to the head, he told himself. Some moved as much as they could, as soon as they could, and retaught their bodies what to do. Others remained forever crippled. He refused to be one of that kind.

You had enough strength to fight the net. Don't let despair make you weak. Waterstrider began to flex one muscle at a time, starting with his left thumb. The agonizingly slow process made him sweat. Simply lifting his left forearm off the bedding was a struggle. As his hand flopped down, he realized he lay on deerhide or maybe bighorn, thick and with cushioning hair on the underside. It was more comfortable than the bedrolls he and Littlecliff had been sleeping on.

Littlecliff. Waterstrider recalled that moment when Littlecliff stood in the moonlight on top of Cloud Mountain, holding a knife left behind by Firesister. *The fact that she could have killed me and didn't . . . is that supposed to make me trust her?* Littlecliff had said yes. But Littlecliff was dead, and Waterstrider was at her mercy.

Swallowing hard, Waterstrider started exercising his right hand. That side seemed to work better than the left. Would the same be true for his legs? How would he ever walk, he wondered, if only one side did what he wanted? He tried again to shift his feet, but they remained obstinately still. *You braced with them before,* he reminded himself. Himself argued, *That doesn't mean you'll become the man you once were.* He silenced the uncertain voice, vowing that, little by little, he would regain control of his whole body.

It was like repairing the canals. First, smaller canals and crosscuts had to be fixed so water could be bled off safely from the midsized distribution canals. Only then would water have someplace to go after being drawn from the river by the main canals. Start pushing water down-canal too soon, and you'd cause more problems than you started with.

Waterstrider redoubled his efforts with fingers and thumbs, bending one and then another.

After a while the desire for sleep crept into his mind. Unwilling to pass into the oblivion that swallowed memories, Waterstrider fought it off by stretching out the fingers of his right hand, then clenching them into a fist. When his right hand began to cramp, he worked the left, then the right again. Bending the right wrist and elbow. Making a fist and stretching. Over and over he worked those muscles, until he could complete the motions on the right side without concentrating all of his attention there. The left side was more reluctant, but he refused to become disheartened.

He would recover fully. On that point he was determined—for what good would a crippled Watermaster be? Waterstrider closed his hands and tapped them against his naked thighs.

His stomach growled, startling him. He suddenly felt ravenous. That was a good sign, he told himself. Dying men had little appetite. Only the living craved food.

Waterstrider couldn't tell day from night in the dark room, so he had no way to judge how much time passed. Meals and water came, often while he was sleeping. Between eating and sleeping and exercising, he gradually became strong enough to use the nightsoil pot placed next to him. Standing was still beyond him, though he could push himself up to hands and knees and tentatively balance there, toppling over whenever he shifted a hand.

After getting a faceful of dust more times than he could count, Waterstrider thought of crawling on his belly, like a lizard. He tried that. His first attempts failed miserably. He realized his movements were more like swimming, relying on arms and legs to draw his body through slick water. He tried using his belly more than his limbs, wriggling side to side as tadpoles do.

His efforts eventually rewarded him with a tiny bit of forward progress. Again he tried, and again, with increasingly long rests between attempts.

Finally, worn out from crawling a distance of perhaps half his own length, Waterstrider lay sweating and panting, muscles spasming, on his right side. At his back was an adobe wall, so no one could come at him from behind. Maybe an unnecessary precaution but reassuring nonetheless.

In a silence between one gulp of air and another he heard something. He held his breath, and the sound repeated: footsteps, heavy and regular, not like the uneven rhythm of Firesister's moccasins, to which he'd become accustomed over the past few days. Air whooshed out of him as he wished for some weapon to defend himself from whoever was approaching. *Not that you could wield it,* the traitorous voice in his head told him. *You're weak as a baby.*

Then came a slithering noise. Waterstrider recognized the sound as that of a reed door sliding across plaster. Dim light appeared around a four-sided patch of darkness. The darkness twitched aside, revealing itself to be a curtain of animal hides sewn together. Beyond the hide curtain was an open doorway. Outside, sunshine beat down, but a man's body blocked out most of the glare. Still, the brightness stabbed at Waterstrider's dark-dulled eyes.

The man entered, ducking his head to avoid the wooden lintel. A twig sticking out of the low ceiling caught one of his pair of braids as he turned aside and fastened the curtain back. Impatiently he tore his hair loose, then cast his eyes on the center of the floor. He spun on his heel and spotted Waterstrider, lying at the edge of the room.

Waterstrider saw no weapon in the man's hands. No food or water either. "Who are you?" As soon as the words left his mouth, he thought that he needed a better question. Where nearly everyone was a stranger, what difference did it make how someone was called?

"You don't remember my name?" The man approached. He squatted next to Waterstrider's chest. "I'm Bearclaw. A friend of Firesister's."

Waterstrider wanted to shove him away, this man who came so close and made a show of friendliness. All he could manage was a twitch of the hand lying limp on his hip.

"Still no better, I see," Bearclaw said.

The childish urge to point out that he'd crawled this far on his own was surprisingly hard for Waterstrider to resist. "What are you here for?"

Bearclaw reached out and nudged Waterstrider's wrist, the right one, attached to the arm pinned between his body and the plastered floor. "You haven't noticed this yet, have you?"

Waterstrider tried to see what Bearclaw was talking about but couldn't get his arm out far enough. Bearclaw rocked Waterstrider's left shoulder back and tugged the other arm free. A fresh tattoo stood out, dark against the red-brown skin above his wrist—a line of dots that seemed to go all the way around, like a bracelet. "What's this?"

Waterstrider asked.

"Have you been gone from the valley so long, you can't recognize the mark of a blood-binding when you see one?"

"A blood-binding." A promise to spend your life together. Waterstrider stared at his wrist. He lifted his gaze to Bearclaw's and demanded, "Who bears the matching tattoo? Firesister?"

He had watched his father's false promises destroy his mother, had avoided making promises to any woman. And now he was trapped into the very situation that had ruined his family. A blood-binding. Undertaken when he was unable to refuse.

"Yes, you—" Bearclaw scrubbed a hand over his face, then started over. "She said you—" He glanced at Waterstrider and didn't finish that thought either. "The healers wouldn't come until she said she was your lifemate and claimed kin-right," Bearclaw explained. "Without her, you would've joined the Ancestors."

"Am I to believe that?" Healers owed service to all in the valley, even strangers. Surely they would have tended the Watermaster who'd come to restore the canals.

Leaning closer, Bearclaw told Waterstrider, "If you had died, so would she. She told the elders if you woke, it would prove that Mother Ge smiled on you and her both. If you didn't, it would be Mother Ge's judgment, and Firesister too would accept death."

"No woman would do such a thing."

Bearclaw's hands twitched.

Waterstrider braced for a blow that never came.

"You don't know her." The other man's voice was low but intense, his eyes fixed on Waterstrider's. "She not only convinced Lightstone to save you, she got the Smokemothers to pray for your recovery. She arranged for food from all the clans and got me to help move you around and take care of you. She dripped pinole into your mouth, coaxed you to swallow some marrow. She even shared her own meat that she'd chewed up nice and soft, as a mother will do for her weanlings when the milk runs out. You owe her your life. That's why—"

Once again Bearclaw cut his words short. He exhaled.

Say it, Waterstrider wanted to demand, but a twisting in his guts kept him silent, a certainty that he wouldn't like whatever the other man was having trouble getting out.

"There'll have to be a recognition ceremony," Bearclaw said miserably.

"Recognition." Waterstrider didn't immediately recall what that meant. Then it came to him. "Of the life-mating? Her clan will have to formally recognize the union?" Relief dawned—he could repudiate her, argue that no one had asked him if he was willing to have her as his lifemate. But . . . could he really afford to do so?

Someone apparently wanted him dead. Under Sister Moon's cold light, Firesister had said the threat came from the Rainsinger, and she claimed to have thrown herself into danger to save him. Waterstrider owed her his life—twice over, if he believed her and Bearclaw. If he trusted them to give him the truth about what had happened. If they weren't the ones who had struck him down.

The other man shook his head. "Firesister is a daughter of the village That means all the clans concern themselves with her. And through her, you." Bearclaw hauled in a deep breath. "The elders will be here soon."

"For a recognition ceremony."

"Yes." Without asking if Waterstrider was prepared to swear his life away, Bearclaw slipped an arm under him and lifted his upper body, then slid behind and heaved upward.

Waves of agony blazed through the back of Waterstrider's head. He cried out and twisted but couldn't escape the pain. His knees buckled and he tumbled to the ground, Bearclaw cursing beside him. A flash of memory: clear sky, laughter, the crunch of gravel behind, a gang of snarling men with partly shaved heads and light-colored ribbons—the yellow of the Serpentgate temple? he couldn't tell—but priests nonetheless, boiling out of the shegoi bushes like ants from a trampled anthill.

Waterstrider swallowed blood and realized he'd bitten his tongue. The throbbing in his head receded as his heartbeat slowed. His clearing mind focused on a thought that seemed important: Firesister was telling the truth in at least one thing. It was priests who had attacked.

As though summoned by his thinking of her, she cried "Bearclaw!" in an accusing voice. Waterstrider turned his head to watch her hasty approach. "What are you doing to him?" she demanded.

Bearclaw rose. "I was just helping him up."

Firesister knelt next to Waterstrider, her brow furrowed in concern.

Waterstrider gazed into her large brown eyes. He wanted to trust her, but so had Littlecliff—with fatal consequences. He mumbled, "Don't blame Bearclaw. Stood too fast, is all."

A shadow fell over him, cast by a slim figure in the doorway, wearing an overlarge shirt nipped in by a sash—a boy, or a girl too young to have a woman's curves. Beyond, someone else, visible for only a moment before vanishing in a swirl of clothing. A skirt, perhaps. The existence of other people proved oddly reassuring to Waterstrider.

Wherever he was, whatever had been done to him, Firesister and Bearclaw hadn't been the only ones nearby. Now the village elders were coming. If he truly wished to extricate himself from Firesister's plan, this was an opportunity to do so—probably his last chance.

"Help me up," Waterstrider said. He pressed his hands against the plastered floor. His muscles shook, unable to bear the weight of his upper body, but they moved in answer to his will. His work in the dark had given him some control, if not strength.

Bearclaw squatted at Waterstrider's right side and motioned for the person in the doorway, who stepped forward obediently. A youth, Waterstrider saw, though a little older than the first impression had indicated. Hair cut raggedly and hanging loose as though in mourning, eyes hollow and red, perhaps from sleeplessness.

"Give us a hand," Bearclaw told the boy.

"I'll do it. I'm right here," Firesister protested.

"It's better for Skyblade to help." Bearclaw took Waterstrider's arm across his shoulders. The boy—whose name, Skyblade, seemed as outsized as his shirt—approached Waterstrider's other side and waited for Firesister to move away, then mimicked Bearclaw with Water-strider's left arm.

The jostling made pain hammer at Waterstrider's skull before subsiding. He stiffened his neck to carry his head high and straight.

Once upright, Waterstrider concentrated on his knees and thighs. He staggered forward a few steps with the help of the tall man and the short boy beside him, the unbalanced support making every movement more difficult. When Waterstrider's muscles gave out, Bearclaw eased him to the floor. Cold sweat beaded on his forehead. His stomach churned. *I'm doing better,* he told himself. He wondered how long ago the attack had been, for him to have become so weak. He looked at his arms and hands, withered like an old man's. Or someone who had gone without food too long.

Bearclaw had said, *"She dripped pinole into your mouth."* Pinole. Marrow. Chewed meat. Foods to sustain weanlings, not men. How long had he been lying uselessly in this room rather than starting to rebuild the canals? The urge to get outside flooded through him. Once he saw what was blooming on the bluffs and foothills, he could calculate how many days had passed since his arrival at Serpentgate.

"Let's try again," he said to Bearclaw.

Firesister bent and grabbed his right hand, the one with the tattooed wrist. He tugged free. "There's no need to hurry," she told him. "You have to listen to your body."

"My body should do what I want," he muttered.

"If wanting filled the river," she said sternly, "no one would ever go thirsty."

He hadn't heard that old saying since leaving the valley. Stifling the sense of homecoming it brought, he turned to Bearclaw and said, "Again."

Bearclaw and Skyblade drew him up. Together they wobbled to the doorway. The sunshine outside overwhelmed eyes unaccustomed to daylight. Waterstrider flinched involuntarily, and Skyblade yelped. Waterstrider supposed he'd stepped on the boy's foot or shoved him into the unyielding adobe. Bearclaw muttered under his breath. He hauled Waterstrider up straight, away from Skyblade.

Waterstrider dropped his left arm from the boy's shoulders. Bracing his knees, he wavered there. He blinked rapidly until the light no longer seemed so intense. "You all right?" he asked.

"Fine," Skyblade said.

From behind, Firesister said, "You should rest. The elders won't be here right away."

"I've rested plenty." The space ahead, bounded by crumbling shoulder-high adobe walls with a gap in the middle, would take only four strides to cross if he could move normally. This day, the expanse seemed broad as the marshes of Earth River. Flecks of mica in the weathered floor glinted in the sunbeams. "Not you, Skyblade." He warded off the youth with one hand. "Just Bearclaw."

The going was easier with only the tall man for support. Waterstrider made it outside to a deserted plaza. Bearclaw shifted him sideways and eased him down the outer wall of the roofless room they'd just passed through. Unplastered adobe caught at the deerskin tunic he wore, hiking it up along his back. Waterstrider, propped against the sun-warmed wall, felt wrinkles in the tunic but was too exhausted to complain. He leaned his head back and let his eyelids close.

He knew where he was now—on top of Cloud Mountain, the Watermasters' largest mound north of the river. All the buildings here had long ago fallen into ruin, their roofs and doors removed, plaster on walls and floors damaged by season after season of rain. That was what he'd found upon the mound when he and the men from the City of Birds had arrived. Since then, in the time he'd spent wandering in his mind, someone had built a new roof for the room he'd been in, put on a new reed door and a hide curtain to keep out the light.

He was in his rightful place. That was good. His authority came from being a Watermaster, and that was reinforced by the high vantage of the mound. From there he could observe what was going on in the river, the upper reaches of canals, and nearby fields. As soon as he was recovered, he would go out and finish inspecting the canals—*As soon as,* the discouraging voice in his head scoffed. *How long will that take?*

The southern edge of the mound would provide a good view of the Greasy Mountains. From there he could tell what was blooming, determine how far spring was advanced. But there was the little matter of moving his reluctant body such a distance. In the meantime, he would have to endure the recognition ceremony.

Firesister squatted nearby. She slipped something onto his head, gently settling it over his hair. He put up a hand and felt it, realized it was an eye shade. The size of the plaits suggested it was woven of cattail leaves. She moved lower and straightened his legs before spreading a cotton mantle over them. Then she seated herself next to him with her legs outstretched like his, her left arm alongside his right one. Their wrists, tattooed with the same design, rested together.

She had placed her mark on his body, claiming him with it.

His gaze shifted to her face. Had she truly believed that was the only way to save his life? Or had some word, some glance, some touch passed between them that made her imagine he would be willing to promise himself to her, and only her, until he breathed his last?

She turned her head and met his eyes.

He looked away first. "What happened to Littlecliff's body?" he asked.

She shrugged. "I didn't know what would be most respectful. Bearclaw and some others wrapped him in a shroud and sang him off. He's buried near where he fell, the grave covered over with river cobbles so he can be dug up and burned, or reburied at his home, if that's what his people do."

As she spoke, Waterstrider's chest tightened with mingled grief and guilt.

Littlecliff had followed him here. If not for their friendship, Littlecliff would still be alive. If not for his own pride, Waterstrider could have ignored the request to return and get the canals running again. He drew in a shuddering breath.

If not for Firesister, Littlecliff wouldn't have been alone; he could have escaped with the other men from the City of Birds. Anger sparked, driving back sorrow.

She asked, "Will you confirm to the elders that we've been blood-bound?"

"Lie, you mean?" For that's what it would be, clear and plain. Although he owed Firesister a great debt for keeping him alive, this life-mating struck too close to his honor.

He had never made promises to a woman. Not even Brightheart, Littlecliff's sister—and he'd been with her for nearly twenty turnings, giving her children, some of whom now had babies of their own. He'd been loyal to Brightheart, if not always faithful. But even with her, he'd never sworn his devotion, never promised to stay with her forever.

He'd vowed that he would never raise expectations that he, as his father's son, would inevitably disappoint. Yet here he was.

Waterstrider knew what he had gained: he remained alive. What did Firesister stand to gain? "Bearclaw said you linked your life with mine to save me. If Mother Ge saw fit to keep me alive, that was a sign that she smiled on us both. Is that the only reason you want to be my lifemate?"

"Are you asking because you fear I'll cling to you? I won't. Having you live was important. Having your life entwined with mine? No." Though her lips curved upward, her eyes seemed shadowed. "I'll go my own way, once you're better."

"How will you do that? Do the elders no longer believe you're a witch?"

Firesister shrugged. "Some may. But they'll keep it to themselves. Mother Ge, in saving you, has restored my reputation too. The Rainsinger is no match for her."

"The Ta'atchul he serves may be. The Ta'atchul may seem more powerful than Mother Ge if the rains are ample this summer and the canals remain dry."

"That won't happen." Her voice was quiet but certain. "Mother Ge saved you for a purpose. First she sent you to us and then she restored you to life."

Waterstrider looked at his legs, stretched out before him. The goddess could have preserved his bodily strength while she was at it. "I don't know when I'll be up and walking, let alone able to work on the canals. You made me dependent on Mother Ge's favor," he continued, "but that goes both ways. If I fail, it may be seen as her failure too."

She shook her head. "I know you can fix the canals." Her gaze sharpened. She reached out and grasped his forearm. "Mother Ge has spoken."

Her heartfelt words made him half believe she could be right.

The elders of the clans began to stream into the eastern plaza, where they seated themselves in an arc facing Firesister and Waterstrider. To their right were blocks outlining the large map-ground where all the canals and clanlands of the Northwind canal system had once been etched deep into the plaza floor. Waterstrider found it interesting that this ceremony was occurring in the same place where the Watermasters had once held hearings to ensure that irrigation water was distributed fairly.

Smiling brightly, Firesister called each new arrival by clan title—Gran Cloudleaf, Uncle Littleseed, one after another.

Waterstrider studied the faces of the old men and women who made decisions for each clan. Firesister asked about sick relatives, new grandbabies, word of kinfolk gone traveling. For Waterstrider, the elders sitting out there, wrinkled and gray-haired, were strangers. Even the clan names didn't map onto fields in his memory, much less the canals that ran between and watered them—or used to. He no longer had a sense of how the clanlands were laid out.

Firesister had saved Waterstrider's life for the sake of what only he could do: get the canals running again, after the farmfolk had failed to do so. Was the life-mating the only way to keep him alive, as she claimed? Perhaps not. But she understood these people, and he didn't. And yet a few days ago they had been willing to give her to the Rainsinger.

Waterstrider shook his head. He had the feeling that he was drifting along the edge of some unseen force, or maybe had already been caught by it, like a current in deep water that could drown an unwary man. There was more going on under the surface than he could perceive.

Bearclaw came into view beside a hard-faced older man. Behind them, Gran Squashblossom hobbled into the plaza, supported by Deeproot. Instead of joining the other clan elders, she stopped beside Waterstrider and turned to face the seated observers. When Waterstrider was a boy, she'd seemed ancient, this grandmother of his friend Tagalong—Tallcorn, he reminded himself. Now, more than twenty turnings later, she still looked the same as he remembered her.

She leaned on her staff and studied the faces in front of her. "Before me I see the elders of all the clans, and it gladdens my heart. Welcome. Thank you for stirring your old bones. For some of you, coming to Cloud Mountain must have felt as long as the Great Salt Journey of your youth. I know it did me." Her rueful admission prompted smiles and a few chuckles.

"Why turn out the whole village?" someone asked. "The recognition ceremony doesn't take more than a handful of witnesses."

Firesister stirred next to Waterstrider.

"There's more at stake than the lives of these two people," Gran Squashblossom answered. "That's what we have come together to discuss."

"I thought we were to make sure Firesister told the truth about this life-mating with the Watermaster," a man said sourly.

The doubter offered an opening for Waterstrider to escape. Again those undercurrents tugged at him. His gaze drifted across the watchful faces, tight with concerns he couldn't understand. Heart sinking, he realized he had to choose a side right now, without knowing what the sides stood for. With the men from the City of Birds gone, Waterstrider's only ally might be his old friend Tallcorn—which meant Squashblossom Clan. And Firesister.

"Thinking so," a woman said in response to the sour-voiced comment, "why did you bother to come?"

Gran Squashblossom pointed at Waterstrider and Firesister. "You can see with your own eyes that these two are blood-bound. Firesister claimed kin-right for this Watermaster. That makes him your clan-son, and mine."

"Son to the healers and hunters as well," said the hard-faced man seated next to Bearclaw. Stiff red-brown feathers twined in his hair marked him as one of the Hawk-Meeters, who determined when, where, and what to hunt. "He can come to us for food, shelter, even work parties. All that in the old days would have been given to the Watermasters freely, without grudging."

After a moment Gran Squashblossom said, "Work parties, yes. Which brings us to the matter at hand: what shall we do for water this summer, with the Watermaster injured and his men driven off?"

The other elders watched her expectantly.

She went on, "As the eldest here, I shall speak first. I remember the old ways, before the coming of the Stormbringers, before they set up the Ta'atchul as the givers of rain. I remember the Long Thirst, though I was only a child during those hard days. What I know, what we all know, is that Mother Ge, not the Ta'atchul, created this world. Mother Ge made Buzzard, who carved out the first canals with obsidian-tipped wings. Mother Ge made Wind, who sweeps the clouds across the sky and brings the rain. And Mother Ge gave this truth to the Ancestors, whose bones rest in her house under the ground and whose spirits inhabit the sky. Soon enough I will walk with the Ancestors myself, and then you are the ones who will have to remember."

A resonant voice echoed from the edge of the plaza: "Looking back to the past serves no purpose."

The newcomer strode toward Gran Squashblossom. The ribbon-bound topknot, shaved hair on each side above the ears, and facial tattoos told Waterstrider this was a priest. The yellow robes marked him as a servant of the Temple of Lightning.

Firesister murmured, "It's the Rainsinger."

Waterstrider studied this man who, according to her, wanted him dead. The priest's jerky, birdlike way of moving, puffed-out chest, and thin limbs indeed resembled the boy Waterstrider had known as Cloudface. The boy who had stayed behind when the rest of the Watermasters left. He'd planned great things for himself. Evidently no one had stood in his way.

The Rainsinger asked the elders, "What use is remembering, when the future is upon us?"

Beside Bearclaw, the Hawk-Meeter spoke up again. "Yes, someone whose ceremony went awry during the River-Binding might understandably wish to encourage forgetfulness."

The Rainsinger glared at him.

"And what of the Watermaster being struck down and left for dead?" the hard-faced hunter continued. "Is that something else you want forgotten?"

"Do you accuse the Stormbringers," the Rainsinger said, quick as a snake, "of striking down the Watermaster and driving off his men?"

The elders looked shocked. They glanced at their neighbors, then gazed at Waterstrider expectantly. "Ask him who it was," Bearclaw called out.

Firesister rose and said, "He doesn't know. They came from behind, so he doesn't know!"

"Is that true?" Gran Squashblossom asked Waterstrider.

Waterstrider could declare that priests had attacked him and his men. But Firesister didn't want him to do that. Neither, he guessed from Gran Squashblossom's tense face, did the old woman. Without knowing which temple those priests belonged to, he could accuse the wrong ones, and that would open him to a charge of lying. "Firesister is right. I didn't see who attacked us." He stared at the Rainsinger. "They came from behind, proving themselves cowards."

Unfazed, the Rainsinger smiled. "No more than the outlanders who ran away, leaving you behind. And the Watermasters who deserted the farmfolk all those turnings ago." He addressed the elders. "Remember the prophecy about flood and drought and the drying up of the canals: 'When Serpent gnaws the bones of the earth and Buzzard pierces the sky, when all the green ribbons have dwindled to dust, the rainbow knife will fly.' The Watermasters fled in fear of that knife. But we Stormbringers, who had put an end to the Long Thirst and made sure such a drought never again afflicted the valley, we stayed. We have shown that you no longer need the canals. Now this Watermaster has come back . . . to do what? Make you depend on him? Give him power over you once again—to say 'This field can have water, but only so much'?"

Gran Squashblossom asked, "Instead we should depend on you and your Ta'atchul, little godlets who are so jealous and petty that they would withhold rain from people who still look to Mother Ge?"

The Rainsinger shook his head, face sorrowful. "This elder who would take you back to the past, her grandson is a special friend of this returned Watermaster. Of course she sees the Watermaster as a boy she was once fond of, rather than a betrayer who ran away with his own kind. Now he lies here crippled and useless, living off your generosity until he leaves again. Is this where you should place your trust?"

Waterstrider looked up at Firesister. "Help me stand," he ordered.

"I don't—"

He lifted his arm and grasped her by the wrist. "Do it!"

Firesister stooped and tucked herself against his chest. She pulled his arm across her back and held it as she strained to help him rise. Waterstrider managed to bend his knees and get his feet flat on the ground, but he didn't have strength enough to push himself up. Someone slipped in on his left side, supporting him there as Firesister was doing on his right. It was Skyblade, scrawny yet adding enough force for Waterstrider to stand, knees locked, braced between a woman and a boy.

Once he felt stable, Waterstrider told the elders, "I returned because

I was asked. To repair the canals. I don't care what you do with them after that. Who gets water?" His eyes drifted to the nearby map-ground. "That's up to all of you. I have no thirst for power." As he said these last words, he stared at the Rainsinger.

"Will you believe him?" the Rainsinger asked the seated elders. "And risk offending the Ta'atchul by doubting that they will be generous with rain?"

No answer came. Most of the listeners glanced from one to another with anxious and troubled expressions.

"Once before," Waterstrider said fiercely, "the People of Two Rivers allowed the rain priests to divide them. It wasn't fear that sent the Watermasters away, it was the struggle between those who believed in Mother Ge and those who believed the promises of the priests. Now you find yourself facing the same choice. I'm not asking you to trust me. I'm asking you to trust Mother Ge. It is said that she saved me from death. If so, she must have her reasons. I'll turn the Rainsinger's question around: will you risk offending Mother Ge, the one who made us, who gave us this land and the crops to grow on it, and taught us how to build the canals to water them? Rain has fallen since the First Days, a hundred generations before the priests arrived. The canals, though, those are ours entirely. What would the People of Two Rivers be without them?"

A man half hidden behind Bearclaw spoke: "Are you promising that the canals can be restored to what they once were, all the way out to Lastwater?"

"Why bother asking for a promise?" someone else said, in a creaky elderly voice that could belong to man or woman. "After all, we've seen what the priests' promises are worth. Too much rain in the winter when we don't need it, too little in the summer."

The Rainsinger growled, "Rain comes to the faithful."

"Your Ta'atchul blame us for going thirsty and hungry," the creaky voice shot back. "They are too cruel, these Ta'atchul of yours. And you as well."

An old man at the back asked, "Why should we believe the Ta'atchul punish only those who lack faith? Uncle Littleseed is loud about his belief in the Ta'atchul, but last season his fields were dry as a bone."

Someone else pointed out, "Those are not his fields, for he no longer has strength enough to work them. His use-right has gone to younger folk who openly doubt the Ta'atchul. Uncle Littleseed may believe, but he permits them to speak their sacrilege."

"Is speaking against the Ta'atchul no longer allowed?" asked Gran Squashblossom.

There was little discussion after that. Waterstrider wondered whether that meant the answer to her question was yes. The Rainsinger took himself off in a swirl of robes. The rest of the clanfolk rose a few at a time and filed out through the passageway. Waiting for everyone to leave was agonizing, but Waterstrider refused to allow his burning thigh muscles to collapse.

"Sit down," Firesister whispered, her shoulders shaking under his arm.

"Not yet." Waterstrider tried to brace against the wall to relieve the strain on her and Skyblade. His vision started to blur at the edges, and the brilliance of the day began to fade. He knew he couldn't last much longer. Another breath, and another and another, counting them, while his legs shook from exhaustion.

At the count of fifty-four, Firesister said, "They've gone."

He collapsed and found himself tangled together with her and Skyblade. She shoved him off while the boy slithered from under him. Waterstrider was left crumpled half on his side, staring into Firesister's eyes. She scooted away and sat upright.

"Don't go," Waterstrider said. "I only need to rest a little. Then . . ." Then what? Let himself be dragged back to that small, dark room to be alone with his thoughts? No. He wanted to get to the edge of Cloud Mountain, see what was blooming in the mountain foothills, figure out how much time he'd lost to his injury.

Firesister chewed on her lip, then crawled forward and helped him sit up against the wall. He half expected her to leave then, but she stayed near, squatting on her haunches with her hands on her knees.

"It was good," she said, "that you didn't deny the blood-binding."

"Did I have a choice?"

She stared into the distance so long without responding that he wondered if she'd heard him. Finally she said, "Believe me or not, as you wish, but I saw no other way. You couldn't be allowed to die."

"Surely if Mother Ge wanted me to live, she would have made it so, with or without you. If the canals are so important, wouldn't the elders have seen to my survival?"

Firesister cast him a sidelong glance. "You saw how few dared speak against the Rainsinger."

"You stood up to him."

"And he retaliated. Why do you suppose I'm the one he accused of being a witch?"

"Surely the elders have more—"

"More to lose." Her mouth tightened. "I've never been willing to do as he wants. And I warn others they're fools for trusting him. He can't bear to be contradicted."

Waterstrider had known people like that, for whom simple opposition was enough to make them into vicious enemies. It was easy to believe Cloudface had grown up into such a one.

Although both Waterstrider and Cloudface were born to Watermaster fathers, they couldn't have been more different. While most of the Watermasters had served the People of Two Rivers with dignity and graciousness, others only took what they could get for themselves. It was obvious from the start which group Cloudface belonged to. That was why the young Cloudface had stayed behind when the other Watermasters went into exile: the priests had power, the Watermasters didn't. It must have been a simple choice for an ambitious boy who got his way through lying, cheating, bullying. But was Waterstrider himself much better? Thinking about the lies he'd just uttered, or at least supported, he shook his head.

"I know the Rainsinger well," Firesister said, apparently taking the gesture as disagreement.

"As a boy, he was the same way. What you say about him makes sense."

Her brows drew together. "Do you think that's why he came after you —not simply because you're a Watermaster but because of the past?"

"It was a boyhood rivalry. Not enough to make me a target for Cloudface, or whatever his man's-name is now." There had been footraces, which Waterstrider had won. Duties as ditchrunners, for which Waterstrider had earned more praise. Then came that day when Brother Sun went dark and Waterstrider left his friends behind with Cloudface at the red rocks of Mother Sleeping. Was that the first time Cloudface had beaten him?

Firesister said, "It's Eaglefeather. That's his man's-name. No one uses it anymore, now that he's become the Rainsinger. It irritates him."

"But you use it instead of 'Rainsinger' whenever you can?" he guessed.

She grinned. The expression brightened her face as if the sun came out from behind a cloud. Struck by the change, Waterstrider stared at her.

"Exactly so." Her eyes glinted with mischief. She shifted and sat next to him with her legs tucked to one side. "Why did you shake your head before, when I was telling you about Eaglefeather?"

The hint of emphasis she gave to the last word made Waterstrider chuckle. Then he sobered. "I was only thinking that with all the lies I agreed to today, I'm not so different from him."

"That isn't true! What was a lie?"

"That we're blood-bound, for one."

"You never had to say it outright. Gran Squashblossom made sure of that."

Waterstrider lifted his wrist and twisted his forearm to show the tattoo, front and back. "You don't call this a lie?"

Firesister's eyebrows drew together. "Is your pride so wounded?"

"It's not my pride, it's my honor." Her face paled, then reddened, as if he'd struck her. He went on, trying to explain. "A promise you can't keep is the same as a lie."

"I won't have any other man as my mate until the day I die. That's the truth, on my side. All it means is that in gratitude to Mother Ge you don't take another woman as your mate here. Will you have so much difficulty keeping this promise while you're in the valley?"

He thought of Brightheart, the many turnings together with no profession of faithfulness or forever from either of them. The many times she had pushed for just such a promise from him.

"Do you have a lifemate back in the City of Birds?" Firesister asked.

He hesitated, then admitted, "There's someone."

She nodded. "I didn't think you intended to stay. I figured you would fix the canals and leave. Isn't that your plan?"

Waterstrider wasn't sure anymore. He'd thought about staying, for the valley had stirred something deep inside, like slaking a long thirst, as he'd looked around at the jagged mountain ranges, gazed up at the sunrises and sunsets painted in the sky, drank in the sounds and smells and heat of his homeland. All those feelings had changed with Littlecliff's death.

That tragedy had twisted everything. Lying in the dark room, he'd considered leaving as soon as he was well enough. But abandoning Serpentgate without repairing the canals would do nothing to honor his friend. It would only strengthen the influence of the priests who had killed Littlecliff—and mark Waterstrider as a coward besides.

Firesister drew her fingers along the tattoo on his wrist. "This only binds you while you're here. You can go back to your woman in the City of Birds with a whole heart and your honor intact."

Her face gave no clue of how she felt about that. Or about this life-mating, which bound her too. Was she eager for him to leave the valley and set her free? Perhaps, he thought. But not until water once more flowed to the fields and the clans were no longer at the mercy of the Ta'atchul and their priests. He studied her, wondering what she was thinking, until her gaze dropped.

With her pointer finger, Firesister began to draw lines in the dirt. "The clans can't see past their own fields," she said. "I was young when the Watermasters left the valley, but I remember how bad things got those first few turnings after. There were floods, big ones. Some places downcanal never recovered."

"We heard. A few clans sent word, hoping we would come back."

"Why didn't you?" She speared him with an intent stare.

"The decision was already made: the Watermasters would stay in the City of Birds." Catching a flash in her eyes, he said, "We're valued there."

"You're needed more here. They've had you for twenty-four turnings."

Waterstrider shrugged. "It's home now."

"Would she come for you if you did stay, this 'someone' who waits for you?"

Thinking of the grandchildren that Brightheart doted on, Waterstrider shook his head. "I wouldn't expect her to."

Firesister continued to scrutinize him. "If we weren't life-mated, would you stay?"

"I'm not exactly welcome here. You warned me off that first night, if you remember, and then Littlecliff—" The words got stuck in his throat.

"That was the priests, not the farmfolk. The clans want you here."

Waterstrider doubted whether that was true. Some of the farmfolk wanted the canals rebuilt, Squashblossom Clan among them. How many others would prefer to cast their lot with the Ta'atchul? Littleseed Clan, perhaps, and who else? Waterstrider eyed the stubborn set of Firesister's jaw and decided not to argue about which of the clans would take his side.

Instead he asked, "If the Rainsinger wanted me dead, why didn't he make sure of it while I was still helpless?"

"He got what he needed."

"What's that?"

"Time. You won't be able to restore the canals before the growing season. He's a patient man. He plans, and he waits. There's no reason for him to come after you now, because he has all summer to bring rain to the fields. If it falls just right, many people will accept that the priests are more important than the canals. Even Gran Squashblossom and other doubters might be forced to support him then. At least not say anything against him."

Her voice made clear that she didn't expect the rain would fall as the Rainsinger wanted. Waterstrider looked at Firesister, a little ashamed that her faith in his ability to fix the canals seemed greater than his own. Though it wasn't really him she believed in.

He thought about the stories of the First Days, when the River Serpents fought one another, breaking the bones of Mother Ge with their thrashing about, creating the buttes and ridges that filled the once-level valley. When at last they quieted, the water that had previously blanketed the valley floor could be found only in the river channels. So Mother Ge had sent Buzzard to carve out the canals with his sharp-tipped wings, and then she taught some among the people how to fill the canals with river water. From that day forward, through the generations, the People of Two Rivers were famous for their canals, green ribbons in the desert. It was his people, the heronfolk, whom everyone else called the Watermasters, who had managed the canals. Until twenty-four turnings ago, when the heronfolk marched southward. All but Cloudface.

"In the City of Birds," Waterstrider told her, wanting to see how she would react, "they don't know Mother Ge."

Firesister's eyes went wide. "How can they not know the Mother-of-All-Creation?"

"They have many goddesses, and gods too. Like a family of brothers and sisters. A goddess who brings children to women. A god of rain."

"Like the Ta'atchul?"

"Perhaps. Some say the first Stormbringers came from even farther south than the City of Birds. Maybe they brought the rain god with them.'

"What is the City of Birds like, if they don't know Mother Ge there?"

Too many people, not enough land for farming, he thought. But canals that worked. "There's a river nearby, and water flows past the people's houses. There's even a well you can walk down into." He wondered what else he should say. She seemed interested. "They have odd-shaped doorways, like an ax, narrow at the bottom and with a top part that's wider, letting the room breathe. There are pens where they raise turkeys and macaws, using the bright-colored feathers to make things for trade." He thought maybe he should miss the City of Birds, now that he was talking about it. But he didn't. Nor did he miss Brightheart.

"What about their pottery?"

"They have a lot of it."

"No, I mean, what does it look like?" Her eyes glowed with an intensity he hadn't seen in her before. "What designs do their potters use?" she asked without giving him time to answer. "Do they have special wood to fire the pottery with? Do they really have plazas in the city where only potters live, as the Far-Traders say?"

"I don't know. I never paid much attention."

"Ah." With that, her inner glow dimmed. She shifted her legs as though preparing to leave.

Waterstrider found himself oddly unwilling to let her go. "Where were the Smokemothers?" he asked. "I would have expected them to take part in a recognition ceremony. If the Rainsinger was invited—"

"He wasn't."

"If he wasn't but came anyway, that makes the Smokemothers' absence all the more curious. I should think they had a hand in my recovery, since Mother Ge saved my life. Yet not one of the priestesses could be bothered to attend this important ceremony."

Firesister's lips compressed. She stared off into the distance for a time before answering. When she did, her voice sounded rough. "The Smokemothers are angry with me right now. It's spilled over onto you."

"Should I ask why?"

"It's . . ." She sighed. "It's not a simple matter to explain."

"Try."

"I accused them of abandoning Mother Ge. It was unfair," she added. "But I was upset. To me, it seems the Smokemothers have lost their way. And they can't see it!" Her voice rose. "They willfully ignore the signs Mother Ge has sent—just as they did long ago, when they allowed the Watermasters to be split off from the farmfolk."

"Signs, you say." Waterstrider's attention sharpened. "What signs?"

Her face twisted. "The latest was the shadowdancer, felled by venom during the Binding of the Serpent. Before that, flood, illness, unseasonable storms, animals retreating to the mountains. The world is going all wrong." Firesister shook her head. "And they simply accept it! Over and over, they bend to the Rainsinger's whims."

Waterstrider thought such occurrences might befall anyplace in this desert valley—and had many times since the First Days. There was no need to attribute them to a vengeful goddess. More likely, Firesister had a personal reason for being upset. "Do you blame the Smokemothers for believing the Rainsinger's accusation of you?"

Her teeth snapped together as her expression darkened. "No."

"What, then? What is it that makes you believe so strongly in Mother Ge but not her priestesses?"

She squirmed under his questions. Shaking her head, Firesister stood. She dusted off her backside. "That's a long and tedious story for another time. You look tired. Let me call Skyblade to help you back in . . ."

"Leave me. The sun feels good. I've spent enough time inside." Waterstrider managed to hold up his head until she had limped out of sight. Then he allowed the exhaustion creeping over him to win. Using his right arm to slow his collapse, he sagged onto the ground and stretched out as best he could. Cottonwood fluff puffed out around him.

Carried on the breeze, it had mounded up patchily along the base of walls around the plaza.

He gazed at the white drifts. When did the cottonwood trees let their seeds fly? He dredged up the names of the spring moons as the People of Two Rivers knew them: Mist first, then Leafing-Out, then Tree Flowers. Vaguely he recalled that cottonwood fluff started to drift when the greenthorn trees were ablaze with yellow during Tree Flower Moon. He'd arrived at Serpentgate soon after the River-Binding sun-festival. The moon was full, halfway through Sister Moon's cycle. That must have been Leafing-Out Moon, for the cottonwoods along the river had been green, their canopy already generous with shade.

If he could stand, if he walked to the half wall that edged the mound, if he looked southward toward the Greasy Mountains across the river, would he see the lower washes dressed in yellow? How much time had slipped away: half a moon? an entire moon? more? He should have asked Firesister.

The previous winter, when Tallcorn's message had found him, Waterstrider had planned to set off immediately for the Valley of Two Rivers. It was Littlecliff who'd asked pointedly who would actually do the work. Waterstrider replied that the farmers would take care of rebuilding.

"The same who let the canals fall into ruin?" Littlecliff asked.

"If I don't go back now," Waterstrider replied, "the farmers will be busy planting and tending their crops. They won't have time to work on the canals. That was always done during the winter moons." At the fastest pace he could take with supplies and tools, he'd calculated that he couldn't get to the Valley of Two Rivers before Mist Moon.

"So you take your own work party," Littlecliff suggested. "There are men without fields of their own to cultivate. Men with strong backs and an eagerness to learn from the best Watermaster the City of Birds has to offer."

Waterstrider had laughed at the flattery, but Littlecliff's reasoning was sound. Together they had sought out men willing to journey far to the north to rebuild the famed canals of the People of Two Rivers.

Now, restored to his proper place on the Watermasters' great mound, with cottonwood fluff tickling his nose, Waterstrider found himself unable to even lift his head out of the feathery drift, let alone finish the inspection of the canals, and those willing men who would have helped him were far away, maybe already back in the City of Birds.

The muscles in his legs shook from overuse, and his arms felt boneless. *What did you do to yourself?* Littlecliff would have asked, forehead rumpled with concern. What could Waterstrider reply: *I stood up?* Once that would have gotten a laugh. But there would be no more laughter from Littlecliff, never again.

A lump lodged in Waterstrider's throat. "Mother Ge, if you're out there, tell me why you've done this. You're killing your people."

Perhaps that was her intention. Who could know, with gods? Perhaps the time of canals was over. Perhaps Mother Ge had sent flood after flood purposely to cut the rivers ever deeper into their beds, leaving the canal heads stranded. Sent floodwaters so strong they overtopped the high canal banks, tearing through to the fields alongside and stripping off the rich soil, only to dump it on the upper floodplain, out of reach of the fields. Perhaps the Ta'atchul were a manifestation of Mother Ge's will and the canals would forever be dry, blowing with dust.

Waterstrider rolled onto his back. On the wall nearby he spotted a small handprint in the plaster, indentations of fingers and a palm barely visible from shadows cast by the high sun. The hand could have been his own, he thought. Plastering was one of the tasks done by the children of the heronfolk, Waterstrider among them.

He'd been proud when he was deemed strong enough, at ten or twelve winters, to dig caliche and haul the heavy clay to mixing-pads, where it was combined with cactus juice and grass stalks and applied to the walls. Digging and hauling tired him down to his bones. Every night, he crawled onto his sleep mat and fell asleep almost before his head came to rest.

He would have scoffed, back then, at the notion that simply standing up during an argument would exhaust him utterly.

Waterstrider realized he must have fallen asleep when he woke to the cool, light touch of a hand on his forehead. A girlish voice sang words he recognized, after a moment, as an old lament: "Where water once ran, the heronfolk man finds but silt and sand. Try as he may, he's been led astray. When new day is done still no water will run."

He blinked to clear his vision and found a pretty young woman leaning over him. Upon seeing that he was awake, she pulled back, startled like a deer: head flung up, brown eyes wide, nostrils flaring. The scarf that had been wrapped around her hair, leaving only her face exposed, slithered down to her shoulders.

"Don't be afraid. I won't hurt you," Waterstrider said.

She scrambled away, watching him fearfully from dark eyes rimmed with white. She vanished in a swirl of skirt and scarf.

Waterstrider couldn't push himself up to track her going, but he supposed it didn't matter. His companions on Cloud Mountain apparently consisted of a girl either painfully shy or touched in the head, a boy more skin than muscle, a witch who'd offended both priests and priestesses, and a jealous hunter who would as soon Waterstrider had never awoken.

Waterstrider heard Littlecliff taunting him good-naturedly: *"Feeling sorry for yourself, are you?"* His big, gentle friend had directed those words to him often enough when they were young. Not so much once Waterstrider had become accustomed to the City of Birds and stopped feeling homesick.

"Leave me alone," he muttered. "It's humiliating enough—"

"What are you talking about?" said a flesh and blood person, neither memory nor Littlecliff's wandering spirit.

He looked up and saw Tallcorn approaching. Waterstrider tried to get his hands under him to press himself up to a sitting position.

Tallcorn came and helped him, then lowered himself to the ground nearby. "I hear tell the Rainsinger has been throwing out threats again. Why do people listen to him?" It wasn't a question needing an answer.

"You might have told me Cloudface became the Rainsinger," Waterstrider said.

"Didn't I? I'm sure I had done."

"I think I would have remembered."

Tallcorn let a few breaths slip by, then asked, "Do you remember how many times I've been to see you since the attack?"

Waterstrider considered the matter carefully, turning it over in his head. Some memories had come back to him. Others probably hadn't. He confessed, "I don't recall seeing you at all."

Tallcorn's mouth twisted. "That's right. I wasn't allowed. Firesister kept everyone away except the healers. It's like she believes she really is your lifemate."

Caught by an odd note in Tallcorn's voice, Waterstrider studied his old friend, trying to identify the emotion he heard. Jealousy? Suspicion? "Let's not talk about Firesister," he said. "I'm grateful to her for saving my life. And continuing to help until I'm strong enough to take care of myself."

"Come stay with me," Tallcorn urged. "You'll be safer under Squashblossom Clan's protection than up here on Cloud Mountain."

Waterstrider shook his head. "This is my place. It belongs to the Watermasters, and I am a Watermaster. Why should I hide like a coward?"

"Because Cloudface is the Rainsinger. He hates you."

"He knows nothing about me, not since we were boys," Waterstrider said. "I did nothing bad enough to make him an enemy for life."

"That race. In his mind, you stole it from him, stole his rightful winnings, too, and embarrassed him."

"Which race?"

"That one where he put the cords across the path to trip you up."

Memories flooded back of that race—of the desperate desire he'd felt to beat Cloudface, who had always been willing to cheat to get his way. "It wasn't intended for me," Waterstrider pointed out. "It was whoever came around the first turn ahead of him."

Tallcorn waved that off. "Everyone knew it would be you. And then he tossed dust in your eyes. And still you beat him by a full pace!"

Waterstrider pulled himself out of the boyhood moment, returning to the plaza and his man's body, injured and infirm as it was. "He's risen high in the world. Why would he still feel bruised from a defeat so long ago?"

"He has a long memory." Tallcorn's eyes glittered. "Remember, you used to say before a race, 'Stay ahead, don't get caught in the pack'? We would answer, 'The hard thing will be keeping up with you.' And Cloudface would wrinkle his mouth like he'd bitten into a hackberry."

"You remember all that?"

"Of course. That day, he came so close, he must've been sure he would win. Now, after all this time, you've returned and will again prove who has the heart for victory. To see his face when you trounce him once more!"

"There's no competition between us. This isn't a race. This is life. Survival."

"All the more important to defeat him."

Waterstrider shrugged. "I came back to repair the canals. Nothing to do with the Rainsinger." But that wasn't true, was it? The priesthood could lose everything if people decided they no longer needed the Ta'atchul.

"He wants his vengeance. I can understand that you would want your own, on him—for killing your friend, if nothing else."

"The Rainsinger might have been behind that, or he might not. I have no proof either way." Just an imprecise memory, lacking crucial details, of priests attacking.

Tallcorn seemed disappointed. "Still, he's coming after you. You shouldn't be alone up here by yourself."

"Hardly alone!" Waterstrider laughed.

"You're practically pushing the Rainsinger to act, since you're living with his enemies." Tallcorn's eyes flashed with suppressed excitement, as if he knew some secret and was waiting to be asked about it.

Enemies. More than one. "You mean Firesister?"

"Not just her. That boy up here—"

"Skyblade."

Tallcorn went on as though Waterstrider had said nothing. "He was a Seeker. His departure from the temple, a handful of moons into his service, was another humiliation for the Rainsinger—and the Smokemothers, too, for he stole the girl they'd gotten into the temple as a seer."

Waterstrider absorbed the information. He had trouble picturing that scrawny youth doing anything so bold. The pretty girl with moon-mad eyes, though—easy to imagine her as a seer.

"Don't let them make you a target along with them," Tallcorn urged. "Come to Squashblossom Clan. Let us take care of you, and help you with the canals too."

Waterstrider said nothing.

"You still think Firesister saved your life?" Tallcorn pushed his face closer, his breath puffing against Waterstrider's cheek. "It was Gran Squashblossom who did that. Firesister has no tie to the clanlands. She doesn't understand how important it is to get the canals running. I don't know why she sank her claws into you, claiming you agreed to be her lifemate—when the world knows you vowed long ago to take no woman as your own—but she's not one of us. She's Near-Kin."

Frowning, Tallcorn straightened, pulling back from Waterstrider and eyeing him carefully. "In fact," he added, "I wouldn't be surprised to find out she's actually a witch, as accused."

Waterstrider's hands closed into fists. He found himself disappointed by Tallcorn's willingness to gossip about Firesister. Though every bit of what his old friend was saying might be true, it seemed mean-spirited.

"After the swallowing of the sun," Tallcorn went on, "there was illness in the Near-Kin enclave. It killed her parents. The rest of the Near-Kin left, but she stayed behind. Why? No one knows." His face twisted with an undefinable emotion. He went on, "Some say she was biding her time, waiting to avenge her parents' deaths. Then, when the people of Lastwater died in the same manner as the Near-Kin—" He broke off and spread his hands with a shrug. "What else is a reasonable man to think?"

Waterstrider, who considered himself a reasonable man, thought otherwise. Firesister clearly did understand the importance of the canals. What's more, she'd proved herself fiercely loyal to the farmfolk—

and to Mother Ge. She might have been born an outsider, but now she was as securely one of the People of Two Rivers as Tallcorn.

Pinning his old friend with a cool stare, Waterstrider said, "She's called a daughter of the village. That seems like ties. She's been feeding me corn, beans, squash soup, and the like, which must have come from the clans."

"From Squashblossom Clan," Tallcorn corrected. "Firesister has always lived off what she could scrounge in the desert. Enough for one person. Not for two."

"Cloud Mountain is my place. I won't turn tail and run."

Tallcorn's gaze held Waterstrider's without wavering. Muscles worked in his jaw, and his nostrils flared. At last he said, "If you insist on staying atop the mound, consider this. There may be a way to appease the Rainsinger." Tallcorn leaned closer. "Wouldn't it be better to have him ignore you than come after you again—at least until you're whole and strong?"

"What are you suggesting?"

"He wants Firesister, the boy, and the girl too. Give them to him."

Waterstrider forced a derisive laugh. "Don't be ridiculous."

"I can understand why you would feel obliged to be grateful to Firesister. But ask yourself why she saved you. In claiming you—a stranger—as her mate, she escaped punishment . . . using you. You deserve some revenge for the wrong she did you. Send her to the Rainsinger as a gift, along with the two others she's dragged into your life."

Ill-concealed eagerness in Tallcorn's eyes sent chills down Waterstrider's spine. Who had his old friend become, to consider giving anyone to an enemy, especially to someone as powerful as the high priest?

And why did Firesister stir up such hostility? Maybe, Waterstrider thought, considering her reserved manner, because a man could never know what she was thinking. But how did that make her different from any other female? Waterstrider admired women, occasionally lusted after them, frequently enjoyed their company, but never claimed to understand them. Their underlying feelings caused them to be unpredictable—like his mother, so frantic to escape the disappointments of the world that she drowned herself. Like Brightheart, declaring her love for him before she even became a woman, insisting that she would be content to be part of his life even if he didn't love her back, then moping around when he didn't.

Men were different. You could declare flat-out that a man was wrong, that he was being stupid. It might start a fight, but after a few punches landed you could thump each other on the shoulder and part—if not friends, at least with a sense of having settled your differences. That was what Waterstrider had always thought.

Did the Rainsinger see things otherwise? Could he have sent Firesister to kill Waterstrider because of a footrace all those turnings ago? Did a boy's hurt pride really explain the priests' attack on Waterstrider and the men of the City of Birds?

Waterstrider scratched the back of his head, where an itchy patch of hair was regrowing around his new scar. Again he sensed undercurrents dragging at him, things happening out of sight and for unknown reasons.

"You can't want her," Tallcorn said, breaking into Waterstrider's thoughts. "Not a cripple like Firesister. Don't let pity keep you from being sensible. She has no one, that's why she clutches at you. All her Near-Kin family went back to the Mountains of Sunrise when she was a child. They left her behind, unwanted. Just as the Watermasters did with Cloudface."

"Cloudface chose to stay." Waterstrider lowered his hand. "Maybe she did too."

"Cloudface had ambitions. Firesister has none. There was nothing for her here, and she was all alone—an sad little orphan, with only the Children's House to go to. Why would she have made such a choice?"

Waterstrider thought about the lightness that had come over him and the warmth in his heart when the familiar red rocks of Mother Sleeping and The Spine appeared, when he spotted the sunset-colored spring flowers covering the foothills and bajadas. He hadn't known, when he'd walked southward with the rest of the heronfolk, that he wouldn't see the mountains of home for twenty-four turnings. Maybe she was wiser than him. "Perhaps she couldn't bear to leave the valley," he murmured.

"She's bewitched you!"

Waterstrider laughed at the absurdity of that.

Ignoring him, Tallcorn went on: "That girl up here on Cloud Mountain —have you seen her?"

"Yes, briefly."

"She's Firesister's daughter. Another witch."

Waterstrider kept his expression neutral. "I don't know why you keep going on about Firesister—"

"The girl was thrown out of the Cornmaidens for trying to bewitch the Rainsinger with earthflower! Can you swear that Firesister didn't do the same to you?"

"I'm not in love with her. I haven't been influenced by any herb." As Tallcorn's gaze slipped to the tattoo on his wrist, Waterstrider felt an urge to place his other hand over it. He forced himself to leave it visible. "Firesister isn't important to me except in what she offers, as a daughter of the village. To satisfy kin-right, the clans have promised to provide work parties."

Tallcorn waved that off. "A few troublemakers here and there at best. To really restore the canals, how many farmers would have to leave their fields, and for how many days every moon? You think they'll be willing?" His eyes glittered. "Just get one canal flowing," he urged. "Even if you get water to only the Squashblossom clanlands, that will show everyone it can be done."

Waterstrider opened his mouth to argue that wasn't how the canals worked. You couldn't put the water here and not worry about over there. Everything flowed together. Instead he said, "Help me get to the edge of the mound that looks out onto the river. I want to show you something."

Obligingly Tallcorn grabbed Waterstrider's hand and tugged it across his upper back. Waterstrider clambered to his feet, glad to feel his leg muscles responding. For the first time since being struck down, he had hope that he would be able to walk, maybe even run, once he was fully recovered. They were halfway across the plaza when Firesister called from behind.

Waterstrider glanced over his shoulder. Her face looked strained as she limped closer.

"Good," she said, a little breathless. "You're up. Can you make it to the side wall, overlooking the storage rooms?"

Tallcorn snapped, "We're headed for the river wall, can't you see?"

Her head cocked to one side, birdlike. "You'll just have to change course, won't you?" To Waterstrider she said, "It's important. Some of the farmers have come to talk with you."

"About what?" he asked.

Tallcorn's neck tightened under Waterstrider's palm. "Probably to complain about you," he said to Firesister.

She ignored him. "The elders must have told them about the canal work being delayed."

Tallcorn opened his mouth. Before he could insult her again, Waterstrider said, "Let's find out why they've come. Help me over to the west wall."

When they reached the edge of Cloud Mountain, Waterstrider leaned on the hip-high wall with Tallcorn's arm around his waist on one side, Firesister's on the other. Far below, on the hard-packed ground that surrounded the great mound, stood a crowd of mostly men younger than himself, a few women interspersed. Their ragged clothes suggested they hadn't had enough water to grow the thirsty cotton for several turnings or perhaps had been growing food instead.

The stooped backs and gnarled hands of the older men and women said these were people used to hard work. It wasn't laziness that kept them from repairing the canals. They probably didn't know where to start, because the damage done by the latest floods was so severe.

A matronly woman with wisps of graying hair poking out of her head scarf said in disgust, "Tallcorn of Squashblossom Clan. We knew you'd come to whisper into the Watermaster's ear."

A man about Waterstrider's age beside her called up, "Is the Watermaster such a loyal friend of yours, Tag, that you expect favors from him?"

As Waterstrider peered at the man who'd used Tallcorn's old nickname, trying to see whether this was another of his childhood companions, the wild-haired matron said, "No more private dealings, Tallcorn. If we hear of you coming to Cloud Mountain again, we'll burn your fields and cover them with clay."

Tallcorn's face paled, then flushed. He pulled his supporting arm away from Waterstrider and set clenched fists on the half wall.

In the City of Birds, where Waterstrider's character was known, he might have tried to lighten the dangerous mood with a joke. Here in Serpentgate, he thought the crowd might take offense to a jollying reply. "Is this what you've become," Waterstrider said, "making toothless threats"—he hoped they were toothless— "against one of your fellow farmers, a man who faces the same risks as you?"

"What concern is it of yours?" someone in the crowd asked.

"You're questioning my honor, not just his," Waterstrider replied.

"When a weed comes up in the corn, it must be hoed down," the wild-haired matron said. Some in the crowd nodded agreement.

Waterstrider asked, "Is it your place to get rid of the weeds in your neighbor's field?" He gave them a few heartbeats to think about that, then went on: "In the old days, claying a field might be done, but only after a clan failed to solve the problem of a greedy clan-son or daughter. Do you doubt Gran Squashblossom's willingness to keep Tallcorn under control? Or is it my integrity you dispute?"

Silence greeted his words. Tallcorn leaned forward and told the farmers, "You only have to talk to the Far-Traders to know why I sent for Waterstrider—not because we were friends long ago, but because he is the best Watermaster in the City of Birds. I'll admit I asked him to get water to the Squashblossom fields first, but that's because ours is the first set of clanlands off the river. If water gets into the Squashblossom ditches, the main canals will be full enough to carry water a good long way downcanal."

It was a good argument, but not quite true. Waterstrider said, "I'll do all I can for you. There'll be no favoritism."

The man and woman who'd originally protested Tallcorn's involvement looked to Firesister. She nodded once, sharply.

Waterstrider felt a dull headache coming on. It made him painfully aware of another reason they might doubt his ability. For the foreseeable future, he couldn't work the same way he was accustomed to. He would have to rely more on his mind than his body. *Turbulence tears through the weak points and leaves only the strong,* he reminded himself. "I'll need your patience," he continued. "And your help. Obviously I'll have to check every canal, every ditch, but I can't do that myself. Not yet."

Many in the crowd shook their head or cast each other bleak glances.

"What about starting up the hearings, as in the old days?" someone asked. "You could do that, at least."

He could, but what would be the point? He didn't remember the details of the network of canals, as numerous as veins in a broad cottonwood leaf, much less where each clan's fields lay. Such information was essential for the hearings, at which farmers used to lodge complaints against each other, each claiming the right to more water. He sidestepped the question.

"First we'll have to make sure the main canals are able to draw water from the river," he said. "I know you're concerned most with the smaller ditches that feed your fields, but let's not rush too far, too fast."

The man who'd asked about the hearings wasn't finished. "Are you planning to stay? Can we count on you to start the hearings when it's time?"

Out of the corner of his eye Waterstrider saw Tallcorn open his mouth. Waterstrider, not wanting his friend to stir up more resistance, cut him off. "That will be up to the village council. It's the clans who will have to decide how to carry on once the canals are running again." Most nodded at that.

"Enough with the hearings," someone said. "What are you going to be wanting from us?"

"That, I'll have to determine, as soon as I can." Waterstrider didn't have answers for them yet. First he had to understand the whole Northwind canal system. Besides the map-ground in the eastern plaza, there had been smaller maps that showed individual canal segments and the fields that drew water from them. "The ditchrunners used to carry parchment maps showing problem areas. Do any of these still exist?"

No one seemed to know anything about them.

"Do you still have ditchrunners?" he asked. People shook their heads.

"Youngsters from each clan could be taught how to be ditch-runners," the matron suggested.

"Maybe two from each," Firesister said. "They wouldn't need to live on the mound, would they, if they report to you here every day?"

"That's a place to start," Waterstrider said. Then he recalled Tallcorn's suggestion that Squashblossom Clan's fields should be restored first. "On the condition that these ditchrunners patrol outside their own clanlands."

Tallcorn folded his arms. Breath rasped in and out through his nose. Waterstrider knew what he would see if he looked over at his old friend: flared nostrils and brows drawn together. Tallcorn didn't like that suggestion. Neither did most in the crowd, whose responses burst out all at once: "But clan-sons know their own fields best—" "Send them to another clan?—" "That's not—"

Waterstrider put up a hand to stop the heated objections. When the crowd below subsided, he said, "They don't need to know the fields. They need to learn how to be ditchrunners."

A harsh voice asked, "How are you going to train them if you can't get out there yourself?"

Firesister jumped in again. "Maybe hunters or traders could help. They walk the full length of the canal paths all the time."

"We don't have to have all the answers right away," Waterstrider said, wishing the headache would ease so he could think more clearly. "Sometimes failure teaches us more than success."

He lifted his gaze and stared out across the landscape. Directly west, the ground was level and flat, broken only by the ridges of canal banks, with no rocky buttes sticking up. It was settled land, tame and obedient, divided into neat, manageable plots by straight and true ditches, the ground tinged green by young seedlings tended by these people and their kin.

He looked down at the crowd, muttering among themselves. They needed more than he could promise at this moment. But they weren't relying only on a lone Watermaster, were they? Their faith rested on a greater authority than his. Waterstrider tried to remember how people spoke about the mother-goddess. A line from an old story came to him, and he recited it: "Mother Ge has given us dirt and water, strong backs, and the good sense to try many different things."

That got them nodding in response. All except the harsh-voiced man, who shouted, "The Rainsinger says the canals will never run again, and that if you promise differently, you're a liar."

The Rainsinger. Cloudface . . . who had once been a ditchrunner. The pounding in Waterstrider's head intensified.

"Do you swear you'll get the canals running as they did before?" the man demanded.

Tallcorn said, "You're just mouthing the Rainsinger's words!" Casting a severe look across the assemblage, he asked, "Are you going to blindly follow the priests to disaster?"

"We don't care any more for your opinion than his," the wild-haired matron shouted up.

"Just think about it!" Tallcorn flashed. "How many times has the Rainsinger claimed rain would fall for the faithful, and then it fails?"

"The Ta'atchul know who truly believes in them, and who is only pretending," the harsh-voiced man said.

As the farmfolk descended into argument among themselves, Firesister touched Waterstrider's elbow. He looked down at her hand. It was trembling, he thought, then realized he was the one who was shaking. His head throbbed.

"You have to end this," she said in a low voice, "before you collapse in front of them. Can't you just promise and send them away?"

He lowered his voice so only she could hear. "No, I can't. For that would be a lie." Returning his attention to the crowd below, Waterstrider called out, "What Tallcorn says is right—I'm very good at getting water to where it's needed. Give me a chance, and I'll prove that I deserve your trust."

Doubt remained clear on their faces, evident in their stiff posture, manifest in their exchanged glances and comments.

Firesister addressed the farmers on his behalf. "Wait a little longer," she said. "Let's not quarrel among ourselves. The Watermaster will soon walk the canals and figure out what needs to be done. Then the elders can decide how each of you can make yourselves useful. Go home now."

Though grumbling, they accepted her order and began to disperse, whether back to their fields or to their clan holdings in the village, but regardless, away from Cloud Mountain, where Waterstrider had run out of ideas and patience.

Tallcorn had had the good sense to remain quiet as Firesister dealt with the farmfolk, but when they were out of earshot, he said, "You should have been more confident. You're a Watermaster! Don't beg them for help, demand it."

Firesister scowled at Tallcorn. "They're worried. Giving orders and expecting to be obeyed isn't going to make them trust him."

Waterstrider's knees slowly gave way, and he slid down into a bank of cottonwood fluff at the foot of the wall. Summoning a few last dregs of effort, he straightened his body and legs and rolled onto his back.

Firesister and Tallcorn crouched beside him. They spoke, but their words faded in and out as he gazed up at the cloudless sky, its blue intensity broken by the white tufts cast up by his collapse.

The headache began to drain away, fading with each heartbeat. A wave of loneliness struck. He missed Littlecliff, a solid, quiet, uplifting friend who spoke only when he had something useful to say.

"Do you want water for your fields?" Firesister asked Tallcorn.

"Of course."

"Then maybe instead of bothering Waterstrider, you should try harder to convince your clan-brothers and sisters—and friends, too, if you have any—to trust him." She pointed at Waterstrider but kept her gaze on Tallcorn. "He needs rest right now. Quiet."

"Who are you to say that to me? You're Near-Kin, no better than an outlander, and a witch too! Now you've dragged Waterstrider into your defiance of the Rainsinger. You're hiding behind his protection. Worse, making him shelter your daughter, too, and that Seeker. It's all pretend for you, isn't it? You don't care if he gets the canals running again, since you don't have fields of your own. You go out and gather enough fruits of the desert to keep yourself going, but you can't feed—"

Waterstrider had had enough. "Go home, Tallcorn. I can't think straight now." Cottonwood fluff danced on the air currents as he spoke. "I won't cast off Firesister." His voice sounded odd in his ears, as though they were underwater. He went on, "The clans know her for my lifemate. So her daughter belongs with me too."

"You're taking her side?" Tallcorn snapped.

Waterstrider explained, "It's not about choosing one over the other. This is the course I must take to do what needs doing. What I came back for. What you called me back for. The canals."

"But—" Tallcorn protested.

"Go home." He closed his eyes and waited to hear his old friend's retreating footsteps. It was a long wait.

Firesister stayed after Tallcorn left. Her breathing was slow and steady. She said nothing, simply maintained a pleasant silence. Sounds of the village drifted to his ears: dogs barking, children's high voices, the rattle of a runningbird, the *who-will, who-will* cry of a dove, shouts and penetrating voices too far away for Waterstrider to pick out the words.

He had no notion of how to heal the divisiveness among the farmers, much less his allies. What would Littlecliff, the peacemaker, have said? Waterstrider couldn't imagine. He felt helpless against the contrary farmfolk, who desperately needed water but had misgivings about the man who could bring it to them.

Can you blame them? Littlecliff might have asked.

No, not really, since he hadn't regained control over either his mind or his muscles. And was a stranger besides, an outlander by deed if not in birth or blood. Twenty-some turnings away from the valley had changed him for the better, giving him experience he could never have gained had he remained here. But the passage of time had changed the valley as well as the people left behind. Not only the canals, with their washed-out and broken banks and plunge pools scoured deep into their once-smooth beds, but even Sky River, which had become wider and rougher at the river crossing.

Waterstrider opened his eyes and stared up at the sky. A crook-necked heron passed over Cloud Mountain on its slow journey toward the river. He envied its freedom. He was trapped on the mound, bound by his healing body, a life-mating he never wanted, and a commitment to restore the Northwind canals.

In the City of Birds, he was known more as a doer than a thinker. Here he had to be the opposite—had to rely on his mind for answers and inspire others to be his hands. Had to pick out what was real in a tangle of competing arguments.

Did the Rainsinger really believe the canals could never be rebuilt? Was that the judgment of Cloudface, the former ditchrunner? Or was it a fabrication, intended to frighten people into doing what the priests wanted?

Waterstrider remembered the day in his boyhood when Brother Sun fell dark, swallowed by a monstrous shadow. Cloudface had claimed to be unafraid of the terrifying experience, and Waterstrider's honesty about his own dread had lost him the ability to influence his friends, who stayed behind and continued to play instead of following Waterstrider back to the village. Why wasn't Cloudface terrified? Where did the confidence come from that turned Cloudface into Eaglefeather and finally the high priest of the Temple of Lightning?

Maybe a better question was, *what are you afraid of?* That was something Littlecliff might have asked.

Waterstrider no longer feared that he would be forever crippled, for each day his condition improved and he became stronger. Was it that he might fail and lose his reputation? No, a reputation could be rebuilt. He thought about the farmers who had stood looking up at him —at the only Watermaster in the valley, who had made himself responsible for their lives. A mere man, of whom they asked but one thing: save us.

Warmth radiated from Firesister, dispelling the chill of the plastered wall and plaza floor.

Tallcorn's complaints about her seeped into Waterstrider's mind. Tallcorn had known her for many turnings, and perhaps his warnings were well founded. What reason other than gratitude did Waterstrider have for trusting her? Had they been thrown together by circumstance— or, as Tallcorn suggested, by her conniving? Waterstrider looked at Firesister and caught her watching him from an open, honest-seeming face. Maybe she was a talented liar and was actually using Waterstrider to shield herself, as Tallcorn had said.

But the villagers seemed to think Tallcorn was after more than he admitted, too. Some even expressed doubts about Waterstrider's true intentions. And why not? Was he certain anymore about his own reasons for coming home?

Perhaps they didn't matter. He was here now, and his life was bound up with Firesister's, this woman who was still a stranger to him. Daughter of the village. Clan-sister to all. Yet somehow seeming as alone, as separate from everyone around her as Waterstrider himself. As solitary as that heron winging across the sky. There was something odd about that contradiction in how Firesister fit into the village.

He twisted onto his side to face her. He felt at a disadvantage lying flat, looking up at her. Struggling to get his hands under his rib cage to press himself up to a sitting position, Waterstrider cursed his weakness. She helped him get upright, then released him. He used his arms and legs to scoot back against the wall.

She seated herself next to him as she had done during the recognition ceremony. This time she sat on his other side, so their wrists lying next to each other were unmarked by the tattoos signifying a life-mating. Waterstrider wondered whether that was deliberate on her part, to avoid reminding him that she'd gone ahead and done what she thought right without asking his permission.

"How many days have passed since the attack?" he asked casually, as if simply to fill the silence.

She tapped her thumb and forefinger together as though counting. "Thirty-eight, I believe."

"So today is near the end of Tree Flower Moon?"

Firesister nodded. "A few days away."

That's why it's so warm. We're easing into foresummer. He let a few moments slide by, then asked, "How did you get me back to Cloud Mountain after the attack?"

Firesister's cheeks paled, but she answered readily, "The hunters rigged a litter, as they would for a bighorn carcass, to get it to the butchering camp."

Waterstrider chewed on his lower lip. "Could I inspect the canals from a litter?"

Slowly she said, "I don't see why not. Only, will it put you high enough to see? Sitting, you'll only be at armpit level. Lower, probably, given the sag of the netting between the two poles."

"Maybe the men could bear the poles on their shoulders."

Firesister frowned and tilted her head down. She worked her heel against a pebble sticking up from the worn plastered floor. "That sounds tricky. They wouldn't be used to carrying a weight so high. They might be able to lift you up at the beginning, but what happens when they need to rest? And then could you hold on if somebody steps out of rhythm with the others, and you're thrown to one corner or another?"

Waterstrider imagined a dead bighorn, bound to the litter with cords and netting. He remembered all too clearly being tied down and unable to move in those first moments of awareness after the attack.

"Maybe," Firesister went on, with increasing enthusiasm, "we could build a bench so you have something to sit on. The men could carry the poles in their hands. The bench would be about knee-high, so your feet could rest on the poles, or maybe add a crossbeam. With that, your head could be even higher than usual."

"Will the farmers be able to spare their strongest men?"

She grinned. "In your present condition, you could settle for weaklings. Let them build their strength as you put on weight."

Waterstrider returned her smile.

More seriously, she added, "Hunters might do it. As the days heat up, deer and bighorn usually retreat deeper into the mountains. Some hunters follow them."

"But not all?"

"Not all." Firesister's expression became thoughtful. "I'll ask Bearclaw."

Her casual tone made Waterstrider wonder whether she knew

Bearclaw's feelings toward her. Though the big hunter would do anything for Firesister, he was obviously jealous of Waterstrider. Maybe more likely to drop him on his head than haul him around.

That reminded Waterstrider of Tallcorn and *his* jealousy, which brought to mind what his old friend had said about Skyblade and Firesister's daughter adding to the Rainsinger's animosity. "Earlier, you said your daughter's story was too long to go into. While I'm resting, why don't you tell me why you brought her and Skyblade to Cloud Mountain."

"It was Skyblade's doing," she said. "He brought her."

"From where?"

Firesister hesitated so long, Waterstrider expected her to either offer another excuse for not telling the story, or construct a lie. "From the temple," she said at last. "How Skyblade got her out, I'm still not sure. He's protecting someone who helped, I think."

"Why don't you ask her? Your daughter, I mean. What's her name?"

"Mistlight. Her name is Mistlight. And . . ." Firesister's expression darkened. "She doesn't really talk anymore."

Waterstrider recognized this as a tender spot, but he pressed forward anyway. "So. Why was she in the temple? Is she a witch, as Tallcorn said?"

Firesister folded her arms as she lifted her chin and looked down her nose at him. "Not a witch, no more than I am. She was caught between the priests and priestesses, that's all. Mistlight is just a girl."

There. That was a lie, the first that Waterstrider had recognized from her. But which part of her reply was untrue? "A girl who doesn't really talk anymore," he said. "That's not like any of the girls I've known."

Waterstrider stretched. His muscles protested, as though he'd run from Mother Sleeping to Sun-Meets-Mountain the previous day, rather than simply hobbling from one place to another on Cloud Mountain. One hand bumped against something that shifted under his touch. He jerked his hand back and looked to see what he'd disturbed.

Rays of morning light angling through the doorway revealed a long shaft of wood with a pair of stubs coming off the top: a crutch, polished from use. Waterstrider thought about Firesister's limp and wondered if the crutch was hers. If so, it would surely be too short for him. But when he managed to stand, he found that it had been made for someone about his height.

His legs felt soft and puny, knees boneless and muscles like sodden leather. He fell as soon as he tried to move. Several times. Because he was alone, with none to watch, he would never have to admit how close he came to giving up. Waterstrider hadn't tried to use a crutch before. It was trickier than it looked.

At last he figured out how to hold it with his upper arm and place it where it was needed. Instead of hopping like a three-legged dog, he steadied himself with two "legs" while moving the third carefully forward. Awkwardly, never getting too far from a wall that would support him if his knees gave way, he went to find Firesister and thank her for the gift that would let him at last get around on his own, after a fashion.

When he got to the edge of the roomblock, he realized she'd been busy with more than the crutch. Strewn across the near side of the plaza were saguaro ribs, leafy reeds, arrowweed rods, cattail stalks, willow switches, and two long poles that hadn't been there the night before. He assumed those were materials for the litter. On the far side of the plaza sat Skyblade, bent over a pair of saguaro ribs. Waterstrider started toward the boy. As he wove between the obstacles, he was careful not to snag the tip of the crutch on anything.

Skyblade held the saguaro ribs crosswise to one another. His tongue poked out of one side of his mouth in concentration as he wrapped a strap over the crossed ribs and pulled it tight. His head lifted, and his gaze roved over Waterstrider, taking in the crutch. Dropping what he'd been working on, he rose and stood still, like an anxious rabbit frozen in place.

Past Skyblade, Firesister knelt at a metate. Waterstrider, distracted by the curve of her breasts, pulled his attention back to Skyblade and motioned the boy over. Skyblade hurried, nearly tripping on his own feet. He reminded Waterstrider of Tag long ago, gangly and uncoordinated, long bones growing too fast for the muscles to keep up, awkward in a rapidly changing body.

"You managed the crutch," Skyblade said. "Firesister knew you would."

At the mention of her name, she looked up from what she was doing and locked eyes with Waterstrider. She offered a too-bright smile. "Did you sleep well?" she called. She straightened to stretch her back and with her arm wiped a lock of hair off her forehead.

The chert knife she held flashed wetly in the morning sun as a thick bead of moisture gathered at the tip. Not blood, too pale for that. Waterstrider glanced at the metate and saw a nopal cactus pad in it. One half had been sliced thinly into strips for cooking, while the other half remained untouched. Cactus juice dripped off the end of the stone, which had been flattened but was not yet hollowed out by use.

As her smile faded, Waterstrider realized she was still waiting for a response. "Well enough." He waved a hand toward the plaza. "All this stuff for the litter?" he asked. "How did you get everything so quickly? No, don't tell me, you're a daughter of the village."

She puffed out a small laugh. "Something like that."

Skyblade said, "She knows where *everything* is. The thickest stand of reeds, tallest willows, saguaro skeletons, everything. Other stuff came from a basket-maker. And the hunters, of course."

"Of course," Waterstrider repeated solemnly.

"She's working on breakfast." Skyblade helped Waterstrider over to where he'd been sitting and showed the panel he'd made. Woven of willow withies on cattail stalks, it was neatly done. Three of the panels would make the sides and top of the bench, with two more for the ends. Waterstrider saw what Skyblade had in mind; the basic design seemed workable. He wondered whether the boy or Firesister had conceived it.

Skyblade said, "I don't know if it will hold your weight, though. I was going to try saguaro ribs. They're stronger. But maybe too heavy."

"Let's try arrowweed instead of cattails," Waterstrider suggested. Arrowweed worked well in headgates, which had to resist force from one direction—not unlike his weight. "The saguaro ribs could be good as a frame for each panel."

Besides the branches, there were yucca-fiber cords and oiled leather lashings to hold everything together. Waterstrider and Skyblade debated what would work best, then tried their ideas. During breaks, Waterstrider observed that Skyblade wielded knife, axe, and adze with an efficiency that indicated a surprising amount of experience and strength.

Firesister eventually called them over for breakfast. She'd lost the ribbon that normally tied her long braid back upon itself, so the braid had slipped forward over one shoulder. It hung nearly to her knees. The white streak that started at the back of her head snaked back and forth all the way down the braid, stark against the black. Cactus juice glistened on her forehead where she'd smeared it. She was walking stiffly, her limp more pronounced as she carried steaming bowls toward them, one in each hand. Two more bowls remained at the fire ring, balanced on one of the flat rocks there.

"Will Mistlight join us this morning?" Waterstrider asked. Lately she hadn't come near enough for him to pick out Firesister's features in her face. He'd glimpsed her a few times while he and Skyblade were working. But she slipped away ghostlike almost before he knew she was there.

Firesister shook her head. "She doesn't eat with us."

She held out a bowl for Waterstrider. He took it and asked, "What makes your daughter so skittish?"

Firesister gave Skyblade his breakfast. Keeping her eyes averted from Waterstrider, she said, "Mistlight was a Cornmaiden until Eaglefeather accused her—both of us—of being witches. Somehow she wound up in the Temple of Lightning, a place where Mother Ge has no influence." Firesister closed her eyes and drew a deep breath. "Something happened to her there. Something that broke her mind."

Skyblade said, "Mistlight used to be . . ." He looked down and scuffed the front edge of his sandal against the ground. "She always talked to everyone. Now she doesn't say a thing." His head came up, and he fixed his eyes on Waterstrider. "It's like men terrify her."

Waterstrider said, "Yet she took care of me."

"Before you woke," Firesister pointed out. "Since you came to your senses, have you seen her? You might say I shouldn't have brought her to Cloud Mountain, but where else will she be welcome? She isn't a Cornmaiden anymore, and we have no other family. She's too old for the Children's House. The same with Skyblade. To rescue Mistlight, Skyblade turned his back on the temple. He has nowhere to go."

"I'm not planning to send any of you away," Waterstrider said mildly.

Firesister nodded, but she didn't seem convinced. She excused herself to take breakfast to Mistlight.

The contents of the bowls she'd brought for Waterstrider and Skyblade had cooled enough to be eaten. They dipped their gourd spoons into the thick blend of beans and meat chunks, boiled with green pot-herbs and topped with strips of roasted nopal. Waterstrider remembered what Tallcorn had said about Firesister feeding him from Squashblossom Clan's crops and whatever she could glean from the desert. The beans might have been from Tallcorn's clan, but the rest of it had come through her efforts. Waterstrider ate with enthusiasm, only partly because he was eating to heal. Her stew was delicious.

Skyblade cleared his throat. "I . . . I thought of something I saw at the Temple of Lightning. In one of the storage rooms where tools are kept, there's a stack of thin skins, dry and mostly flat but curly at the edges. You said ditchrunners used to carry maps made of parchment and would mark washouts and plunge pools and the like on them. Could those skins at the temple be the parchment maps you were talking about?"

"Could be. How many were there?"

Skyblade indicated the stack was about thigh high.

Waterstrider thought back twenty-four turnings. On what turned out to be their last day of work in the Valley of Two Rivers, the ditchrunners had piled their maps in a small storeroom. Waterstrider had looked for them the first day he'd come back to Cloud Mountain. He'd been deeply disappointed to find they were gone.

"I could go get them," Skyblade said.

Waterstrider shook his head. "A disgraced Seeker? You would hardly be welcomed in the temple precinct."

"I could sneak in."

Waterstrider bit back a smile at the thought of the slight youth trying to sneak out a heavy stack of skins. "No. I won't ask that of you."

"I probably wouldn't get caught. No one saw me when I lived there."

"I won't get them back through theft."

"How, then?"

Waterstrider hesitated. It must have been Cloudface, the former ditchrunner, who'd taken the maps to the temple. If he'd only wanted to keep anyone from using them, he could have burned them—or left them where they were until rain and time destroyed them. Yet he'd preserved them. "By right," Waterstrider said.

Skyblade's forehead creased in puzzlement.

"I'll go and tell the Rainsinger to hand over the maps."

The boy's eyes went wide with shock.

Waterstrider smiled. "Do you fear he'll kill me? Firesister says not. Do you believe her?"

"You think he'll just give them to you?"

"Why not? They belong to the Watermasters. And they don't do him any good." Stuffed away in a storeroom, they were useless. Just as Waterstrider, trapped by his unhealed body on Cloud Mountain, had been no good to anyone. It was long past time to change that.

"Let's get back to work on that litter," he told Skyblade. "When it's done, the first thing I'll do is go to the temple and get those maps back."

Waterstrider eyed the sliver of moon high in the midnight sky. He stretched out on his cushioned sleep-mat. Tired of the close confines of the room, he'd had Skyblade place the bedding in the middle of the eastern plaza at the south end of Cloud Mountain. Crisp air seeped around the deerhide blanket as he stared up at the White Starry Path and worried.

Not about the litter, for that was done; he and Skyblade had worked all day and finished it before sunset. He'd looked then for Firesister to tell her that the first test of the litter would involve going to the temple to retrieve the maps. Upon failing to find her, he'd asked Skyblade. *"She's gone to talk to the hunters,"* the boy had said. Waterstrider hadn't asked why Skyblade knew that and he didn't.

He'd waited for her—until sunset, until darkness drew close and the night turned cold, until moonrise and beyond. And still she hadn't returned.

Had Eaglefeather done something to her? She'd said the Rainsinger wouldn't move against either of them, but Waterstrider thought now that was wishful thinking rather than certainty.

Unable to sleep, he pushed the deerhide blanket away. He worked his limbs, hands first, then arms, and then legs, from hips to knees to feet. The past few days, whenever he was unobserved, he practiced the repetitive movements: flexing and relaxing, flexing and relaxing, to loosen and warm the muscles. Blood pumped through his body without starting his head pounding. Though that was an improvement over his condition a few days earlier, the movements still required too much effort.

He needed to look strong when he insisted on the return of the parchment maps. Instead he would be hauled like meat through the village, sitting on a peculiar construction carried by men who had no loyalty to him or his mission. That was assuming Firesister proved successful in convincing the hunters to convey him where he wanted to go. He trusted that she would. But still he found her absence unsettling.

At last, cold gray whiskers of dawn tickled the eastern sky. Waterstrider struggled into a kneeling position and saluted the Sentinels, the two mountains in the east that Sky River ran between on its descent to the valley. He sang a few words from a song he hadn't thought of for many turnings: "Day is come, it begins in the east, and the morning comes up with the sun." What was next? "River is come, it flows from the east, and the Sentinels send us its water."

Waterstrider heard a noise behind and twisted to see if it was Firesister returning from wherever she'd gone. It was the girl, Mistlight, who normally whisked about without making a sound. Waterstrider wondered if she'd made the noise on purpose.

Her fingers were knotted so tightly together that her knuckles were white. "Don't let them drive you away, heron-man," she whispered. "Your people will need you before winter." Then she slipped around the corner of the wall in a flutter of skirts.

"Mistlight!" he called after her. He reached for the crutch and managed to stand, but she was long gone. What had she meant? *She doesn't talk much,*" Firesister had said.

Waterstrider snorted. Mistlight had found something to say to him. Not that it made sense. Bemused, he shook his head.

Pinks and oranges of oncoming sunrise began to fill the sky, reflecting off thin clouds too high to offer the possibility of later rain. Birds warbled in full voice from the cottonwoods and willows along the river.

On such a morning a man could believe he was the only one alive.

Waterstrider wasn't, of course. He heard Firesister's voice on the other side of the plaza wall and felt a surge of relief that she was all right.

Immediately after, male laughter boomed out.

Waterstrider shuffled through the gap in the wall separating the eastern and western plazas in time to see Firesister step out of the passageway, with Bearclaw right behind. She'd changed into a pottery-red skirt with an undyed overshirt nipped in by a sash at the waist. A cotton cloak, fastened at the neck, flowed partway down her back. Her long braid was now neatly bound behind her head and held in place by two bone pins.

Several other men followed Bearclaw. Some wore wide bands of leather slantwise across their chests, while others had sleeveless vests made of leather squares laced together. Their kilts consisted of the hairy pelts of small animals. Leather belts around the men's midsections held knife sheaths and loops from which heavy stone-headed clubs dangled. Obviously hunters by their clothing, the men strode into the western plaza and collected around the fire-ring.

Upon Waterstrider's clumsy approach, unfriendly faces turned toward him. He wasn't sure how his plan to go to the Temple of Lightning would be received.

In the end, it wasn't the hunters who argued and called him stupid. That was Firesister, who rounded on him with a pale face and flashing eyes. "He tried to kill you! Twice!"

"You said he wouldn't attempt it again," Waterstrider said. "Have you changed your mind? Besides, I'm under Mother Ge's protection."

She folded her arms and looked away.

Bearclaw said, "We agreed to carry you along the canals. Not to the temple. You expect us to haul you to the Rainsinger's door? Then what? Wait for him to invite us for breakfast?"

"Just get me close to the temple precinct. I want to walk through the gate on my own two feet."

Grudging respect came into Bearclaw's eyes, but Firesister snorted at what she probably saw as a man's useless pride.

Bearclaw said, "We're supposed to let a crippled man go alone into the priests' territory? I know it was priests who attacked you and drove off the outlanders. You would be helpless against them if they try again."

"I have to chance it," said Waterstrider.

Firesister told him, "There's no purpose to it. You can't believe anything Eaglefeather says. His corruption is deep, his heart cold."

"I'm not interested in his words," Waterstrider replied. "According to Skyblade, he has something I want."

Bearclaw asked, "What's so important you'll risk your life for it?"

"The Rainsinger took the ditchrunners' canal maps. I need them back."

"Why?" one of the hunters asked. They'd left the fire-ring to crowd around him.

"The maps show the details of the entire Northwind canal system—from mains to crosscuts, along with every little ditch and the clanlands they water. Piece by piece, all marked on thin parchments carried by ditchrunners."

Another of their party nudged one of his fellows. "How can something so large be made small enough to carry?" he whispered.

Firesister said, "It's like a drawing of lightning or mountains as a tattoo or on pottery. You recognize it, a large thing made small."

Waterstrider nodded at her apt description. "You don't use maps?" he asked the puzzled men. "How do you tell somebody where the deer are collecting or where to find a kill?"

"Every place has a name," a hunter drawled, as though the answer should be obvious.

Bearclaw said, "If the Rainsinger indeed has these maps, they're twenty-some turnings old. Why not make new ones?"

Waterstrider looked at him, then glanced around the listening men. "On the northmost canal, how many paces are there between the first distribution canal and the second?"

"I don't know," Bearclaw said impatiently. "Let's walk it and find out. Then you can mark it on your own parchment map."

Waterstrider tucked the crutch more deeply under his arm. "The first thing ditchrunners have to learn is how to take paces precisely this distance—" he measured the length of a pace with his hands "—every time and count their steps. Try it yourself when we go to the temple. It's more difficult than it seems. You're six men, not all the same—"

"Seven!" called a young voice from the east side of the mound.

Bearclaw muttered something under his breath. "My brother, Ninetoes," he told Waterstrider. Raising his voice so his brother could hear, he added, "Who was not asked to come along."

"You can see Mother Sleeping from here," Ninetoes said. He stood outside the south doorway of the observation room, with its unusual opening to the northeast.

During the winter sun-festival, Brother Sun's setting light passed through the room and pointed to the Belly of the Mother, in which the blaze announcing the New Fire ceremony would be lit once darkness fell. A watcher posted in the room would look for that fire and, upon seeing it, would call out to another watcher in a tower at the south end of Cloud Mountain. The large pile of wood waiting there would be set alight. In response other fires would be kindled to the east, west, and south, and so the message would be passed to every village in the valley.

When Waterstrider looked at that room, he imagined in the shadows his father, who had been the watcher all those turnings ago, on the day of the dark-sun. The room lay exposed to daylight now, its ceiling gone, its mysteries revealed. And Longflute, his father, had joined the Ancestors nearly five turnings ago.

Ninetoes went on, "I didn't realize you Watermasters were among Mother Ge's faithful."

Bearclaw said, "Stop poking around where you don't belong." He gestured for his brother to join the group.

Waterstrider felt sorry for the boy, who looked over his shoulder at the odd room and then, passing the map-ground, with its strangely cut block walls and eroded floor, craned his neck to peer in. Ninetoes seemed nearly the same age as Skyblade, but there the resemblance ended While Skyblade was slight, Ninetoes was tall and muscular already, though nowhere near as large as his brother. The differences between them reminded Waterstrider of himself and Tag those many turnings ago.

"I've heard . . ." the boy trailed off. He came a few steps closer and gazed at Waterstrider with intense curiosity. "They say Mother Ge made the rivers and the Watermasters made the canals but then became overproud, angering the mother-goddess, who sent them into exile."

Bearclaw snapped, "It doesn't matter why they left."

"It matters to me," Ninetoes shot back.

"What matters," Firesister said firmly, "is that Mother Ge has faith in Waterstrider. She saved him for a purpose. Not to risk his life."

An old saying came into Waterstrider's mind, something his father used to tell him: *A mind blinded by fear becomes foolish.*" He spoke the words aloud and received a scowl from Firesister in return.

He reminded her, "I came back to restore the canals. I can't do that if I allow myself to be frightened off the best path to that purpose."

"Is it some kind of magic, then," Ninetoes asked earnestly, "getting the water out of the river and taking it to the fields? 'Water flows always downhill,' they say. But the fields are uphill from the river. And the canal banks are higher yet."

Waterstrider wondered how to explain. "It's not magic," he said. "You've seen weirs built across the river, yes? They're sort of like tall beaver dams." Sky River had several, one for each of the major canals. Somebody would have to be blind to not notice them.

Ninetoes nodded.

Waterstrider continued his explanation. "Behind the weir, the water rises higher and higher, until it finds a place that's lower—the bed of a canal. The banks are there to make sure the water stays in the canal, so it doesn't really matter how high they are."

"Unless there's a flood," one of the hunters put in.

"Unless there's a flood," Waterstrider agreed.

Bearclaw said dryly, "Glad as I am that you're willing to answer my inquisitive young brother's questions, maybe we could get back to exploring whether to take you to the temple or the river, as Firesister planned."

Before Ninetoes had asked how the canals worked, Waterstrider had felt the hunters inclining toward his way of thinking. Now they seemed bored. "Carrying me through the village will be easier than the path to the river," he said.

"We don't need easy," Bearclaw said.

"It'll be quicker, too," Waterstrider added. "Once I get the maps back, it won't be necessary to lay eyes on every canal right away. Just the mains, between the mounds." Cloud Mountain wasn't the only one of the Watermasters' mounds in the Northwind canal system. All the way down the canals, mounds topped with observation towers stood about three thousand paces apart. That seemed a reasonable distance to walk while carrying the litter. "From the top of the mounds I can figure out how each parchment fits with the others."

"What good are old maps?" Bearclaw asked. "Big floods have changed the canals past recognizing, so the farmers say."

Past recognizing? Hardly. Canals were more persistent than that. "If we know how the canals used to look when they carried water, we can figure out how they need to look now."

Bearclaw turned to Firesister. "What do you think? Is it the truth, that he really needs these maps? Or does he have some other reason for wanting to confront the Rainsinger?"

"What reason?" Waterstrider asked.

Bearclaw's hand fell to the blackish green head of the axe in his belt. "Vengeance. You might want to trick us into having your back, while you go after the Rainsinger to avenge your friend's death."

Firesister sucked in a breath.

Waterstrider glanced at the other hunters. They didn't appear reluctant to fight the priests—instead, fingering their axe heads and knife hilts, they seemed curious to see how he would respond to Bearclaw's speculation. "It's not for me to seek vengeance," he said.

"No?"

Shaking his head, Waterstrider started, "Little—" but stopped when Firesister's drawn expression and tightly folded lips reminded him that the names of the dead were not to be spoken. "My friend had a brother, Ravenchild. I can't answer for what he will do once word of his brother's death gets back to the City of Birds. But for me to take that kin-right from him—no. It's as I said. I need those maps."

Firesister stirred, shivering—not, Waterstrider thought, from the cold but out of concern for him. Her worry seemed just like his the previous night, when she hadn't returned to the mound. Was this what being a lifemate meant? He felt if he was being pushed into a new life, as inexorably as water being pushed into a canal by a weir, lifted out of his old, comfortable ways and set on a new course, unexpected, uncertain, turbulent, and irreversible.

"Then," Bearclaw said, "we'll take you to the temple. The priests won't drive *us* away." His visage bore a mixture of determination and anticipation, an attitude reflected in the other men of his company.

Firesister turned away. Over her shoulder she said, "It's too early to go to the temple. The priests won't be stirring yet."

The hunters laughed, though some looked envious of the priests. Waterstrider knew what was in their minds. Every man in the valley could imagine the contented, exhausted sleep of those priests who had satisfied themselves with Cornmaidens the previous night.

"I'll make breakfast," Firesister added.

That got such enthusiastic approval, Waterstrider figured the hunters had all eaten Firesister's cooking before. He watched her direct some of the men toward storage jars, the water olla, piles of wood for a cook-fire.

Beyond the wood, the litter caught his eye, that untried contrivance. *Maybe try it before looking too far ahead on your life-path,* he told himself. *Get to the temple and see what happens.*

Jolting about on the litter proved more wearing than Waterstrider expected as the hunters hauled him through the village, periodically complaining that his seated weight was more difficult to balance than a carcass lying flat. His legs ached from the effort of holding himself in place on the bench he and Skyblade had made. He gritted his teeth and bent forward to brace his forearms on his thighs.

People stared and dogs ran behind, growling and barking at the spectacle. At the gate of the temple precinct, the guard in the tower didn't challenge the odd party right away.

Bearclaw, holding the left pole at the front of the litter, said, "Stunned into silence, you reckon?"

His comment prompted a laugh from the other hunters. Waterstrider was just relieved that the jolting was over. "Set the litter down here, while they're wondering what to do."

"We can carry you in."

"No, I'll—"

From the tower came a blast on a ram's horn, followed by, "Who are you, and what business do you have at the Temple of Lightning?" The voice was high pitched and cracked a few times.

Not a full priest but a Seeker, Waterstrider guessed, unsure of himself and nervous about a party of armed men coming to the temple. "Set me down," Waterstrider said.

At a nod from Bearclaw they complied, so unevenly that Waterstrider's back twisted and his teeth snapped together. He cursed under his breath. It was hardly the arrival he'd envisioned.

He informed the young guard that he'd come to see the Rainsinger. Soon a wiry Seeker wearing only a breechcloth ran from the tower toward a low building near the temple.

Waterstrider's gaze traveled up the impressive temple, its walls slightly longer than they were high, with two gaping doorways rising one above the other in each smoothly plastered face. On the top perched a smaller structure. He'd passed the identically constructed Temple of Mist and Temple of Thunder on the journey from the City of Birds, though at such a distance that they seemed tiny. Here the Temple of Lightning loomed over him, making him feel small. Annoyance over that unwanted sentiment gave him the strength he needed to rise from the seat on the litter.

Once up, supporting himself on the seat, he started to reach for the crutch. One of the hunters handed it to him. He took it with a word of thanks and got himself straightened up as the Seeker emerged from the building, waved toward the gate, and disappeared around the small building, headed somewhere else. A moment later, the young voice from the guard tower said, "You may enter. Wait for your escort."

A pair of large priests in the yellow robes of the Temple of Lightning, their faces tattooed with the marks of lightning, wind, and rain, their hair shaved on the sides and bound up in a club at the back of their head, came around the corner where the messenger boy had disappeared. They bore no visible weapons.

For a moment, struck by a fragmentary memory, Waterstrider wondered if they were the ones who had attacked him, split his head open, and left him for dead. He wished briefly that the hunters were bristling with spears, with bows and arrows, not just axes and knives, which were good only for close-in battles. The last men who'd accompanied him had been attacked in brush that hid the attackers until the last moment. Here, in the open, arrows could stop a skirmish before it started—but in doing so, start a conflict that would tear apart the People of Two Rivers.

Waterstrider hobbled forward to meet the oncoming priests. Leaving the hunters outside the temple precinct, he passed through the gap in the thick adobe wall, shivering as he encountered the cold that lingered in the shadows. The priests didn't speak. Neither did he.

They fell in on each side of him. Normally they wouldn't have been quite as tall as he was, but stooping to use the crutch put him at a disadvantage. They stayed with him until he got to the doorway of the low building where the boy had gone to announce his arrival.

Waterstrider paused at the edge of darkness and light to let his eyes adjust.

"So, there will be no more racing for you," he heard from the dimness within. The voice was rich, compelling, persuasive.

Waterstrider fought the urge to agree. "My head was broken, not my legs. They only need time to get strong again." Something moved in the room. As Waterstrider peered more closely, he made out a dark face and hands against yellow robes. The features quickly resolved into the beaky nose, sloping forehead and chin, and shallow-set eyes of Eaglefeather, not vastly changed from the boy he'd known long ago as Cloudface.

"It will be a new experience for you, not winning," said Eaglefeather, folding his hands upon a blocky shape waist high in the middle of the room.

Moving forward as smoothly as the crutch would allow, Waterstrider commented, "It never mattered so much who won."

"You only say that because, in the end, I will be the winner."

Waterstrider refused to be baited into a reply.

Eaglefeather went on, "I should thank you for keeping my secret. If you had told anyone I was not going to leave with the rest of the heronfolk, I might have always been second best."

"Why did you stay behind?" Waterstrider asked, curious to hear how the other man would explain that fateful decision.

"When the sun was swallowed by darkness, I saw how desperately people cling to certainty and strength in times of trial." Eaglefeather's versatile voice twisted into contempt. "The Watermasters are weak, as you proved that day, as all the heronfolk proved when they left the valley. Do you think if you had stayed, anything would be different today? The Stormbringers would still have won out over the heronfolk, just as the Ta'atchul are beating the goddess."

Eaglefeather puffed out his chest, reminding Waterstrider of a bird of prey preening itself. "Maybe things would be otherwise if you had broken your promise to remain silent. My father might have dragged me along, as yours did you." He sounded proud of himself and his decision.

That pride gave Waterstrider the opening he'd hoped for.

As a boy, Cloudface had only a nodding acquaintance with the truth, and Firesister's low opinion of him suggested he'd only gotten worse. If asked outright to give the maps back, he would likely laugh and say that Skyblade had seen nothing more than a pile of skins used for some other purpose. But he might be tricked into admitting he had them tucked away.

Waterstrider said, "Yet you kept the ditchrunners' maps. Why, if you no longer wanted to be a Watermaster?"

After the barest hesitation, Eaglefeather said, "A lot of time went into those, some of it mine. It seemed a shame to let them molder in the rain."

Waterstrider kept satisfaction out of his voice. "You never thought to use them?"

"They are useless. The canals cannot be restored."

"You've said that before. What makes you so certain?"

Eaglefeather chuckled. "You may find out. If you are as skilled as Tallcorn claims." His tone made clear that he doubted Waterstrider's skills. "In any case, there can be no harm in your trying. Once you fail, the farmfolk will see there is nothing more to be done. Ultimately, they will be happy to abandon the canals."

Waterstrider thought back to what he'd seen at the river crossing while the water level was still high from spring runoff. The Southwind canals, which drew from Sky River upstream from the crossing, had been running full and fast, so the river should have been only knee-high when he waded across. Instead he'd gotten wet past his hips. "Is it the river that's changed, or the canals?"

Eaglefeather laughed, then said, "You are persistent, I see. That may be good. In any case, I am grateful to you for taking responsibility for the witches. But I wonder: Do you not fear them?"

Fear them? Waterstrider quickly figured out who Eaglefeather was talking about—Firesister and Mistlight. "Over that absurd accusation of witchcraft?" He shook his head. "Of course not. But I wonder: Were you surprised to find me still alive, since you sent Firesister to kill me?"

"What surprises me," Eaglefeather said, "is that you tolerate Firesister at all, since she is a mother who deserted her child."

Long ago, Cloudface had learned that Waterstrider's mother was a sore spot, and he'd poked at it as often as he could. It didn't stir Waterstrider into a rage anymore. Catching Eaglefeather's gaze, Waterstrider said levelly, "Firesister's daughter seems to have forgiven her."

Eaglefeather smiled. "Have you forgiven your mother? If you want to make peace with her memory, I could tell you what clan she belonged to."

Waterstrider's blood heated. He cautioned himself to hold onto his temper. "It doesn't matter," he said.

Her kin hadn't been interested in him when he was young. Indeed, they'd taken their disinterest to such an extreme that he didn't even know the name of the clan that shared his blood. His father would never speak of her or her family, and when Waterstrider had asked other Watermasters, they always said he was better off not knowing. He'd left the valley before there was any need to find out, either to avoid the appearance of favoritism or to keep from being slandered by spitefulness. He wondered now whether the harsh-voiced man in the crowd of farmfolk, the one who had seemed hostile toward the canals and Watermasters and even himself, was one of his mother's kin. Maybe he should find out. But not from Eaglefeather.

"I'll take those maps now," he said.

As Waterstrider returned to the gate, followed by the priests who'd been his escort, he felt uneasy over Eaglefeather's readiness to surrender the ditchrunners' maps. The encounter with his old rival had gone too smoothly. He hadn't embarrassed himself by a failure of mind or body, but it was a close-won thing. The effort of covering the short distance from Eaglefeather's workshop to the open gate wore him out and left his leg muscles quivering.

"You're lucky he didn't refuse," Bearclaw said after the priests dumped the parchment maps on the ground and retreated into the temple precinct.

Waterstrider gazed at the skins, thin and pale, flaking around the edges. They had slithered over one another, scattering, coming to rest against the boots of the hunters who stood around the litter. He'd remembered there being more maps, but here he counted at least thirty. Enough to give him a good start on reconstructing the master map on Cloud Mountain. "Yes, lucky." Surprisingly so. He nudged the nearest map with the tip of the crutch. "First thing is to get these back to Cloud Mountain. I can't pick them up, so if you would . . ."

Some of the men stooped and started to gather the maps. Bearclaw didn't move. He asked, "What're you going to do with the skins? Hold them on your lap?" At the challenge in his voice, the other men stopped what they were doing. "That's a lot of weight. More than just carrying you around."

"We'll get them," said Skyblade, popping into sight from behind a nearby house compound. At his heels was Ninetoes, who cast an apologetic glance at Bearclaw. Both boys carried burden baskets in their hands rather than on their backs.

Bearclaw started to snarl at his younger brother, but Ninetoes said, "You told me I wasn't strong enough to help with the Watermaster. Let me at least take some of the maps."

The brothers drew aside for a low-voiced argument filled with gestures and grimaces. Waterstrider tottered over to the litter and collapsed on the seat, calling forth an ominous creaking as the woven branches protested the abuse. He dropped the crutch and leaned forward, placing forearms on thighs to stretch his back. Tilting his head sideways, he saw Skyblade picking up the skins one at a time and placing them in a burden basket. He considered telling the boy to roll them up, as they were stronger that way, but decided not to. They might need to be moistened before they would roll without cracking. "Thanks, Skyblade, for coming to help."

Skyblade replied, "Firesister sent us. She knew you'd get the maps."

Bearclaw clouted his brother on the shoulder gently enough to prompt a good-natured smirk in return before Ninetoes joined Skyblade in gathering up the maps.

With a jerk of his chin, Bearclaw set the men in position around the litter. This time he took his place beside Waterstrider rather than in front. A moment later, Waterstrider was once more off the ground, bracing with overtaxed muscles against the swaying, stomach-churning movement of the hunters stepping rhythmically, as though to an unheard song.

"River or Cloud Mountain?" Bearclaw asked as they started off.

Cloud Mountain, Waterstrider wanted to say. But that would be admitting a weakness he couldn't afford. Somehow he had to endure. "Take me to the canal mouths on the river."

In silence they walked southward, retracing their steps through the village. Not as many people craned their necks to see the strange procession this time. Dogs came and barked at them but didn't follow. At last even the dogs dropped away.

Bearclaw lifted his free hand and scratched at his chest, shifting aside the bone whistle that dangled from a thong around his neck. So deep was the quiet that Waterstrider heard the clack of the whistle against one of the fearsome claws the hunter wore as a necklace.

"You never asked where Firesister was last night," Bearclaw said.

"No," Waterstrider replied.

"Don't you care?"

Are you jealous? Waterstrider might have asked in return. He didn't need to, because the answer was obvious. "I assumed she was safe, since she's a precious 'daughter of the village,'" Waterstrider tried to hold back the question hanging on his tongue, but he lost the struggle. "Was she with you?" *Are* you *jealous?* asked a mocking voice in his own head.

Bearclaw said, "No. She went home."

The words startled Waterstrider. He hadn't considered that Firesister would have her own place. He'd only seen her at Cloud Mountain: first disheveled but not cowering in the shadows of the storage room, then crouched over him in the moonlight as she strove to convince him she meant no harm.

"It was hard on her, that's why I'm telling you about it." Bearclaw said. "They smashed her pots and burned everything else, even her clothes."

"Who did?" Waterstrider asked.

"Who else? The priests from the Temple of Mist, when the Rainsinger accused her of being a witch." The hunter scowled. "She hadn't been back home until last night. Only a few of her things survived the fires. She brought them with her to Cloud Mountain this morning. You might not have spared her a thought, but she's lost much in the past few moons."

"Why are you telling me this?"

"I'm warning you to be careful of her."

The path narrowed and became rougher. Waterstrider looked away from Bearclaw and saw that they were surrounded by shegoi bushes, bristly cholla cactus, and ocotillo rather than the adobe walls of the village. The last time he'd been out in this kind of landscape, his head had been bashed open. He hoped that wouldn't happen again.

Waterstrider turned his attention back to the hunter. "I'm not planning to hurt her," he said.

Bearclaw grunted. "I'll put it a different way. Don't try to get close to her. She's suffered too much already at the hands of men."

"What do you mean by that?"

"Sixteen turnings ago, or thereabouts, she was attacked by a madman." Bearclaw's voice was soft but filled with anguish, as though the words hurt his mouth. "She's been afraid of men ever since. Unwilling to be alone with a man."

Waterstrider had trouble reconciling this view of Firesister with the boldness she'd shown toward Littlecliff and himself. *Is it you, Bearclaw, she doesn't want to be alone with?*

Then he thought of her limp and what she'd said about knowing what it was to lie hurting and alone in the dark. Mistlight was about fifteen—was she the child of this madman Bearclaw spoke of? Waterstrider's chest tightened with an unfamiliar ache. Absently he rubbed at it.

The big hunter went on, "Firesister was just beginning to trust again, and then this accusation of witchcraft . . ." He shook his head. "Don't hurt her. If you do, I'll hunt you down, however far you run." His voice rang with forbidding promise.

"I'm her lifemate in name only," Waterstrider said.

"I know that. But . . . it's in some men to be careless with women. I'm warning you not to believe you can play with Firesister's feelings." He kept his gaze forward.

Waterstrider's temper rose, and along with it the old shame of being too much his father's son. "I have no intention of playing with Firesister in any way." A severe jolt from the litter nearly sent him flying into a nearby willow. They had reached the floodplain.

"That's good, then. You'll be able to go back to the City of Birds alive."

"Stop here," Waterstrider ordered. He stared at what remained of the canal mouths, perched high on the sharp-cut banks of Sky River.

His stomach twisted. Eaglefeather might be right about the canals.

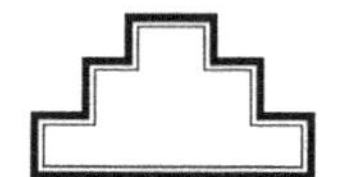

Voices

*Drink, my friends,
    the sweet saguaro wine,
    red as blood.
    Drink deep
        and sing to Mother Ge.
Be beautifully drunk.*

—FRAGMENT OF SONG FROM THE SIT-AND-DRINK CEREMONY

Relieved to have gotten the maps back safely to Cloud Mountain, Skyblade sped up for the last few steps in the passageway. He forgot about the burden basket on his back and knocked it off-kilter against the wall when he turned to enter the plaza. His face flushed, and he yanked it straight again, shifting an offending pole away from his backbone.

Without commenting on his embarrassment, Ninetoes came up beside him and pointed at the map-ground. "Is that where the skins go?"

Skyblade understood why he sounded doubtful. What remained of the Watermasters' plaster map of the Northwind canals lay open to the sun and rain. It was surrounded by squared-off thigh-high blocks with gaps between, through which the ever-present mound-top breezes whistled, piling up cottonwood fluff on the windward side. Empty postholes for roof supports gaped on the upper edge of the blocks. On the map-ground's floor, patches of color showed through wherever plaster had broken away. Like everything else on Cloud Mountain, it was a ruin.

"The maps go here." Skyblade indicated the small, square storage room beside the map-ground. He turned Ninetoes and took off the other boy's burden basket, then had Ninetoes do the same for him.

Ninetoes glanced into the storage room and said, "It needs clearing first."

He was right. Cottonwood fluff had reached such a height within that it spilled out the doorway. Skyblade walked toward the piles of branches left over from building the litter.

Catching up, Ninetoes said, "There's no roof. The skins would get more protection in there." He gestured toward Waterstrider's sleep-room.

Skyblade glanced at the sky and said, "It won't rain anytime soon." He stooped and picked up some arrowweed.

"How do you know?"

"I just do." He smoothed the arrowweed stalks together and held them tightly with both hands. They were bristly enough to serve his purpose.

Ninetoes asked, "Is that something you learned from the priests? Or are you weatherwise?"

Unsure how much to admit about himself, Skyblade stared at his hands. He could say, *My spirit-guides made me weatherwise.* But the other boy might ask him to prove it, just as Puckermouth had. Skyblade suspected his claim to predict the coming of rain was another thing that had gotten him on the wrong side of Puckermouth. He hadn't even told Waterstrider or Firesister yet. He said, "I don't think I learned anything from the priests."

As Skyblade returned to the storage room, Ninetoes trailed behind, confiding, "I'm a dowser. Whenever we're out hunting and need water, I can find it. I have a feel for water."

His boastfulness didn't bother Skyblade like Puckermouth's did, maybe because Ninetoes seemed friendly rather than aggressive. Skyblade glanced at him. "I've never seen a dowser at work." They were said to hold sticks out in front of them, and the sticks would turn in the dowser's hands to show where water lay hidden underground. It sounded like magic, but so did much of the trickery performed in ceremonies by the Stormbringers.

"Want me to show you?"

Skyblade, sorely tempted, hesitated before answering. There was work to be done. He didn't want to be found lacking and get sent away . . . not after gaining something like a family here on Cloud Mountain. Besides, he needed to prove his usefulness to Waterstrider before confessing what he'd done while still a Seeker. "Maybe after we put up the maps," he said.

Stepping into the storage room, which he could span without fully stretching his arms, Skyblade began to sweep the cottonwood fluff out into the plaza. The other boy coughed and moved out of the way as the little white tufts soared on the breeze.

Skyblade set one of the burden baskets beside the doorway of the storage room. He lifted out a handful of maps and stacked them in the room.

"I'm hungry," Ninetoes declared. "Is there anything to eat up here?"

"How can you be hungry already? You ate before we went to the temple."

Ninetoes headed toward the western plaza with its roasting pit and fire-ring and, at the north end, the room Firesister had chosen for herself. "There was a little bit left," he called back over his shoulder.

Skyblade looked at the maps he held, placed them on top of the others in the storage room, and started after Ninetoes. After two steps he halted, frozen in place by what his father would have said about leaving a task half finished. He sighed and turned back to the burden baskets, letting his friend go on without him.

Friend. The idea was so unfamiliar, Skyblade rolled it around in his head as he finished stacking the parchment maps.

In Lastwater, the only boys had been a few turnings older, and in Serpentgate, he'd made only enemies among the other Seekers. On Cloud Mountain, where he'd spent the past moon, there were only Firesister and Waterstrider, old enough to be his parents—and Mistlight, beautiful as ever but walking in a world of her own. Now, suddenly, there was Ninetoes, as impossible to dislike as a tail-wagging pup and following Skyblade around. Could friendship be that simple?

He turned from the little room and saw Ninetoes approaching.

"I still think those maps are gonna get rained on," the other boy said.

He offered a mesquite journeycake to Skyblade, who wasn't hungry but accepted it anyway in the spirit of friendliness.

Speaking around a mouthful of journeycake, Ninetoes said, "Maybe we could put a roof on. Don't you think? I mean, I know you said it wouldn't rain, but it will someday."

"Let's do it," Skyblade said.

The two boys collected the branches and saguaro ribs that would be needed for a temporary cover over the precious maps, as well as reeds for a door to protect against blown-in rain.

While they worked, Ninetoes asked, "Aren't you scared up here on the mound?"

"Why would I be?"

"Folks say Firesister is a witch. They say she killed your whole family, everybody in Lastwater."

The comment surprised Skyblade, who had thought the hunters loyal to Firesister. "Don't be ridiculous."

"And you're not hoping to get revenge on her?"

"Of course not," Skyblade answered, before recalling that only a few moons ago, after finding out what had happened to his parents, he had indeed desired revenge. But that was because of the Rainsinger. "She's no witch," he said with a shrug, "and anyone who claims she is, is just stupid."

That seemed to satisfy the other boy.

After carrying an armful of saguaro ribs to the storage room, Ninetoes wandered off while Skyblade sat and sorted through the leftover reeds. A startlingly white dove flew up to the top of Waterstrider's sleep-room and started its mournful call. Skyblade's hands stilled at their task as Mistlight sidled out of the passageway, following the dove, and stood in the plaza looking up at it.

Ninetoes emerged from the southern doorway of the room that lay just east of the map-ground, the odd little space with two entrances. "It seems strange—" he began.

Mistlight scuttled back into the shadows of the passageway that led to the ruins on the north half of the mound.

Ninetoes stared after her. "Is that the moon-mad daughter?"

Scrambling to his feet, Skyblade remembered how he'd found her in the temple—bleeding, bruised, bewildered. Mistlight had indeed been touched by Mother Ge and left moon-mad, but she deserved sympathy, not scorn. His hands formed into fists beside his thighs, and his voice shook as he said, "As kin, Mistlight has more right to be here than either of us."

"Sorry. I didn't mean to offend."

Skyblade saw no malice in his friend's eyes. No lust for pretty Mistlight either. Ninetoes wasn't like Puckermouth—he really hadn't intended offense. Skyblade's surge of temper faded, and he let his fisted hands relax.

"It seems strange," Ninetoes said, "that there's no room like this facing south, toward the river. Where did the Watermasters view the canals from?"

Skyblade pointed to the ruined tower in the southwest corner. "There. It doesn't look like much now, but once it was a lot taller." The massive footings were evidence of that.

Ninetoes studied the remaining walls, barely higher than his own head. "If it was so big, where did all the adobe go?"

"People keep coming and taking it away." As a Seeker, Skyblade had made many trips to do just that. "A lot of the adobe from the mound has been reused for house compounds in the village. Poles and branches from the roofs too."

"Ah." Ninetoes nodded.

In his friend's ready acceptance of what he said, Skyblade found an unfamiliar sense of pride. He wasn't used to being listened to.

Skyblade gathered up the reeds he'd set aside. "Bring those saguaro ribs, would you?"

Ninetoes complied agreeably. In front of the storage room, he let the saguaro ribs slide onto the others he'd brought earlier. "The top of the wall doesn't look very even," he observed.

"We're going to fix that."

It wasn't quite that simple. First they had to find chunks of adobe to set in where the walls had crumbled. Skyblade used rocks from the fire-ring to turn smaller pieces of adobe into powder, which he mixed with water, cottonwood fluff, and some of the cactus juice Firesister had set aside for that purpose. "Mortar," he told Ninetoes in answer to his friend's question. "The cottonwood fluff makes it stronger, and the cactus juice keeps it from cracking as it dries."

"You know a lot about this building stuff," Ninetoes said. "Could you teach me?"

Hearing desperation in the words, Skyblade stopped mixing the mortar and eyed his friend. "Why do you want to know?"

"Waterstrider seems to respect you. If I could make a good impression on him, maybe he would let me be a ditchrunner."

"You want to be a ditchrunner?"

Defensively Ninetoes said, "I could do it. I'm strong. Fast, too. And have a feel for water."

"Finding water, at least," Skyblade muttered.

"Don't you think that could be useful?" Ninetoes hesitated, then said, "I do want to be a ditchrunner, though my brother won't be happy. Could you help me convince Waterstrider to take me on? If I can get him to agree before I tell Bearclaw . . ."

Skyblade wasn't sure how to respond to the request. Torn between suspicion that he was being used, a desire to help his only friend, and the practical voice in his head that said Waterstrider needed workers, Skyblade went back to stirring the mortar, rather more vigorously than it deserved. "I don't think ditchrunners do much with plaster," he told Ninetoes. "I guess they look for washouts, erosion, broken headgates, missing turnout stones. I'm doing this"—*to be useful*—"because the Watermaster needs the big plaster map before he even sends out any ditchrunners."

"Oh. That makes sense." Ninetoes sounded disappointed.

As days passed, Skyblade regretted showing that he knew how to work with adobe, for that skill mostly restricted him to the top of the mound. The farmers accepted Ninetoes, with his sturdier frame, on the crew doing the heavy work of rebuilding the weir.

They preferred farmfolk as ditchrunners, so as clan-sons were assigned areas to patrol, the clanless Skyblade was left out, despite learning the skills of a ditchrunner: calculating using knots, marking maps, understanding how water moved, judging the lay of the land. When Waterstrider complained that most of the ditchrunners were unable to pace off a set distance, Skyblade even came up with the idea of tying knots in a long cord to measure a number of paces that would be consistent no matter who was doing the measurement.

But he wasn't really a ditchrunner. Nor was he helping rebuild the canals. Instead, he spent most of his time getting the map-ground ready for Waterstrider's use later, once the weir was done. He told himself that was important too.

Waterstrider, overseeing construction at the river, had set aside crotched poles for the shelter to be built over the large map, and Skyblade mortared the poles into postholes in the blocks surrounding the map-ground. Because some of the holes needed to be enlarged, just putting up the poles took more time than expected. Then branches, which twisted and wrenched out of his hands in errant gusts of wind, had to be laid between the poles and secured with rawhide straps. Working alone except when Firesister came to help, Skyblade wrestled them into submission. More branches laid across the shorter dimension of the map-ground completed the framework, with saguaro ribs crosswise to hold them in place.

At last the shelter was ready to be thatched. That was the task ahead of Skyblade as he stood outside the map-ground looking eastward. Because the map would need to be protected from rain, the shelter couldn't be the customary vatto, which only provided shade. A thatched shelter wouldn't be watertight, of course, but if it was done right, not much rain would drip through the thatch and onto the map carved into the plaster below. Most would slide off the overhang outside the map-ground. Or so Waterstrider had said. The People of Two Rivers didn't do much with thatch. Most roofs were solid so you could walk on them and store corn and other foodstuffs out of reach of animals.

Skyblade placed his aching hands one on each side of his waist, thumbs behind and fingers pointing forward to stretch them. What would be the best thatching material? He bit his lip, unsure who to ask.

Every evening, after being carried home by the hunters in purple twilight, an exhausted Waterstrider examined Skyblade's progress and praised what he'd done. The Watermaster then retreated into his sleep-room and wasn't seen again until dawn. So it went, day after day, with

Skyblade wondering how long Waterstrider could push himself before he collapsed entirely.

Firesister didn't look much better. She'd been busy recruiting work crews among hunters, healers, crafters, traders . . . everyone she could think of, sometimes talking so much that she became hoarse. She didn't rely on just her voice, either, but took baskets full of food to the workers in exchange for their efforts. The food had to be gleaned from the desert, which took her away from the mound, leaving Skyblade alone most of the time.

Alone and, he had to admit, a little lonely.

Tilting his face skyward, he asked Mother Ge, "What did you give us for thatch? You must have created the perfect thing." Upon hearing a throat cleared behind him, he spun around.

Mistlight, for that's who his gaze fell on, pointed at the room with two entrances and said, "She hears better in there."

Skyblade was so shocked to find the elusive Mistlight standing right there, and not only that but speaking to him, that he could think of nothing to say in reply.

"Go in and ask her." After a few heartbeats, Mistlight held up her hands and pressed the air as though to push him forward.

Though she was too far away for him to actually feel her touch, his chest became hot as though she'd laid her palms on him. Skyblade's heart leaped against his ribs. He gulped.

Obediently he left the map-ground and walked toward the still-roofless room she'd pointed out. He entered it from the southern doorway. Gazing toward Mother Sleeping, and feeling rather foolish, he repeated his question: "What would be best for thatch? Seepwillow? Arrowweed?"

After a moment, Mistlight called, "Did you hear?"

Skyblade looked out of the narrow doorway and saw that she had followed him and now stood just outside the room. He shook his head.

"She says arrowweed." Mistlight cocked her head as though listening to something he couldn't hear.

He studied her delicate face closely, thinking her cheeks were more rounded, their color brighter than when she'd been a Cornmaiden. His gaze went lower, and even though he felt his own cheeks flush, he was sure her breasts were larger, more womanly—and her waist thicker.

Mistlight laughed and skipped away, scrambling childlike over the remains of a tumbledown wall before vanishing into the ruins of the north half of Cloud Mountain.

That night, sitting under the stars with Firesister after gulping down the usual journeycakes and jerky that had become his regular fare since she'd become busy providing food for an ever-changing work crew, Skyblade said, "Mistlight spoke to me today." It was dark, before moonrise, and he thought that would make it easier to get through what he wanted to say.

"Really?" Firesister sounded doubtful more than surprised.

"Have you taken a close look at her lately?" His cheeks grew hot again. He hoped Firesister would say yes, so he didn't have to voice his suspicion that Mistlight might be with child. As a Seeker, he'd heard a lot of speculation from the priests about which of the Cornmaidens and Smokemothers carried new life in their belly. To his inexperienced eye, Mistlight seemed to show most of those signs.

"I haven't seen much of her since Waterstrider recovered," Firesister admitted. "Why do you ask?"

Embarrassed to be talking about woman things with someone he'd come to think of as almost a mother, Skyblade said, "She just seems different, is all. Like she's . . ." The thought of Mistlight's breasts and hips made his face flame hotly.

"She's what?" Firesister prompted.

"Going to have a baby?" He forced out the words, though they half strangled him, and he wondered if Firesister would even understand them. *Don't make me say it again,* he begged inside his head.

She was slow to answer. "The Smokemothers said no, when Mistlight was a Cornmaiden."

"That was before she went into the temple."

Skyblade didn't have to see Firesister's expression to know she was remembering Mistlight on the night he'd rescued her from the temple— broken in mind, body, spirit. Bleeding from places that no one, man or woman, should be losing blood.

Before going to the temple, Mistlight hadn't wavered in her devotion to the Rainsinger despite his cruelties to her. Now she might carry a baby conceived in violence and pain and yet treasure it, as blood of the Rainsinger's blood, flesh of his flesh. What would come of that tangle?

Whenever Skyblade looked at Mistlight he felt something far more complicated than the stirrings of longing and desire that had gripped him since the first moment he'd seen her. She now seemed beyond his grasp, as unreachable as the stars in the evening sky, more even than when she'd been a Cornmaiden and he only a lowly Seeker. Touched by Mother Ge, Mistlight had become something other than a woman.

"If she's with child," he asked, dreading the answer, "could the Smokemothers ask her to become one of them?"

"She isn't a Cornmaiden."

"Not now. But she could become one again at the summer sun-festival, couldn't she?"

Haltingly, Firesister said, "The Rainsinger would have to agree."

"Wouldn't the decision of whether she became a Cornmaiden again be the Smokemothers', not the Rainsinger's?"

"Haven't you ever wondered why the Smokemothers always let the Rainsinger get his own way?" Firesister asked after a moment. "I used to believe it was out of fear. But I've come to suspect it's something thornier than that."

She didn't say any more, and Skyblade didn't press her. Whatever guided the Smokemothers in their decisions, no man was likely to understand. "Should we ask a healer or even the Childcatcher to come look at her?"

"No Smokemothers! And no healer, not yet. Let's be sure first."

Skyblade sat back on his heels and wiped sweat from his brow with the back of a tired hand. He'd just used the last bundle of arrowweed, securing it to the saguaro-rib braces through which willow branches were woven to form one large mat roofing the map-ground's shelter. A measuring glance over the unfinished section told him he would need at least ten bundles of arrowweed thatch to cover the rest of the roof.

Where to find more arrowweed, that was the question. Firesister had said it grew near the river, its gentle resinous scent sweetening the heavy odors of pondweed and brackish water. But "near the river" could describe anything from the riverbank to the flats beyond. Lastwater, where he'd grown up, didn't have arrowweed thickets.

He supposed he could hope that Mother Ge would lead him to what he needed. He was sure that's what Firesister would say. She urged everyone to trust Mother Ge, claiming that the goddess had given her people all the bounty of the desert. Unlike Firesister, Skyblade found such unwavering faith hard to come by. If Mother Ge existed at all, why had she allowed everyone in Lastwater to die?

Skyblade slipped a gray chert chopper, with one sharp edge, into a deerskin sheath. He unfastened his sash and hung the sheath from it.

Next he picked out a burden basket large enough for five bundles of arrowweed. He tied a long-handled corn knife to it. Between the corn knife and the chopper, he should be able to hack the stalks free no matter how tightly clumped they grew. He put a few journeycakes in his belt pack and filled a gourd canteen with water before slinging it over his shoulder. Satisfied that he was ready to set off, he shrugged into the burden basket.

Skyblade left the mound for the first time in many days. As he turned onto the path to the river, he decided to head downstream first and see the progress on the weir, find out exactly where to find arrowweed, maybe coax Ninetoes into helping him haul it back to Cloud Mountain. Having some assistance would save him a second trip, so the map-ground would be completely protected and ready to be plastered anew.

Birds sang, shegoi bushes scented the air, and trees along the washes were covered with pink or yellow blooms. Skyblade found himself whistling as he strode down the path. He couldn't remember how long it had been since he'd felt so cheerful.

The exhilaration of joining the Seekers had worn off quickly, leaving behind mostly fear and resentment—but not enough to make him break off from the life-path that his father and old Dustwind had set him on. Miserable as a Seeker, he'd thought many times about what his father would have to say if he ran home to Lastwater. When his parents died, the question changed to *Where can I go if I run away from the Temple of Lightning? What can I do?* At least with the Stormbringers, he'd had a purpose.

Then he'd seen what the Rainsinger had done to Mistlight, and that had broken him from his life-path as a Seeker. He'd taken Mistlight to her mother and had remained with her on the mound, and his purpose had changed. His life-path now ran alongside the Watermaster's. He could still help the farmfolk get water for their fields, but through the canals, not with the summer rains.

If the canals get rebuilt, said a voice in his head that sounded like the Rainsinger. Skyblade stopped whistling.

As he followed the path around a bend, his spine tingled in warning. His head came up, and he scanned the surroundings, trying to see through shiny-leafed shegoi bushes and cholla cactus stems so thickly thorned that they seemed fuzzy rather than spiny. He heard the crunch of gravel to his right, a sharp whistle from ahead, and a laugh behind him.

Puckermouth stepped into view on the path ahead. Skyblade knew the Seeker wasn't alone—he never went anywhere by himself. Three other boys oozed out of the bushes.

Skyblade reminded himself he was no longer a Seeker. He didn't have to worry about Puckermouth anymore.

"Grab him," Puckermouth said.

Skyblade staggered as the burden basket was ripped off his shoulders. Hands took hold of his right arm and tightened on his sash. He wrenched his arm free, spun about to put the cholla at his back, and drew the chopper from its sheath, waving it in front of him. "Get away," he warned his attackers.

Puckermouth laughed. "You think we're scared?" He jerked his head, signaling the other Seekers to advance on Skyblade, but they didn't move at first. "Grab him," he repeated, sounding irritated.

This time the one on Skyblade's left approached. Skyblade slashed at him with the chopper. The Seeker jumped back. Skyblade took a kick to his right knee. That leg crumpled, and before he could regain his balance, the Seeker on the left came in low and fast and knocked him down. Someone tried to take the chopper from his right hand, but Skyblade clung to it and struck out blindly with the left.

There was a flurry of movement, sandaled feet and brown legs dodging, whirling, hoarse grunts and exclamations, and then the Seekers backed off, leaving Skyblade blinking up and wondering why they'd set him free. He spotted Ninetoes, holding an axe in one hand and a hunter's sturdy knife in the other.

"Four against one?" Ninetoes said. "That seems a little unfair. Whose fight is this?"

Puckermouth stepped toward Ninetoes, but a small gesture from the knife stopped him. "Not yours," the Seeker growled.

"It's mine as much as theirs." Ninetoes waved the axe toward the other three Seekers. He asked Skyblade, "You all right?"

"Yes. Fine." Skyblade scrambled to his feet. He tore the corn knife from its tethers on the burden basket and faced Puckermouth. Four against two now.

"I'll keep these three busy," Ninetoes said.

Puckermouth laughed again, less amused, a touch of nervous strain in the sound this time. "Sure, I'll match myself against Skyblade. But to make it a fair fight, he should have to put down his weapons."

Skyblade didn't need the barely perceptible shake of Ninetoes' head to know how stupid that would be. "Why did you come after me at all?" he asked the Seeker.

Puckermouth scoffed. "You think we followed you? Nah. We were just walking along, minding our own business, when you showed up."

"No, I mean what do you have against me?" His existence shouldn't bother them at all, now that he was no longer a Seeker and they didn't have to look at his ugly face every day, which was Puckermouth's former complaint.

"Traitor!" one of the other boys hissed.

Startled, Skyblade glanced at him. Puckermouth sprang and brought his joined fists down on the hand that held the chopper. The blow made Skyblade drop the tool, more out of surprise than pain. A moment later, Puckermouth grabbed the wooden shaft of the corn knife, placing his hands on either side of Skyblade's left hand and twisting. Skyblade got his other hand on the wood. He and Puckermouth wrestled for the corn knife, yanking and shoving each other.

Skyblade knew the contest could only end one way, with him losing to the stronger boy, and that was what happened. Puckermouth pulled the corn knife away with a shout of triumph. Seeing his chance, Skyblade kicked Puckermouth in the stomach, then dropped to the ground and scrabbled for the chopper.

The corn knife came down on his arm, slicing deep. It didn't hurt, not at first. Blood welled up quickly, coming in spurts, and Skyblade knew that was bad. He brought the chopper around and struck Puckermouth behind the knee, tearing through something tough—muscle, tendon, ligament, Skyblade didn't know.

Then the pain in his slashed arm hit. He dropped the chopper.

He supposed he should scream, as Puckermouth was doing—but all he could do was crouch helplessly on hands and knees and try to keep breathing. He focused on dragging air into his lungs, as his sluggish mind wondered if he was breathing mostly dirt, for the air around him seemed unbearably thick and heavy.

Ninetoes grabbed him by the arm—the good one, not the bleeding one—and hauled him up. "Come on."

He found himself being hustled down the path. They didn't go far.

When they stopped, Skyblade looked down at his arm. Blood flowed from a long gash in fitful spits and spurts. How easily a sharp knife could slice through flesh, he thought, bemused. What once was whole could be divided in an instant.

Ninetoes wrapped Skyblade's sash tightly around and around the bloody cut before tying it off with a deft motion, as Skyblade had seen his mother do many times.

It won't stop the bleeding, he might have said, *just hide it for a while until it soaks through.* But he couldn't get his tongue to work.

Ninetoes grasped his elbow and pulled him onward. "We better keep moving. Get you to a healer before you lose too much blood."

Skyblade thought his friend was probably right. Simply placing one foot in front of the other took all the strength he could muster, and his head seemed to be floating away.

Mistlight danced like a child in her joy at being the only one on the mound. In full view of Mother Sleeping, she leaped and whirled, making herself dizzy. The tattered cotton skirt caught at her legs, while stitches on the much-patched shirt tickled her skin and caused her to giggle. It was the first time she'd been alone in so long!

Firesister and the big, wounded water man and the thin, quiet boy— one or another stayed always near. Today they had all gone off somewhere, and Mistlight's quick feet matched the flight of her heart, so pleased was she at having no one watching, suspecting, judging.

Her happiness shattered with the sound of voices. Men's voices. Many men's voices, echoing off the adobe walls so their presence engulfed her. She froze, shuddered, wrapped her arms around herself, and retreated into the shadows of Mother Ge's room.

"Run and fetch Lightstone," she heard. The voice was familiar. This man had been kind. A friend of Firesister's while the water man lay injured.

She crept to the southern doorway of the room and poked her head out, craning her neck to see what was going on. Through gaps in the blocks surrounding the map-ground she saw several men carrying something between them. They took it toward the plaza where Firesister cooked food for her.

Mistlight slipped out of the room through the northeast doorway and picked her way, bending low and breathless at her daring, through the rubble-strewn plaza that lay to the north. At the corner of the plaza, where one wall stubbed up against another, the joint had begun to crumble, leaving a low spot. She scrambled over, flew across the open space to the next tumbledown wall, and hopped over it. There she paused, torn between curiosity and caution.

Curiosity won out. Snaking along the north side of the plaza wall toward the back of the room that had become Firesister's, Mistlight made herself silent and invisible. She stepped onto the block of adobe she'd placed there some time ago and peered over the wall into the plaza.

Most of the men stood back from a crumpled figure on the ground near the fire-ring. One, wearing a necklace of bear claws, told a boy around her age, "You, go get Lightstone. If he's not there, one of the other healers." His was the familiar voice she'd heard. His name escaped her, though, for Mother Ge's near-constant whispering drove out little things like names.

The boy, with streaks of blood on his face and clothes, said, "The gash is really deep."

"Yes, so go quickly."

The boy took off. His racing footsteps crunched over the rough plaster of the plaza. Mistlight cocked her head, listening as he pounded down the passageway she'd crossed a few heartbeats ago. What if she'd been slower? He might have seen her!

"Where's Firesister?" asked the necklace wearer, Firesister's friend.

Out gathering, Mistlight might have told him, impatient with his stupidity.

"You." Firesister's friend pointed at one of the other men. "Build up a fire. Take him off the litter and put him down here, close to the fire-ring."

"A fire?" someone asked. "He's already sweating."

Somebody else said, "We should put down a pad first. Make him comfortable."

"There's bedrolls over there."

"Grab a couple and lay them down for him," said Firesister's friend.

"Should we unwrap the bandage?"

Firesister's friend shook his head. "Wait for the healer. The bleeding seems to have stopped with pressure."

"But if it's too tight . . ."

"Leave it for now. Get the fire started, will you? That wound will need cleaning. Then stitched, I'm guessing, from what Ninetoes said. Where does Firesister keep her cook-pots?"

Mother Ge told Mistlight, *"Help them. You can do it, as you did for the Watermaster."*

She hadn't done much for the Watermaster. The healers had fixed his head wound. She'd just tended his fever. "I'm scared," she confessed, though of course Mother Ge knew it already.

"What was that?" said Firesister's friend.

Mistlight clapped her hands over her mouth and retreated from the wall, scuttling into the roomblock on the north side of the exposed space.

"You cannot hide forever," Mother Ge said.

Listening for any hint of pursuit, Mistlight closed off Mother Ge's voice inside her head. But the voice returned, beating at her inner defenses like a drum, until she placed her hands over her ears . . . and still she heard it: *"Go, go, go, go."*

Mistlight thought back, *"What do you want from me?"*

"You must not wait for the healers."

Into her mind came the memory of the shadowdancer lying in the prayer room, breathing his last.

"The boy needs your hands," Mother Ge told her, urging her out of her refuge, out to where strangers waited to leap on her.

Mistlight's heart thudded against her ribs as she began to tremble. "No," she whispered. The word bounced off the walls and returned to her manyfold, seeping through her hands into her ears and burrowing deeper until at last she could bear it no longer. Unable to resist Mother Ge's urging, she left the room and slunk through the maze of open spaces and walls. Finally she huddled at the edge of the wall outside the plaza where the men collected around the one who had been injured. She peeped within.

Flames leaped up in the fire-ring. Evidently the men had found the wood and the firestarter kit. The water olla leaned precariously to one side. There was no sign of the heavy-walled, corrugated gray pot that Firesister used for cooking stew and boiling jerky. Mistlight lost her feeble hope that these men might be able to do what needed to be done, without her.

She crept forward, into the plaza.

"It's the crazy—"

Firesister's friend cut off the speaker with a quick slash of a hand.

Painfully aware of every shuffle of a foot, every breath, every brush of leather, the stench of man-sweat and dead animals, Mistlight located the pot in the corner, under the reed mat Firesister used when cooking. She took the pot to the water olla and filled it, then set it on the three rocks of the fire-ring placed just so, to keep the pot level and stable. After, feeling eyes on her back, she went into Firesister's room and rummaged for the moontime cloths every woman kept separate from the rest of their clothing. She hesitated at the doorway, cloths in hand, weighing the danger.

Most of the men had left. Only Firesister's friend still stood in the plaza, and he was way over by the outlanders' packs. Watching her. Her heart raced as though she'd been running full-out. Her breaths sounded raspy to her sharp-pricked ears.

Eventually, alert for any hint of movement, she dared to leave her refuge. Mistlight let her gaze drop to the slight form lying by the fire. There she saw the boy who had stolen her from the temple, where her world had been torn apart by learning that Eaglefeather had never cared for her, that he hated and despised her for even wanting him. Eaglefeather had rejected her heart utterly. She hated him. And loved him still.

Mistlight bit her lip. She spread her fingers over her belly and reminded herself that she might not have Eaglefeather, but she soon would have his baby to love—and to receive worshipful devotion from, unconditionally and forever, as a child naturally felt for its mother.

She looked again at the boy, at his right arm, bound with strips of cloth soaked through with blood, glistening in the sun. He was small, about her own size, and looked to have been beaten, as she had been, with bruises and welts darkening his red-brown skin. Pity overtook her.

"Child."

"Yes," she answered Mother Ge.

"You must begin."

Mistlight laid Firesister's mat beside the wounded arm, positioning it well away from the blood that had seeped into the pitted surface of the plaza. She began to sing the song of healing: "When Mother Ge made up this land . . ." Her voice faltered, for her mind's eye gazed on the shadowdancer rather than her rescuer. The hands she reached out toward the bloodied boy seemed no more than wispy trails of fog moving through the air. "I can't," she told Mother Ge. She withdrew her insubstantial hands and laid them in her lap.

"Wait for the healers," Firesister's friend told her soothingly. "The water will be hot by the time they arrive. You've done well."

She was tempted to do as he said. Sorely tempted to leave the boy to the healers, to escape into the silence of the ruins. But Mother Ge wouldn't let her. Sighing, Mistlight reached out and touched the bandage, letting the goddess feel the wound through the cloth.

The boy's eyes opened. They fixed on Mistlight's face.

"It's all right," she whispered.

His other hand, blurry around the edges, came over his body and wrapped around hers. His touch felt faint and indistinct. "I was the one," the boy said in a voice that barely reached her ears. "I told the Rainsinger that Waterstrider was coming. I got his friend killed. I never admitted to it, never asked forgiveness."

This pitiful boy had come to her when she was wandering alone in the shadows after something terrible had happened, and she'd taken his hand and gone with him. She thought of that as she looked down at their hazy fingers linked together.

"Take the bandage off slowly," Mother Ge instructed.

Mistlight pulled her hand free and placed the boy's left arm back at his side. She fumbled at the knot, but the bandage was pulled too tightly to work loose. She drew a sharp knife from her belt and sliced through the twisted cloth—hard to do cleanly when she couldn't quite focus on the knife or the bandage.

Firesister's friend uttered a hard exclamation and started forward, covering half the plaza in a few long strides. "Stop it!"

"Stay back." The voice that came out of her throat was a deep thunderous roar, so unlike her own that she stopped breathing for a moment.

The man halted. A strange expression swept across his face. The boy on the ground beside her said something.

She told the boy, "Trust me."

Her gaze returned to Firesister's friend, big and powerful. To him she announced, "This is Mother Ge's will."

The three of them remained still for the space of ten heartbeats, an eternity for Mistlight as she waited for the big man to advance and knock her away from the wounded boy.

Hoarsely, the boy called out, "Let her do as she thinks best."

"You're still bleeding!" But the big man stayed where he was, on the other side of the fire-ring.

Mistlight peeled away the top layer of soggy bandage. She cut the next strip of cloth that became visible, moved it aside, and did the same with the next and the next one after that. The blood began to feel sticky, as though starting to dry.

"Gently, gently," Mother Ge advised.

The motions came readily enough, with her hands seeming to know what to do. Mistlight knew the goddess was working through her. But that hadn't saved the shadowdancer.

Mother Ge said, *"The shadowdancer was not meant to live."*

"And this one is?"

The answer that came to Mistlight was no answer, simply the blanket of reassuring warmth and love the goddess wrapped her in whenever she became too frightened or tired to go on.

The boy's eyes drifted closed, and Firesister's friend shifted restlessly. Mistlight flashed him a threatening glare. He froze into immobility but said, "You'll kill him!"

"No. You'll see." Mistlight repeated what Mother Ge told her: "The cut's already starting to scab over."

Firesister's friend shook his head. "It's too deep for that. The healers will need to stitch it."

"No need for stitches."

"You can't know that—you weren't there."

"Mother Ge was." As she uttered that unassailable truth, Mistlight removed the last strip of red-tinged cloth and laid the wound bare. A crust of blood angled across the boy's forearm, following the cut. The cloth had been damp enough that its removal hadn't stripped away the drying blood that sealed the wound.

Mother Ge said, *"It will stay closed. If you are careful."*

Mistlight was careful. She took fresh cloths one at a time and dipped them in hot water, let them cool briefly in the air, and gently wiped the smears of blood from the boy's arm, cleaning all around the gash before, at last, placing a clean cloth on top to protect the wound from the wind that puffed cottonwood fluff and dust into everything on the mound.

Soon another man arrived, bony and tall and smelling of herbs. Mistlight scrambled away from the boy. She retreated into Firesister's room. Jangling nerves made her want to scream and claw at herself. *"Make them go!"* she begged Mother Ge, who soothed and caressed, easing the panic.

Firesister's friend asked, "Where's Lightstone?"

The new man said, "He'll be along."

"Mistlight wouldn't let me get close. I couldn't stop her from taking off the bandage."

The new man lifted the cloth away from the boy's arm, then let it settle back into place. "The girl did well enough," he said. He turned and looked straight at Mistlight, smiling at her.

Mistlight, wishing Mother Ge would emerge and drive away the intruders, bared her teeth in return. She pushed herself back from the doorway and slid over to the side wall of the room, out of view. Closing her eyes in an effort to shut out the masculine voices did no good. Still she could hear them, the deep rumble and growl. More voices joined them.

"The boy must be moved now," someone said.

"It might be too much for him."

Their words faded as Mother Ge drew a veil over Mistlight's senses. The distance from the world of men made her feel like a Cornmaiden again, hidden from view and untouchable. Sadly, the feeling of withdrawing into somewhere safe within herself didn't last, for all too soon Firesister's voice penetrated her remoteness.

"What are you doing?" Firesister demanded.

A man said, "Taking him to the healers' compound. He's been injured."

After a few moments of silence, Firesister said accusingly, "This is no accident. It's a knife cut, clean and deep."

The recognizable voice of Firesister's friend said, "He was jumped by some Seekers."

"And you want to take him off the mound?" Firesister asked.

A man said, "The healers can take care of him better—"

"Put him down," Firesister commanded.

"But—"

Firesister said, "The Watermaster was attacked by priests. This boy was once a Seeker, turned against the priests, and now has been attacked in turn. Do you really want to be responsible for keeping Skyblade safe?"

"Better us than you," a man said. "They got the boy this time. You might be next. Leave the Watermaster. Get yourself away from the mound before it's too late."

Firesister said, "You idiot. Skyblade wasn't hurt here."

"What makes you so certain?"

"The mound is guarded," she said. "There are always hunters stationed nearby, watching."

Firesister's friend said, "She's right. My brother was with Skyblade. They were near the river when the Seekers came upon them. It was an unprovoked attack, though I'm sure the priests will claim otherwise. This time we know for sure who's to blame."

The words flew back and forth, then swept away like a cloud of bats as Mistlight heard a baby begin to cry. Her baby. While she huddled in the room, trapped by the crowd of men in front of the room's doorway, her baby wailed inconsolably somewhere outside.

"What do I do?" she asked silently, rocking back and forth in time with the infant's cries. No answer came from Mother Ge. Her anguished heart swelling until pain sank its talons into her chest, Mistlight sat in misery, desperate to rescue her child but unable to force herself out where the men lay in wait.

After an agonizingly long time, she heard Firesister say, "They've gone. You can come out now."

There was no sign of anyone at the door, no voices rumbling in the plaza. Mistlight's skin no longer crawled with the sensation of being surrounded. She eased toward the doorway, ready to either retreat or run away if Firesister was lying. But there was no one in the plaza except Firesister and the injured boy, who lay beside the fire. Mistlight crept closer. His eyes were closed, but his chest rose and fell.

Firesister spoke again, startling her: "The bonemender said you did a good job closing the wound. You were right—it wasn't deep enough to need stitching. Skyblade will have a nice scar to show off."

Mistlight shuddered. She turned away and hurried toward her baby, winding through shadowed passageways, picking her way across plazas and courtyards strewn with chunks of adobe, drawing ever closer to the alcove where the crying was coming from. She reached in, grabbed the swaddled form, held it to her breast, and bounced it gently to make it stop crying.

Firesister's voice startled her: "What's that you have?"

Mistlight whirled around.

Closer Firesister came, and closer yet, until her hot breath puffed out on Mistlight's shoulder as she bent near. Her thin, grasping fingers twitched the cloth off the baby's face. "It's a jar! An old one, too, judging by the pattern."

"It's mine! My baby!" Mistlight knocked the probing hand aside. She stepped back until she came up against a wall, then sidled away, eyeing the woman who would steal her child.

"It's not a baby. Just look . . . there's birds painted on it—"

Mistlight turned and ran. She clutched her baby close as she fled through the maze of ruins, counting on speed and the many twists and climbs and narrow spaces to prevent being tracked to her bolt-hole, the secret place hidden inside one of the tumbledown buildings where she stashed her sleep mat, blankets, clothing, food. Once there, she crouched in the corner, hugged her bundle, and rocked in time to her heartbeat while she waited to be discovered.

Mistlight woke with an image in her mind's eye: *an arrow dark against the sky, the Rainsinger tumbling from the top of the temple.* Her heart clenched and she gasped for breath as she lay rigid in the dark. Horror washed through her, though she was safe in her bolt-hole, far from the temple. She'd had the same vision for a long time, but it was coming more often of late and frequently kept her from sleeping at night. It had begun to appear as it pleased, day or night, whenever she could no longer stay awake.

Mother Ge said, *"Cleanse yourself so the malignant spirits following the boy do not find you weak from dreaming."*

Mistlight rummaged through the basket of herbs she'd collected. Upon finding the tender tips of desert-broom, she swept them across her hair and face to start the rite of cleansing while she spoke the words of the invocation: "Spirits of the Ancestors, draw the dream-vision from my fleshly body. Wipe it from my eyes like tears, breathe it from my nose like fog, drift it from my ears like music, melt it from my shoulders like the dew." She moved to her breasts, down to her stomach and thighs, all the way to her toes, and sent the taint of dreaming deep into the ground.

"Now go to him," Mother Ge ordered.

At first Mistlight was afraid to stir from the bolt-hole, but Mother Ge reminded her of the earth-magic that lay strong beneath her feet here on the mound, reassuring her that no one moved nearby and it was safe to emerge.

She went to the boy. He lay still, his arm bandaged. Sweat beaded his brow, and his breaths sounded ragged. His eyes were closed. The scent of hot willow bark hung in the air, wafting off a squat cook-pot beside the embers of the earlier fire.

He was not the shadowdancer, she reminded herself. This open space, lit warmly by Brother Sun, was not the prayer room where the shadowdancer had passed over to the Ancestors. This innocent boy's wound was a clean slice, not the strong spring venom of serpents. She wouldn't lose him. Mother Ge had promised.

Lines of pain around the boy's mouth made him seem old and frail. She took up a gourd spoon and dipped it into the willow-bark decoction, then squatted beside him, reached for the bandage, and began peeling it back gently. Whenever the cloth stuck, she poured a few drops of the warm decoction onto the scab below.

She felt eyes upon her and glanced up from her task to find him gazing back. Her hand trembled, spilling some of the decoction on the ground.

"Don't be afraid," he said.

The spoon dropped from her nerveless hand. She rose and stepped back before spinning around and running from the plaza. She'd gotten partway down the passage that led to the north half of the mound when she heard voices echoing off walls somewhere beyond the narrow passageway. Wildly she gazed about, unsure where the people were. Forward, there were open spaces on both sides where she would likely be spotted, but going back to the plaza would expose her even more. She stood still and begged Mother Ge for guidance as the voices grew louder.

The light voice was Firesister. The deep one belonged to the water man. "Don't be afraid," Mistlight whispered to herself. Yet she trembled so hard, she couldn't bear to stand there waiting to be discovered. She turned to the east, toward Mother Sleeping, and scrambled over the low point where two walls joined. Crouching low, she pressed her back against the wall and covered her mouth with one hand.

Firesister and the water man drew near, then stopped on the other side of the wall. Mistlight didn't move, hardly dared breathe.

Quietly but with an edge sharpening his deep voice, the water man said, "Skyblade isn't the only one at risk. I'm getting reports from farmers of mysterious damage to the ditches. They're sleeping in their fields and they hear nothing, then wake in the morning and find the turnout stones smashed or a hole deep enough to swallow a half-day's water allotment right outside their field. Some blame it on witchcraft. It's too dangerous for you and Mistlight on the mound."

There was a silence. Then, "Where would we go?"

"Gran Squashblossom would take you in."

"Putting us closer to the farmers who are already afraid of us? I think not. Eaglefeather works through fear. Those who refuse to cower before him and instead place their faith in Mother Ge will defeat him in the end. There's no need for you to worry about us. In truth, I would rather you didn't. I can take care of myself and my daughter."

The water man said, "You chose me as your lifemate. That gives me the right to worry about you."

For a while, nothing more was said. Mistlight, hoping the two of them were ready to move away, took her hand off her mouth and listened hard for their footsteps to start up. The water man spoke, dashing her rising hope.

"Early on, you said Skyblade shouldn't be a ditchrunner. Did you know something like this would happen?"

"Suspected," said Firesister, "from what he told me of his life as a Seeker. It's why I tried to keep him busy on the mound, had you send up branches and brush so he could work steadily. He must've run out and gone for more."

"He had to have known the hunters were guarding him as long as he stayed here. How could he have been so—"

"He may be only a boy, but he has his pride. I let him believe it was Mistlight they were guarding. But it wasn't, not really. Eaglefeather was happy to be rid of her. The Smokemothers were the ones who wanted her in the temple, not Eaglefeather. He only used her to threaten me with. I would like to know what curse he placed on her, to make her imagine that she loved him. He broke her mind, and for that, I can never forgive him. I want him dead!"

The world darkened around Mistlight. She remembered the dim room, the dizzyweed, Eaglefeather's hot breath and hurting hands roaming over her body as she screamed. And then he was falling from the top of the temple. *"I want him dead!"* But that hadn't happened yet, had it?

Tears blinded Mistlight. She stumbled away, unseeing. How long she wandered through the passageways and courtyards in a vain attempt to escape those words echoing in her mind—*want him dead, want him dead*—she didn't know. At last she stubbed her toe, and the stab of pain brought her back to the top of the mound, where Brother Sun shone on her face and dried her tears.

Later, back in her bolt-hole, Mistlight hugged her bundle close as she considered Firesister's words. They should have hurt. She'd loved Eaglefeather. She'd ached for him, craved his devotion more than food. And the agony of learning how little he cared for her! But now that she had her baby, she understood that what she really desired wasn't Eaglefeather's heart, nothing so burdensome. What she'd wanted all along was simply love.

Mother Ge had given her that.

She was a mother now. The most important person in someone's life. That was enough.

Standing in the mound's west plaza, Firesister wished for a headscarf to cover her black hair, baking under Brother Sun's fire. The hot, dry days of foresummer had set in. When she was gathering mesquite pods or cactus pads or berries for Waterstrider's work crews, she always made sure to finish before the heat of the day and prepared the food in the shade of the cottonwoods by the river.

Today Skyblade's injury had interrupted that routine. Bearclaw had sent for her, and she'd run back to Cloud Mountain as quickly as she could, leaving nopal pads in the burden basket where she'd placed them after slicing them loose from the cactus. Their slimy juice would soak through the netting of the burden basket, maybe ruining it.

She would have to send someone after the food. And who would cook for the work crew?

Wishing there were three of her to make sure everything got done, she placed both hands on top of her head to protect her from Brother Sun's enthusiastic rays.

The movement brought Waterstrider's eyes to meet hers. Bare-chested and sweaty, he leaned on his crutch. She flushed and looked away, casting her gaze down at Skyblade, who lay in the plaza, eyes closed and chest heaving with ragged breaths.

The bandage had been peeled back to reveal a clean wound, the edges of the skin already sealed with dried blood. Firesister ached for the boy, who deserved better than this latest tangle with the Seekers, most likely those who had bullied him while he was one of their own.

Waterstrider asked, "Are you sure you can take care of him?"

Firesister eyed Waterstrider's drawn expression and the way his weight sagged on the crutch. The hunters had used the litter to haul

Skyblade to Cloud Mountain, leaving Waterstrider to walk from the river by himself. She said, "Unless wound fever sets in, I should be able to manage."

Skyblade stirred restlessly. He muttered something but didn't open his eyes. Some of the willow-bark decoction had spilled next to him, and a gourd spoon lay nearby.

Firesister knelt, picked up the spoon, and set it back in the pot holding the warm liquid. She lifted out a few spoonfuls and poured them over the wound, then replaced the bandage and soaked it with the decoction. Rest, regular applications of willow bark to provide relief from pain, and the resilience of youth would soon have Skyblade up and around again.

In the meantime he needed some shade. His exposed skin, damp with sweat, had begun to redden. Firesister knew she wasn't strong enough to drag him into a room by herself. But Waterstrider was in no condition to provide help.

"Don't worry about Skyblade," she said. "He'll be fine. Go take care of yourself. You need rest."

"Do I look that pathetic?" Waterstrider put up his free hand to cut off whatever she might say. "No need to answer. I'll go lie down for a bit."

Her gaze followed him to the sleep-room. Within the thick adobe walls that held onto some of the coolness of night, Waterstrider would be comfortable enough. Firesister wished Skyblade would be too. *"Water doesn't flow for wishing it so,"* as her mother used to say. Wishes were useless. Firesister sighed.

The quiet on top of Cloud Mountain was broken only by the chatter of a runnerbird perched on top of Waterstrider's sleep-room. The plaza where materials for the map-ground roof had lain for several days was empty now; the diligent Skyblade had tidied up all the brush and branches. Firesister saw nothing with which to make a shade for Skyblade as she had for Waterstrider when he'd lain unconscious among the shegoi bushes, and she thought, not for the first time, that Mother Ge's desert was more generous than the places built by men.

Should she leave Skyblade alone? She could go find a few of the hunters, convince them to place the injured boy in one of the rooms. But that might take a while. Perhaps Mistlight could watch over him while Firesister searched for someone to help.

More likely not. The girl, even if she could be found, might be of little use, for her madness seemed to have worsened. She now believed she was no longer carrying Eaglefeather's baby but had actually given birth. Firesister's hands tightened into fists at the thought of what Eaglefeather had done to Mistlight. What he had done to all the wounded people who had taken refuge on Cloud Mountain—Skyblade being the most recent.

"Yah!" she called up to the runnerbird, which cocked its head and rolled a yellow-rimmed eye at her before rattling its bill impudently. "Go ask Mother Ge how we are to endure all this."

The large bird extended its wings and flew down to the litter. After clicking its bill a few times it took flight, skimming over the low wall and out of sight somewhere below the mound.

Firesister looked at the litter, which now consisted of little more than two poles with saguaro braces between them. The bench had been cut away and left behind at the river so Skyblade could be carried flat, not seated as Waterstrider had been for the past several days.

She went into her sleep-room and found the headcloth she'd been wishing for earlier. She moistened it with water from the drinking olla. Back in the plaza, she propped up the two poles of the litter and tied the damp cloth between them to shade Skyblade. The breeze on top of the mound should cool him without disturbing the delicate balance of the poles and cloth. In a few moments the boy's restlessness eased, and he seemed more comfortable.

Footsteps and voices echoed up the passageway that led to the north half of Cloud Mountain. The first man who strode into the plaza was Lightstone, the chief healer, his red robes flapping. She summoned her usual bright smile, the one she always used when there was little to smile about.

Several young, strong healers followed their senior into the plaza. Red robes swirled festively around their ankles, but their faces were grave. They would be capable of hauling Skyblade into the shade. She didn't think that was what they intended.

"Greetings of the day!" Lightstone stopped several paces away and inclined his head with distant dignity.

The formality of his words and gesture disturbed Firesister, even though his voice was, as always, soft and caressing like the touch of a feather. She'd often wondered how much of his power as a healer came from his voice, which soothed the listener's heart with the warmth of a well-tended hearth in a winter storm. Today something felt amiss. Her smile faded. Try as she might, she couldn't bring it back.

Wordlessly Firesister looked an inquiry at Lightstone, who explained, "A Seeker with a deep wound in his leg accuses this boy of striking him from concealment, to settle a grudge. The elders will consider who is telling the truth—the aggrieved Seeker or this boy. Until they assign blame, he is to be tended in the healers' compound."

"And if they blame Skyblade?"

"If he is innocent, he has nothing to fear."

Nothing to fear when the priests were involved? Firesister held herself still, hands at her sides, though she wanted to fly at the chief healer and smack him for his stupidity. "You stood by me," she reminded him, "when I was accused of witchcraft. Skyblade deserves the same consideration."

"Everyone in the village knows you are no witch, yet we were unable to keep you out of the Rainsinger's clutches. He has gained too much influence with his promises."

"Not promises. Lies."

"This is the best solution for everyone. Especially you. We cannot permit you to take such a risk after what the Rainsinger did to you last time."

To me? He did nothing to me but set my life-path alongside Waterstrider's! It's Mistlight he tore to pieces. Firesister tried to tamp down her anger rather than letting it flame up into a conflagration of words she could never take back. "That's my choice, not yours."

"You do not have the right to say who stays on Cloud Mountain and who goes."

Waterstrider said, "You're wrong."

Firesister spun around and spotted him leaning on the waist-high wall that separated the east and west plazas.

Though his face was drawn, his voice was implacable. "My lifemate can say exactly that."

Firesister's heart skipped a beat upon hearing those words. She told herself sternly not to be foolish.

He went on, "Skyblade is a ditchrunner. By long custom, he belongs wherever he can be most useful. I have assigned him to Cloud Mountain for now. Would you argue that I lack the right to say who stays on Cloud Mountain and who goes?"

Lightstone said, "Do not put yourself in the middle of this matter. If the Rainsinger involves himself—"

"Skyblade is mine," said Waterstrider. "There's no question of taking him."

Skyblade said, "Let me go." Staring across the plaza at Waterstrider, he added, "You don't know what I've done."

"I know you took care of me when I was recovering. You helped train the new ditchrunners. You rebuilt the map-ground."

Skyblade took a deep breath and let it out. After a long moment he said, "I overheard something I wasn't meant to, and I told the Rainsinger of your return well before you arrived. I nearly got you killed. Your friend did die." He turned his head away, evidently too ashamed to face Waterstrider. "It's all my fault. If Firesister and Mistlight won't be safe as long as I'm around, I should go."

"Tcha!" Waterstrider scoffed. "It doesn't matter that you told him of my return. He probably heard it from Far-Traders anyway. We were a large party and didn't bother with a stealthy approach."

He cast Firesister a meaningful glance. She picked up his argument. "Skyblade, the priests from the southernmost temple ran up here and informed Eaglefeather that a Watermaster was coming. That's when he went after Mistlight and me—as a way of getting to Waterstrider. When that failed, he had the priests from the other temple attack Waterstrider and the outlanders. Never blame yourself for the things Eaglefeather chooses to do."

From beside her Lightstone muttered, "Still calling him by the name he gave up when he became the Rainsinger? Such disrespect is unwise."

"Eaglefeather deserves no respect," she hissed at him.

"Many others disagree," Lightstone said. "You should not make your contempt so clear. This is no time to turn stubborn. What if the Rainsinger claims the boy is still bound by his Seeker's vow to obey?"

Waterstrider gazed at the wide-eyed boy absorbing the words that would determine his future. "Skyblade is a ditchrunner now."

Lightstone said, "Be reasonable. Would you jeopardize everything for the sake of this one boy?"

"I'm not the one who needs the canals in order to survive," Waterstrider replied. "I can always return to the City of Birds. You said the clan elders will decide? Let them try to take him." Waterstrider's gaze roved over the healers, who stared back, openmouthed, as though they'd picked up something they thought was a stick and it turned out to be a rattlesnake.

Firesister shivered, suddenly afraid that she would find herself going against every instinct for self-preservation if she was not very careful. Waterstrider created feelings inside her that she had never felt before. He could easily be the making of her, or the death of her. She couldn't decide which was the more likely.

He'd resisted taking her as his lifemate but had eventually accepted the situation grudgingly, and then Skyblade had come bringing Mistlight, and Waterstrider had allowed them all to stay without argument. Firesister had assumed that he found herself and Skyblade useful for his goal of rebuilding the canals and simply ignored Mistlight, that he wasn't overly concerned with the lives of any of the people who'd come to Cloud Mountain because they had nowhere else to go.

But now here he was, defending Skyblade as though the boy really was important to him, and as more than a ditchrunner, more than someone who worked cheerfully and attentively. Firesister reeled internally with a realization that felt more dangerous than anything she'd experienced at Eaglefeather's hands—Waterstrider's defense of Skyblade seemed like a fatherly love.

Firesister had gone from having no one to having something very like a family, and she was terrified that she would lose all these people she had so unexpectedly come to care for. *Mother Ge,* she prayed silently, twisting oddly cool, stiff fingers together, *please let me keep them. Don't let Eaglefeather destroy them.*

She watched Lightstone gather the other healers and lead them in stiff-backed offense from the plaza, the hems of their red robes drifting in the breeze. She couldn't look at Waterstrider or poor Skyblade.

Late in the morning of the next day, Firesister was thinking about how Eaglefeather might retaliate. She was certain that he would not let the injury to his Seeker pass. Anxiety lodged deep in her bones, chilling her even as Brother Sun blazed high above. Several women worked nearby in the littletree cactus patch, but none of them could see her face within the headscarf she wore. She was glad her expression was hidden. Besides fretting about Eaglefeather, she couldn't get Waterstrider off her mind.

Upon discovering that she'd arranged to go out picking cactus buds, Waterstrider had tried to forbid her going. *"I won't be alone,"* she'd explained. *"There'll be a group of us. And several of the hunters will go with."* She and Waterstrider had thrown words back and forth, until it was settled that Firesister would do as she planned, since Waterstrider's work crew needed to be fed. That was the practical thing to do.

Skyblade—though still weak—would accompany Waterstrider, well guarded by hunters, older men but capable of warding off any direct physical attack from Eaglefeather. Several of the most respected elderly hunters would guard Mistlight on the mound. And off the mound, as always, Bearclaw wouldn't let Firesister out of his sight.

Yet all the provisions for protecting herself and the others didn't reassure Firesister. Eaglefeather was a trickster. He would wait until she least expected the next attack, and then he would do something completely unforeseen. Frustrated, she shook her head as she viciously twisted the last bud loose and dropped it on the others.

After setting the saguaro-rib tongs on top of the buds that filled the basket, Firesister interlaced her fingers behind her cotton shirt and arched her back. The air sucked up the sweat so quickly that her shirt and skirt were dry, leaving her skin prickling.

Her face pointed upslope toward the red-hued mountain known as The Spine, which was said to be the remains of one of the great river-serpents that had formed the Valley of Two Rivers. The shadows had shrunk as the morning advanced, flattening the canyons and ridges into a featureless block that loomed against the painfully brilliant blue sky. Firesister placed a finger and thumb at the corners of her mouth and gave a piercing whistle. When the women working nearby in the cactus patch looked up, she waved and called out, "Time to go. We have enough by now."

She'd been productive, filling two baskets with cactus buds. The other women had worked hard too. Between them, they had picked enough buds for several roasting pits: one for each clan that participated in the communal task and another for the men rebuilding the weir.

A few days earlier, some of these women had begged her to show them a generous patch of littletree cactus. She'd known them from her time in the Children's House, but that they would come to her was a surprise. Older than she was, they had little to do with the scrawny girl she'd been back then, a child of the Near-Kin.

Her people, who had come from the Mountains of Sunrise during the Long Thirst, were looked upon with suspicion because of the staying-sickness that swept through their enclave and struck down so many, her parents among them. Firesister was spared, but many of the other children who'd been orphaned as the staying-sickness spread throughout Serpentgate kept their distance from her, not only then but for many turnings after.

She gazed at the crowd of high-spirited, chattering women. Their faces peeped out from headcloths the same color as the desert pavement, the same color as their ankle-length dresses, which swayed with the movement of their hips as they walked between baskets filled with food they wouldn't have but for her.

Early this morning they had shown up with daughters and clan-sisters, a whole companionable throng, and had followed Firesister to this spot north of Serpentgate, a place well known by the Near-Kin. The women hadn't quite picked it clean, but there wouldn't be many cactus fruits left for the deer and birds. Firesister offered a silent apology to Mother Ge.

Bearclaw came up to her. "I think we brought enough drags for all the baskets."

Firesister turned a grateful smile on him. He had volunteered the services of the hunters to haul the gathered buds back to the village, enabling the women to pick more than they could carry by themselves. *"We'll be there anyway to make sure nothing happens,"* he'd said. "The drags were a good idea," she told him. "Let's get the baskets tied on."

In the end, Firesister didn't have to do anything. She stood back and watched as various hunters competed to see who could carry the most baskets, showing off their muscles and speed but taking care to not spill any of the precious cactus buds. The women fastened the baskets onto the drags with nets, like the one Firesister had used on Waterstrider to keep him from flailing around when his wits were wandering. As the hunters placed baskets into the clan-sisters' hands, appreciative glances flew back and forth and hands seemed to linger longer than necessary.

Firesister realized this occasion might be unusual on both sides. The hunters didn't spend much time in the village, coming in from their hunting grounds mainly on trade days and for the sun-festivals, like the upcoming Cloud-Summoning of midsummer. During such celebrations, they were gambling, eating, dancing, racing. There weren't many opportunities for clan-sisters to see them working.

One lovely younger woman, with a delicate face and large, expressive eyes, seemed especially taken by Bearclaw. Firesister hoped he noticed, but she suspected he was oblivious, for he was busy making sure the nets were tightly secured.

"All ready," he said at last.

With the hunters taking turns at the drags, the contented party of men and women descended from the foothills of The Spine, winding through the open spaces that surrounded shegoi bushes, avoiding the scatter of spiny greenthorn trees, saguaros, ocotillos, and various cactuses. At last they turned onto the path that would take them south to Serpentgate. The path lay before them broad and relatively straight and smooth, and everyone else began to walk more quickly.

Everyone but Firesister. The chill she'd felt earlier returned, deepening as she neared the Temple of Lightning, which lay at the north end of the village. The temple was an imposing structure, as tall as some of the buttes near the river. It had stood there her whole life, pale except for the three gaping holes in each face, black rectangles stacked one on top of another, deep shadowy openings that seemed to have no end. Firesister hurried to catch up with the rest of the party. She usually didn't travel at this pace because it made her limp more conspicuous, but she suddenly felt anxious about being alone.

Her limping haste proved unnecessary, because the others halted soon after. When Firesister peered past the women's pale dresses and the hunters' broad, leather-vested backs, she saw the yellow robes of the priests of the Temple of Lightning.

Eaglefeather, she realized. He had moved more quickly than she'd expected. That he hadn't made her wait too long was almost a relief, though her heart began to beat fast and hard against her ribs.

She moved through the group, who had fallen silent, their laughter and easy banter gone. She spotted Eaglefeather: his flat yellow eyes, the rounded chinless head and long, scrawny neck, the thin chest puffed up with pride. Hatred welled up in her. This was the man who had ruined Mistlight and attempted to do the same with Firesister, who had ordered the attack on Waterstrider—she was sure of it—and probably on Skyblade too.

Her desire to kill this evil man grew so strong, she nearly choked on it, and her fingers curled so that her nails dug into her palm. Firesister reminded herself that he had gained the position of Rainsinger by being smart, dangerous, and unpredictable. She had neither of the latter characteristics. That meant she had to be smarter. Deliberately she tamped down the hunger to see Eaglefeather punished for his malice. Another thing her mother used to say: *"Strong emotions get in the way of sensible thinking."*

Bearclaw shifted his weight as if he planned to shield her from Eaglefeather, but she waved him off.

"You should go on ahead," she told the other women, who were eyeing her curiously. "Get the buds in the roasting pits. There's no sense in everyone standing in the sun." She didn't want them to overhear what might pass between herself and Eaglefeather, who excelled at twisting words.

Physically she would be safe enough, she assured herself, moistening her lips. Eaglefeather could do nothing to harm her with Bearclaw nearby. Yet when the hunters disappeared into the brush, she shivered, overcome by a disquieting sensation that the temple's shadow would cut her off from any rescuers. She kept her hands at her sides, open and ready to grab one of the sharp bone hairpins at the back of her head if Eaglefeather gave her reason.

Before the women were out of earshot, he began speaking in a resonant voice pitched to carry, and a few stragglers glanced back in curiosity.

"Long ago," he said, "when the Temple of Lightning was being built, one of the original Stormbringers was killed, struck down from behind after bringing the rains back to the valley to end the Long Thirst. Since then, it has been the Stormbringers who have suffered for trying to do what must be done, while witches such as yourself make the task more difficult."

"You know well I am no witch."

Eaglefeather smiled crookedly. "Pity the same cannot be said for Mistlight. She did, after all, attempt to sway my mind and heart with an earthflower charm."

"What is it you want?"

His eyes raked down her torso, lingering on her breasts and belly in a way that made her skin crawl. "That, you will find out soon enough. You made a mistake siding with the Watermaster. When his best efforts fail—and they will—and the farmfolk understand that the canals will never run again, who will they turn to?" His voice slithered into her ears in that insinuating way that persuaded the weak-minded to believe him.

Firesister refused to let him divide her from Waterstrider. If it was Mother Ge's will, the canals would run again. "Too many people know what you are," she replied.

"You believe that will make any difference to them?" He sneered. "Desperate people are the easiest to influence."

Firesister shook her head. "Mother Ge will stop you."

He laughed. "Mother Ge is powerless against me—or soon will be. If you imagine the Smokemothers will protect you once the Watermaster leaves, you are as moon-mad as Mistlight."

Hearing her daughter's name on his tongue made Firesister's anger flare, for who was it that had driven Mistlight mad? She went very still and told herself not to react, though sorely tempted to strike him down like a mother bear protecting her cub.

"You are going to lose everything and everyone, Firesister. I will have my revenge in the end."

"Why?" she demanded. "What did I ever do to you?"

A half smile twisted Eaglefeather's face. He stepped closer to her.

Repulsed and suddenly afraid, goosebumps rising on her arms, she backed away. He said nothing, but she sensed his arousal.

Since Waterstrider came into her life, she hadn't experienced that visceral fear of a man with anyone but Eaglefeather. Her mouth went dry. Hoping to drive out fear with defiance, she asked, "As part of your revenge, did you send those Seekers after Skyblade?"

"Certainly not. If I had known there was such bad feeling among my Seekers, I would have rooted it out long ago. No, Puckermouth and the others acted of their own volition. Understandably, they were concerned about Mistlight's safety."

"Her safety?"

Eaglefeather placed a hand on his chest as though wounded. "Oh, I see. You blamed me. You may think me a monster, but I am far from it. Mistlight entered the temple of her own will. What reason would I have, or any other of the Stormbringers, to mistreat her?" He shook his head sorrowfully. "If she came to you a little bruised, ask yourself who had the opportunity to do that. After all, Skyblade always showed an unhealthy interest in Mistlight."

Firesister recalled how Skyblade had noticed changes in Mistlight's body, and she wondered whether the boy really was as true-hearted as she'd come to believe. Then she considered Mistlight's willingness to be in Skyblade's presence, even to speak with him when no one else could draw words from her. Firesister clamped her jaw closed, reminding herself that nothing Eaglefeather said should be believed.

He leaned forward, his flat eyes searching her expression. With some effort she kept herself rooted in place as his face came closer. He wasn't much taller than she was, but still she felt the masculine threat of him.

Pulling himself up straight again, Eaglefeather nodded. "You trust the boy, I see. Even though he was the one who accused you of being a witch? You never wondered at his willingness to join you after that?"

"He was only delivering your message."

"He needed little encouragement. His entire family died at Lastwater."

Firesister's hands slowly closed into fists. Not content to warn her away from Waterstrider, now Eaglefeather would set her against Skyblade?

"He felt honor-bound," Eaglefeather continued, "to see the one who killed his parents be punished. Did he fail to tell you that, when he brought Mistlight to you and offered some story to wring your heart? Never mind. If you feel comfortable having him beside your daughter, that is on your head. He has nowhere else to go, after all. You are simply proving your kindness for all to see."

Firesister didn't feel kind. She felt quite violently unkind. "Why did you seek me out today?"

"To allay your worries about poor Skyblade," Eaglefeather explained. "That is, if you mean to stand by him, as the Watermaster did you. Though the situations are not precisely the same, since Skyblade made no attempt to kill you." An unspoken *yet* hung in the air between them.

"Allay my worries in what way?" She drew herself up straighter and crossed her arms, meeting his malicious gaze without flinching.

"To begin with, my dear Firesister, there will be no need for the village elders to convene a hearing. The wounded Seeker has withdrawn his accusation. Indeed, he is no longer a Seeker, for he has been sent home to his family. We cannot condone violence, no matter the reason."

Firesister huffed out a laugh at the absurdity of that claim coming from Eaglefeather.

He smiled benignly and continued, "The divisions among our people distress me. This seems an occasion to bring everyone together. Surely you can understand that? Skyblade has been clever enough to make himself valuable to the Watermaster, so no matter what else he might have done, of course he should continue along that path." Eaglefeather placed an open hand over his heart. "The Stormbringers are dedicated to aiding the Watermaster in whatever way we can, for the good of all the people of Serpentgate and beyond." He slid half a step closer and said, so softly that she barely heard, "Then, when he fails and once again runs away to the City of Birds, everyone will lose their faith in Mother Ge."

Waterstrider won't fail, she wanted to say. *He won't leave.*

"And you, too," Eaglefeather went on, relentlessly, "since you were so insistent that your goddess saved Waterstrider to restore the canals. You, an accused witch, will be left alone here to endure the vengeance of those who feel themselves betrayed. Come to me when you are in need of protection. You will not be able to refuse me forever."

He turned and strode down the path toward the temple. The other priests fell in behind him, leaving Firesister burning with anger—at him, at herself for listening to his insinuations, at the unfairness of having somehow attracted his attention and ill will. At the fact that she couldn't simply run up behind him and slip one of her bone hairpins between his ribs.

Bearclaw approached and asked, "What did he say?"

She turned her head. "Skyblade won't have to face the elders over that fight."

"That's good, isn't it?"

Firesister considered what Eaglefeather demanded in exchange for Skyblade's freedom: *"You will not be able to refuse me forever."* She smiled at Bearclaw and said what he expected to hear. "Of course."

For several days, Firesister found herself watching Skyblade whenever Mistlight flitted past, for Eaglefeather's poison had seeped into her head. She could see no changes in Mistlight's body. But such changes would be hard to see past that old jar with the birds painted on it, which Mistlight carried about with her, crooning to it like a sleeping baby.

Skyblade was not often on the mound during the day. He generally accompanied Waterstrider, carrying tools, food, and water and even descending into the canal beds to measure depths and widths, prod fissures, and perform other tasks the Watermaster still couldn't do for himself.

They worked well together, Waterstrider told her once, for instead of driving each other hard, they tended to slow each other down out of consideration of the other's wound. Skyblade was stronger than he looked, a good worker, and smart.

Upon hearing the praise, Firesister thought that Skyblade might be strong enough to hurt Mistlight and clever enough to hide it. Then she felt guilty for doubting him. She began to avoid Skyblade and Waterstrider in the evenings, after they returned to the mound after their day's work. She left stew out for them in a pot kept warm with stones and retreated to her sleep-room, pleading exhaustion.

Waterstrider sought her out after a few evenings had passed in this way. Leaning against the doorway of her dark sleep-room, he asked, "What are you doing?"

Firesister, huddled in a corner and wrapped in a deerhide against the evening chill, considered pretending she didn't know what he meant. Something deep inside tugged her toward Waterstrider despite her past, despite everything she thought she knew about herself. He didn't want to be tied to her, yet he was. She didn't want to be drawn to him, yet she was.

"Are you asleep?" he asked.

Moonglow outlined his form but hid his features. She didn't need to see him to be certain that he knew she wasn't sleeping, even though he couldn't have spotted her in the dark corner.

During his recovery, she had stared surreptitiously at his face until she'd memorized it, from the curve of his chin and the angle of his nose to the shape of his ears. The way his neck swept into his shoulder. The hollow of his throat above his chest. The long, tapering fingers that ended in large fingernails with a white crescent at their base. The habit of moving his jaw to one side while thinking, the tongue that touched the corner of his mouth and swiped halfway across his teeth when he thought something he didn't want to say. Did he know her as well as she knew him?

She looked at him and thought of a song: *"I was dreaming of you in the dance of the wind, while I lay in the arms of another."*

This was Waterstrider, a man who would never stay. Her heart would suffer when he left, but she'd endured terrible pain before and knew she would survive. Would it be better to make him believe she was avoiding him rather than admitting that Eaglefeather had poisoned her against Skyblade?

She'd remained silent too long. He straightened up and turned away, striding into Sister Moon's gentle light.

From the shady place under the cottonwoods where she was pounding dried mesquite pods into powder, Firesister saw that the weir was coming along well. Heavy piers of stripped pine trunks stood tall in the knee-deep river. Between each pier were willow branches, planted in the hope that some would root deeply enough to withstand the floods of the following winter and spring. Boulders had been seated in the riverbed to brace the piers and keep the willows upright against the current. The next step would involve weaving brush horizontally, in and out of the vertical framework, from the top of the weir down to the riverbed, to halt the water's flow and push it into the thirsty canal mouths.

Tallcorn was overseeing construction now that Waterstrider had turned his attention to the canals. Firesister had to admit that she took little notice of the weir since Waterstrider was no longer working on it. She lowered her gaze. The tattoo on her wrist reminded her that she was bound to Waterstrider even when he wasn't near. Deliberately she looked past the tattoo, following her hands to the stonewood pestle they held, down the long, thick shaft to the rock mortar in which it rested. Chunks of mesquite pod lay on the mortar's surface, testifying to her carelessness at the task.

She drew in a deep breath, stretched one hand after the other, pulled the pestle out of the round hole, and brushed stray pod fragments back into the mortar. She started pounding the pestle into the mortar again: down with a twist, and lift, and down with a twist, and lift.

It was monotonous work, unthinking, uncreative, and boring. She hated it, but pounding away by herself in the shade was less exhausting than picking mesquite pods while surrounded by chattering women.

A voice eventually rose above the noise of the pestle striking the mesquite pods below. When she stopped pounding, she heard her name called. Raising her head, she saw one of the hunters trotting along the path. Bearclaw stepped out to meet him. After a few words were exchanged, Bearclaw gestured for her to join them.

Eaglefeather! was her first thought. Her stomach twisted in fear. She dropped the stonewood pestle and hurried toward the two men. Her alarm abated only slightly when she learned that Smokemothers had come to Cloud Mountain looking for Mistlight. Firesister rushed back to the mound.

There she found all four of the high priestesses. They clustered in the east plaza and gazed toward Mother Sleeping. The musty smell of tobacco from their smoke-gray robes and headscarves made the plaza seem smaller and darker, reminding Firesister—as always—of the many moons she'd spent helpless in their care. Her leg throbbed for a moment as it once had, many turnings ago. She gasped from the shock of it.

The noise caught the attention of the Truthspeaker, youngest of the four. She stared down her long nose at Firesister. "Where," she demanded, her sharp features tight, "is Mistlight?"

Firesister inwardly cursed the pain in her leg and the breathlessness from hurry that she feared would make her sound weak. She pulled herself up tall and folded her arms. "Mistlight is none of your concern."

"How dare you speak so?" the Truthspeaker hissed.

How dare I? Firesister's throat constricted. Her heart, which had begun to slow after her exertion, sped up again, pounding in her chest. With her arms crossed, she found it hard to breathe. She dropped her arms and linked her hands together in front of her, a more respectful posture.

Her gaze flicked toward the Childcatcher, the white-haired, stooped priestess who had led her out of despair so long ago. "I owe you my life," she said. "I know that." Turning to the others, she continued, "You spoke up for me when I was accused of being a witch, and for that I am grateful. But when Mistlight needed you, you all turned your back on her."

The Truthspeaker pointed at Firesister and declared, "You know nothing of this matter."

Firesister lifted her chin, determined not to allow old habits of deference and gratitude to shake her resolve. She owed the Smokemothers, yes, but there were limits. "Did you blame Mistlight for the death of your son, the shadowdancer?" she asked. At the discomfiture on the priestess's sharp features, she leaned forward and said quietly, "Oh yes, I know he was yours. I was there when you birthed him, remember?"

Nostrils flaring, the Truthspeaker said, "You are mistaken about the shadowdancer. This was never about him."

"Why else would you give Mistlight to Eaglefeather?" Firesister asked.

The Childcatcher answered: "Mistlight loves him. It was her choice to go to the temple."

Firesister eyed the white-haired priestess, the oldest and most venerated of the group, and forced a scornful laugh, though it pained her to treat the Childcatcher so ungraciously. "Would you let babies put their hands in the pretty fire, too, if they chose to do so? You need to protect these girls who don't know how cruel the world can be."

The Truthspeaker pointed out, "It was her choice to make the earthflower charm, hoping to bind the Rainsinger to her."

The Dreamwalker spoke over the last few words in the portentous tone she favored for her pronouncements: "The daughter of the daughter of the village must be in the temple. This was foreordained by Mother Ge herself."

"Mother Ge wouldn't ask such a thing of any woman." Firesister's hands shook at the memory of Mistlight's bloody body and ruined mind when she came to Cloud Mountain. Mistlight must have suffered the same terror and helplessness that Firesister had endured at the hands of a man. The agony, mental and physical, that had lingered long after the attack. The mind-numbing panic at the thought of ever facing her attacker again. The eternity of not submitting to a man's touch after that.

The Dreamwalker gazed serenely at Firesister and said, "No one can halt the onrushing storm." Her pupils were immense black circles barely ringed with brown, pools in which Firesister felt she could drown.

The Truthspeaker freed Firesister from that compelling stare by saying, "Mistlight must be in the temple to witness the Rainsinger's fall."

"Do you mean Mistlight will bring about Eaglefeather's death? Or a loss of power?" Firesister asked slowly.

The priestesses glanced among themselves but made no answer. Maybe they didn't know which possibility was more likely. Not that it mattered to Firesister. What mattered was that the Smokemothers hadn't done right by Mistlight so far.

All their plotting and scheming had come to naught, dividing Mother Ge's people just as Eaglefeather did. As Firesister saw it, the high priestesses were as wrongheaded as the priests. To survive, everyone would have to work together. Wasn't that Mother Ge's intent in bringing Waterstrider back to the valley and keeping him alive?

Firesister saw no softening in the Truthspeaker's expression, no backing off from the resolve to take Mistlight. "Neither course is right," Firesister argued, "whether death or downfall. Such a path is dangerous. It might begin with good intentions but can only end by corrupting whoever walks it. Punishing Eaglefeather is for Mother Ge to do."

The Truthspeaker stated flatly, "You know nothing of Mother Ge's will."

Without thinking, Firesister asked, "Are you really vain enough to believe that only the Smokemothers can understand her will?"

The priestess flinched as though she'd been slapped. Her eyes narrowed. "You cannot keep us from taking Mistlight to the temple."

"She's no longer a Cornmaiden," Firesister replied, choosing her words carefully, though she feared it was too late—her earlier comment had likely turned the Truthspeaker into yet another enemy. "Mistlight doesn't answer to you."

But the Childcatcher, who'd left the group without Firesister noticing, had found the normally elusive Mistlight and was leading her toward the other priestesses. Mistlight held the swaddled jar tightly against one breast. Her clothes were tattered, her eyes were vague, her mouth moved with inaudible words.

The Smokemothers looked shocked at her appearance. Firesister took no satisfaction in that but hoped it would make them understand that Mistlight wasn't fit for their dread purpose. She pointed toward her daughter. "This is how Eaglefeather left her. There were more wounds inside and out. Only the ones that were visible have healed."

The Truthspeaker grabbed Mistlight's shoulder. "You are going back to the temple, girl."

"Don't touch her!" Firesister hurried forward and struck the priestess's arm, knocking it down and away from Mistlight, tearing the girl's dress at the shoulder.

Freed so suddenly, Mistlight cried out and backed away. Her free hand clutched at the torn fabric. Shrieking, she ran across the east plaza and clambered over the wall. Three of the high priestesses stared wide-eyed and stricken after the moon-mad girl.

Only the Dreamweaver seemed unaffected by Mistlight's flight. She nodded as if an inward suspicion had been confirmed. "Mistlight will return to the temple before the Cloud-Summoning of midsummer."

"I won't allow that to happen," Firesister snapped. "Now go." She gestured toward the passageway. "Leave Cloud Mountain and never return."

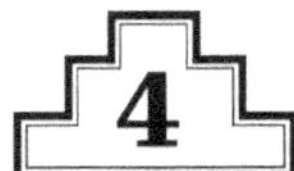

Barefoot, Waterstrider curled his toes around slick cobbles. River water bearing the chill of its birth in the Mountains of Sunrise licked halfway up his legs, cooling him despite the strength of Brother Sun's rays as summer approached. Waterstrider balanced with the help of two saguaro ribs, one in each hand. Now that he'd regained most of his strength, the crutch had proven too limiting, so he'd left it at the mound the past few days. On flat paths he was able to walk without aid, but the cobbles of the riverbed rolled underfoot, forcing him to lean heavily on the saguaro-rib staffs.

He cursed his weakness as he assessed the mood of the work crew surrounding him, their faces dark with confusion and budding hostility. "It's not yet time to finish the weir," he repeated.

Tallcorn, arms folded across his chest, took a step closer and said, "The posts are in place. What more needs to be done?"

Waterstrider wished his friend would be quiet. Some of the listeners undoubtedly assumed his own loyalties lay with Tallcorn and Squashblossom Clan. No matter what he said next, they would distrust his motivation. "The canals need reworking before you can send water into them."

"They're deep enough already," Tallcorn argued. "We made sure of it."

Clinging to his last shreds of patience, Waterstrider said, "Depth isn't the problem. That's why the weir had to be built higher, to raise the water level at the canal mouth back to where it used to be."

"So let's close off the weir now," Tallcorn said.

Waterstrider turned his head toward the broad canal bed, pitted and pocked like volcanic stone. The channel down the midline—which must have taken great effort to carve out—had already eroded into snaky curves. Resting his weight on his left side, he lifted the saguaro-rib staff in his right hand and pointed toward the canal, its mouth gaping high in the bank as it waited thirstily for the river to rise to meet it. He said, "Water won't run true unless the canals are smooth, their beds level and plastered."

Leaning against the steep riverbank was the harsh-voiced man who had, before the rebuilding of the weir began, advocated letting the canals die. A half smile twisted his mouth. Waterstrider had learned his name: Digger, of Cornhill Clan. Though a good worker, he was the only one of his clan among the crew and kept to himself.

Digger asked, "Are you saying the channel is the problem? The channel Squashblossom Clan put in?"

Tallcorn flushed and drew himself up straight. "Summer draws near," he said, "and the rains with it. If we don't finish the weir, all that water will run downriver and be lost to us."

Angry muttering followed, as many among the work crew either agreed with Tallcorn or, like Digger, distrusted him and Squashblossom Clan.

Waterstrider understood the resentment over putting in so much time on the weir and then hearing more needed to be done. But closing the weir before the canals were ready to drink from the river would only cause more damage from scouring and washouts.

He was balanced on a knife-edge, being pressed to choose between Squashblossom Clan and Cornhill Clan. Taking any side would be a betrayal of what it meant to be a Watermaster. To be a true Watermaster, he had to remain neutral and think only of one thing: how to get the most water to the most fields possible, day after day. That meant working slowly, being cautious, advancing one step at a time.

"We should close off the weir," said someone at the back of the group.

"And not listen to the famous Watermaster who returned to save us all?" Digger asked. "Tell me, do you trust Tallcorn of Squashblossom Clan to do what's best for you?"

A new voice asked, "What, then? Are you prepared to take more time away from your own field to do the Watermaster's bidding? I'm not. I say we should complete the weir and go home."

"That's because you get water from the Squashblossom canals," Digger shot back. "Anything that benefits them, benefits you."

"So all of us should risk losing water by not closing off the weir in time for the summer rains?"

As Waterstrider prepared to wade in and stop the bickering, his attention was caught by a flash of movement. He lifted his head and spotted Skyblade racing along the canal path, his arms and legs silhouetted against the sky.

The boy stopped and glanced over his shoulder. He nodded to someone Waterstrider couldn't see, then scrambled down the bank, grabbing onto seepwillow branches to slow his descent. On his arm, sunlight caught the fresh scar, shining pink against the red-brown skin.

Skyblade ran across the rocky shingle at the river's edge, skirting the work crew as he approached Waterstrider. Slowed by the deepening water, he splashed along until he drew near enough to grip Waterstrider's sleeve. "Trouble," he gasped out. "It sounds bad."

Above, Ninetoes appeared on the canal path, followed by a wiry man Waterstrider didn't recognize. Boy and man left the path and were screened from view by underbrush along the riverbank.

Skyblade tugged on Waterstrider's sleeve. "You have to come."

Waterstrider released one saguaro-rib staff and with that freed hand grasped the boy's shoulder. He bent close. As he did so, the tattoo around his wrist caught his eye—the tattoo he'd resented so much at first, marking a bond he'd never before imagined for himself. "Did something happen to Firesister?" he demanded.

Fear settled sharp and cold in his belly, roiling his guts. *"You did well,"* Waterstrider remembered telling her. He'd praised her for protecting Skyblade and Mistlight, keeping them out of the hands of those who would harm them. He'd trusted that Firesister would be safe on the mound because it was Watermaster territory. Had he been wrong?

He shook the boy. "What happened to her?"

"Not Firesister. Not Mistlight." Skyblade hauled in a lungful of air.

"Tell me what happened."

"A friend of my father's. Far-Trader. Says there's outlanders coming north."

Waterstrider took the words as a punch to the gut. Skin tingling, suddenly dizzy, he knew what the coming of the outlanders must mean. It was indeed trouble, and of a sort he should have expected.

Pulling Skyblade along, he turned upriver, toward the backwater where the bank flattened out. The staff in his left hand got caught between two stones, so he dropped it. His foot slid, creating a wavelet that surged over his ankle. He cursed under his breath.

The outlanders he'd talked into coming to the valley were young and adventuresome and filled with themselves. Being driven away by the famously peace-loving People of Two Rivers must have stung their pride. For them to head north as summer loomed suggested they were driven by a strong motive: revenge. Southlanders had a tradition of avenging slights to their honor. Dismayed, he shook his head.

"This way." Skyblade gestured toward a tangle of reeds and seepwillow.

Waterstrider could see nothing in the undergrowth but, trusting Skyblade's young eyes, headed for the river's edge. Farther upriver, under towering cottonwoods, light feminine laughter rang out.

The rounded stones of the riverbed became smaller, coated with decaying pondweed and black mud, the last remains of a stagnant pool. As he squelched through the muck, it oozed between his toes.

Skyblade glanced down. "I'll go back for your sandals," the boy said, "once you've met Blackstar."

Before Waterstrider could respond, they pushed through the underbrush and entered the gravelly floodplain beyond. Ninetoes stood beside a man who'd seen several more winters than Waterstrider. He was lean, as befitted someone accustomed to traveling long distances. His skin was dark from the sun and weathered like mesquite bark. A strap supporting a burden basket through many journeys had left its mark as a straight-edged depression in his skull. Even if Skyblade hadn't identified this stranger as a Far-Trader, Waterstrider thought he would have guessed.

Respectfully, as one should do with an older man, Waterstrider extended both hands, palms outward, and bowed his head. "I am Waterstrider, of the heronfolk," he said. Out of the corner of his eye he saw Skyblade retreat.

"Blackstar." That one word was all that the trader saw fit to reveal about himself. He went on, "Word is, several hundred outlanders approach from the south. Which means perhaps fifty."

Fifty? I brought only twenty with me. Waterstrider shivered despite the warmth of the sun.

The chill settled deeper as the trader said, "But those fifty are said to be armed with clubs and spears." The man pierced Waterstrider with a hard gaze. "Their leader is named Ravenchild. You know him?"

"He's brother to—" *Littlecliff.* His dead friend's name caught on Waterstrider's tongue. The name would mean nothing to this Far-Trader.

Voice sharpening, the trader asked, "Why has this Ravenchild come?"

Waterstrider said, "Most likely, to punish those who killed his brother."

The trader nodded, as though that answer confirmed a rumor already flying. "But who might that be? Who has he come for?"

Waterstrider had no answer. The attackers had been priests, according to his slippery memory, but from which temple? It wasn't the first time, or even the hundredth, that he'd wondered that very thing.

Had the men of his party seen the attackers well enough to identify them as priests, well enough to see the color of ribbons binding their hair? Or did Ravenchild have a more general target—such as all the men of Serpentgate? Or even Waterstrider himself, who had led Littlecliff on this fool's journey? It seemed ominous that Ravenchild, who had adopted Waterstrider as a second brother, hadn't sent him a message warning of the arrival.

A brittle silence stretched for too long. Waterstrider broke it by asking, "Where are the outlanders now?"

"Probably Sun-Meets-Mountain. A group like that, they can't travel as quickly as the messenger who brought word." Blackstar gave a few polite words of farewell, then struck out along the path that led toward Mother Sleeping, away from Serpentgate.

Waterstrider calculated the distance to the fist of rock that was Sun-Meets-Mountain, which rose from the desert floor well south of the southernmost canals. Ravenchild would get a fair ways north of there before Waterstrider, still recovering his strength, could cover much of that distance. To meet him, Waterstrider would have to correctly predict the route he would take. Would Ravenchild follow Earth River to the Temple of Mist? Or cut through the desert and come straight to Serpentgate? It all depended on who Ravenchild wanted to punish for Littlecliff's death.

On a heavy sigh, Waterstrider decided there was too much chance of going the wrong way and missing Ravenchild if he set out now. He had to wait. And explain to Firesister that he had to leave but would come back.

"Are you going to Sun-Meets-Mountain?" Ninetoes asked. "Can I come?"

Skyblade trotted up, dangling Waterstrider's yucca-fiber sandals. "Sun-Meets-Mountain?" He sounded incredulous.

Waterstrider grimaced. Before the injury, he could have run there in two easy days. Now, in his condition, the journey might be beyond him entirely. "No," he told the boys. "It makes more sense to find out where Ravenchild is heading."

Days later, Waterstrider's hollow stare took in the Temple of Mist, which lay empty, the corpses of its priests still smoking among the ashes of funeral pyres laid in the center of the plaza. His stomach heaved, though he'd already vomited once and there was nothing more to bring up. Swallowing his gorge, he pulled his attention away from the horror to focus on Ravenchild's soot-streaked, haggard face.

"It wasn't my doing," Ravenchild said. "I wanted to avenge Littlecliff, but not like this." He waved a bone-weary hand, blistered and burned from the funerary fires that had borne the priests' spirits upward on reeking smoke.

Waterstrider wanted to believe Ravenchild, who had been a friend— no, more, a brother of the heart—through twenty-four turnings. "Who, then?" he choked out. "Who ordered this?"

A narrow-eyed stare, almost accusing, clashed with Waterstrider's tortured scrutiny. "It was the men you led up here. The priests of this temple drove them off—and so deserved to die."

Waterstrider knew the People of Two Rivers, accustomed to peace for generation after generation, would never understand such bloody reasoning. They didn't even have a word for murder, let alone war. The rough men of the City of Birds, in contrast, had several. To them, besmirching their honor was reason enough for this slaughter.

Leaning against the wall on legs so exhausted they shook, Waterstrider drew the stench of burned flesh into his lungs and coughed. Blame for bringing killers to the valley did indeed lie with him, though he hadn't foreseen such a result. "The priests from the Temple of Mist, they were the ones who attacked us?"

"You didn't know?"

Waterstrider understood what Ravenchild was really asking: *Why didn't you avenge Littlecliff? Why are you still here, helping the people who killed him?* "I never saw the attackers," Waterstrider said. "I was struck down and left for dead. It took me time to recover."

Ravenchild swept a glance over him. When his gaze met Waterstrider's again, the harshness in it eased into sympathy. "I believe it. I almost didn't recognize you when you came up," he said. "You move like an old man. Come. We'll feed you, let you rest."

Waterstrider peeled his back away from the wall and found that his legs had begun to stiffen. Thigh and shin muscles protested the renewed abuse but had regained enough strength to bear him along, one tottering, agonizing step after another.

A smooth-faced woman in the gray robes of a Smokemother appeared in front of him and Ravenchild. Two flames tattooed over her eyebrows indicated that she'd birthed two children for the village. A wild light blazed in the amber eyes below. Bruises were visible on her wrists. She bowed her head and said slowly, as if dragging each word from someplace dark, "Thank you for sparing us. Come. Let the Smokemothers feed you."

Ravenchild said nothing in return. His face didn't change expression.

In the language of the City of Birds, Waterstrider said, "Are you pretending not to know their speech? That's an ill trick on people who wish you well."

Ravenchild's head swung toward Waterstrider. "Do they? Wish us well?" he asked in the same tongue. "These Smokemothers served the priests."

"Not so," said Waterstrider.

"They were welcome in the temple precinct; other women were not."

"They are servants of Mother Ge," Waterstrider told him, "the goddess who made the People of Two Rivers. Her priestesses are of an ancient order, from the time of the First Days. The priests have been here only a few generations."

Ravenchild grunted.

"Come." The Smokemother gestured toward the gateway that led away from the massive temple and the smoldering fires of the plaza. Her gaze brushed against Waterstrider's. She hastily lowered her eyes. "I know what those other men intended for us," she said in a rush. "Many of my sisters would have killed themselves rather than be taken by force."

She grasped Ravenchild's muscled forearm. "Let me stay with you," she begged. "Give me your protection. Even if you don't understand my words, can you hear what my heart says?"

Ravenchild eased himself free.

Still in the language that she couldn't know, Waterstrider asked Ravenchild, "Where are the rest of the men from the City of Birds?"

"Hunting priests. Some got away, running like rabbits from a fire. Pursuing them distracted the more merciless from the priests' women here."

"I tell you, Smokemothers aren't the priests' women." Waterstrider wondered if any of those who escaped the temple precinct were Seekers, like Skyblade. He hoped so. Not yet tattooed as their priestly masters were, Seekers could fade into the village and rejoin their families. Where could the tattooed priests hide? And would they continue to run, or would they eventually turn and fight?

The Smokemother pointed toward the gateway. "Come," she urged again. "We give food—" she pretended to eat "—and sleep." She laid her head across folded hands and closed her eyes. Then she ran her hands suggestively down her body, though her taut expression belied the gesture.

"Do you want to go with her?" Ravenchild rumbled, still in the language of the City of Birds.

Waterstrider shook his head. What if the surviving priests fled to other temples—such as the Temple of Lightning? That would draw the vengeful men straight to Serpentgate, where Firesister was. Waterstrider's mind froze. He staggered, dizzy.

Ravenchild steadied him. "Here stands a pretty woman offering you food, sleep, and bedplay, and you're turning her down? You must be completely done-in."

"She's offering herself to you, not me. Besides, I—" What could he say: *I have a woman I'm bound to*? "I need to get back to Serpentgate."

The Smokemother shifted her gaze uneasily between the two men. Waterstrider shook off Ravenchild's support and circled around her, leaving his friend to disentangle himself.

A few heartbeats passed before Ravenchild fell into step beside him. "Surely you aren't such an idiot as to leave now. The day wears on. It'll be dark soon."

Waterstrider shrugged. "Night walking is the best time."

Ravenchild grabbed him by the shoulder, stopping him before he got to the gateway. "I wasn't intending to come north at all. I was half crazy, mourning both my brothers, Littlecliff and you. Then we heard you were still alive but in the clutches of a witch."

A witch? Waterstrider felt confused until he realized his friend was talking about Firesister.

Ravenchild continued, "I came for you, Waterstrider. To rescue you. You're free now. Come with me, home to the City of Birds. Whatever vengeance you want—"

"It's not vengeance. It's . . . ." Fear that he would return too late to save Firesister—from the outlanders if they believed her a witch, from farmfolk loyal to the priests and suspicious of anyone associated with the outlanders, from Eaglefeather and the Smokemothers. Waterstrider pulled away from Ravenchild and began walking again.

He would force his legs to carry him northward until they collapsed under him, and then he would crawl. But no, he thought. It had taken the better part of two days to get to the Temple of Mist. Another two days to get back to Serpentgate might mean Firesister would face the fate intended for the Smokemothers here.

He would have to run. Waterstrider extended his stride and immediately pitched forward. He caught himself on his palms and rolled to avoid injuring his wrists. Panting, he lay on his back and looked up at the flower-petal colors painting the sunset sky.

He slammed his fists against the ground. His mind filled with Firesister as he'd seen her first, held captive in the storage room beside the mound, her hair a mess, face dirty, spitting a challenge at him. Then he imagined one of the outlanders holding her down by the wrists, ramming into her with such force that her defiance collapsed into a desire for death. As Bearclaw had told him, Firesister had been raped before. That experience had wounded her in ways that hadn't fully healed. He couldn't let it happen to her again.

Ravenchild squatted beside him. "Why are you so concerned for these people? If they're stupid enough to side with the rain priests over the Watermasters, let them dry up and blow away. And need I say, they tried to kill you, Waterstrider, my brother."

Waterstrider rolled onto his side and sat with his legs out in front. Massaging his thigh muscles to loosen them, he muttered, "It isn't right to punish everyone over the faults of a few. You know this. It's why you protected the Smokemothers."

"Serpentgate is where the Temple of Lightning is, yes?" Ravenchild asked. "The high priest of that temple ordered the attack on you. If it's revenge you want, there's no need to go all that way yourself. The others who came north with me, they'll continue on to the Temple of Lightning and kill the priests."

Waterstrider's mouth went dry. It was Eaglefeather that his friend spoke so casually of killing, along with the rest of the priests. What would the Serpentgate clans do then, with no canals working and all those who called down the rains dead? Who would they turn on when their crops failed and the outlanders had vanished southward again? Would they even accept that Waterstrider, who had brought the outlanders in the first place, simply wanted to help? And what of Firesister, his lifemate?

Ravenchild said, "Rest here a few days. Then we'll head for home and leave these people to the mess they've made."

"I have to go to Serpentgate," Waterstrider insisted.

Ravenchild stood and walked a few steps. He placed his palms on his waist and bent his head, shaking it as he inhaled deeply and exhaled on a sigh. He turned around. Folding his arms, he scowled at Waterstrider. "All right. You need to go to Serpentgate but can't wait until tomorrow, like a sensible man. Stay here and rest. I'll find travel rations and water for us."

"You don't need to come."

Ravenchild barked out a humorless laugh. "As if you're strong enough to stop me." He went off, passing through the shadowed gateway, a space in the wall that set the temple precinct apart from

Crookstaff Village.

Waterstrider stared into the darkness long after Ravenchild disappeared from sight. He lay flat, with an arm covering his eyes, and thought about why he didn't want his friend to come along. Ravenchild still acted like the same man who had long been his friend, even his brother . . . but everything about Waterstrider's life in the City of Birds seemed foreign now.

Here, Ravenchild didn't fit. None of the outlanders did. Everything about them was wrong. Their quest for vengeance was like a flash flood, sudden and destructive, tearing away everything in its path, and Waterstrider saw no way to stop them.

What, then, could he do? Perhaps he could save Firesister. And then what? Convince her to leave the doomed village? Or stay and try to rebuild the canals, the task that had occupied him these past moons? Waterstrider felt Brother Sun on his face, Mother Ge supporting his back.

He thought of the people who had become important to him: Firesister, Skyblade, Tallcorn, Gran Squashblossom. Even Digger—hostile, watchful Digger—and the rest of the work crews, along with their clansisters who had been feeding them. Was Waterstrider, with Firesister as his lifemate, a son of the village now, not bound to a single clan through kinship but responsible for all? Was this what it meant to be a Watermaster? Was this what the farmfolk had given up when they sent the Watermasters into exile?

Forced to choose between new ways and old, the clans had tried to have both: the rains called down by the priests of the Ta'atchul, and the canals given by Mother Ge. And now, with the coming of the outlanders, would the people of Serpentgate and nearby villages have neither rains nor canals?

The people of Crookstaff Village didn't seem upset that their rain priests were gone. But their canals still flowed with water. So did the other canal systems of Sky River and Earth River. Only the Northwind canals, which began at Serpentgate and continued westward, were dry. The words of the prophecy came back to Waterstrider: *"When Serpent gnaws the bones of the earth and Buzzard pierces the sky, when all the green ribbons have dwindled to dust, the rainbow knife will fly."* Had the time of prophecy come?

Not all the green ribbons—the canals, bands of intense green within the muted tones of the desert and fields—had dwindled to dust. Not yet. Were the Northwind canals a harbinger of the end for all the People of Two Rivers? No, surely Mother Ge would never do such a thing.

But as the old saying went, *Hope won't fill the river.* He wasn't sure he could get even one of the canals running. And if he did, how long it would take. Exhaustion soon swept away the worries clogging his mind.

They waited for moonrise before following the canal path out of Crookstaff Village. Ravenchild had agreed: "Night travel may be best, at least until we get well beyond the village."

It was just the two of them, Waterstrider and Ravenchild. The rest of Ravenchild's men had been left behind to hold the temple against any priests who escaped the hunt and returned to Crookstaff Village, or any of the farmfolk who might try to oust the outlanders rather than waiting for them to leave.

In each hand, Waterstrider held a spear disguised as a walking staff, their lethal tips covered by feathers and ribbons. Ravenchild, several steps ahead on the path, bore a finely netted burden basket lined with cloth. At the bottom, Waterstrider knew, were knives and clubs for him, matching the ones hung on Ravenchild's broad belt. Above the weapons were two sets of reed chest armor rolled around leather helmets, along with two leather war kilts. "For when we catch up with the avengers," Ravenchild had said.

As Waterstrider looked at the burden basket on his friend's back, he smelled again the stench of death at the Temple of Mist, and bile rose in his throat. He quickly shifted his thoughts to the top layer of the basket, which held such trade goods as powdered cacao, beautiful quetzal and macaw feathers, copper bells, mica mirrors, embroidered headcloths, toys—the sorts of things that could be traded for food and would suggest peaceful intent if anyone challenged the two travelers.

"Why did you come to find me?" Ravenchild's words carried in the still night air.

Waterstrider owed his friend some form of the truth. "I didn't expect you to journey north. Not to avenge Littlecliff's death, and certainly not —since I knew I was in no danger—to rescue me. Nor did I think the men of my original party would seek vengeance."

"Why not?"

Waterstrider considered how to answer. Back in his homeland, his thoughts had slipped into old habits. There was no reason to expect danger here, among the People of Two Rivers. *And yet the priests struck you down,* a voice in his head argued. He reminded himself, *The priests are not the people.* The original rain priests came from the southlands long ago, and maybe they taught violence in the temples.

Who was there among his people who would defend themselves against other men? Would the hunters launch their arrows or spears against human prey? Waterstrider couldn't even guess.

As younger men, he and Littlecliff and Ravenchild had talked about this difference between their two peoples many times. Littlecliff had admired the unfamiliarity of violence among the People of Two Rivers, who had never faced invasion or warfare, for their land was so difficult that no one wanted it. Ravenchild had never understood. That was why he'd remained at the City of Birds while Littlecliff had come to see the People of Two Rivers for himself. That was why Ravenchild was alive and Littlecliff dead.

"Things here are just different," Waterstrider told Ravenchild at last.

For two days and three nights they traveled, resting often and consuming journeycakes between rest stops. "To feed your muscles," Ravenchild had said when Waterstrider suggested conserving their travel rations.

There was no one to trade for food with. The first day of travel saw them across the desert separating the Earth River settlements from the southernmost Sky River settlements. The fields and villages they passed on the second day mostly lay empty, though Waterstrider felt anxious eyes watching. A few people seemed determined to work their fields regardless of the danger. These farmfolk turned blank, shocked eyes toward plumes of smoke that rose to the east and far to the west, beyond the Old Man Mountains, and then looked back at the ground, wielding their heavy stone hoes and digging-sticks ferociously.

On the third day, Waterstrider saw smoke plumes to the northwest, where Sky River and Earth River joined. Sweat broke out on his forehead, and his heart raced with the knowledge that once the vengeful outlanders reached the confluence of the two rivers, they could quickly follow Sky River upstream to the Temple of Lightning.

The canal path stretched out to the horizon as Waterstrider hobbled along, held to a slow pace by his body though his mind was aware of time slipping by, as his feet crunched into the gravelly path and lifted again and again. He would have given up many times if not for Ravenchild, who seemed to know whenever Waterstrider was about to collapse from exhaustion and pressed food, water, and rest upon him.

At last they reached the crossing of Sky River. Smoke hung in the air over Serpentgate, concealing Cloud Mountain at the south end of the village and the Temple of Lightning to the north. The air tasted heavy and acrid as Ravenchild and Waterstrider splashed across the river.

Waterstrider's hands tightened on the spear shafts that helped him keep his footing on the rocks of the crossing. The smoke meant the avengers had beaten him to Serpentgate. He'd been too slow to warn Firesister. If the outlanders truly saw her as a witch who was allied with Eaglefeather, they might have stopped at Cloud Mountain first. He faced the terrible thought that if they had done so, it was too late to save her.

But surely, the reasonable part of him argued, they would have sped directly to the Temple of Lightning in pursuit of Eaglefeather, who had caused the dishonor they were avenging. Besides, if Firesister was in danger, Bearclaw would defend her.

Waterstrider, knowing he would never forgive himself if he was wrong, took the path that led directly to the temple, bypassing the village.

Serpentgate wasn't silent. There were shouts of anger and cries of terror, wailing children, barking dogs, clash of stone against stone. Was this was what the other villages had sounded like, Waterstrider wondered, before they became the silent, fearful ones he'd passed through during the past three days and nights? He drew ahead of Ravenchild on the winding path and looked for the Temple of Lightning to rise above the vegetation that interrupted his sight line.

There it was at last, a small room perched like a head on the massive shoulders of the buff-colored temple. Waterstrider pressed forward on knees that threatened to give out and hips that made each step torture.

He wasn't far from the wall surrounding the temple precinct when a blast from a conch-shell trumpet split the sky. A lone figure stepped out of the uppermost room and stopped behind a low wall atop the temple. It was Eaglefeather, garbed in the ceremonial yellow robes of the Rainsinger, neck curving birdlike under a chinless face. A mica mirror gleamed and flashed upon his forehead.

No priests challenged Waterstrider and Ravenchild as they passed through the narrow gateway and entered the plaza, where several groups of people clustered, their attention focused on the Rainsinger. Waterstrider and Ravenchild halted behind the assemblage.

Eaglefeather lifted his arms dramatically and declared, "Little minds flinch at shadows. Great minds bring forth the light and drive them away." The flash of his mirrored forehead was echoed suddenly in each hand, drawing gasps from the crowd.

Waterstrider missed the next few words. Then he heard, ". . . the brave souls at the Temple of Mist, those who have swept aside the shadows that veil the spirit world, those who have faced the monsters wearing the bodies of outlander men." A crash as of thunder echoed off the walls of the plaza, causing many in the crowd to jump and hiss in fear.

"You are like children, afraid of shadows in the night." Eaglefeather drew his left arm around in a graceful arc. Drops of water trailed behind his gesture. They hung sparkling in the air before drifting downward. "Listen now to the promises of the Ta'atchul," he proclaimed, "which they have granted in response to my prayers on your behalf." He stepped forward as an eerie humming began, seemingly from nowhere.

Ravenchild snorted as though unimpressed, but his muscles tensed and he craned his neck, looking all about him. Waterstrider could have told him the noise was produced by a priest with a wind-roarer, a flat piece of wood on a length of cord being swept through the air in an unending circle. Long ago, when the Watermasters went into exile, a young priest had gone with them, turning his back on the priesthood. He'd shared some of the tricks used by the priests during ceremonies. The wind-roarer was one.

Eaglefeather lifted both arms to the sky and intoned rhythmically in his powerful, carrying voice, "The night-spirits warmed me and made my heart light, so I roused in the morning and sang. Into the waters of darkness I leaped, and the spirits led me home. For as long as the Ta'atchul inhabit the sky, there is nothing to fear in this land."

As the words settled into the minds of the listeners, even Waterstrider felt the hope and surety of the Rainsinger's pledge, tempting him to believe that there was indeed nothing to fear.

A flash of movement distracted Waterstrider, too fast to follow with his eyes. Then it became all too clear.

An arrow with black fletching lodged in Eaglefeather's throat. He wavered upon his perch, uttering a wordless scream and clutching at his neck. Blood streamed onto the yellow robes as he stood, mouth open, mirror flashing in all directions as his head twisted. With agonizing slowness he leaned forward until at last his hands dropped away from his neck and his arms opened as if to fly.

His body, limp and ungraceful, plummeted downward. There was a sickening thud and then silence. Through a gap in the stunned crowd, Waterstrider saw the body of the Rainsinger of the Temple of Lightning, limbs twisted at impossible angles. Blood began to soak into the hard-packed plaza.

Waterstrider scarcely breathed as he gazed at the corpse. The hair on the back of his neck lifted. Coldness washed over him.

This was not just death. This was an execution carried out in public, ending the life of the most powerful man north of the river. A man who had been killed while calling on his gods and promising safety.

Waterstrider had counted Eaglefeather as an enemy all this time, and yet the death meted out to him was monstrous. Shocking. Appalling. What the outlanders surely saw as rough justice, what Waterstrider might eventually consider a necessary evil to end Eaglefeather's influence, right now was too awful to accept.

And if Waterstrider felt that way, what must the people of Serpentgate feel? What would they do in response?

No one approached the crumpled body. As Waterstrider gazed around the silent watchers, he noted that all the women had the upper half of their faces painted black, while all the men wore cloths wrapped around their heads, under which their faces were painted white or daubed with mud. There was a disturbing sameness to everyone, as though they had made a deliberate attempt to erase the differences between them.

And yet his eyes were drawn to one woman, standing immobile at the left side of the temple—Firesister. The bone hairpins holding her long braid in a knot at the back of her head made her instantly recognizable. With the face paint, he couldn't tell what expression she wore. Was Firesister glad Eaglefeather was dead? Or was she frozen in horror, appalled by the outlanders' vengeance? Did she understand that Eaglefeather had brought his death upon himself through the killing, intended or not, of Littlecliff?

She moved suddenly, stooping beside another woman who had collapsed. Mistlight, he supposed.

The keening of grief broke the silence in the plaza. Low at first, scattered, it quickly gathered strength.

Then a few heads turned away from the body and lifted upward toward the temple. Waterstrider too looked in that direction as an arrow arced up, its flaming tip trailing dark smoke. It slammed into the reed screen covering one of the openings of the temple. The screen above had already begun to burn. Smoke went up from all four sides of the temple as arrow after arrow hit the screens, the only vulnerable parts of the thick-walled adobe temple.

Waterstrider gripped Ravenchild's shoulder. "Is this how your outlanders took the Temple of Mist?"

"No," Ravenchild said quietly. "There, the priests had no warning. As we arrived, they swarmed out of the temple like angry wasps and made themselves easy targets, killed with arrows one by one."

"We have to stop this," Waterstrider breathed.

"Why?"

"People here are more desperate. The priests have a stronger hold. You saw for yourself, coming north, how all the canals south of Sky

River run full, taking water to the fields. Not so here. In Serpentgate, many see the priests as the only hope for the crops."

The stubborn set of Ravenchild's jaw didn't ease.

The crowd pressed forward, tightening around them. Waterstrider, looking over the heads of those before him, saw that the reed screens had largely burned away, exposing three doorways gaping open one over the other in the front face of the temple. Outlanders wearing armor and helmets advanced on the temple. They struck out with clubs and axes at anyone in their way, but carelessly, as though they couldn't be bothered to inflict significant harm.

Waterstrider pushed forward as the dangerous mood of the farmfolk darkened further. These were a peace-loving people, yes, but even a rabbit could bite when threatened.

Smoldering fragments of the screens rained down. A spark burned his shoulder and he blew it out. He reached the nearest doorway before the first of the outlanders, who were slowed by their swinging of clubs and by the press of the crowd.

In their tongue, he called out, "Stop!" He crossed the spears in front of him to reinforce his order. Though he gained the outlanders' attention, they kept advancing toward him.

He shouted, "Perhaps the high priest deserved to die for the vile things he's done, not only to you but to others here—including me. But the other priests here have done you no harm. Why should they be hauled out of the temple and slaughtered, or burned alive within?"

Ravenchild joined Waterstrider, standing between the outlanders and the priests they saw as their prey. Shoulder to shoulder, the two men faced a rising storm, too, in the clans of Serpentgate.

The old saying *Fear turns a man foolish* came into Waterstrider's mind, and he wondered who was more foolish right now, him or the massed gathering before him. One wrong word, one careless action could push this entire community onto a path of destruction from which they might never recover. He sought the right words.

Before they came to him, Ravenchild said in the language of the City of Birds, "Rattail, I see you." He began naming the outlanders in the plaza. "Dogeater. Bigspear." He continued as other outlanders emerged from the places from which they'd shot the flaming arrows. They held their bows loosely while the rest stopped plying their clubs and gathered around Ravenchild and Waterstrider. "Put away your weapons. You have had your revenge. It is time to go home."

The people of Serpentgate fell back, waiting and watching. Waterstrider knew what they saw in Ravenchild: A hulking, craggy-faced man taller and broader than Waterstrider. A man with such presence that he could with his voice alone either stir other men to violence or ward off a fight. A man speaking a strange tongue and standing next to Waterstrider, who had left the weir unfinished and had never promised to restore the canals.

Not far away, the Rainsinger who had made promises to the farmfolk lay dead, brought down by an outlander arrow. If the would-be avengers obeyed Ravenchild and set their weapons aside, would the people in the plaza let them go—or set upon them with vicious intent? What was certain was that the outlanders would kill everyone indiscriminately if provoked.

Waterstrider said to the farmfolk, "These outlanders came for the Rainsinger, who ordered the attack upon them. Now that they've had their revenge, they will leave. Let them go."

"You stand with them!" came a harsh voice that Waterstrider recognized as Digger's.

"I stand with my friend, brother to the man who died protecting me," Waterstrider replied, hands tightening on the spears he still held crossed in front of him. "The violence started with the Rainsinger. These outlanders have a different way than ours. They seek blood for blood, for their gods are petty and quarrelsome. We are not that way. Mother Ge would not be pleased to see you become like them."

Feet shifted, stances eased, eyes became less piercing in both groups.

Ravenchild spoke again to the outlanders in their language. "Head for the mound," he said. "I will be along shortly, with Waterstrider."

They didn't move until Ravenchild gave them a sharp nod. Then they clumped together in a defensive formation with arrows nocked against attack from all directions. Moving as one they slipped out of the temple precinct.

Ravenchild stayed with Waterstrider.

From behind, Waterstrider heard rustles and scuffs and whispers. He stepped away from the thigh-high doorway and gazed up into the room, in which a big priest walked forward, the wall's thick shadow sliding over his body at a steep angle.

The priest halted at the edge of the doorway. His face, though fully lit, bore no expression. He wasn't looking at Ravenchild or Waterstrider but stared past them.

A hand slipped into Waterstrider's. He glanced down and saw a slender wrist that bore the same tattooed line of dots as those on his own. Firesister had come to him.

"Thorn," she asked the priest above, "will the Stormbringers seek vengeance in return? Or will you accept Eaglefeather's death as the end?"

"Is that what you would advise, Firesister?" Thorn replied.

When she nodded, he said, directing his question to someone beyond Waterstrider's shoulder, "What say you, Gran Squashblossom?"

An old woman said, "Haven't we had enough killing?"

"I will see what the other Stormbringers choose to do." But he didn't retreat back to the temple. Instead he looked at Ravenchild and waited.

Ravenchild revealed his ability to speak and understand the language being used by everyone else: "This peace will last so long as no one from your side strikes. I shall stay here to make sure of it."

Bringing a searching gaze to bear on Waterstrider, Thorn asked, "Can this outlander be trusted?"

"I have known him since I was a boy," Waterstrider declared. "He will do as he says."

Thorn seemed to accept that, for he disappeared back into the temple. Another man deeper in the shadows came forward then and showed himself to Waterstrider. They exchanged glances before Bearclaw followed the priest into the darkness. If the outlanders hadn't left after killing Eaglefeather, Waterstrider realized, they would have become the hunted. The priests here had been prepared for the attack.

Once the confrontation was over, Waterstrider's legs collapsed under him. His muscles knotted and cramped enough to make his eyes water.

"Get him some food," Ravenchild ordered Firesister.

She tugged her hand free. The skin on Waterstrider's palm tingled where it had touched hers. His eyes met her dark-brown orbs, black at the center, surrounded by bloodshot whites, set deep within a face painted half black. She seemed like something out of a tale of the First Days. "I'll come back," she said, shooting Ravenchild a hard look.

Waterstrider watched her limp away. He was fiercely glad she had come to him, laying her hand in his. Skyblade and Ninetoes approached, their faces painted white. Both boys greeted Waterstrider with what seemed like relief, though their manner was subdued and they kept casting Ravenchild sidelong glances.

Ravenchild handed Waterstrider a journeycake. Before he took the first bite, he asked Skyblade about the face-paint.

"As soon as messengers brought word of the Smokemothers and Cornmaidens being in danger," Skyblade said, "they returned to their clans. Most of them, anyway. Gran Squashblossom sent for Mistlight and Firesister, since they didn't have anyplace to go. Some of the clan-sisters wanted Firesister to give them tattoos matching the Smokemothers, but somebody said it would be easier to just blacken everybody's skin. Somebody else said only the top half needed to be painted."

"And the men?" Waterstrider asked.

Skyblade shrugged. "White to hide the priests' tattoos. Cloths to conceal their shaved heads," he admitted with another glance at Ravenchild.

"Clever," Ravenchild said.

A new cramp stabbed at Waterstrider's shin. He sent the boys for water.

Once they were alone, Ravenchild said, "That woman who came and held your hand . . ."

"Firesister."

"What does she mean to you?"

Waterstrider wasn't sure how to answer that. He kept his reply simple. "She saved my life."

"Is she the reason you had to return to Serpentgate? The reason you drove yourself past exhaustion?"

There was more to it than that. "This is home," he said.

Ravenchild stared hard at him, took a breath, let it out, and took another.

Waterstrider cocked an eye at his friend. He pretty well knew what was coming: *"Brightheart is waiting for you."*

"My sister loves you. She's expecting you to return to her."

Waterstrider, who had many fond memories of Brightheart, smiled. "She found pleasure with me, but in the end she didn't ask me to stay. She has her children now, and grandchildren too. I will miss her, I suppose."

Ravenchild grunted. "If that's the most you can say, why did you stay with her for so long?"

"To keep her children from feeling the shame of a father who disrespects their mother. I know that shame." He knew it all too well. "I won't be going back to the City of Birds," Waterstrider told his friend. "My people need me." *And I've come home.*

Epilogue

The night-spirits warmed me and made my heart light,
So I roused in the morning and sang.

—DEATH SPEECH OF THE LAST RAINSINGER
OF THE TEMPLE OF LIGHTNING

Whistling, Skyblade sauntered along the path to Mother Sleeping. His melody rose and fell against the rasping of the kuhtpul, the thick-bodied insects whose noise marked the approach of the summer rainy season. Rain wouldn't fall today or tomorrow—of that he was certain. Five winters had passed since he'd done his naming-quest and received the gift of predicting rain. He had learned to interpret the feel of the air.

Though the morning was well advanced, he was cool enough, for a dampened head-wrap kept Brother Sun's rays off his black hair and his pace was measured. He didn't need to hurry. As long as he reached Mother Sleeping before midday, he would be fine.

Above the shegoi bushes ahead, he saw two of the broad, shallow baskets that women used when gathering saguaro fruit. The baskets bobbed along as though floating on water, though he knew they were carefully balanced on the gatherers' heads, held in place with a woven grass ring, while the women took cautious steps to keep from losing any of the precious contents.

As Skyblade rounded a bend in the path, he spotted the basket bearers. Skirts of undyed cotton drifted limply around their coppery-hued legs, both skin and cloth streaked with purple-red saguaro juice. Head scarves covered their hair, framing their faces. They looked weary and sweaty. They must have been working hard since dawn gathering saguaro fruit on the north slope of Mother Sleeping.

Back at Serpentgate, jars of saguaro syrup were fermenting into liquor for the upcoming midsummer sun-festival, so Skyblade guessed this late picking was intended for eating, or maybe drying into fruit leather. The lack of reliable water for the fields forced the people of Serpentgate to rely heavily on desert foods provided by Mother Ge. It pained Skyblade to see them struggling to feed themselves and their children. He was doing all he could to help bring forth a good crop from the fields, but whether his efforts would be successful . . . who could say? A generous harvest depended on Mother Ge's will, as Firesister always said.

Several other women came into view behind the leaders. Most bore baskets, but a few carried the saguaro-rib staffs used to knock ripe fruit off the top and high arms of the giant cactus. The staffs were tied together in bundles so only the crossbars at the tips were visible over the women's shoulders.

So normal was the scene that for a moment Skyblade was yanked back several turnings in his memory, to the days before everything had changed. He could hardly breathe for yearning to see his mother and the other women of Lastwater walking home from picking saguaro fruit in the foothills. But his mother was long dead and these were strangers, their faces within the scarves unfamiliar.

The women stopped when they saw him. The ones carrying the staffs inclined their heads in the gesture normally reserved for clan elders. Those with the baskets seemed uncomfortable, as though they wanted to do the same but didn't dare risk dumping the fruit. They all lowered their gaze to avoid meeting his eyes. "Greetings, honored son of Mother Ge," said the foremost one, whose face bore the dignity of age. The others, clumped together as closely as their baskets would allow, echoed her words.

"Greetings to you," he offered in return, unused to being treated with such respect. Word of his naming-quest had gotten out a few moons ago, and he'd gone from being an unknown ditchrunner to being much in demand among the farmfolk of Serpentgate, as proof that Mother Ge hadn't deserted them.

The woman who first spoke began to walk again. Skyblade moved out of her way. The one directly behind her remained in place. "I am of Littleseed Clan," she said. "We're grateful for your prayers."

"Oh. Yes?" He cleared his throat and remembered what Thorn had advised him to say: "May Mother Ge bless you and yours with the rains that are to come."

She stepped forward and laid her fingertips briefly on Skyblade's shirt over his heart, as though by doing so she could draw forth some of the power with which Mother Ge had supposedly imbued him. "Thank you."

The others touched him in the same way as they passed. He endured, though his heart pounded with embarrassment and heat rose in his cheeks. Toward the end of the pack he saw, finally, one familiar face.

"Shiningdawn!" he exclaimed.

She looked up, startled. Her expression eased into a smile that dispelled the awkwardness he felt over the reverential attitude of the other women.

Skyblade ducked beneath the basket to press a quick kiss on her cheek. He'd grown quite a bit during the turnings that had elapsed since the downfall of the priests, and though he hadn't caught up to Waterstrider, he was taller than any of the women.

Shiningdawn eyed him sidelong. "What are you doing so far from the fields?"

He placed a hand on her large, round stomach and felt a kick from within. "Another one? Who's the father this time?"

She grinned at him. Lifting the full basket off the grass ring on which it rested atop her head, she held the basket in the crook of her elbow and slid the ring onto her wrist. With her free hand, stained dark with saguaro juice, she pressed his forearm. "You, of course."

Counting back to when he'd last lain with her, he laughed. "I don't think so." One of her children might be his, but the other was from her service as a Cornmaiden. Most recently, she'd spent much time in the company of one of Ravenchild's outlanders, a likable man with a rich, hearty laugh. Skyblade suspected that fellow was the father. It seemed good to have love and children joining the People of Two Rivers together with the outlanders, after the violence of the initial revenge-fueled invasion.

"But what brings you here?" Shiningdawn lifted her hand away from his arm. "The way the farmers have been demanding your blessing, I'm surprised you have time to wander about."

"I'm not wandering." Skyblade gestured toward Mother Sleeping, where the Skywatchers had long ago designed a way to track the sun's path through the seasons. "I came to check how long until the Cloud-Summoning ceremonies start."

"Why? What does that have to do with you?"

Fearing that she might think he was bragging, he glanced down and rubbed the side of his nose before admitting, "Thorn has been teaching me the words for the Sit-and-Drink. I'm to be one of the overnight celebrants."

"But you were never even a priest!"

Her scoffing tone stung. "Being a priest isn't necessary for the ritual. The elders performed the Sit-and-Drink for untold generations before the priests came to the valley."

"You aren't an elder either."

"I don't need to be."

She lifted her chin as though to argue.

"All that matters," he went on quickly, "is Mother Ge's willingness to hear our prayers."

"Is that what Firesister says?" She put a nasty twist on Firesister's name.

To Skyblade, Shiningdawn's hostility seemed ill-timed, given that she was undoubtedly coming back from picking saguaro fruit in a place Firesister had recommended. What Firesister didn't know about Mother Ge's bounty—what to gather, when, and where—wasn't worth knowing. He responded coolly: "No, it's what the farmfolk say when they ask me to bless their fields." What Firesister said was, *"With the canals still not flowing, people need hope above all else."* He added, "I give them hope that Mother Ge is listening."

Shiningdawn rested a hand on her belly. She gazed after the other women, the last stragglers nearly out of sight, then spoke without looking at him, as though she didn't want to see his face: "I fear you're getting caught up in matters too big for you. Thorn may have renounced the Ta'atchul and now claims to serve Mother Ge, but many still see him as a priest. It may prove dangerous to be so closely associated with him. The Smokemothers are jealous of the influence he retains. They're resentful, too, about Firesister and Mistlight claiming to speak directly with Mother Ge. Now you step forward as another link with Mother Ge. Besides all that, there's the five turnings you've spent working on the canals for Waterstrider and the outlanders—with little to show for it. Take care, Skyblade. When you fly so high, it's a long way to fall."

She slipped the grass ring off her wrist and placed it on her glossy black hair, then lifted the basket with the purple-red ripe saguaro fruit from the curve of her arm and set it carefully on the ring. Without another word, without so much as a glance at him, she turned and walked away.

As he watched her go, he felt a pang of regret. Shiningdawn had been his first lover, introducing him to the pleasures young men and women could experience together on starlit summer nights. When the passion cooled between them, she moved on to another man, while Skyblade continued to count her as a friend. But those last words to him didn't sound like friendly advice. Was she separating herself from him, for fear that she might fall along with him?

Taking part in ceremonies, blessing the fields, allowing people to believe that his naming-quest revealed Mother Ge's beneficence—those were all risky endeavors. Skyblade might very well fail and suffer the consequences.

But not to try at all? No. Then it would be the people of Serpentgate who would surely suffer.

If he'd learned anything from Waterstrider and Firesister, it was that allowing fear to control one's actions was a sure way to stumble into disaster. A man had to try with all his might. Then if he failed he could take comfort from having done what he could.

Skyblade sighed. He pulled his gaze away from the sway of Shining-dawn's skirt and continued up the path toward Mother Sleeping. The sooner he finished this task, the sooner he could return to Cloud Mountain and Mistlight.

Mistlight's hand began to shake as she finished outlining a black petal on the wall. She laid the brush across the paint bowl and studied the wind-willow flower. It didn't look much like the flower she remembered from the days when she used to gather herbs with the Childcatcher. She hadn't been off Cloud Mountain to see flowers since Eaglefeather's death—however long ago that was now. Time was slippery. Memory even more so.

Thoughts of Eaglefeather had once brought such pain as she'd never before known, agony beyond enduring. She'd loved him more than herself. And then she'd hated him with equal passion. And then he had died and for an eternity haunted her dreams night and day. Looking back, she understood why. She had foreseen the arrow to the throat, the fall from the temple—and feared that meant her vision caused it to happen. For a long time, guilt had clawed at her throat whenever Eaglefeather came to mind.

Gradually she had become aware of many things—sunshine shifting into cool darkness, the scent that preceded rain being cleared away by falling droplets, people moving about and talking at her. Little by little, Eaglefeather's ghost had faded from her dreams and Mistlight found her way out of the darkness in which she'd been too long trapped.

But she hadn't quite returned to the world. The flowers had begun to fade from memory. She missed them. Enough to venture away from this room on Cloud Mountain where she was enfolded by Mother Ge's warmth and love?

Mistlight crept to the doorway in the center of the room's east wall. Brother Sun had shone through the narrow opening when he rose that morning. His light had pierced Mistlight's closed eyelids, waking her abruptly. Time to add more pictures to the wall, she'd thought, and had slipped out to grab a bowl of face-paint that Firesister had prepared for some purpose other than painting black flowers. Now the doorway lay in shadow, for Brother Sun had mounted high overhead.

The previous night, she'd dreamed again of standing hand in hand with Skyblade and a child under a sunset sky. That dream-vision was coming regularly. It was a relief.

Some of the terrifying dreams Mistlight had experienced under the influence of Eaglefeather's vengeful spirit—a flaming mountain shooting out ash, a bright moon blazing across the sky dragging all the stars into darkness behind it, a toothed frog monster eating Brother Sun —made her wonder how much longer she could go on. Ending her life would end the dreaming, she'd thought sometimes. A knife to the heart, perhaps. Or choking herself with a twist of cloth until the rush of blood in her veins stopped. Or throwing herself from the top of the Temple of Lightning.

Then Mother Ge would whisper comforting words in her ear and send Mistlight into a dreamless space where she felt safe. That place now seemed cramped and confining.

Mistlight left the shadowed room and stepped out into Brother Sun's brilliance. She gazed northeast, toward the red ridge of Mother Sleeping, where Mother Ge was said to be strongest.

The rasping noise of the kuhtpul became louder, filling the air. Mistlight asked Mother Ge, "Could I come and visit you there?" A warm breeze caressed her face. The rasping of the kuhtpul faded as a small twister picked up a column of dust out on the desert, moving slowly northward.

"Come to me," Mother Ge said. *"Free yourself from this trap of your own making."*

Mistlight wavered. Did she dare leave the mound? She remembered a dream-vision from a few nights earlier. The vision had begun with her scuttling through a long cave filled with ice, the mountain above her gushing out ash and fire. As she emerged from the cave, a bird swallowed her and she lay in its belly. Pushed out, she fell and dropped into a hollow reed borne on floodwaters. In desperation she sealed the end closed, then floated in the reed until it came to rest on solid ground. She broke the seal and found that she'd been tossed up on top of Slant Mountain, at the edge of the Mountains of Sunrise. To escape from angry people there, she crawled into a round jar covered with painted birds. Down she rolled from the mountaintop, shaken and battered as the jar tumbled from the ridges. When the jar stopped, Mistlight fought to get out, but the walls wouldn't break and she crouched alone in the dark.

"Stop," someone had told her. The voice belonged to the woman she'd called Mother, the one who had raised Mistlight as her own. The woman who had been the caretaker of the Children's House.

"Let us help," someone else had said.

A crack had appeared in the jar, a streak of light. Pieces broke away, revealing a dream-world of misty trees covered with spring blossoms. Two women stood among the blooming trees, Mistlight's mother and the Childcatcher, whose face had lost its wrinkles and whose hair was the blue-black of a raven's wing. "Be reborn," the Childcatcher said. Then they had vanished.

The dream had meant nothing to her when she'd experienced it. Now she thought she understood.

Mistlight turned away from Mother Sleeping and went in search of the bird-patterned jar she'd swaddled in bloody cloths and carried around for so long, convinced it was a baby. Not just any baby, either, but Eaglefeather's. The man who had betrayed her, stolen her mind, left her with memories so painful and dangerous that she'd turned away from the world. Now she saw the way to break free.

She found the jar propped against one of the adobe blocks outside the bolt-hole where she'd slept until recently. Mistlight snatched up the painted jar, strode to the half wall at the edge of Cloud Mountain, and heaved the heavy vessel as hard as she could. A satisfying crash followed. She leaned over the wall, precariously balancing on her stomach, and surveyed the potsherds scattered on the gravel far below.

With rising confidence she started for the main passageway to the north half of Cloud Mountain. As she emerged from the cluster of buildings into the open space overlooking the storage rooms, the sweet aroma of saguaro syrup came to her nose.

The scent took her back to the day she'd become a Cornmaiden, so long ago, after her first moontime. Thick red syrup had been painted in a circle on her forehead, which was then dusted with yellow corn pollen. Following a ceremony filled with lofty and inspiring words,

Mistlight had dedicated one full turning of her life to Mother Ge. It was supposed to have lasted from one summer to the next.

Instead she'd gotten tangled in her mind and lost her way.

Mistlight walked to the half wall. She laid her hands on the warm adobe and stared down at the activity in the roomblocks. One work area held a fire-ring with several pots that bubbled with syrup. Piled against the compound's wall were jars filled with a mix of syrup and water, left to ferment into saguaro wine for the Cloud-Summoning ceremonies.

In the adjacent work area, women were painting rainbows on thin hides stretched over basketry frameworks, to be worn on their heads during the ceremonies. Each woman had her own pot of color. Mistlight envied the variety as she thought of the black paint she'd been using on the walls of her little room.

Movement at the gap in the high wall surrounding the mound caught Mistlight's attention. Skyblade was there, strong thighs bunching and releasing as his kilt shifted with each step. Below the short sleeves of his shirt, ropy muscles rippled down his arms. The shirt, a little too tight, pulled across his chest. She wondered when he had turned into a man.

Surprised by her curiosity, she reminded herself that she had Mother Ge's love. Surely that was enough. A moment later she realized it wasn't. Suddenly she wanted the physical love that a man could provide. *Maybe a child too,* an inner voice suggested, as a long-banked yearning sparked to life again. Her hands tightened on the edge of the wall.

Skyblade looked up at where she stood. He waved a greeting.

Slowly, Mistlight waved back.

Firesister watched children playing in the old ballcourt, an oval surface dug deep into the ground. Their voices—raised in mock screams, taunting, and wild laughter—drifted on the breeze along with the buzzing of the kuhtpul. The outlanders' children were indistinguishable from the children born to Mother Ge's people. They all ran about nearly naked, clad in dust and joy.

She glanced sidelong at Ravenchild, Littlecliff's brother. The two were so similar physically, she found it almost painful to look at him. But Ravenchild made sure the too-frequent conflicts between the adults of the outlanders and the People of Two Rivers were resolved peacefully. Perhaps more important, he was Waterstrider's best friend.

Relaxed, he leaned against a house-compound wall as they waited for Waterstrider, who'd been waylaid by an irritated farmer. Only one of the Serpentgate canals ran full with water all summer. The farmer had demanded to know why, with a witch as a lifemate, Waterstrider didn't have her simply conjure water into the other canals.

Firesister told Ravenchild, "Thanks for pulling me away before I said something awful." Now that her flare of temper had subsided, she felt embarrassed at how quickly she'd lost control. It was just that she'd been trying so hard to help everyone survive without the canals.

More and more people from the City of Birds had followed the initial invaders to the valley. They had quickly taken the best-yielding fields. Those among the People of Two Rivers who resisted, early on, were beaten or killed. The rest of the clanfolk learned quickly and gave up their fields to the newcomers. That meant more farmers trying to work less land, and fighting each other over it, until few clans remained whole. Displaced families from south of the river drifted northward, to Serpentgate and beyond, where there was desert, lots of desert, from which people could glean enough food to stay alive, if they knew how. The sensible ones came to Firesister and asked for help.

Not enough were sensible.

Firesister returned her gaze to the children playing below, oblivious to the tensions between the adults. She couldn't remember being that innocent. When she was seven, the Watermasters had been driven out of the valley. When she was fifteen, she'd been attacked and left for dead. At twice that age, she'd seen the downfall of the priests. And now, five turnings later, authority seemed to come from a willingness to use violence.

She sighed, admitting to herself that she too had become hot-tempered, tempted to strike out at people when they got in her way. Mother Ge was surely disappointed in her.

"That is strange," Ravenchild said beside her, tensing as he often did when startled by a Serpentgate custom.

She followed his gaze toward the house compounds of the village. A small clot of people broke apart to reveal several Coyote-Tricksters moving through, using willow switches on anyone too slow to step aside. Brown and tan stripes were painted on the Tricksters' bellies, arms, and legs. Sweat from the rising heat of the day had caused the stripes to sag and run. Coyote pelts were wrapped around the shoulders of the lithe figures, and fur kilts wrapped around their hips. On their heads were basketry masks giving them long muzzles and sharply pricked ears.

Ravenchild asked, "Are they not early? The midsummer ceremonies have not yet begun."

Firesister frowned. The Tricksters—who normally targeted people guilty of quarreling, crying, or complaining during the four sun-festivals —were indeed early. And they seemed to be coming for her.

Ravenchild stepped between her and the Tricksters.

"No, don't," she told him. "Don't interfere. I'll be fine." She didn't know what was going on, but whatever it was, Ravenchild could not get involved.

Reluctantly he moved aside, and the Tricksters surrounded her. Their willow switches tapped the back of her knees, thighs, ankles, not hard enough to raise welts but with enough sting to urge her forward.

"What are you doing?" she asked the nearest, who glanced at her sidelong and said nothing.

Another light tap to her thigh got her moving. Every time she slowed, she received another flick of the willow. They weren't being rough; it wasn't like the time the southern priests had attacked her in her home and forced her to run through the village. The Tricksters accommodated her limping pace. People they passed appeared startled but not concerned by the Tricksters being out so early.

As she neared the temple, Firesister reminded herself there was no reason for fear. Eaglefeather's spirit had long ago been sung to rest. The Temple of Lightning belonged to Mother Ge now, for the Smokemothers had claimed the heights left behind by the priests.

Sweat stung her eyes, and she wiped the moisture away with the edge of her sleeve. It was too hot for this trotting about, she thought. Too hot even for walking. She wouldn't have left the mound at all today except that Tallcorn had asked her and Waterstrider to visit.

Firesister stumbled but regained her balance. Grim curiosity, rather than the little flicks against her skin, kept her moving. What could the Smokemothers want with her?

As the Tricksters urged her into the temple precinct, the song of the kuhtpul rose, a sign sent by Mother Ge to reassure her people that the rains would soon come. White clouds mounted into the sky above the temple, building higher as Brother Sun drank up the sweat from the village and poured it into the clouds.

Firesister expected the Tricksters to stop in the plaza, but they urged her onward, straight into the Temple of Lightning. Blinded by passing from brightness into shadow, Firesister stopped. Someone bumped into her from behind and uttered an exclamation. A burst of laughter followed, reminding her that once the masks came off, the Tricksters were just boys.

Her skin prickled from the chill of the thick walls. Eyes adjusting, she saw a doorway. Beyond was a slender, upright figure enveloped in pale cloth. "Come," the Smokemother whispered before moving away.

Firesister left the Tricksters behind and followed the graceful priestess through the maze of rooms, some lit by the rectangular openings in the temple walls, others closed off from the world. Around and around they went, and up a ladder, around again, up again, around and up, until at last the Smokemother stood aside and sent Firesister up one more ladder into Brother Sun's brilliance. She emerged at the top of the temple. Though no higher than Cloud Mountain, the temple felt so narrow and hemmed-in, with so little earth under her feet, that she felt dizzy.

She blinked a few times and tried to steady herself. She saw, in place of the adobe room that once perched on the top of the temple, a rainhouse—fat and round like a cook-pot but woven of branches rather than formed from clay. Five Smokemothers wearing gray robes, with ragged edges at hem and sleeve, stood in front of the rounded hut: the Truthspeaker, the Seedkeeper, the Dreamwalker, and two lesser servants of Mother Ge, including Willowbundle, who had once been Firesister's most loyal friend.

Even before Bearclaw, there had been Willowbundle. And now Bearclaw was exploring the southlands with the Far-Traders, and Willowbundle was here wearing an expression that looked sly rather than friendly.

Firesister demanded, "Why was I brought here?"

Wrapped in the scent of tobacco, the Truthspeaker stepped forward. Her bony nose and chin had softened over the past turnings, as her wrinkles became deeper. "You must know, the Childcatcher passed recently."

Firesister understood what was left unsaid: they wanted her to replace the old priestess, whose death left the Smokemothers diminished, with too few in the order to do all that needed doing: to welcome newborns and send off the dead, to bless seeds and give thanks at harvest, to pray for peace, to call down rain.

She crossed her arms. She wanted to do good things for her people, for the Smokemothers in particular, because they'd saved her life long ago. But to join their order, to live by their rules and give up the life-path she'd begun to walk, the happiness she'd found with Waterstrider? That was asking too much. "I was never a Cornmaiden. I can't be a Smokemother," she said.

The Truthspeaker told her, "You fulfilled the most important requirement of a Cornmaiden—you bore a child and gave it to the village."

Firesister eyed the Truthspeaker with dislike. *"Her,"* she said with quiet emphasis. "I gave *her* to the village. And I took her back when you refused to protect her."

The Smokemother had the grace to look embarrassed.

"Why did you scheme so to give Mistlight to the Rainsinger?" Firesister demanded.

The Dreamwalker lifted her chin and spoke: "She had to be at the temple to witness his downfall." Her voice throbbed with conviction.

The Seedkeeper added, "Everything we did was to bring down the Rainsinger. He could not be allowed to gain more power. That you and Mistlight were caught up in our plans, we can only apologize."

"I'm life-mated," Firesister reminded them. "My first loyalty can never be to Mother Ge. I have taken a different oath."

The Seedkeeper stepped forward. Loose gray hairs curled around her face as her eyes, deep and wise, locked with Firesister's. "Yet you still serve Mother Ge in everything you do. Can you deny it?" She stooped and picked up a bowl filled with saguaro wine.

In low, compelling tones, the Truthspeaker said, "Drink the wine and speak to Mother Ge. Help us weave our words and call down the rain. This is where you are needed."

The Seedkeeper, her intense eyes trapping Firesister's, held out the bowl. Firesister's hands lifted of their own volition and accepted the heavy vessel. The surface of the red liquid caught the light, rippling and gleaming like blood. Firesister gazed into the depths of the bowl where the wine rested still and dark.

A distinctive odor lifted from the wine. Dizzyweed, she realized, which brought visions and desires. Her hands tightened, trembled. A few drops of saguaro wine spilled onto her wrist, covering part of the tattoo that marked the vow she had made with Waterstrider.

The vow that had saved his life. The vow Mother Ge had led her to make.

The Smokemothers might believe she belonged with them, but that was not where she needed to be. She would do Mother Ge's will by living in the community and helping people survive. Not drinking herself into the madness of dizzyweed and imagining herself more important than others around her. Not by leaving the man she had opened her heart to.

Firesister pressed the bowl back into the Seedkeeper's grasp. "This is not the way I serve Mother Ge."

Waterstrider strode toward Ravenchild, who waited near the old ballcourt. From the vantage of the mound, Waterstrider had seen no sign of Firesister or the Tricksters, so he figured they'd already reached the temple. He remembered the first time he'd seen her, held in the storage room next to the mound—her clothing dirty and disheveled, hair wild, eyes locked fearlessly with his—and remembered, too, the tragic events that followed his refusal to become involved with her affairs. Littlecliff's death. The outlanders' invasion. The killing of Eaglefeather and the end of the priests.

He hadn't suspected, five turnings ago, how important she would become to him. He was responsible for her. He owed her his life. And she held his heart.

Ravenchild approached. His brow was furrowed, the lines beside his mouth deep and harsh. He turned and matched Waterstrider's pace so there was no need to slow down. "The Tricksters came for Firesister."

"So I heard," Waterstrider replied. "Ninetoes said the Smoke-mothers sent them. Let's go get her back."

Ravenchild grabbed Waterstrider's elbow and pulled him to a halt. "Firesister told me not to interfere."

Waterstrider yanked his arm free. "She didn't tell me." His gaze lifted to the temple, its upper walls rising above the other structures in the village. His gut tightened at the possibility that he might no longer see Firesister's face across the cook-fire, feel her hand on his arm, hear her voice raised in song and laughter. With a rising sense of urgency, he started forward again.

Ravenchild's heavily muscled arm shot out, blocking him. Waterstrider knocked the arm away and kept moving. "If it is the Smokemothers who summoned her," Ravenchild called after him, "she is in no danger. They will do nothing but talk." With a few quick strides, Ravenchild placed his body between Waterstrider and the temple.

"You don't know that. You don't know what they want with her." What if they resented Firesister's ability to speak directly with Mother Ge? What might they dare to do if they feared they would be deemed unnecessary? Waterstrider tried to step around his friend, but Ravenchild shifted again to block the way.

"She went calmly enough," Ravenchild said, "as if she expected the summons. Might they ask her to join them? I heard one of the old priestesses died."

"True." Considering that possibility, Waterstrider ran a hand over the top of his head, hot from the sun and prickling with sweat. As he lowered his arm, the tattoo on his wrist caught his eye.

"Would she agree to join the priestesses?" Ravenchild asked.

Waterstrider turned his wrist, following the dark line of dots encircling it, a reminder of the vow he shared with Firesister. "No," he said slowly. His earlier urgency subsided. "They've wronged her too many times." Especially in taking Eaglefeather's side when Firesister was accused of being a witch. He knew she still felt bitter about that. "But I don't trust them."

"No more you should. Still, you need to show that you trust her. If you do."

"Of course I do."

She was the one who held Serpentgate together. The other communities of Earth River and Sky River still had working canals, but their clans were so busy fighting with each other and with the outlanders that no one was deciding where irrigation water would be most effective. By contrast, in Serpentgate only one canal was working as it should, but because of Firesister the clanfolk trusted Waterstrider to distribute the limited supply of water fairly. Because of Firesister they believed in Mother Ge's bounty: there would be food enough in the desert to see them through lean times, sufficient rain from the sky to water the crops. Because of Firesister the clans of Serpentgate were patient, working diligently every winter to rebuild a few more lengths of canal to irrigate more fields.

Granted, it was a frustrating, tedious process. Waterstrider suspected that only if Mother Ge sent the River-Serpents to reshape the valley would the canals ever be fully restored. But Firesister said she was sure he would find a way. She had more faith in him than he had in himself.

"Let her deal with the Smokemothers," Ravenchild advised. "Trust her that much. She is strong."

Waterstrider looked toward the temple, which glowered at him from the north end of the village. He did trust Firesister. She would return to him.

He gazed past the lighthearted children to the clusters of young men and women pretending not to notice each other. In a few more nights, the dancing would start, and some of those determinedly oblivious youngsters would pair up and go into the bushes together. The short hair still favored by outlanders and the long hair of Mother Ge's people would spread out together on the desert pavement in the dark. Through bedplay and children, the two peoples were becoming joined so tightly that they could never be completely separate again.

Nighttime pleasure had joined him and Firesister as well, on many occasions. He smiled as recent memories drifted across his mind. They had become lifemates in truth.

Ravenchild asked, "What did you do with that farmer who wanted her to use witchcraft for his benefit?"

"I told him if he insulted Firesister again, I would tie rocks to his arms and legs and throw him in the canal."

Nodding solemnly, Ravenchild said, "Not the best idea. His corpse would poison the water. Toss him in the river instead."

Waterstrider grinned. "Good thinking."

Ravenchild thumped him on the shoulder. "I imagine for Firesister's sake you might actually do it, never mind the consequences."

Waterstrider shook his head, but his friend was right.

Eyeing him closely, Ravenchild said, "You returned to the valley out of loyalty, you said before you and Littlecliff left the City of Birds. Called home by an old friend, you felt a sense of obligation. I suspected then that you wanted to prove it was a mistake to force the Watermasters into exile. Whatever you originally intended, your reason for staying has become something different. It is Firesister that keeps you here. Am I wrong?"

Waterstrider met his friend's inquiring gaze levelly. Ravenchild was partly right, but it wasn't just Firesister. Waterstrider now had a family of sorts.

It didn't consist of blood relatives, even though he'd found his mother's kin—for Digger, of Cornhill Clan, had turned out to be Waterstrider's uncle. Cornhill Clan still had nothing to do with him. The only way to be accepted by his mother's people, Waterstrider had realized some time ago, would be to get water to their clanlands. Like the rest of the farmfolk, even Tallcorn, his mother's clan valued him only for what he could give them.

He wasn't sure how to tell Ravenchild what he was feeling. Of course, Ravenchild knew that bonds between those who found kinship through the heart could be stronger than blood, for he'd looked upon Waterstrider as a brother ever since their meeting nearly thirty winters ago. Hadn't he, and Littlecliff too, taken on Waterstrider's responsibilities as theirs? Though Littlecliff was gone, Ravenchild remained, still Waterstrider's brother. And the ties stretched to include Firesister as his lifemate. The sons he'd found in Skyblade and Ninetoes. A daughter, Mistlight, through Firesister's blood. Those were Waterstrider's family.

Waterstrider decided to ask a question he'd wondered about many times in the past few turnings and never dared voice. "If the canals failed utterly, would you go back to the City of Birds?" As surprise appeared on Ravenchild's face, Waterstrider explained, "Without the canals, there would be no reason for you to stay and help me. It could even become dangerous." His chest tightened as he waited for the answer. A yes would mean he'd be alone in pressing forward with an idea that had recently come to him, while a no would mean he'd have Ravenchild beside him—a powerful ally.

Ravenchild turned his gaze upon the house compounds beyond the busy ballcourt, then looked up at the tall white clouds building with promise. Cocking his head, he admitted, "I would have a hard time leaving. There is something special about this place. I see why you needed to return. It has become home for me too."

As the bands of tension around his chest released, Waterstrider nodded. "Then would you be willing to risk trying something different to save your new home?"

"What do you have in mind?"

"Those canals where water is seeping up from below." He gestured westward. Ravenchild knew the places he referred to. "What if we trapped the water there, maybe with headgates?"

Ravenchild's brow puckered as he thought. "It could work," he said. His eyes narrowed as his attention fixed on something to the north, beyond Waterstrider's right shoulder. He jerked his chin that direction.

Waterstrider followed his friend's gaze and found Firesister limping toward him with her usual unhurried gait. Her face was serene, as though she had been out enjoying the morning rather than being harried by the Tricksters and harassed by the Smokemothers. The rasping of the kuhtpul rose as she neared, like ceremonial music sent by Mother Ge. Glowing in the sunlight, she smiled warmly at him.

"Thank you, Mother Ge," he whispered. Waterstrider lifted a hand and rubbed his chest, for his heart felt so full, he feared it might burst. Mother Ge in her wisdom had set him on this life-path, which he had never thought he wanted for himself. She had brought him home and given him a family.

In return, he vowed, he would figure out a way to save her people.

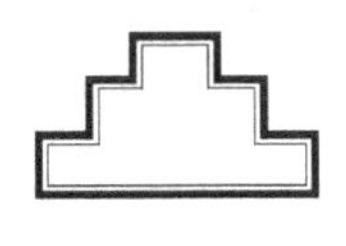

Glossary

Some of these words are my own coinages, some are from the modern-day O'odham, and others are used in Arizona to describe things found there.

blood-bound: A man and woman sworn to each other for life, wearing matching tattoos around their wrists; they are called lifemates

bonemender: A person, often one of the hunters or healers, called in to tend injuries

caliche: Hard calcium-based layer in soil; often mixed with other components to make a water-resistant plaster

Canalmaster: The Watermaster in charge of a village's canal

clanlands: Use-rights to these fields are passed down from mother to daughter, reverting to the clan when no daughter inherits

clan-sister, clan-gran, clan-daughter: A person within the same clan but not in the immediate family

comal: Flat pottery griddle for cooking directly on a fire or balanced on hot rocks

Cornmaidens: Handmaids to the goddess, Mother Ge; after being impregnated by the Stormbringers in fertility rites, some few are selected to become Smokemothers, while the others return to their clans to raise their children

digging-stick: Heavy farming implement made of stonewood, with a large, flat blade at one end for digging and hoeing and the other end tapering to make a hole in the soil for planting

earthflower: A light-colored lichen that grows on rock outcrops of mountains and foothills; used in love charms

Far-Traders: Traders who connected the People of Two Rivers with groups outside the valley, bringing in goods such as copper bells, bright feathers, and tanned hides of exotic beasts

greenthorn: Paloverde, *Parkinsonia* spp.; a spiny tree in the legume family with smooth green bark on its trunk and branches

kuhtpul: Locusts whose buzzing indicates the start of the summer rains, called male rains because of their violence and short duration

life-mating: The joining of a man and woman, either temporarily (signified by a cord braided of their commingled hair and tied around their wrists) or permanently (signified by a line tattooed around their wrists); they are called lifemates

Long Thirst: The generations-long drought ended by the Stormbringers

makai: A magic-wielder (pl., mamakai), found among the healers as well as those chosen to be priests or priestesses

mesquite: A deep-rooted tree, *Prosopis velutina,* of the legume family; leaves drop during dry spells and help fertilize the soil, while the beans can be pounded in a stone crusher to produce a protein-rich flour

moontime: The days of women's regular bleeding, tied to the cycles of the moon; women during their moontime go to the clan's hut to avoid contaminating those in their family who may need to hunt or harvest food or perform healing ceremonies

Mother Ge: The Mother-of-All-Creation; the goddess of fertility served by the Smokemothers and formerly worshiped by all the People of Two Rivers, before the coming of the Stormbringers and their introduction of a new religion

Namers: The elders who gave adolescent boys and girls their adult names upon completion of their naming quest; before the quest, they may have one or more child names, often based on appearance, and afterward, they may be better known by nicknames or may even have their names changed by some significant event

obsidian: A black volcanic stone that breaks along fracture lines to create a sharp but brittle glasslike knife

ocotillo: A thorny shrub, *Fouquieria splendens,* that puts out small green leaves and, at the tip, a stalk of scarlet flowers after the winter rains; when planted close together in a row, ocotillos make a fearsome living fence

old blood: Those who trace their ancestry to the days before goddess-worship; one born of the old blood and outlander was prophesied to save his people from a cataclysm

olla: Large fired-clay jar with a wide mouth and narrower neck used for storage, especially of water

orders: Cross-clan groups, especially religious based, that draw members from nearby villages because of skills rather than kinship; the most notable are the Skywatchers, Stormbringers, and Smokemothers

outlanders: Those who are not born of the People of Two Rivers

piki bread: A thin batter of ground corn drizzled onto a hot comal to cook; typically eaten for breakfast

Rainsinger: Head of the Stormbringers for each temple; referring to the Rainsinger by his name rather than the title is disrespectful

remembrancer: A man who keeps the calendar stick for a community, recording important events and narrating them in story form

River Council: Joint council of Canalmasters for Earth River and Sky River

saguaro: A giant columnar cactus, *Carnegiea gigantea;* the fruit ripens at the start of the summer rainy season and is fermented to make a celebratory alcoholic beverage

shadowdancer: A young priest who dances with snakes during the spring River-Binding ceremony

shegoi: Desert bush, *Larrea tridentata,* whose resinous leaves are most strongly scented during the summer rains

Skywatchers: Group formerly responsible for tracking the sun through the seasons, dictating the timing of the four sun-festivals, particularly the Sun-Turning

Smokemothers: Priestesses of Mother Ge; the four high priestesses give up their names and are referred to by their position (Childcatcher, Truthspeaker, Seedkeeper, Dreamwalker)

stonewood: Desert ironwood, *Olneya tesota;* the wood of this long-lived tree is dense and hard, making it useful for digging and chopping tools

Stormbringers: The priests who worship the Ta'atchul; originally outlanders, they ended the Long Thirst and now are responsible for singing the summer rains into being as well as conducting essential ceremonies during the sun-festivals

sun-festivals: Occurring four times each year, at the solstices and equinoxes; River-Binding in spring, Cloud-Summoning in summer, Heart-Gathering in fall, Sun-Turning in winter

Temple of Lightning: Northernmost temple of the Stormbringers, headed by Eaglefeather as the Rainsinger

Temple of Mist: Southernmost temple of the Stormbringers, headed by Morning Green as the Rainsinger

turning: A unit of time consisting of a full year; at the Sun-Turning ceremony of midwinter, the sun reverses its path along the horizon, and the days start to become longer

vatto: A shade structure made of branches woven into a flat roof supported by mesquite posts

Watermasters: The ancient sect that kept canals and ditches operational and allocated the water equitably to the farmers; they call themselves heronfolk

White Starry Path: The Milky Way

Author's Note

In the modern-day state of Arizona, where the Salt and Gila Rivers meet, the aptly named city of Phoenix rose from the ruins of an ancient civilization. Long before Europeans gazed on this blistering desert valley ringed with mountains, people called the land home.

Here they lived, creating beautiful things, some of which linger in the painted pottery, jewelry, and rock art passed down to the valley's present inhabitants. Here they built vast systems of irrigation canals, astronomical observatories, cities containing walled family compounds and multistory buildings, and immense platform mounds that may have served as artificial mountains, bringing them closer to sacred beings in the sky who sent life-giving rains in answer to their prayers.

Then they vanished.

Perhaps they died, most of them, leaving a pitiful few to be absorbed into the O'odham people that indigenous origin stories say came from the south soon afterward. Perhaps they left, joining the better-known Hopis on the great mesas to the north. Perhaps they stayed and changed with the coming of the Apaches and, soon after, Spanish explorers and missionaries, becoming a new people quite different from their ancestors. Whatever became of these Ancestral Desert people, the Akimel O'odham, who inherited their land, named them the Hohokam, "those who are gone."

Was it an environmental cataclysm that brought about their downfall? Or the creeping weariness of a civilization past its time and torn apart by internal strife? Or invasion by another desperate people? Or were many factors mixed in a terrible conjunction—not of stars, but of individuals whose lives were driven by ambition, despair, envy, fear, love, courage, pride, and honor?

This is a story of what might have been.

Water—sometimes too much, usually not enough—established the timeline for this chronicle of the collapse of the Hohokam civilization. A generation-long drought parched the American Southwest in the late thirteenth century AD, leading to unprecedented migration across the region. Once the drought was over and the summer and winter rains returned, these people did not enjoy a cultural blossoming. They merely hung on.

Then something happened. Droughts, floods, eclipses, dust storms, volcanic eruptions, tornadoes and microbursts, and other calamities had occurred before, yet the farmers of the Valley of Two Rivers persevered. What happened after more than a thousand years of irrigation farming to cause their disappearance?

Decades of research and personal experiences in the Arizona desert inspired me to create a world in which canals run like green ribbons through a quilt of adjacent fields. Villages of neat adobe compounds, punctuated with platform mounds, ballcourts, and greathouses, stand straight and tall, statements of these inventive people's mastery of their homeland.

Desert washes shine with pink-blooming ancient ironwoods, sunshine-yellow clouds of paloverde blossoms, and the graceful pink to purple flowers of desert willows. Rivers carry water through groves of cottonwoods and willows and past bosques of mesquite trees filled with a panoply of birds, singing and calling out a warning when people intrude. Beyond lie grasslands populated by rabbits and other small animals. In the desert flats, immense saguaros tower over creosotebush, barrel cactus, flame-tipped ocotillo, and, in the spring, a multicolored carpet of flowers that pop up and as quickly fade.

This is a landscape of richness and contrast, fraught with hazards yet achingly beautiful.

In this world the worst dangers come from other humans: the ones most trusted by the People of Two Rivers.

Acknowledgments

I am immensely grateful

To the many readers whose valuable comments helped shape this book over the decades: Agnes Bennett, Matthew Boyington, Sara Drane, Karen Edwards, Delores Everts, Patti Hodge, Rosalie Kerl, Dave King, Margo Uri Simmons, Alison Valentine, Adam Vucelich, and friends and colleagues from my time in Arizona who read earlier drafts;

To the Knoxville Writers' Guild Advanced Fiction Writing critique group: Robert L. Beasley, Pamela Schoenewaldt, A Jordan, and Bonny Millard;

To the cover designer, Kara Hudgens, who took my vague idea and turned it into a stunning piece of art;

And to the many archaeologists, anthropologists, ethnologists, museum curators, biologists, historians, astronomers, and others whose dedicated research and sharing of knowledge gave me a foundation for the world of the Watermasters.

Any errors, omissions, and obscurities are entirely my responsibility.

About the Author

Sally Bennett Boyington fell in love with the Southwest during a childhood vacation in Flagstaff, Arizona. Later visits to ruins and a memorable kachina coloring book spurred a lifelong fascination with the history and people of the Southwest.

During the twenty years she lived in one Arizona city or another as an adult, she witnessed devastatingly beautiful sunrises and sunsets, experienced spine-tingling moments of awe, and came to understand the fragility of human existence.

Brought up in a family of readers, at four years old she demanded that her mother teach her to read. Three years later, she had a Halloween poem published in the newspaper. Creative writing had sunk its teeth into her and never quite let go.

For a long time (300 books' worth), making a living with copy editing took priority over writing, but personal changes and recent developments in the publishing industry convinced Sally to share her imagined worlds with readers. She hopes they stimulate thoughts, conversations, and a new perspective on the real world in which we live.

(Author photo by Kara Hudgens Photography Co.)